Tears of the West

Ted York

Tears of the West

Matador
9 Priory Business Park,
Wistow Road, Kibworth Beauchamp,
Leicestershire. LE8 0RX
Tel: 0116 279 2299
Email: books@troubador.co.uk
Web: www.troubador.co.uk/matador
Twitter: @matadorbooks

ISBN 978 1785891 885

British Library Cataloguing in Publication Data.
A catalogue record for this book is available from the British Library.

Printed and bound in the UK by TJ International, Padstow, Cornwall
Typeset in 12pt Aldine401 BT by Troubador Publishing Ltd, Leicester, UK

Matador is an imprint of Troubador Publishing Ltd

For all my family

"An eye for an eye only ends up making the whole world blind."
Mahatma Gandhi

Characters in *Tears of the West*

HARRIMAN SECURITY

Colonel John Harriman
Deidre 'Dee' Cox – Colonel Harriman's goddaughter
Major Smith
Captain Johnston
Captain Harrington
Captain Norlington
Sergeant Quick
Corporal Williams
David Sturridge
Doheny
Amanda Hodge
Mack
Raza and Jafar Bhutani
Captain Sutherland
Commander Cunningham

MI6 (SIS)

Sir Anthony Greenwood – Chief of the Secret Intelligence Service
Caroline Bland
Adam Runfold
Joseph Dyer
Ricky Matthews
Charles Standing
Spencer Mortimer

MI5

Sir William Villiers – Director General
Simon Tomlinson
Sebastian Masters-Buchanan

CIA

Samuel J Goldmuir – Director
Jack Clarke – Deputy Director
Willis Coogan – Field Agent
Uhmed Abaid – Field Agent
Estenso and Walker – Field Agents
Wilson McCourt – Field Agent
Meredith Marchonais – Field Agent
O'Hara – Field Agent
Hearne – Field Agent
O'Reilly – Field Agent

FBI

Bud Ruskin – Director

AL-QAEDA

Osama bin Laden
Ibrahim Belardi known as Mansur Ahmedi, Asad Meshgi and Mohamed Sarraf
Al-Rashid-Bin Ibrahim (Ibrahim) known as Kadar, Syed Jagir and Sameer Jagirani
Abu Khan
Abdul Suleman (originally Europe Commander K/A 'Blue')
Safiyah Jamil, known as Karim Basilah
Umed Zamal – London agent
Ali Omar – Iranian assassin

Amadou Masrat – Libyan assassin
Abail (later Europe Commander K/A 'Blue')

'Red' – Mexico, USA and Canada Commander
'Green' – Africa Commander
'Black' – Middle East Commander
'Blue' – Europe Commander
Ursaan Alvi – Bodyguard
Navid Sassan – Bodyguard
Saarik Fahd k/a Aban Razak

BILLIONNAIRE SUPPORTERS OF AL-QAEDA

Alexail Pankov – Russian
Cheng Kuang – Chinese
Farid Al-Kazaz – Saudi
Madura Chatterjee – Indian

OTHER SUPPORTERS OF AL-QAEDA

Lt. General Akif Gandapur – Pakistan Security Service (ISI)
Lihua Nha Ping – Ministry of State Security (MSS), Chinese Secret Service

PAKISTAN SECURITY SERVICE (ISI)

Colonel Akrim

CHINESE INTERNAL SECURITY SERVICE

Liu Hong – Head of Ministry of Public Security

Ted York

FRENCH PLAYERS

Paul Foncard – Editor, *Le Mistral*
Bridgette Corfour – Reporter
Georges LeForge – Head of Investigations, French Customs
Serge Votre – French Customs

PAPARAZZI

Daniel Ribert
Jason Long

UK GOVERNMENT

Prime Minister
Deputy Prime Minister
Jonathan Gould – Foreign Secretary
Keith Landers – Health Minister
Sir Geoffrey Mason – Attorney General
Sir Henry Park – Chief Scientific Officer
Brian Scott – Defence Minister
Justin Hayward – Press Secretary
William Morgan – Chief Spin Doctor
Humphrey Dawes – Home Office

UK GOVERNMENT ADVISOR

Professor G Endleson – Essex University

US GOVERNMENT – NATIONAL SECURITY COUNCIL

The President
Vice President

Franklyn Andrew Browne – Secretary of State
Dawson Treat – Secretary of the Treasury
William Collins – Secretary of Defence
General Bradley Paterson – Chairman of the Joint Chiefs
Chad Newton – Assistant to the President for National Security
Walter Fairchild – Director of National Intelligence
Maxwell Liddle – Health Secretary
Ryan Brundleson – Attorney General
Lance Manley – Secretary of Environment Protection Agency

US GOVERNMENT ADVISORS

Professor Eugene Rendle – Harvard University
Professor Brian Flavier – Harvard University
Vice Admiral Dearing – Special Operations Commander

Author's Notes

UNDERSTANDING NANOTECHNOLOGY

A centimetre is one-hundredth of a metre, a milometer is one-thousandth of a metre and a micrometre is one-millionth of a metre. But these are huge compared to the nanoscale.

A nanometre (nm) is one-billionth of a metre; smaller than the wavelength of visible light and a hundred-thousandth the width of a human hair

Three hundred million nanoparticles each 100 nanometres wide can fit on the head of a pin.

NANOENCAPSULATION

The coating or enclosing of a substance, as if within a capsule, with another material at the nanoscale level.

TOXICOKINETICS

A description of what rate a chemical will enter the body and what happens once it has.

Prologue

Professor Dolen found himself thinking once again about the mysterious ingredients in the Stardust range of cosmetics. One of his brightest PhD students studying Drug Delivery and Microbiology, Deidre Cox, had come to see him a month ago about her thesis: 'Is nanotechnology being properly controlled?' She had examined the ingredients in a wide variety of cosmetics and, in some ladies' face creams, she had discovered nanoparticles. One brand in particular, Stardust, was causing her a concern. She felt certain that its range of cosmetics, shampoo, hairspray, toothpaste, nail polish, shaving cream, sunscreen and deodorant all contained nanoparticles. The problem was, despite her best endeavours, the pharmaceutical company who manufactured the range, ExCy, was not replying to her emails, letters or telephone calls asking for a list of ingredients. The ingredients listed on the packaging did not include nanoparticles but when Deidre had conducted experiments, removing each of the stated ingredients, something was left behind. But what?

Professor Dolen was the senior Professor of

Biotechnology at Imperial College, London and had been intrigued when Deidre showed him her findings. Could there be nanoparticles in these Stardust cosmetics, a brand that was being widely advertised and sold in most supermarkets? His friend, a fellow student from his days in the 1960s at Oxford University, Professor Endleson, was a specialist in nanotechnology at Essex University, and he was on his way for a coffee with him in Upminster, a short underground train journey. He was deep in thought as he contemplated the intriguing possibility that nanoparticles were included in these cosmetics; if so, what was their composition and purpose? The platform was still crowded with commuters as he waited to catch a tube on the underground at South Kensington station for his 10am meeting. A person behind him had a terrible cold and kept sneezing. He was daydreaming when he felt the wind and heard the distant sound of the approaching train. As the train hurtled into the station he felt a shove on his back. Suddenly he was in the path of the oncoming train – next: excruciating pain and darkness.

1

Colonel John Harriman had left the SAS in 2001 after a distinguished career and formed his own security company. He had joined the army after graduating from Cambridge University and, at twenty-one, had undertaken officer training at Sandhurst Royal Military Academy in Surrey. He transferred from his regiment, the Coldstream Guards, when he was twenty-three to the SAS regiment. He rose through the ranks from second lieutenant to acting brigadier and retired on a high. He then built up his firm into the largest private security firm in London. Today he was having lunch with his goddaughter at the Savoy Grill in London.

Deidre Cox, Dee to her friends, told him her final year thesis was taking shape. She explained to her godfather that she was researching the manipulation of nanotechnology by various pharmaceutical companies, particularly those using nanoparticles in day-to-day cosmetics and personal care products. Initially, she had looked at established household names where she found nanoparticles in face creams and toothpaste. But a relatively new company selling cosmetics,

ExCy, trading a range it called Stardust, had attracted her attention.

The problem was that the examination and analysis of the ingredients in their various cosmetics and products were not simple. As she was explaining over lunch to her godfather, the list of ingredients shown on the Stardust products' packaging did not identify if nanoparticles were included.

"But surely you have to list all ingredients?" asked the colonel.

"Ah, but if the ingredient is virtually invisible, why should you? Particularly if the manufacturer believes the consumer isn't ready to understand this new technology," replied Dee.

"Are you telling me these nanoparticles are invisible?"

"That's about the size of it. Look… let me explain. Nanotechnology involves the creation of structures on the scale of atoms and molecules. One nanometre is one-thousandth of a micrometre and one-billionth of a metre." She took out her purse. "You see this pin you might use for pinning up a dress? One billion nanoparticles would fit on the head."

Colonel Harriman looked at the pin. "Wow! You really wouldn't be able to easily detect something that small. But what's the problem? Isn't this progress, as you young ones keep telling us?"

"Sure. It's amazing if used correctly, but there are some proven instances notably a study by Japanese researchers last year showing that the transfer of nanoparticles of titanium dioxide from pregnant mice to their offspring caused brain damage, reduced sperm production and caused nerve system damage." Dee went on. "Fullerenes – these are hollow-shaped particles made of carbon atoms that are so remarkably small they have bioavailability – could be coated with or contain a dangerous substance." She glanced at her godfather. "Sorry. Am I boring you?"

"No, not at all. It's fascinating." He tried not to look bemused as he struggled to follow what his goddaughter was explaining.

"Where was I? Yes. Fullerenes and nanoparticles, minute in size, have been found to cause brain damage in fish, kill water fleas and have bactericidal properties."

"You're losing me again, Dee," grinned Colonel Harriman.

"It's quite simple really. There has been insufficient research into the cause and effect of using fullerenes or nanoparticles in cosmetics and they are being used now! Nanoparticles can be linked to biological molecules that can act as directional tags to direct the particles to specific sites within the body. What if the coatings, or what the nanoparticles are made of, are toxic chemicals and dangerous?"

"I don't understand how these nanoparticles can enter the body," replied the colonel.

"Nanoparticles can be absorbed into the bloodstream through the skin, inhaled or swallowed, and can be directional."

"Ah, here's your father," said a relieved Colonel Harriman struggling to understand what his goddaughter was telling him.

A smartly dressed, fit-looking man, slightly greying at the temples, approached the table.

"I hope I'm not too late. A business meeting ran over," he said, kissing his daughter on the cheek and shaking hands with his old friend. He sat at the table.

"No problem, Dad. I was just educating John on nanoparticles."

Martin Cox looked quizzically at his daughter, taking out his spectacles.

"Don't ask," said John Harriman.

"Ah, but there is a point." A waiter hovered to take their order.

"G & T please," Martin ordered, glancing in front of John and Dee, noting they both had drinks. "Sorry, darling, what is the point you wanted to make?" he asked.

Dee paused for a second, not entirely sure what to say.

"I'm doing my final thesis on nanotechnology. When I began my research on which cosmetic and personal toiletries companies were currently using this technology I hit a brick wall. You see, the list of ingredients in a certain manufacturer's cosmetics it sells as the Stardust range, which includes sunscreen, deodorant, shaving cream, hairspray, nail polish, soap and shampoos, all in everyday use, doesn't state if nanos have been included."

"But perhaps they haven't," interrupted her father.

"Dad, when you test a cosmetic at a laboratory, removing each one of the stated ingredients, and you're left with something, even though it's so small you cannot detect it through a microscope, then we know some pharmaceutical companies, and this company ExCy, which trades as Stardust is a prime example, are adding nanos."

"So how do you establish the inclusion of these particles?" asked John.

"A computer program has been developed by my professor at Imperial College, and we have a particle counter that he has let me use, which enables us to test for nanoparticles," Dee replied.

"So, darling, what's your point?" asked her father.

"I need to identify what type of particles this particular pharmaceutical company is including, and the composition of the particles, but I can't. I've asked the manufacturer and so has my professor, but they won't reply. Then last week..." she paused and her eyes filled.

"What is it, darling?" asked her father.

"Professor Dolen, who has been helping me with the research, died."

"Died," said John, "how?"

"He fell under an underground train at South Kensington station," she replied.

"God, that's awful for you," said her father.

"No, it's worse, Dad. The laboratory technician, who was also helping me – sending emails and making calls to the manufacturer – was murdered… also last week."

Both men sat bolt upright.

"Murdered," said her father.

"Yes, he was stabbed walking down Kensington High Street in broad daylight. The police said it was a mugging gone wrong. But it seems an amazing coincidence to me and I'm frightened."

The lunch had finished in time for Martin Cox to return to his desk at the Swinford Merchant Bank in the City, but Colonel Harriman had decided to escort Dee to the flat she shared in Princes Road, Kensington. He had also gone to the men's room to telephone for one of his operatives, Amanda, to meet him there.

The black cab pulled up outside her student lodgings, Dee got out and the colonel paid the fare.

"Ah, there's Amanda." John explained that he had arranged for one of his operatives to act as a companion until he could look into the deaths of Dee's professor and the laboratory technician. Dee had not objected. She had continued at lunch to explain more about the new nanotechnology and the billions of pounds that could be involved. Basically, she said only Greenpeace and Friends of the Earth were actively exposing the lack of research into the dangers for humans.

Amanda was waiting by the steps leading to the front door.

"Afternoon, Amanda," said Colonel Harriman.

"Colonel," she replied.

All the employees at Harriman Security were ex-military or special branch, SAS or SBS, and they continued to call him by his old rank.

"Meet Dee, who you will be watching over. Dee has a spare bedroom as her roommate is on a field trip. Please accompany her at all times and wait when she attends lectures at the university," he said.

"Dee."

She opened the front door and turned towards her godfather.

"John?"

"It's important that you make sure Amanda knows your movements. Don't leave the university without her; not even for a few minutes."

"I think I'm even more frightened now, John," she said.

"Don't be – just taking precautions," he replied.

Colonel Harriman knew Dee was in good hands. Amanda had left the SAS two years ago when she realised she was omitted from all dangerous operations; or worse, left in the rear. Querying this with her commanding officer got her nowhere. She had not fought her way up through the Blues and Royals to second lieutenant, and then gone through SAS training, to sit back as her male colleagues had all the fun. When her suspicions were confirmed that her father, a retired general, had something to do with it she resigned.

Leaving the women, Colonel Harriman went back to his HQ on Park Lane in London to check out the mysterious deaths his goddaughter had told him about. He thought a visit to his old friend Sir Anthony Greenwood at MI6 was warranted.

2

During the lunch with his goddaughter, John remembered that Dee had particularly referred to the giant industrial chemical company ExCy. She had explained that ExCy appeared from nowhere about two years ago. Based in London and Zurich, it had bought up several large companies, notably British Chemicals Plc and Lorego in Zurich. Then the two companies had changed direction. Whereas previously both companies had considerable earnings from industrial chemicals, their plants had been adapted to manufacture, produce and bottle hairspray, soap, shampoo, deodorants and other personal cosmetics. In two years ExCy had changed its operation to establish a strong market growth in the EU and the USA, marketing heavily. The stock market had welcomed the new broom in the boardroom and its shares were trading at a premium. Dee's interest in them was the ingredients in their products. She had explained that she had been unable to identify what appeared to be nanoparticles in its Stardust range of cosmetics. Approaching ExCy had produced no response, and that was when her tutor, Professor Dolen, and one of the lab technicians had taken up the challenge.

Colonel Harriman explained all this to his old friend Sir Anthony Greenwood, the head of MI6.

"I know this is not a security issue but can you do some digging for me on these ExCy people?" he asked.

"Certainly, old boy, leave it with me. How is Martin?" Sir Anthony referred to Dee's father. Colonel Harriman, Sir Anthony and Martin Cox had all been to Eton before parting to go to different Oxbridge universities.

"Oh, you know Martin – making loads of money."

Colonel Harriman left the Thameside offices of the security services and returned to his HQ in Park Lane. In his sixty-fourth year, he let his operatives do most of the legwork and so decided to call a meeting of his senior staff. The investigation they were about to commence would be thorough and would start with a bogus VAT inspection at the ExCy London office, as he intended to send Harry Sutherland, one of his operatives, to check it out.

"Harry, organise the paperwork and gear up your pal at the VAT office in Knightsbridge in case they phone to check out your credentials."

The colonel looked at Harry Sutherland, one of his recruits from the Special Boat Services, known as the SBS, and then turned towards his second-in-command, Major Smith, who had been the colonel's first employee at Harriman Security.

"Can you carry out a check at Companies House and ask our contact in Zurich to identify its office personnel? I would like to know who runs this ExCy company."

"Are we treading on anyone's toes here, John?" asked Major Smith.

"No, I don't think anyone is interested. The two deaths, on the face of it, have been an accident and a mugging gone wrong."

The meeting broke up after a brief résumé of their other operations: protecting pop stars and actors, guarding

Russian oligarchs and acting as security for rich people. And now they were part of the Royal Protection Squad. These were their day-to-day meal tickets. Colonel Harriman had recognised, when he left the SAS, that there was going to be a need for private security, and set up Harriman Security. Investing most of his savings and recruiting ex-SAS and SBS members his business had grown exponentially since 2001.

3

WANDSWORTH, LONDON

The grey dog, a lurcher, bounded toward Harry, whirling around Rocky, his two-year-old westie. Rocky was on the lead as, given the freedom, he was inclined to head off across Wandsworth Common at speed. More than once Harry had found himself pounding after his loveable terrier. Rocky wanted to play with this bigger dog. *Fearless*, thought Harry. *That's why I called him Rocky*.

Captain Harry Sutherland was part of the investigation team working for Colonel Harriman. Harry had been recruited in 2007 shortly after the colonel had been involved in a major investigation, which had stretched his resources. Nobody discussed the earlier investigation but from snippets Harry had gathered they had 'lost' two good men.

Leaning down he released the lead and Rocky darted away, chasing after the bigger dog. *Got some guts has Rocky*, he thought. Harry Sutherland had served in Northern Ireland, Iraq and Afghanistan before leaving the SBS. At twenty-seven he had been promoted to captain after leading a successful incursion into a Taliban-held stronghold on the border with Pakistan. Two British soldiers had been rescued and his unit of eight men had returned unscathed. He smiled to himself as the light rain continued. *It's a good soft day,* he thought, referring to his father's Irish expression for a steady soaking.

Harry had an instinct. It had kept him safe undercover in Northern Ireland for six months at a stretch. He noticed the dark-haired man in the anorak approaching on the path across the common and, at the same time, he pretended to be preoccupied watching Rocky whirling around the lurcher, who was beginning to tire of his young playmate. What was it? Later, Harry would say it was the hat he was holding in his hand, but there was no logic – it was raining! As the man got closer he drew a gun, dropping his hat; Harry's instinct and training took over. He dived sideways as the man fired; a bullet whistled close by. He heard the 'phut' of the silenced pistol again and was knocked backwards on the ground. He had been hit; a shoulder wound.

"Hey," a male voice called out. Harry didn't see this man as his training took over. The assailant turned and fired at the man who had shouted at him, who clutched his stomach and lurched forward. Harry reached for the Beretta in his shoulder holster, smoothly drew the pistol and, rolling over, fired two rapid shots.

The man took at least one bullet but continued moving towards him firing his pistol. Harry fired another double tap. This time he was accurate. The man dropped to the ground and remained motionless.

Harry grimaced as he picked himself up, gingerly holding his shoulder. He walked across to the assailant and kicked away the silenced pistol – a Walther, he thought. The stranger, who had probably saved his life by diverting attention for a precious second, moaned. Harry knelt beside him.

"All right mate, stay still. I'm calling an ambulance."

The man looked at Harry, went to speak, then blood came out of his mouth and he slumped over.

★

A week later, recovering from his shoulder wound but still on leave, Harry pondered on the attempt on his life. Why had that man – no identity on the body but probably Albanian, a conclusion drawn from labels in his T-shirt and underpants – tried to kill him? Thank goodness the guy who shouted out had made it. It had been touch and go for a few days and despite his wound, Harry had insisted on staying with the man, Edward Croucher, and his sister Susan in a bedside vigil until he came out of the drug-induced coma. During the two days, he had got to know Susan very well.

"Typical of Edward," she had said, "someone's in trouble and he's there."

Edward Croucher was a probation officer, and from the way Susan described her brother he was the most dedicated probation officer in London. It was not as though Harry minded sitting with Susan – she was stunning. She worked as a translator at the Foreign Office and had taken a week off to be with her brother. Harry fell in love during those few days. Her brown eyes sparkled as she talked about her brother. Harry just listened, enjoying her account of Edward's life. Edward had got a first-class honours degree at Guildford College of Law but chose to become a probation officer. "The law stinks, was what he said drove him towards the Probation Service," said Susan laughing.

Harry was returning to partial active duty tomorrow but looked forward to spending one more day with Susan. He walked up the stairs to the second floor at West Brompton Hospital. The colonel had arranged for Edward Croucher to have a private room. Tapping lightly on the door he went in. The room was empty. He went to the nurses' station.

"Where has Mr Croucher been moved to?" he asked.

The man looked up. "Are you a relative?"

"Yes," Harry lied.

"He's been moved to Hammersmith Hospital."

"Why?" asked Harry.

"Complications. You'll need to ask the nursing staff there."

Harry thanked the nurse and hurried towards the stairs, taking out his mobile as he walked.

"Susan? Harry – is Edward okay?"

"Oh Harry, I am sorry. I didn't have a chance to phone you. He's not good. They have taken him to an intensive care unit at Hammersmith Hospital."

"All right. I'll be with you in twenty minutes." Harry dialled again.

"Colonel H, please. Harry Sutherland."

"Harry." Colonel Harriman was a man of few words.

"Edward Croucher has been moved to Hammersmith Hospital – complications. He's in intensive care and I'm going there now."

"Right. Do you need anything?"

"No thank you, sir." Harry rang off.

Enquiring at the front desk and once again feigning he was a brother, Harry found Susan sitting by Edward's bed in a room on the tenth floor.

"What's the prognosis?" he asked.

"The doctor wouldn't tell me." Susan's bottom lip trembled and Harry felt like sweeping her into his arms and protecting her from this heartache.

His mobile rang; he saw it was the colonel.

"Bad news, Harry, and it's likely his sister doesn't know. They've discovered Edward has full-blown Aids." Harry's faced dropped.

"Harry, what is it?" Susan asked.

"I need to talk to the doctor. What's his name?"

Harry excused himself and went to find the doctor Susan had met – a Dr Hargrean.

It was difficult tracking down Edward's doctor but Harry persevered and found him in A&E.

"Dr Hargrean?" Harry approached the middle-aged man who was about to leave. The doctor looked tired.

"Yes," he replied.

"I'm Edward Croucher's brother."

The doctor thought for a moment.

"Ah yes. The man with the stomach wound."

"Yes that's right, but I understand there's another problem."

"Come with me," said the doctor.

They went back to the tenth floor. The doctor asked Harry to sit, pointing to some chairs outside the ward, and then went to the nursing station. A few minutes later he returned with the patient's notes, which he was reading.

"Hmm… look, it's not good news, I'm afraid."

"Can I stop you there? I need to get my sister."

Harry rushed to the room where Edward was being treated and beckoned Susan to come with him.

"This is my sister." The doctor nodded as Susan looked quizzically at Harry. "Can you explain Edward's condition to us both?"

The doctor opened the file again.

"Mr Croucher is recovering from a bullet wound to the stomach." He looked up. "Yes, I expect you know that. Unfortunately he has contracted pneumonia which has complications."

"Complications?" said Susan.

"Miss," he paused, not knowing Susan's surname. "Your brother has HIV/Aids."

Susan looked at him.

"I beg your pardon," she said.

"I am sorry but your brother is HIV positive and has Aids."

Suddenly it all made sense. The warning notice on the door of the room, 'Careful – bloods', and the nursing staff were wearing gloves.

"But where did he get it?" Susan asked.

The doctor had been on duty for fourteen hours non-stop and was exhausted, but managed to follow hospital protocols.

"That would require further investigation," the doctor replied.

"Is the condition and the pneumonia very serious?" asked Harry.

"Yes, I'm afraid it is. The next twenty-four hours will be critical."

Susan and Harry sat by Edward's bed, not talking much. Harry understood her need for silence. Then at 11pm the alarms which were connected to Edward went off. Harry had been dozing but immediately awoke. Nurses rushed in. Susan and Harry were ushered out of the room. Thirty minutes later a doctor came to find them sitting silently in the passageway.

"You are Edward Croucher's sister and brother?" Harry had not explained anything to Susan about his small deception and she did not ask.

"Yes," Harry replied.

"Come with me, please."

They followed the doctor to a small office marked 'Staff only'. Inside, the doctor sat them down. Then the bombshell.

"I'm sorry to inform you that Edward died twenty minutes ago."

Susan cried out, "No! no!" and started to slump forward. Harry reached her and kneeling by the chair held her.

Regaining her composure Susan said, "Can I see my brother, please?"

★

Five days later Susan, a few distant relatives – her parents were both dead – friends of Edward and many dodgy-looking characters who Susan said were his charges, and Harry, attended the cremation at Highgate Cemetery.

Harry had been to Susan's flat in Knightsbridge every day. She seemed to be coping, but when the coffin started rolling towards the curtain she burst into tears and clung to Harry, sobbing her heart out.

Later, upstairs in The Red Lion pub opposite the crematorium, there was a wake organised by Harry. Friends, relatives, and some of Edward's charges, told Harry more about the remarkable man who had been Edward Croucher. Many of the men who attended the funeral were on parole and came over to Susan to tell her about her brother. More than once she cried. Harry stood, gently holding her when needed. Finally everyone had left and Susan stood alone with Harry.

"Susan." He looked at this fragile woman he knew he loved.

"Harry, you've been very kind and I'm so very grateful, but if you were thinking we might continue seeing each other – don't. Please try and understand."

Harry looked crestfallen, but nodded.

"I'm sorry. Another time, a different set of circumstances, but every time I saw you I would be reminded why my brother was dead." A tear rolled down her cheek.

The bombshell hit Harry hard but he managed a polite smile.

"At least I can get you a taxi home."

"No, I want to walk." She looked at him. "On my own for a while."

She kissed Harry on the cheek.

"I'm sorry. Goodbye." Another tear ran down her cheek.

Harry went to hold her but stopped himself. *Let her go. She's right. It would never work*. Susan walked away. Harry paid the landlord of The Red Lion – it was the least he could do – and phoned Colonel Harriman to report for light duty.

4

"The Macedonian Airlines flight MA264 to Paris is boarding at Gate 15." There was a general flurry of activity as dozens of people got up from the uncomfortable plastic seats at Bogota Airport.

"Macedonian Airlines announces the departure of flight MA264 to Paris," a dark-skinned uniformed airline stewardess announced to the passengers who were sitting in front of Gate 15. "First-class passengers only, please." A few people got up. "Please now board the aircraft by seat number."

She began to relay the order in which the waiting passengers could go through the gate to board the aeroplane. Families and single women with children were invited to board first. Then seats 70–102, and so on. The first-class passengers had been invited through the gate ten minutes before and Serge Votre had taken his seat, nervously looking around the cabin. *Have I made it? Am I going to evade them?*

Serge was a French customs officer. He had been sent to Bogota in Colombia to check on a chemical company called ExCy that was exporting a huge amount of, supposedly, pharmaceutical chemicals to a French chemical company just outside Marseille. Large bulk liquid tankers arrived at Marseille from the Colombian port of Cartagena all with correct bills of lading and immaculate documentation. The French customs service, suspecting drug smuggling, had checked every shipment but nothing had been found, only what appeared to be liquid soap and shampoo. Now he sat back and accepted the glass of champagne offered by a petite brunette stewardess with the name Lola on her name badge. Not since he had investigated strange shipments of agricultural machinery coming from Cuba, when he had narrowly escaped an attempt on his life, had he felt in as much danger.

Two days ago, he had decided to try to gain access to the ExCy factory but had been approached outside the gate in the Bogota suburbs and bundled into a car. On his way, by appointment, to visit the factory, he had been handcuffed, his mouth taped and a hood put over his head. He had feared for his life when he was bundled out of the car and frogmarched into an empty building, he estimated, about an hour's drive away. He hadn't a clue where he was, and nobody was backing him up. The hood was removed and the tape torn from his mouth. A large, well-tanned man with dark piercing eyes and dark hair came into the room and sat opposite him. Two other men remained; one stood behind him. He was interrogated for about ten minutes then warned that he should leave the country immediately. Dumped in an alley opposite his hotel, he was happy to oblige and booked the next flight to Paris. What he hadn't told his inquisitors, and he had been tempted when they were slapping him about, was that he had acquired a small sample of the substance they were exporting. A customs officer at the docks had taken a hefty bribe and opened one of the canisters marked for Houston, Texas, and filled a thermos flask Serge had given him with the liquid he found inside. Yesterday he had brought the liquid to Serge's hotel.

The steward on the flight began the safety warnings and the screens in the top of the seat in front of him began to repeat in English and French the usual information, 'In the event of landing on water…'. Serge closed his eyes. It had been very frightening when he was captured by the unknown men. Probably Colombians but at least one looked to have Middle Eastern origins.

The plane, an A380 Airbus, began to taxi then with a roar from the jet engines hurtled down the runway. Serge breathed a sigh of relief and took out his mobile. He had the adapted version of a Nokia allowing use during the flight but when he tried to make a call there was nothing. He opened the battery compartment – gone. It was gone. A stewardess, not the polite Lola but a tall dusky woman called Marilyn, was giving out complimentary drinks in the first-class area.

"Excuse me." He held up his hand.

"*Oui, monsieur.*" *Clever how the stewards check who is sitting where in first-class,* he thought.

He spoke in English to avoid misunderstanding.

"The battery for my telephone has fallen out and I need to send a text message to my office – have you a battery I can buy or borrow?"

Marilyn looked at the phone.

"I don't think so, *monsieur*, but I will check." She turned off towards the galley.

Five minutes later she returned.

"I am sorry, *monsieur*. We have no batteries but I will ask the captain when I get an opportunity. The captain, first officer or the flight engineer may have some spares."

"Thank you." He reminded himself of her name by glancing at her name badge (and noticed her ample bosom). *Steady*, he thought, *time to think of amore when I'm back in Paris.* Serge looked at the in-flight movies, decided to watch a film called *La Vie en Rose* and settled down. Fifteen minutes later he was asleep.

Serge awoke as someone announced into the earphones he was still wearing, "*Mesdames et messieurs*," and then in English, "the captain has switched on the seatbelt signs. Please return to your seats." And then the captain's voice on the sound system. "Ladies and gentlemen, this is Captain Voulan. We are encountering a storm, which means some turbulence will be experienced. Please remain seated until we clear the area."

Serge's screen had returned to blank where the film he had started watching had finished. He began to set up the film to watch again. He had been enjoying it until he fell asleep.

A stewardess – *what was her name,* he thought – approached, leaned over and handed him a mobile phone.

"The first officer says you can use his phone to send a text."

"*Merci, mam'selle*," replied Serge as he started to type his message to Monsieur LeForge, the head of investigations for French customs in Paris.

He was halfway through his message when there was a loud explosion from the front of the plane. The plane lurched and began to spin. They were diving very fast. Passengers were screaming in the cabin. A stewardess fell past him. The oxygen masks dropped down – he tried to reach his but the rate of descent and the dive were so fast. He pressed the transmit button on the mobile, they hit the water, the plane broke up, then darkness.

★

In Paris, Georges LeForge heard his mobile beep and picked it up. It was a message from Serge but not from his number. Strange he hadn't finished.

"I am returning with a sample. Suspect not drugs but some other dangerous substance. I have…" then nothing; the message had ended abruptly. Ten minutes later his telephone rang. He listened, sighed to one of his contacts, then put the phone back on the old-fashioned cradle. He picked up the internal telephone and pressed three buttons.

"Simone, Serge's plane – he was travelling from Bogota to Paris on Macedonian Airlines – has disappeared. Ask Maurice to go to Charles de Gaulle Airport and monitor the situation with the authorities. It is Macedonian Airlines flight MA264.

5

CIA agents Walker and Estenso drove in silence in the black Toyota Land Cruiser towards the dockyard at Mogadishu. They had bribed a Somalian guard on the gate of Pier 6 and expected to gain access by simply driving in. Approaching the gate the man they had paid one hundred dollars to appeared, nodded, opened the barrier and waved them through.

So far so good, thought Walker, the senior officer. Walker and Estenso were CIA field operatives working on code name Project S. For some time the CIA had been monitoring a company called ExCy Chemicals, which was exporting from Africa massive quantities of liquid soap and cosmetics to an ExCy chemical plant near Mexico City. The shipments were then transferred by road tanker to a factory outside Houston, Texas that manufactured the popular Stardust range of ladies' cosmetics widely on sale in the United States. Stardust was a trade name owned by Regal Cosmetics, an ExCy company, which was in turn traced to a Cayman Islands' company Imperial and Regal Chemicals. An in-depth investigation into Imperial and

Regal Chemicals had produced nothing and the director of operations had decided to send a team to extract a sample. Agents had broken into an office of ExCy's in Grand Cayman only to find it empty. Two agents had tried to break into an ExCy chemical plant near Mexico City but had triggered a sophisticated alarm system and been arrested by the local police. They had been initially apprehended by armed guards at the ExCy plant. This, together with the dead end in the Caymans, prompted CIA head of operations, Samuel J Goldmuir, to order an attempt to infiltrate another known plant in Somalia to obtain a sample of the liquid they were exporting to Mexico by bribing a guard or breaking in. The Somalians were usually open to bribes and Agent Walker had little difficulty in persuading a burly local man to help them. Another CIA agent, Ben Livesey, a resident in Mogadishu, had given them a dossier on the guards at the plant and they had chosen this man as he lived alone and spent a lot of money at a bar in the town buying drinks and girls.

They approached warehouse number 6, parked the car a hundred yards away and set out on foot. Agent Livesey had given them a map marking warehouse 6, and a quantity of plastic explosives to blow the door. As they approached all seemed quiet. *Too quiet,* thought Walker. During fifteen years of field craft you learnt nothing was easy.

After attaching the plastic explosive and timing device to the door lock, they backed away. A small explosion broke the lock and they entered. Both had silenced Walther PPK pistols provided by Livesey. It was dark inside, there were no windows, and as they accustomed their eyes to the interior they saw two large containers. Walker touched his colleague's arm and they approached the first container. There was a door at one end. Gingerly, Estenso tried the handle. It opened silently and he went inside. Walker didn't see the men. They were dressed in black and carried Uzi sub-machine guns. Four men, who professionally fanned out so as not to hit each other, then opened fire.

Walker was caught by the first burst from four machine guns and fell immediately. Estenso came out of the door firing his pistol but was caught in a hail of bullets. Just before he died, he pressed the button on his mobile. His mobile had the text message, 'Operation failed'. The four men kicked the two bodies and one of them picked up the two pistols. Another pulled the dead men to the exit door. Two other men came in, picked up the bodies and put them in a van. Later they would be dumped from a speedboat to be eaten by the sharks offshore. The leader of the four men pulled off his black balaclava and the three Somalian men did likewise. He handed each man a wad of dollars and they all smiled in anticipation of the women and booze such treasure would buy.

The light-skinned man, a Moroccan, using a false Somalian name of Ashkir Abdi, phoned to report their success. "The two CIA agents are dead." Walking to the dockside he threw the mobile in the water. The man had told him to dump the mobile, not bothered that the CIA global satellite would pick up the message confirming the agents were dead. *What a waste*, he thought. There wasn't anything in the containers as they had moved the contents when the Americans arrived from Italy three days ago.

★

Agent Meredith Marchonais sat in the black Toyota Land Cruiser two blocks away from the dockside area waiting for the two field agents to return. She didn't usually do field work and was apprehensive, what was keeping them?

6

The helicopter hovered briefly then set down on Battersea helipad in London near to the River Thames. Two men identically dressed in dark blue suits, both carrying overnight bags, alighted and were met by Caroline Bland, the deputy head of MI6. Formalities exchanged, they got into a black Audi with darkened windows and headed towards MI6 headquarters on the south bank of the River Thames. Driving into the building's underground garage they alighted and followed a silent Caroline Bland to the lift. They got out at the fourth floor.

"Follow me, gentlemen, please."

Caroline was not one for small talk and, whilst her main responsibilities were with MI6, she had recently been co-opted as liaison by Max Ramsey-Taylor to work with MI5 on the project they called Project U. The 'U' was for unknown. The visitors were shown into a small office and offered coffee. A few minutes later, the director of MI6, Sir Anthony Greenwood, entered by the second door followed by a tall lean man of military bearing.

"Gentlemen." Sir Anthony Greenwood knew both the

men sitting at the table opposite. "Can I introduce Colonel Harriman?" He motioned towards the older of the two men sitting. "Jack Clarke, deputy director, CIA, and Mike O'Leary representing the president."

"Colonel." Both men had been briefed that Harriman would be at their meeting and had seen his dossier. The colonel was ex-SAS and had commanded a unit in 1975 at the Balcombe Street siege. He had also worked with the Americans extensively in both the Iraq wars and in Afghanistan.

"The prime minister has asked that you pass his compliments to the president," said Sir Anthony as he looked at Mike O'Leary who nodded. "Gentlemen, to business; after coffee we'll adjourn to the operations boardroom. Meanwhile, some paperwork to read."

Sir Anthony passed out a thick file in a green cover marked 'Top Secret Project U' to each person. Caroline Bland had already read the report, indeed had written most of it, and excused herself to ready the boardroom or 'Ops room' as it was called internally.

Ten minutes later the four men entered the boardroom as Caroline was bringing up the visuals.

They sat around the large boardroom-style table, without formality.

"Gentlemen, I have prepared a brief résumé of what we," – she stressed the word 'we' – "have on this matter we are calling Project U." She pressed a button and the lights dimmed. The commentary coming from the screen was hers.

"Late in 2007, MI6 intercepted a message destined for bin Laden in Afghanistan. The message was in a code not known to us. It took our boffins a month to decipher the code and you can hear the message now."

She didn't elaborate that an SAS snatch squad had picked up a man on the Pakistan border who had been carrying the coded note.

"Operation Tears of the West is underway, the note said. This made little sense to anybody, including you gentlemen at the CIA." She nodded towards Jack Clarke. "Two months later, Colonel Akrim of the Pakistan Security Service passed us the transcript of a conversation one of his operatives had had with a terrorist they apprehended in Islamabad. This man was, it seems, a high-ranking official in the Taliban. This is his statement, translated of course."

"You will die like the dog you are, a traitor to Allah. Shortly the western scum you align with will be reduced to nothing. Our beloved leader, and al-Qaeda, has planned something so devastating the American devils and their British lapdogs will be destroyed – forever." The tape stopped.

Caroline continued. "There was a lot of other information and most has been substantiated. Despite extensive drugs and the attention of Pakistan's best, the man has refused to say any more about the operation he referred to on the tape. He has now been moved, courtesy of our Pakistani friends, to your holding place in Romania." Caroline referred to the CIA establishment near Tanin in Romania, a transit point before sending prisoners to Guantanamo Bay or Morocco.

"Since then," continued Caroline, "we have been using all of our resources to try and discover what the code name Tears of the West refers to." She paused. "It was Colonel Harriman," the colonel looked up, "who provided a clue. Colonel, will you explain?"

"Yes, Caroline. In December last year my firm was asked to help with an extradition. A man – a self-styled Somalian sheikh – wanted to leave his country in a hurry. We found out why of course – he was about to be ousted in a coup. This man, Sheikh Ali Ibrahim, had met me at Sandhurst in '68 and insisted my firm organise his swift exit. He also said that in return for being paid one million dollars he had some information for the British Secret Service.

This information he said concerned the Tears of the West. Now, we in Harriman Security didn't have the faintest idea whether this information would be useful so I rang Sir Anthony. To cut a long story short, we extracted the sheikh and his entourage of three wives and fifteen children, overland and by sea at the end of January. We encountered a little local difficulty but were able to proceed."

A little local difficulty; Colonel Harriman didn't elaborate on the three units of the Somalian army pursuing their convoy of Land Rovers to the port of Mogadishu. A firefight broke out outside Mogadishu town which resulted in extensive losses for the Somalians and none of the colonel's men injured.

"Having extracted the sheikh we met with Sir Anthony and Caroline in London."

Caroline played the recording of the meeting with this self-appointed sheikh. He was known to respond well to attractive women and Caroline was certainly that.

"Your Highness," she had begun by referring to the title he bestowed on himself, "you sent a message to Colonel Harriman and referred to the Tears of the West. What did you mean by that?"

The camera zoomed in on the sheikh's face as he started to speak. They would later test his honesty and integrity when he answered questions by measuring the pupils of his eyes; a new computer program the boffins had perfected for determining if a person was telling the truth or lying.

"I will tell what I know," he paused, "but before I do I want a letter from the prime minister confirming that I and my retinue may reside indefinitely in the UK, and one million dollars."

The tape had stopped at that point. One day later, the tape was dated and timed. Caroline began again.

"Now, Sheikh, you have the letter from the home

secretary and the promise of the money. Tell us what you know of the Tears of the West."

"Very well," he replied. "In June 2008, one of my trusted colonels brought a man to me. He was an Arab and said his name was Saarik Fahd and that he represented the ExCy Corporation. His name was false. A friend in the Russian Security Service told me his real name was Aban Razak, a Lebanese national. This man wanted to lease from me exclusive use of three large warehouses on the dockside. I already knew that the ExCy Corporation had built an extensive factory outside Mogadishu earlier in 2008. They showed me around that factory in January of that year."

"What do they make at that factory?" asked Caroline.

"Soap and shampoo," replied the sheikh. "Now, returning to my office, Colonel Hasan said he had arrested a Somalian man for the rape and murder of a woman in a village outside Mogadishu. The man, a known criminal, would have been executed had he been found guilty. He said he had some information that I would find very valuable. The colonel extracted the information and passed it to me."

They all waited as he took a sip of water. He was clearly enjoying the drama.

"Well, what did the man tell you?" asked a patient Caroline.

"He said that all was not what it appeared at the ExCy plant. He said that they didn't make soap or shampoo. When one of the workers at the plant stole a small bottle full of the liquid they manufactured, he was taken away and never seen again. Another man tried using the liquid to wash grease from his hands. The grease foamed up but wouldn't come off and later he developed a terrible rash on his hands and up his arms. Another stole a small quantity of the liquid in a small plastic bottle and gave it to his wife to wash her hair with. Within a week all her hair had become dull – he described it as lifeless – and clumps began to fall out."

He waited for the implications of what he had said to sink in.

"I conclude that the liquid in the vats in the warehouse was not liquid soap and shampoo, and there is also something else."

"Yes, Sheikh?" replied Caroline.

"What my security thought was a high-ranking official of the Saudi Embassy visited the plant and the warehouses two months ago. The man was thought by the security people to be Mahmoud of the Saudi secret police. He spoke on his mobile thinking he was safe in his embassy, but one of the cleaners overheard the words, Tears of the West."

"That is excellent. Is there anything else?"

"My accommodation in London; I asked for the top floor at the Ritz and I find myself in Claridges. Can you make the necessary arrangements?"

The screen went blank.

"So, in summary," said Caroline, "there is a code name – Tears of the West. We believe this means a plot is underway and it appears to be connected to ExCy, a chemical company. We have tracked the ownership of this company to a dummy corporation in Grand Cayman. This company, ExCy, has factories in Mexico exporting cosmetics to the United States, originating and transported from Somalia. Colonel Harriman can add something else."

All eyes turned to John Harriman who turned towards the CIA man.

"One of my employees is an expert computer programmer recruited after he hacked into a number of security computers." He referred to David Sturridge, a young man who was nothing short of a genius. He had cracked the CIA code at Langley, Virginia, the headquarters of the CIA, and penetrated secure parts of its website. In addition, he had planted a message inside MI5's website demonstrating he had penetrated its firewall by adding 'Arsenal for the cup' in a sensitive section. British Special Branch arrested him in 2007. The Americans demanded he be extradited. Instead of employing the young man, the home secretary proposed a lengthy prison sentence as a deterrent for others who might try to have fun at the expense of the security services. The prime minister, guided by Sir Anthony, proposed that his talents be 'on tap' so to speak, but he was not to be directly employed by the state. He knew just the person to rein him in – Colonel John Harriman. The sixteen-year-old boy responded to the colonel's brand of discipline and early on he lived with him in his Chelsea mews house. During the past year he had proved invaluable on more than one occasion. An example was a computer analysis he carried out for a detective at Scotland Yard during a recent series of murders, which had resulted in them reaching the correct conclusion long before the truth finally came out, and the culprit was caught. The boy was a genius.

The colonel continued, "We've hacked through the firewall of ExCy's office in London and found the message 'Tears of the West should commence'. There are various emails but are all non-descript and from various people in their other chemical manufacturing companies in Somalia, France, Spain, the Middle East, Colombia and Mexico. A list of the factories and, where known, storage facilities, is in your file."

"Thank you, Colonel," said Sir Anthony. "We can add something else, Caroline."

"MI6 has been covertly watching most of the known ExCy factories and storage facilities and there is a definite build-up. They are apparently transferring liquids from converted petrol tankers to secure storage in the USA, France, the UK and Mexico. The liquid arrives by ship, we think from Somalia, but this has proved difficult to track." Caroline switched off the screen.

Jack Clarke, leaned down, checked his case and produced five red folders with the CIA gold crest on the front cover.

"Perhaps you would like to spend a few minutes reading our take on this," he said, passing out the files marked ExCy.

The report began:

Field Officer Hearne – Mexico City

A reliable source has indicated to me an involvement by a known member of al-Qaeda, an Arab, and a further man of Arab origin so far not identified, with the company ExCy which manufactures and exports the Stardust brand of cosmetics to the USA and Canada. My source reports that security at the plant outside the port of Veracruz, Mexico has dramatically increased. Several dozen men of Arab appearance are now controlling the external area and internal security around the warehouse at the docks. All employees are frisked and their bags searched on arrival and on leaving the plant. A source tells us that several of the workers have had internal body searches. Deliveries of a liquid are received by tanker from Somalia to Mexico City through the port of Veracruz. The new head of security in Mexico City, who comes and goes, is a man called Belardi who we also know as Mansur Ahmedi – a known member of al-Qaeda. This man has been linked to terrorist activities in Afghanistan.

Recommend action: Agents penetrate holding warehouse in Mogadishu, Somalia and ascertain content (obtain sample) of large vats. Agents also penetrate factory in Mexico City and Veracruz and take sample of apparent cosmetics.

Note: Border patrol to carry out routine search of imports to USA checking for drugs. Inform Drugs Administration, FBI and local police. Photograph of unknown Arab meeting Belardi, taken in Mexico City, seemingly heading up operation, attached. Do full search. Carry out full trace ownership of ExCy Corporation.

The report was flagged with an 'URGENT' sticker. Turning the first page, Caroline continued to read.

CIA field officers Walker and Estenso assigned to investigate Somalia, Mexico City and Veracruz warehouses.

Then a gap.

Message by secure email. Agent James Walker,

Following meeting with Deputy Director Clarke, Estenso and I have taken a look at the ExCy operation in Somalia with regard to shipments to Mexico City and the warehouses at Veracruz docks. These installations in Somalia are heavily guarded but we have bribed a guard to let us in the docks when the workforce leaves at 5.50pm, November 10.

The factory in Mexico City will require a number of additional operatives if we are to penetrate; security is extensive. Estenso, posing as a Mexican factory inspector, reports:

Penetrated target factory November 7, acting as assistant to a legitimate Mexican factory inspector we had bribed. Extensive security – I was body-searched and accompanied around the factory by three guards at all times. The guards are Arabs of undetermined nationality and carry Uzi submachine guns. On entry to processing plant they appeared to be manufacturing shampoo and liquid soap. The shampoo is branded Stardust, the soap Simply Stardust Pure. The liquids are mixed in massive vats: *unable to obtain samples*. They are then bottled and boxed in another plant for export probably to USA and Canada. Later tracked containers marked Stardust, which carry goods to USA using Merlin Line Shipping Company from Veracruz to Houston. *Note*: Check where ExCy distribution centers are in the States and check Merlin Line Shipping Company for connection to ExCy.

Caroline, who was used to speed reading, finished the first page and turned over to read the next heading.

Report on ExCy by internal officer Agent O'Reilly.

ExCy is a Cayman Islands company owned by Regal Cosmetics Inc. This company is also registered in the Caymans. This company (Regal Cosmetics) is owned by a company called Imperial and Regal Chemicals Inc; you guessed it, also registered in the Caymans. Agent O'Hara to visit Grand Cayman to track Imperial and Regal Inc.

The pharmaceutical company trading as ExCy exports cosmetics, including shampoo, hairspray, deodorant, toothpaste, nail polish, shaving cream, sunscreen and liquid soap to the States using the brands Stardust and Simply Stardust Pure. Stardust has a lemon, lime or orange shampoo range sold at budget price through thousands of independent outlets and the larger supermarkets. Likewise sold as Simply Stardust Pure is liquid soap, shaving cream, toothpaste, deodorant, nail polish, sunscreen and shampoo, some of which are in a dispenser (applicator). All are budget products retailing at less than ten dollars. Extensive TV advertising started in California in February 2007 and has now extended nationwide. We estimate that primetime slots are costing twenty million dollars.

Customs at Mexico/USA border confirm twenty plus trucks per day, seven days a week, cross the border at Matamoros loaded with boxes of Stardust merchandise in containers. The trucks head for distribution warehousing on the Amtrak Railroad emanating from Houston. Inventories from the Amtrak Rail network indicate at least 800 smaller containers of goods are being despatched to US cities each week and some to Vancouver, Canada, also by rail, each week. Trucks transport supplies to smaller towns and cities from train stations via distribution warehouses in San Francisco, Delaware, Kansas City, Columbus, Phoenix and Chicago. The goods are now available throughout the States and Canada from virtually all supermarket chains.

Note from FBI Head of Scientific Research

Samples of Stardust range of cosmetics and Simply Stardust Pure have been purchased in fifty states and are being analysed. All samples contain extracts of the following – a big list of ingredients followed.

Conclusion

These are legitimate cosmetic products, although some have questionable ingredients, but no illegal/toxic materials were found. We are analysing old stock of the Stardust range we have acquired (according to sell-by dates).

Colonel Harriman was the last to put down the report.

"As you can see, Caroline and gentlemen, we are on the case. The problem is, what case? What is it we are looking for – a load of soaps? Is someone bullshitting us?" Jack Clarke paused before continuing. "Then we considered the involvement of the Arab, Mansur Ahmedi (known as Ibrahim Belardi), a known al-Qaeda terrorist. We do not consider he would legitimately be head of security for this firm ExCy without a terrorist connection, and why do security guards at their plants carry Uzi sub-machine guns? Bit over the top. Who wants to steal soap? We're missing something and have sent agents to obtain samples from the trucks at border crossings and Somalia.

"The dummy corporations are being investigated but you know what it's like breaking Cayman Islands' security." He paused.

"However, the unknown Arab, referred to in the report, has been identified."

He passed a grey folder to all three. Caroline grunted.

"This man," – a photograph showed a dark-skinned

man – "is known to us as Kadar, surname unknown, and has been long-suspected as being a banker for al-Qaeda. The president is treating this as a hostile situation. It could be they are fronting up this soap, we used the term disparagingly, to cover something much more sinister. US customs has started searching every vehicle that enters the USA and the FBI is doing random searches of their factories and distribution depots in the USA. So far, nothing."

As he finished the sentence his mobile rang. Clarke listened without talking. His face remained passive, and nobody would guess he had received a call informing him of the death of two of his agents.

Ending the call he continued, "Well, that's where we're at with this. We'll keep you informed." Which Caroline thought probably meant they wouldn't.

With the meeting obviously over they exchanged pleasantries and left the boardroom. The Americans said they were returning to Washington on the red-eye.

Sir Anthony, who had been previously informed that Colonel Harriman had got one of his men into the ExCy headquarters in Mayfair, London, asked him to stay. Sir Anthony knew that after John's meeting with his goddaughter, who told him about her suspicions and the deaths of two of her colleagues, Harriman had tasked Harry Sutherland to penetrate the ExCy HQ in London.

"How is Harry?" Captain Sutherland had been shot a day after his visit, posing as a VAT inspector, to the ExCy office in London.

"He's fine. The bullet creased his shoulder. He was fortunate he moved to pet a dog."

"And what about the Arab-looking man he shot dead?" asked Sir Anthony.

"Your excellent Spencer Mortimer," – who was Sir Anthony's PA – "told me when I came in that he had been identified as an Albanian, Sokol Fakaj."

"Any connection with al-Qaeda?" asked Sir Anthony.

"No. Not as far as Spencer has traced."

There was a pause as Sir Anthony summoned tea.

"It seems more than coincidental that having visited the ExCy office in Mayfair suddenly a hit man attempts to kill him."

"Tell me again. What did he find?" asked Sir Anthony.

"Very little, actually. He posed as a VAT inspector and insisted on seeing all their invoices and accounts."

"Anything show up?" asked Sir Anthony.

"Well, one possible lead. A Saudi company, the Ulema Corporation, invoiced ExCy for delivery by tanker of petroleum spirit; we presume a derivative of petrol but it could have been anything. It was returned as incorrect as the invoice should have gone to the French office of ExCy in Marseille."

The tea arrived and Sir Anthony paused to pour both of them a cup. "Milk?" Colonel Harriman nodded.

"Are you checking out the Saudi company?" asked Sir Anthony.

"Yes. Through contacts in Riyadh."

"We'll ask the French to check out the Marseille factory. What did you make of the Americans?" asked Sir Anthony.

"Guarded as usual. Probably not telling us everything they know."

"Quite," muttered Sir Anthony, who had never understood why the 'Special Relationship' wasn't that special.

Colonel Harriman was about to leave when Spencer Mortimer knocked on the door.

"Spencer?" said Sir Anthony.

"Air Macedonia jet gone missing – left Bogota, Colombia and has simply gone missing," he replied.

"Anything for us?" asked Sir Anthony.

"We're checking the passenger list. I'll let you know."

Colonel Harriman left MI6 headquarters and went by taxi to his offices, a suite on Parkside, Park Lane, next to a large BMW dealer. Several messages and two meetings later the colonel headed to his mews house in Chelsea, Captain Johnston dropping him off. As the captain left the neat row of houses in his black Audi, he noticed the BMW parked at the end of the mews with darkened windows, but thought nothing of it.

Two men dressed in boiler suits got out of the rear doors of the BMW. Both men were olive-skinned with black hair, and walked towards the colonel's house. A car came into the mews. They carried on walking. A woman in her fifties got out and rang the doorbell of Colonel Harriman's house. A light went on in the hall. The woman turned and looked at the men walking towards her, then casually she put her hand into her shoulder bag. The door opened; suddenly both the men yanked Uzi machine pistols from the bags they carried.

Caroline Bland was the best pistol shot in MI6 and took down the nearest man with a head shot, then fired two body shots into the second man. Both fell; one dead, the other mortally wounded. John Harriman came charging out of the front door, Walther pistol in his hand and very little else. He was wearing his Harrods dressing gown but his appearance made Caroline laugh out loud.

"God, John, you would certainly scare me wearing that dressing gown."

"Are you okay?" he asked.

"Sure," she pointed, "but they're not." She used her mobile to summon a clean-up squad.

"Charlie, send a disposal squad to John Harriman's mews house in Chelsea. Outside the house you will find two bodies." She then phoned Special Branch to update them; you cannot go around killing people on British streets. She didn't notice the black BMW slip away at the end of the mews.

"Hold on, Caroline, this one's not dead," said the colonel, feeling a weak pulse in his neck. She made another call.

"Well, you have certainly got the bad buys after you, John Harriman."

She leaned upwards and kissed him on the cheek.

"I'm lucky to be in love with the best pistol shot in MI6," he chuckled.

Caroline smiled. John Harriman had been her lover for eight years, since the Americans first went to Kabul. Before he formed Harriman Security he had led a deep cover SAS unit on the Afghan border. It was to be his last act before he retired and as SAS commander-in-chief he shouldn't have been there.

Caroline was a field officer working for MI6, endeavouring to persuade a Taliban commander to change sides. The man was reputed to control over one hundred fighters but later Caroline admitted she had been naive to completely trust her source. As her Land Rover approached the rendezvous, near the small village of Qamar Din Karez, John and his unit of eight SAS men stepped into the road. Later she reflected that her first words were not complimentary – 'We could have thought you were the enemy and run you down.' She realised after the later debriefing that the SAS unit had saved her life, as the Taliban commander she was expecting to meet had set up an ambush. Her informant, an Afghan village elder named Malik Khan, was found beheaded the following day on the outskirts of Kabul.

"I guess that makes us even, John Harriman." She smiled as she picked up the Uzis from the pavement.

"Oh no, I saved you from at least fifty men – you've forty-eight to go."

Caroline laughed as a black van pulled up. The bodies were unceremoniously dumped in the back after the clinic's ambulance arrived and declared both men dead.

Caroline instructed the two men who arrived to pick up the bodies to take them for forensic examination where every item of their clothing would be checked for identification. Their photographs and fingerprints would be sent to the CIA, FBI, Scotland Yard and Interpol.

"They look Eastern European, John. What have you been up to?" asked Caroline.

"I've been racking my brains and can only assume this is all to do with Harry's investigation of ExCy."

"Just in case they've got some friends, why don't you stay at my place tonight?" asked Caroline.

"I'm not going to be driven out of my house by terrorists or whatever they are," Harriman replied.

"All right." Caroline touched his arm. "Why don't I stay the night?"

"I thought you would never ask." He grinned at her and wrapped an arm around her waist.

*

Captain Johnston was to later confirm that he had seen a black BMW at the end of the mews.

"Did you get the number of the BMW?" asked Colonel Harriman.

But the sharp-eyed captain had not. The car was probably stolen anyway.

7

Meredith Marchonais sat in the Toyota two blocks from the dock. It had been two hours since field agents Walker and Estenso left her 'filing her nails', as Estenso had put it. The dark-haired CIA agent, Estenso, hadn't said a word until he left. *Tension*, she thought. But the two agents hadn't returned. *What do I do? Phone Langley?* No, she was the field agent on the spot; she should go and have a look. Leaving the car, she removed her Beretta M9 pistol from her handbag, put a round in the chamber, and slipped the gun into her jacket pocket. She checked that she had a spare clip and, walking close to other parked cars, approached the dock gates. Walker had bribed the guard yesterday to access the warehouses and she had a one-hundred dollar note in her hand to do likewise. The man on the gate, a Somalian, looked up as she approached.

He pointed to a sign. "No come in here," he said in French.

"I have a message for my friends, who you let in earlier," Meredith replied in French and passed him the hundred dollar note. He looked at it and a toothy grin broke out on his face. He leaned down and then the electric gates guarding the dock entrance began to move.

Meredith nodded and walked in. She gingerly approached warehouse 6. Meredith Marchonais – her colleagues called her MM for obvious reasons – was the youngest daughter of Clare and Alain. Her grandparents had emigrated from Scotland in 1961, after her grandfather Peter was offered a job in California. Some years later their daughter, Clare, married a French man, Alain, after a whirlwind romance in Paris. Meredith's mother, who was eighteen at the time, was meant to be on a round-the-world gap year before taking up a place at Harvard studying law. Instead she met Alain, a young French student, and shacked-up in Paris. A year later Estelle was born, then Claude in 1982 and Meredith in 1983.

Meredith had always been the most adventurous of the siblings. She loved going to the States and staying with her grandparents in California. It wasn't a surprise when she won a scholarship to Yale to study law. Shortly before her finals she was approached by Michael Benning Jnr at a recruitment fair. He told her that the FBI and the CIA were recruiting. That sounded very exciting. Meredith applied and was accepted by the CIA. She had spent the past two years at Langley, mostly on training courses. Then she was assigned to Somalia at the American Embassy in Mogadishu, not a very glamorous posting.

This was her first field action and Meredith's legs felt heavy as she approached warehouse 6. She wasn't inclined to perspire but a bead of sweat trickled down her face. *Stop this. Hold it together,* she told herself. Her hand trembled as she tried the door, which opened. She looked in – complete darkness. In the distance she heard water – was someone hosing something down? Meredith drew her pistol from her pocket and went in. Suddenly a large hand caught hold of her wrist. Struggling, she kicked out and caught someone, then she felt a blow to her head and blacked out.

As she regained consciousness she struggled but realised she had been tied up. Her hands were behind her back and her legs tied. She tried to bring her arms around but couldn't. The rope must be secured to something behind her head, she thought. Light streamed in as a door opened and she saw she was on the floor in a small office with no windows. Three men – Somalians she thought – came in laughing, talking in French. The first one through the door had won something. When he reached Meredith he tore at her blouse, ripping the material as the buttons parted. Then he yanked her bra, hurting her breasts as the clasp gave way. She kicked out but then he hit her around the face. Blood trickled from her nose into her mouth. He grabbed hold of her legs. He was a big man. She couldn't fight him and he undid the rope, loosened her belt and pulled down her trousers. A whoop of delight came from the other two men behind him. He tore down her panties and she closed her eyes. They were going to rape her and there was nothing she could do about it. She decided struggling would achieve little. He spread her legs, then she could feel him trying to enter. He hit her again. She tried to relax. When he finished, another man unzipped his trousers and tried to enter her. She cried out in pain. Then the third man raped her – the pain was excruciating.

All three men were laughing and joking, when the door opened and someone else came in. He barked an order, approached Meredith, turned her over and then raped her again. Meredith cried in pain as tears and blood spattered her face. The men finally left her on the floor, stark naked. Later, two of the men returned. One of the men tried to penetrate her again; she screamed in pain, he hit her. When he finished he undid the rope behind her, leaving her hands still tied, picked her up and walked towards the door. She realised she must have been their prisoner for hours as it was getting dark. They carried her to the dockside, picked up a heavy-looking chain, laughed, and then wrapped it around her legs. *God, they're going to drown me.* The pain from her vagina and anus was intense and just fleetingly she thought it would be a release to drown. But the will to live took over and just as they threw her into the water she took a deep breath.

The weight of the chains dragged her down and they had left her hands tied together. Meredith knew the meaning of the phrase, 'Your life goes before you', as she tried not to struggle. *Conserve oxygen*, she told herself as she tried to dislodge the rope securing her hands. Then a strange thing happened. She thought she saw a figure in a mask. An air-piece was shoved into her mouth. The figure picked her up and despite the weight of the chains around her legs struck out for the surface. As they went up she sensed he was struggling and might not make it, but somehow he did. She now realised, her brain having cleared breathing the oxygen, that it was a white man who had rescued her. As they reached the surface he clung onto a stanchion holding up the dock, breathing deeply and heavily.

"You must help me push you up. You're bleeding and it'll attract sharks." He undid the knot and released the rope holding her hands tied.

He managed to push her until she was sitting on a shelf under the dock just above the water level. He unwrapped the chains and dropped them.

"Don't move. I'm going to get my rubber dingy." She had muffled a cry of pain as he had pushed her onto the shelf, but he had to get her out of the water. Meredith sat thinking about the man who had a deep, British voice, blue eyes and dark hair. Meredith nodded as he put the mouthpiece back into his mouth and dived silently into the depths.

For what seemed like an hour or more, but was

probably much less, Meredith sat shivering. *Delayed shock*, she thought. Then she heard an outboard motor and saw a small craft approaching where she was hiding. Meredith prayed it was him.

Adam Runfold was a British Secret Service MI6 agent sent by Caroline Bland to obtain a sample of the liquid in the vat at the warehouse in the Somalian docks. He had approached the area from the marina in a rubber dingy and tied up the boat, deciding to swim underwater the last two hundred metres to the dockside. Intending to climb up on the ledge underneath the dock he planned to take off the aqualung and mask, and retrieve the waterproof bag he had dragged with him. Suddenly a splash from above and a young woman in chains headed past him fifteen feet to the bottom of the harbour. Adam's instinct to help a damsel in distress kicked in. It had tested all his strength to bring the woman to the surface. Luckily the chains were not that heavy, otherwise he would have failed.

Now approaching in the rubber boat he checked no inquisitive eyes were watching from the dockside. Cutting the outboard motor, the momentum carried him to where he had left her. He pulled close to the dockside.

"Can you move?"

"Yes," she said, eager to get away from this area.

"Right, drop down into my arms," Adam held out his arms. Meredith looked at the dark-haired man and gladly slid off the shelf. A sharp pain shot through her inside. She grimaced, trying not to scream, then fainted.

Adam caught the woman and carefully placed her at the bottom of the boat. He took out his shirt from the waterproof bag and gently covered her nakedness. He pulled the starter and headed towards the Mustang cruiser he had moored at the edge of the marina. Adam whistled as he approached the sports cruiser and Jocelyn appeared on deck.

"Help me with this woman." He lifted up the still unconscious woman and passed Jocelyn the line to hold the rubber outboard as he stepped onto the platform at the back of the cruiser. Jocelyn tied up the boat then helped Adam get the woman up the metal steps at the back of the boat. Jocelyn noticed she was naked except for Adam's shirt.

"Christ, Adam, you were sent to get a sample and you come back with a nude woman."

"I'll tell you in a minute. Let's get her below. Someone's hurt her badly."

Adam gently placed the woman on his bed in the aft cabin.

"Call HQ. She needs a doctor fast," he instructed Jocelyn.

Using the satellite mobile on the secure channel Jocelyn phoned Caroline Bland, as Adam changed from his wetsuit.

"I'm telling you, he has brought a naked woman onboard who is unconscious. We need a doctor quickly."

Jocelyn listened then passed on the message.

"As arranged, the destroyer HMS *Coventry* is waiting three nautical miles at coordinates…" she read out the figures. "They have a ship's surgeon onboard."

Adam went to the wheelhouse, started the engine and headed out to sea using the Mustang's sophisticated direction finder system. The boat was more than adequate for cruising the area but was not a speedboat. It took fifteen minutes to reach the destroyer circling in the distance.

As they came alongside, dwarfed by the warship, two crew members took the woman in a blanket up the steps. Jocelyn had earlier given her a morphine injection as she moaned unconscious on the bed, and this seemed to help. The navy surgeon, Lieutenant Noel Cummings, directed the men to put the woman on a stretcher and take her to the infirmary. The captain, Roy Holden, knew Adam from earlier missions and shook his hand.

"Where did you find this one, Adam?"

"Oh, you know, Roy, they follow me about. Look after her; I think they have hurt her badly. Now we must go. *Au revoir*," said Adam.

The two men shook hands and Adam returned to the Mustang cruiser.

"Right, Josie," – he called Jocelyn by a shortened version which infuriated her – "back we go. Let's get the job done."

Jocelyn poked her tongue out and started the engine.

"Any idea who she is?" she asked.

"No. But in the few words she spoke I think she's American."

"Poor thing," muttered Jocelyn. Adam was not sure whether she was sympathising with her injuries or that she was American.

"Drop anchor where you did before," said Adam.

Jocelyn dropped the anchor as far away from the dockside as possible, about a quarter of a mile out to sea, and Adam pulled in the rubber outboard.

"If there has been activity on the dock they might be more vigilant so get ready for a swift getaway," he said as he went below.

Adam put on his wetsuit, collected a new oxygen cylinder and stepped onto the rubber boat. Gunning the engine he set off, with only the moon to guide him. He decided not to go as far in this time and tied the boat to a buoy near the entrance to the harbour. Entering the cool water he got his bearings and set off. The swim to the dockside took less than five minutes. Adam hauled himself onto the ledge where the woman had rested and took off the aqualung and his flippers. Taking out his canvas shoes and the silenced Walther PPK from the bag he carried, he climbed the rusty metal ladder to the dock. Once again the moon aided him as he sought warehouse 6. As he silently approached, a match struck up in the darkness and Adam saw a black man lighting a cigarette. He had an Uzi sub-machine gun slung around his neck. *Careless,* thought Adam. *Not a professional.* He got close and shot the man in the head; the only sound a 'phut' from the silenced pistol. *Perhaps he was one of the bastards who hurt the girl,* he thought.

Adam frisked him, removing a Beretta and putting it in his belt. He found a set of keys. After a few failures finding the key, he unlocked the door and dragged the body inside. He heard footsteps outside the warehouse. A man's voice called out in Arabic; it sounded like a question. The door handle turned, and the moonlight lit up the man's silhouette as he entered the warehouse. Adam dropped him with a double tap to the head and chest. He pulled the man inside alongside the other corpse.

Using the pencil torch he carried, he silently went forward. The narrow beam of light picked out a large metal object. *Must be the vat*, thought Adam. He walked all around the vat which was at least fifty feet in diameter. *Shit,* he thought, *no obvious outside tap to take a sample*. He had seen a ladder on the far side and went around again. Climbing up, he reached the top and shone his torch inside – empty. Bloody empty. His torch beam picked up a small residue of liquid on the bottom. The ladder continued down the inside of the vat. Adam reached the bottom and got out his sample bottle. He filled it and started back up. Suddenly the overhead fluorescent lights came on.

"Moses, Ruben, where are you?" a man's voice called out in French. Adam climbed up the ladder and peered over the top. Another black man had entered the warehouse. It was only a matter of seconds before he would see the dead bodies. Adam risked a noise to get out of the vat and climb down the rail. The man turned as he heard something and unslung his Uzi.

"Come on, man, don't piss about."

Then he saw the bodies.

"Come out where I can see you," he called in French.

Adam put the Walther in his belt behind his back and held out the Beretta, barrel first.

"*Bonjour*." He came out from behind the vat holding one arm up and holding out the pistol.

"Down," the man said, pointing to the ground.

The Beretta clattered on the ground.

"Kill him, Tim." Adam pointed behind the man who half-turned. Adam pulled the Walther and shot him in the head. He thanked God he had spent all the hours on the practice range doing head shots. "Only head shots guarantee a kill, son," said Sergeant Major McCall at the practice range of the SBS. He was right; the black man was dead. Adam kicked away the Uzi and left the man where he fell.

The moon had gone behind a cloud; Adam thought *this is my lucky day,* when he heard more voices. *Time to get out of here.*

Retracing his steps he found the rusty ladder which went to the ledge under the dockside. He strapped on his aqualung, put on the flippers and entered the water. Reaching the rubber outboard he clambered onboard just as a powerful searchlight began to sweep the harbour side. *They'll probably switch to the water soon,* he thought and gunned the small boat back towards the motor cruiser. Suddenly the searchlight began to sweep the harbour then the beam found him. A machine gun started firing. Adam ducked, picked up the waterproof bag, tied it to his waist and dived overboard. Swimming underwater he surfaced after a few minutes to verify direction. There was the cruiser, tied to the buoy, fifty yards away. Jocelyn had heard the commotion and started the engines. The spotlight illuminated the cruiser as Adam climbed the short ladder and got on the diving board. The machine gun opened up again. *Out of range,* thought Adam, as bullets dropped into the water metres away.

"Go, Josie. Go!" he shouted.

The cruiser, startled by the surge of power demanded by the engines, leapt forward.

Adam reached the bridge. "Close-run thing, Josie. Keep your foot down."

Suddenly two machine guns opened up. This time the bullets sprayed the cruiser. Adam saw two speedboats one hundred metres back and gaining ground. He picked up the grenade launcher he had put onboard earlier that day. Firing at the nearest boat, the grenade went off next to it. A huge plume of water soaked the three men onboard. The man at the front returned machine-gun fire and a hail of bullets hit the cruiser.

This is going to be a close-run thing, thought Adam as he fired a second grenade. He aimed forward of the speedboat and if the driver was stupid enough not to zigzag he would have a bull's-eye. A huge explosion sent part of the speedboat hurtling up in the air. The second speedboat was gaining and in a few minutes they would be in range of the man who held what looked like an Uzi machine gun. Adam fired another grenade. This driver was more sensible. He changed direction and the grenade landed ten feet to the left of the speedboat, spray momentarily obliterating the boat. The man with the Uzi opened up and the side windows of the cabin on the cruiser shattered.

"You all right, Josie?" Adam looked inside.

"Yes, just a scratch." Adam saw blood running down her left arm. He picked up the SA80, his assault rifle of choice. *Okay, you want to play? Now we play.* He lay down on his stomach and tracked the speedboat. The driver continued to zigzag. Two men were now firing at them. Adam switched to fully automatic and opened fire; the driver slumped over. The speedboat swerved as the driver let go of the wheel. Adam fired again; another hit, the man dropped down. The third man realised the speedboat was out of control and moved towards the front of the cockpit. Then 'boom!' a large gun opened fire, and shells landed close to the speedboat. Another 'boom!' and the speedboat exploded. Adam looked north and saw HMS *Coventry* was firing from her front turret and steaming towards them.

Ten minutes later the Mustang cruiser was lashed to the stern of the destroyer, and Josie and Adam were enjoying a coffee on the bridge as the captain scanned the horizon.

"Bloody pirates and their speedboats," said Captain Holden, knowing he would have a dressing-down for opening fire in Somalian territorial waters.

"Right. Best let Lieutenant Cummings take care of your arm, Josie," said Adam. She nodded and was led away.

"Quite a stir, Adam. I hope it was worth it," said the captain.

Adam, who was forever the optimist, said, "I think so. How's the American woman?"

"Cummings has got her sedated. Terrible what they did to her. Raped her. More than one of the bastards, Cummings thinks."

Adam bit his lip. *I hope I killed all the bastards that did that to her,* he thought.

A day's sailing on HMS *Coventry* brought them to Cape Town. Josie and Adam disembarked and were rushed to the airport for a BA flight to London. The American woman was transferred at the airport, at the request of her embassy in Somalia, to an ambulance taking her to hospital presumably.

Adam had looked in to see her before he left.

"How are you feeling?" he asked.

"Awful," she replied. "Are you the man who saved me?"

"Hi, I am Adam." He gazed at a beautiful brunette with the cutest little nose and brown eyes.

She held out her hand. "I'm Meredith. Thank you, Adam. I owe you my life."

"My pleasure. We must do something more relaxing next time."

She laughed, and then grimaced.

"Still painful?" he asked.

"Yes," she replied. "They're taking me off at Cape Town and sending me back to the States. If I don't get the chance will you give me your telephone number in the UK so I can call you and thank you again?"

Adam was only too pleased and found a pad in a drawer and noted down his phone number.

"I'm not there often but leave a message," he said, passing the note to Meredith.

"I know it sounds crazy but I keep dreaming I've drowned," she said.

"You'll get over it, and I mean all of it, with some help," he replied. "But don't fight the guys who'll be trying to help you. I know from bitter experience the shrinks have a place in the scheme of things."

She looked at him curiously.

"That's a story for when we meet again," he said and kissed her on the forehead and left.

8

Caroline Bland motioned to Colonel Harriman to sit down as she continued her conversation on the telephone. She put down the receiver.

"Trouble?" asked the colonel, sensing the tone of the call.

"You know what it's like; people expect miracles. We all know something's going on, but what? We can't guess and aren't mind-readers," she replied.

"Any news?" he asked.

"My man has a sample from Somalia. He's landing tomorrow at 3pm at Heathrow. We should have some answers soon."

"Harry Sutherland is working with young Sturridge, Harriman Security's computer boffin, but nothing so far. I can't help feeling Harry saw something they think he passed on to me otherwise why the attempt to kill me?"

"Yes, I agree. Let's talk to Harry again and go through what he found at ExCy's London office."

★

Harry was still fretting. He couldn't get Susan Croucher out of his mind, especially when he lay down to sleep. His mobile bleeped and Harry looked at the display. Colonel H wants him – he answered.

"OK, I'll be with you in thirty minutes."

Summoned to the security services' headquarters on the Thames Embankment, Harry sat in the back of a black cab pondering his heartache. Perhaps he should call Susan. *No, don't be silly, she made it very clear. Why prolong things? There was no future with her.* Harry daydreamed and uncharacteristically didn't notice the black leather-clad rider on the BMW motorcycle who followed the cab. Captain Johnston did though. Colonel Harriman had instructed Captain Johnston to tail Harry, keeping undetected if possible. Harry would be mad. But better mad than dead. The people they were up against had tried to kill Harry once and had made an attempt on the colonel. Since then all Harriman Security had been put on a 'red alert', their highest rating. It meant all personnel had to be doubled-up. Captain Norlington was tailing the colonel, with Captain Johnston covering Harry Sutherland. The colonel knew Harry well and expected him to object. So he didn't tell him.

Harry's cab drew up on the south side of the Thames, just past Battersea Bridge. Harry paid and looked to cross the road. The BMW motorcycle sped towards Harry, the rider had something in his hand. He spotted the danger and was about to hit the ground when a black Mini Cooper roared up behind the big bike and nudged the rear wheel. The motorbike rider lost control and dropped the bike. The screech of metal and the sight of a leather-clad rider hurtling through the air caused a woman out walking her dog along the Embankment to scream. The rider hit the ground with a thump and lay still. The bike continued, the metal screaming as sparks flew off until it hit the front of a bus coming in the opposite direction.

The police were on the scene very quickly after the bus driver called 999. Accidents outside this particular address in London prompted an instant response. He was explaining to a policeman how the driver of a black Mini had rammed the motorbike, causing the terrible accident. Then the Mini had driven off at speed. No, he didn't get the number. The police officer knew that CCTV on the road would have captured full details and didn't pursue the matter. Harry had got up and gone across the road, not bothering to check the motorcycle rider; he could see his neck was broken. The security at Thames House called Caroline, who came downstairs.

"Harry, trouble seems to be following you!"

"Who was that in the black Mini – one of yours?"

"Good Lord, no. The colonel will explain," she replied.

Caroline picked up the internal phone in reception.

"Sir Anthony, another attempt on Harry Sutherland. Yes, just now outside our building. The police are on the scene. Can you deal?"

Caroline knew Sir Anthony would phone the chief constable and arrange for the body of the motorcyclist and the CCTV tape to be delivered to MI6 immediately.

They went upstairs to the tenth floor.

Colonel Harriman was sitting in Caroline's office as they entered.

"Problem, Harry?" he asked.

"Not for me. Plenty for a motorcycle rider who was about to shoot me. Caroline tells me that my guardian angel wasn't one of hers."

The colonel knew he had to come clean.

"No, it was Captain Johnston."

"Johno!"

"Yes, I've declared a red alert. Since the attempt to kill you, and the attempt by the two men at my house, it's clear our adversary is trying to eliminate us both." He held up his hand. "I know you can take care of yourself and prefer to work alone – but we always double-up when there's a red alert. You know the rules." He looked at Harry. "What happened, anyway?"

"A motorcyclist on a big bike, probably a BMW, had a pistol drawn and was about to fire when Johno hit the rear wheel with his Mini Cooper. The man flew off. The bike was wrecked."

"Do we have the assailant?" asked the colonel.

"Yes, but he's quite dead," said Harry. "Broken neck."

"Damn. Another lead to nowhere," replied the colonel.

"Those people are really after you two. Time to think safe house, I believe." Caroline looked at John Harriman, knowing he would object.

"Let's adjourn to the boardroom," said Caroline. "Matthews, one of my people, has something to show you."

They entered the boardroom and a short, prematurely balding young man stood up from the table.

"Ah, Ricky, this is Colonel Harriman and Harry Sutherland. Harry is the person who infiltrated ExCy's London office. Harry, tell us again, the whole episode. We're missing something," said Caroline.

As Harry spoke, Ricky Matthews, typed into a laptop.

"Acting as a VAT inspector, I bluffed my way into the Mayfair offices of ExCy. The receptionist, an olive-skinned, dark-haired woman, aged about thirty, called for someone else. She spoke Arabic. I couldn't determine the dialect but it wasn't Urdu or Pashto." Harry had studied the Afghan language and Urdu at Cambridge University before joining the Royal Marines. "A man was summoned. He was 5'10", again olive skin with black hair and a distinct Arab look but dressed in western clothes. He introduced himself as Abdul Suleman and said he was the office manager. He had gold teeth, didn't smile a lot and was completely businesslike. He listened to my request to inspect the VAT records, asked for my ID and told me to wait. He told the receptionist to arrange for coffee. Later, my pal at Customs and Excise Investigations Division told me a Mr Suleman from ExCy Pharmaceuticals had called to check my credentials. The receptionist brought coffee. Thick, black coffee, Arabian style."

"Describe her again. Did she have make-up? What was her accent?" asked Caroline.

"She wasn't English but had an educated accent and a distinct look. Not Arabian, more Mediterranean, say Lebanese," replied Harry, "and she spoke English with no trace of an accent."

"But spoke impeccable English, you say?" asked the colonel.

"Yes."

"What else about her?" asked Caroline.

"She had no make-up, no nail polish and her black hair was cut short. Her clothes were expensive. She wore a small Rolex watch. She was pleasant enough without being friendly."

"What happened next?" asked Caroline.

"The man who introduced himself as Abdul Suleman came back. He handed me my ID and told me that all the records I wished to view were stored in a secure computer. He would have to sit with me. He had arranged a room." Harry took a sip of water.

"Go on," said Caroline.

"We went up in the lift to the third floor to a small office and in the centre of the room was a mahogany desk with a leather swivel chair behind the desk and another alongside. There was a picture on the facing wall – I recognised the mosque at Mecca. He asked me to sit next to him, and switched on the computer."

"Was there an access code?"

"Yes. He typed in a code. I thought he typed the Arabic letters that looked like three Js but I couldn't be sure."

"Carry on, Harry, you're doing well," said Caroline.

"He had on a gold watch, also a Rolex, no rings. After he logged in I saw the home page and all the words on screen were Arabic. He went into an accounts section and asked me for the period I wished to check. All the text was in Arabic. He hovered over an icon and the screen changed to English. The headings were Date of Entry, Item, Amount, VAT, Payee and Comments. He clicked 'Headings'. The screen brought up Transaction number, Date, Payee, Amount, VAT, Comments. He clicked on Transaction number. A dropdown list of transactions appeared."

"Can you remember them?" asked Caroline.

"Yes. He would not permit a copy of the list even though I insisted."

Most SAS and SBS operatives had skills honed by continuous physical training and the use of weapons. Harry's memory was good but he admitted not perfect. He shut his eyes.

"The dates were 1st August 2006–31 August 2007. This is the list." He drew a notebook from his pocket and reeled off a list.

"The heading was Payments, then another list:

Arabic Consumables

BMW Park Lane

Royston Taxis

Battersea Heliport

Royal Ascot

Shewards Bank – a large sum of £100 million was shown

Harrods

D Ali

A – ? – sorry, cannot remember this one,

Arabic Consumables

Ergon Oil

Ergon Oil

BMW Park Lane
Rules Restaurant
The Ritz Hotel
Shoreham Harbour Authority
Arabic Consumables
Dr Rashid."

He paused, looking up from his notes.

"Ergon Oil.

Sorry I'm beginning to reach the end of my list."

"Try to continue," coaxed Caroline.

"Ah yes,

The Kitty Club
Mr A Ibrahim.

I'm sorry, that's about it I'm afraid, but there were a few others I'm not absolutely certain of." He continued reading out loud.

"Kensington and Chelsea Borough Council
Tilbury Dock Authority
Rules Restaurant
Colorado Oil and Gas
Wright, Smith and King
Kensington and Chelsea Borough Council'
M Lord
Carrington Fuel.

That's it now. In any case I think that's all there was."

"Great recall, Harry," said Caroline. "Now, can you add dates and perhaps the amount of money?"

Harry looked at his notebook again.

"Ricky, put them up on the screen," instructed Caroline.

Ricky, the office IT expert, pressed two keys and a display appeared on the wall. He pressed another key and a list of names appeared.

"Okay, Harry, there's your entries. How about dates and amounts?"

Harry went through the list missing some dates he didn't have and approximating others. Some amounts he had remembered and written down; others – no recall. Caroline wasn't bothered about some of the entries but others she asked Harry to think about.

When Ricky had updated the laptop he clicked the button and four hard copies appeared from the copier in the corner. They all studied the list.

"A few things stand out," said Colonel Harriman.

"Go on, John," said Caroline.

"Someone has paid what I presume is a parking fine twice. Perhaps we can trace the road and then look at CCTV to see where the person went and who they were."

Caroline noted that down.

"The Kitty Club – Harry can go there and check it out? The Ritz Hotel on the date Harry mentioned will be able to look up who was staying and supply a list if you pressure them, and they have CCTV. BMW has supplied vehicles – let's check that one out and get registration numbers and put details into the police computer. Try the motorcycle that's just crashed. Battersea heliport will have details of a landing and any departure. They also have a CCTV camera – let's check the footage. There are five Arab names – let's put them through intelligence computers, including CIA. Royston Taxis on the 5th or 6th of August. Where did they take the passenger? Some of the London cabs have CCTV. We might be lucky. Royal Ascot in August will be frantic but these sorts of people go first-class, and there's surveillance at Ascot as the royal family often attends."

The colonel paused, looking at his list, and Caroline took up the analysis.

"Shewards Bank – a deposit of one hundred million pounds. We won't get far with the conventional route enquiring at the bank but perhaps our boys can take a look." She looked at Ricky. "Or your expert, John?" She referred to David Sturridge, a young IT whizz kid whom Colonel Harriman had taken under his wing. They all realised cracking the bank's firewall and security codes would be a masterstroke but if they couldn't, perhaps CIA might be able to assist.

"Shoreham Harbour Authority and Tilbury Docks you can leave to us," said Caroline. "John, can you check out Arabic Consumables? It's probably a shop in North London. We'll check out Ergon Oil and Colorado Oil and Gas," she said. "Oh, and Carrington Fuel," Caroline added.

"Wright, Smith and King sound like lawyers. We'll check them," said Colonel Harriman.

"Finally the name M Lord – add that one to the Arab names. We'll run them through the computers," said Caroline.

Ricky typed on the laptop, pressed a key, then about forty photographs appeared on the fifty-inch wall screen.

"One by one please, Ricky," said Caroline. "These are all the people that have gone in and come out of the ExCy building since the attempt on Harry's life. We began watching the premises the following day," she said.

Ricky clicked through the photographs.

"Stop," said Harry. "That's the man calling himself Abdul Suleman."

A dozen photographs later Harry stopped them again.

"That's the receptionist," he said.

Caroline paused at the photographs marked 31 and 43.

"These two are dead; I shot them outside your house, John."

"So we now have a definite connection with ExCy," said Colonel Harriman.

"Yes, but they could claim the two men were not known to them and make up a plausible reason why they were seen coming out of their London HQ," replied Harry.

"Hmm… take your point," said Colonel Harriman.

"We'll work on finding further evidence and then move against ExCy as soon as possible," said Caroline.

"Are you going to keep our cousins across the water in the loop?" asked the colonel.

"In the fullness of time," replied Caroline.

There was a knock on the boardroom door. Caroline looked up and beckoned a dark-haired man to come in.

"Sorry to interrupt, Caroline. Can I have a word?" he said.

Caroline got up and left the room.

"Can we have copies of the rogues gallery you've photographed coming out of the ExCy HQ, Ricky?"

"Yes, if Caroline approves," he replied.

Caroline returned and sat down.

"Caroline, we'd like copies of the photographs you've just shown us. Is that okay with you?" asked Colonel Harriman.

"Sure, no problem – Ricky will organise. I also have a link to a plane. You will recollect a Macedonian Airlines jet went missing three days ago en route from Bogota to Paris." They turned to look at her. "One of the passengers was a French customs officer who Interpol tell us was investigating ExCy imports from Colombia to France."

"Have you asked for a meeting?"

"No, you know what the French are like – won't share, don't like Americans and naively think they're the best. Need I go on?"

"Let's all meet again in two days and review our findings," said Colonel Harriman.

"Sounds good, John." Caroline winked at him thinking no one spotted it, but Harry had!

9

CANNES, FRANCE

When the British government disposed of the Royal Yacht *Britannia*, previously used by the Queen for royal tours, it was purchased by an unknown buyer in Kuwait. Since then, it had been refitted and renamed the *Good Queen Bess* – someone had a sense of humour. The yacht was now leased from its base in Cannes, South of France. The crew and captain, who usually manned the yacht, had been given two weeks paid leave. The person who chartered the boat wanted complete privacy and had appointed their own crew.

The new captain, a Lebanese man named Emile Nasr, had sailed the waters of the Mediterranean since he was fourteen years old. His instructions, since picking up the yacht at Cannes, had been to steam to Paphos in Cyprus where four people boarded. Then he moved on to Dubrovnik in Croatia, where two further passengers boarded. Six more guests were picked up in Naples and a similar number in Corfu Town. Other than the man,

Al-Rashid-Bin Ibrahim, who had hired him and the crew members he knew, he had no idea who the guests were. There were no women. Even the stewards, who changed the guest beds and furnished them with clean linen, were men.

The chef, a renowned French man called Pierre Van Duble, was not introduced to the guests. The Lebanese man thought it odd, but his fee of fifty thousand dollars for two weeks' cruising was irresistible. The only clue he had to the nationality of the men was that he thought they were Muslims. They all left their sandals outside the spacious lounge and dining room. They ate alone, and armed men patrolled the boat. Only the chef and one waiter were allowed in the dining room. As the captain, he would have expected to dine at least once with the guests. Not in this case. The chef and the waiter were both searched as they entered the dining room. Cameras and mobile phones were banned on board the yacht. All of the crew had been searched, including their luggage. Mobile phones were taken away. One of the crewmen objected and was promptly fired. The others, who were each paid two thousand dollars for each week, did not make a fuss. The yacht rarely berthed at the marinas they called at. Only in Cannes had the majestic vessel been tied up to the marina. All the other pick-ups were made by anchoring outside the marinas and sending the yacht's rubber inflatable to collect the passengers.

★

Jason Long was a particularly daring member of the paparazzi. He had been tipped off by Manuel Sendardo, one of his many tipsters. These were contacts who gave him the nod when a target he might want to photograph was coming to Cannes, or hiring a boat. Manuel, an experienced first mate, had been recruited by a Lebanese captain to sail the magnificent yacht, the *Good Queen Bess* for a two-week cruise. Jason sniffed a killing – only the very rich could afford that charter. It must be someone who wanted absolute anonymity to let the usual crew go on paid leave and employ a new crew. The usual captain of the yacht had no idea who had chartered the boat. More and more intrigue. Jason bribed an assistant chef to take photographs. That was another funny thing – no women were being hired. The man Jason bribed to take photographs couldn't tell him his excellent Nokia, the phone he was going to use to take the sneak shots, had been taken from him.

Jason had decided to follow the yacht and chartered a speedboat – his favourite method of approaching a large yacht or cruiser. Come in fast, take twenty or thirty shots then speed away. Or stand off and use the telephoto lens. Jason had very sophisticated telephoto lenses, which enabled him to snap the guests from a distance. That way you got shots when the subject least expected their picture to be taken. Jason had chartered a more expensive speedboat than he usually did. The *Belle Époque* had a canopy and radar. He could track the bigger yacht and keep at a distance until he wanted to swoop in for snapshots or use the telephoto lens. Reine was his long-suffering partner. He would steer when Jason needed to take the pictures. Last year Jason had earned four hundred thousand dollars from various sets of pictures. The best coup had been the Italian prime minister kissing and fondling an attractive young girl on board a large cruiser in Cannes. The subjects clearly had not realised the sophistication of a night vision lens. The girl was later identified as a twenty-one-year-old Brazilian model. Another success was a member of a European royal family's drunken departure from a Nice nightclub with two blond girls later identified as goodtime girls.

Jason had been following the luxury yacht for a week

and had tried three approaches at high speed outside Paphos, Dubrovnik and Naples. He wasn't sure he had got anything of significance but he hadn't had time to print the pictures yet.

Abdul, who had been stationed on the bridge with Captain Nasr on the *Good Queen Bess,* had been told by the radar operator about the three approaches and had reported to Ibrahim the speedboat was following them.

Jason had to anchor some distance from the yacht. He or Reine watched the radar day and night waiting for the big ship to up anchor. They didn't take any notice when a powerful launch came towards them from the east. The *Good Queen Bess* was anchored outside Corfu Town Marina. Jason and Reine were anchored a half mile away. As the approaching speedboat pulled alongside Jason's boat, three men sprayed the decks with machine-gun fire. Jason and Reine died in a hail of bullets. One of the men jumped across onto the speedboat, dodging broken glass. He found Jason's camera and case, and then placed a small device on the deck by the petrol tank. They left in the direction they came.

The chef, Pierre Van Duble, was organising the serving of a fine prawn cocktail when they all stopped talking. An explosion some distance away. The group of men Pierre served resumed its conversation. Chef Pierre thought the conversation was in Arabic but really didn't care if it was Martian if they enjoyed his dinner this evening.

★

After an uneventful breakfast the following day, the passengers on the *Good Queen Bess* were summoned to a meeting. The six men sat in a semicircle in the lounge of the yacht and faced the giant screen on the wall. Their bodyguards patrolled the decks and guarded the doors. The picture flickered. Then an Arab in headdress appeared.

Osama bin Laden was rumoured to be dead. If so, this was a good lookalike. Each of the men in this two-way transmission acknowledged and saluted the man whose face was on the screen. Each of them had a code name. They never referred to their real names.

Blue, an Iranian based in London, was the manager in Europe. Red was Lebanese and managed their operation in Mexico, USA and Canada. Black, a Pakistani, acted for the group in the Middle East, and Green, an Iranian, managed the African operation. The two other men in the lounge were not known to any of them.

"Green," said the figure on the screen, speaking in English. The voice was heavily distorted but the man known as Green looked up. He was an Arab from Iran but was born in Iraq. The man, code name Green, spoke.

"We have had some difficulty in Somalia. The infidel Americans sent three operatives to check our ExCy warehouse at the dockside in Mogadishu. We eliminated all three. We believe that they were CIA."

"You say they might be CIA and are dead?" asked the figure on screen.

"Yes," he replied.

"Then who later killed the nine men – six were killed pursuing a man and a woman leaving the harbour in a speedboat, and three were found dead in the warehouse by the docks?"

Green spluttered slightly. How did 'the figure' know about this? Green's number two in Somalia, the Moroccan Ali Aghmati, reported the deaths of the useless Somalians chasing the couple in the harbour two days ago directly to him.

"We haven't yet established who they were," replied Green.

"Did they get a sample?" asked the figure on the screen, his voice clearly distorted.

"We must assume they did," replied Green, somewhat sheepishly.

"Good. That will keep them wondering. But, Green, you must be more careful. One more mistake by your number two in Somalia then replace him."

"Very well," replied Green.

"Blue," said the figure on the screen.

"Yes," Blue replied.

"You decided to eliminate the French customs officer?" He asked a question that he already knew the answer to.

"Yes, he had obtained a sample from Bogota. When Red informed me that the Frenchman had bribed one of the Colombians and obtained a sample, I thought it necessary to eliminate him," Blue replied.

Red shifted in his seat. He was the manager in South America and one of his men had been bribed into giving this French customs officer a sample.

"Red," said the voice from the screen, "what have you got to say? This is a serious breach of security. The Frenchman has a sample of the compound, not useless soap."

"The Colombian who took the bribe has been eliminated and as you know the French customs officer is dead. The sample is at the bottom of the Atlantic Ocean."

"Nevertheless, the operation was nearly jeopardised. This was careless. Eliminate your number two. I will send a replacement."

"Yes," replied Red.

"Black," – a Pakistani with a sharp-hooked nose looked at the screen – "are the production factories on-target to produce the compound to specification?" asked the figure on screen.

Black replied, "The factory in Yemen, outside the port at Aden, has had a local difficulty which I briefed you on through the encrypted email. But they are on-target to produce ten tons of the compound."

"Ah yes, the local harbourmaster required a bribe to allow our tankers to use the local marina. Have you paid him?" asked the man on screen.

"Yes, one hundred thousand dollars," replied Black.

"Later we will eliminate him," replied the figure on the screen. "Continue, Black."

"The plants in Beirut and Yemen are on-target – ten tons are awaiting shipment to the processing plants in Columbia, Marseille, Mogadishu, Rotterdam and Mexico City."

"That is good. And the production plant in Oman?" asked the figure on screen.

"One of the local policemen is demanding access to the plant. So far we have resisted but he is a powerful local man," Black answered.

"Very well. Leave him to me," replied the figure on screen. "Finally, only use the encrypted email we purchased from the Chinese for urgent matters. The CIA and the infidel's code breakers at the NSA complex in Utah may be working on a solution. I have set up a series of messages; don't write them down. They are all single transmissions. Don't use the message more than once. Memorise the one-off messages now." He showed six messages on the screen.

"Finally, Blue," he paused, "three times you have been given instructions to eliminate people in London interfering with our plans."

"But I have sent assassins, Romanians, who have failed."

"This man, Colonel Harriman – take great care; he is very resourceful and a dangerous adversary. The woman the British fools have appointed deputy head of their MI6 – kill her now. She is too clever for her own good. Use the men I will be sending you, not the Romanian scum."

"Yes," replied Blue.

"And, Blue, this is your last chance."

All the men sitting around the screen knew what that

meant. This man, if he was Osama bin Laden, was merciless. Failure meant death.

The screen went blank. The men got up to give instructions to their servants and bodyguards that they were getting off the boat that evening. They did not talk to each other. All four men regarded Ibrahim with suspicion. He was likely to have installed cameras and microphones on the yacht to report to the figure they all thought was Osama bin Laden. Ibrahim was a Saudi and they were all convinced that this was a Saudi-backed operation.

The yacht, which had been anchored outside Corfu Town, upped anchor to sail to the Lebanon to drop off the four men, the worldwide managers of the operation, and their entourage at Beirut. Each would travel by different routes back to their control areas.

The other two men who had sat in during the broadcast left the yacht in Corfu. The other passengers had no idea who they were except they were not Arabs and neither had spoken a word. Black suspected one was a Pakistani but you didn't discuss their presence onboard, if you were required to know you would have been told. In fact it was two of the billionaire backers, the Russian and the Indian, who had insisted on seeing the second tier of the management of this operation for themselves.

10

Jack Clarke was the deputy director of the CIA. A career spy, he had done his time in the field during the first 'Bush' war in Iraq and subsequently in Afghanistan. Now aged fifty-two, he doubted he would make director but he sure as hell was going to try. This Tears of the West stuff was his opportunity. Something big was going on. The British had spotted it and so had the CIA. But what? Everything linked to the ExCy company. A manufacturer of soap. He suspected it was a red herring and was actively following it up. He had returned from London two days ago but Caroline Bland had not been able to add anything to what he already knew, most of which he was not sharing with the Brits. Nice folks but these days a second-rate nation. He buzzed his intercom.

"Lisa, find Willis for me," he said.

Willis Coogan was one of Jack's principal investigators. An ex-Harvard law graduate, he had been recruited in the intake of 1995. Willis hadn't wanted to join the CIA. His father, General George Coogan, wanted him to follow an army career and join the marines. Willis went to Harvard and studied law and languages. He was a gifted linguist. Almost without effort he learnt Urdu and Arabic. When in his final year his roommate was busted by the local police department, they found both of them in possession of cocaine.

All that earlier work – wasted. Until that is, local agent Merve Murray, the CIA recruiter for Harvard, Yale, Stanford and other major colleges, stepped in. In return for arranging for the charges to be dropped, Willis had to commit five years to the CIA. At first he had resisted. At worse he would be sent down. But his best friend, Jackson Furley, was also in the frame. His father, Senator Morgan Furley, would be furious. And it was election time. An attempt by Jackson to bribe Willis with Sally Hobb, a beautiful second year he had been admiring, and fifty thousand dollars, cost him their friendship. Jackson had inherited his grandfather's trust money when he was twenty-one but he had gambled and owed bookmakers a considerable sum. Between a rock and a hard place Willis joined the CIA. His father was angry but calmed down when his son was sent, after initial training, to Iraq.

Willis had dark skin and became a master of disguise. He had been an excellent shot since an early age and had a natural ability to speak Urdu and Arabic. He went undercover and quickly established a formidable reputation. Much of the intelligence gathered for the second invasion of Iraq was thanks to Willis. He had spent long periods in Bagdad. Now Jack needed his talents to find out some answers on the ground. There was a tap on the deputy director's door.

"Come."

"Hi boss." In breezed Willis, tanned and now sporting a long beard. Working in Afghanistan undercover as a Lebanese businessman he had to have the compulsory beard otherwise the Taliban were likely to shoot first and ask questions later. The Taliban controlled much of the business between Pakistan and Afghanistan. Willis was considered by the Taliban to be a Lebanese businessman who could supply many things, from Land Rovers to Uzi machine guns. His background cover was immaculate. But Jack needed him to sniff around the bin Laden radicals and the Taliban to find out what he could about this Tears of the West business.

Jack briefed Willis, who looked despondent. This was his first leave of absence from the Pakistan/Afghan border for twelve months and the pressure was telling on him. "And Willis, I know I promised a period in the States. But first things first; find out what you can, someone must know something."

Willis flew to Karachi the following day as Muhammad Tanvir.

★

The deputy director studied the CIA field agent's reports on all the known ExCy manufacturing units, warehouses and dockyards. Every person who went to or from any of these establishments was now being photographed. The recognition computer, an extraordinarily powerful computer with clever facial identification software, then checked the photographs against people on the CIA database. So far they had identified Belardi, a known al-Qaeda terrorist. Since his agents, Walker and Estenso, had been killed in Somalia, Jack wanted vengeance against the perpetrators. He had had the unpleasant job of telling Walker's wife and Estenso's partner that their men were dead. He wanted to make swift progress, track down the leaders and eliminate them. So far, progress was slow. A British agent had obtained a sample in Somalia where his three agents had failed. That irked him. Once again, though, the sample proved nothing. The agents had risked their lives for liquid soap. Jack sat with his hands on his head. What were these guys up to? It must be connected with ExCy but how? His internal buzzer went. It was Lisa, his PA.

"Jack, big chief wants to see you," Lisa said.

"Ah, I was wondering when he would want a progress report."

He picked up the photo ID of a man known as Belardi. The report on the liquid sent by the Brits made up his mind on a course of action and he went upstairs.

Samuel J Goldmuir was the director of CIA. Climbing the promotional ladder had not been easy for a man from Brooklyn, New York. Samuel had joined the marines at the age of eighteen having flunked most of his studies. He only excelled in Spanish but found his fluency useful. He served with distinction in the Vietnam War and had been awarded a Silver Star and the Congressional Medal of Honor. The army had been his life. He transferred to the Rangers in 1981 and was again decorated. By then he had risen up the ranks to captain. The army examinations seemed that much easier. His fluency in Spanish made him a popular officer with the Hispanic conscripts. In 1983 he was wounded in an ambush in Granada. He returned stateside and after six months' recuperation reported to the base at Benning, Georgia expecting to be a training officer. Much to his surprise, 'Big Ron' Rawlins was in the company commander's office. Ron Rawlins was a CIA man. Samuel and a unit of Rangers had saved his hide in Vietnam in 1968 when he had been cut off near the city of Hue with the Vietnamese closing in. At the time all the CIA colleagues of Big Ron had written him off. 'In too far this time' they had said.

Ron, a master of infiltration behind enemy lines, had gone deep into hostile territory seeking to talk to South Vietnamese fighters who were stalling the Viet Cong push they later called the Tet Offensive. He had got cut off. Only a desperate incursion by a platoon of Rangers, led by a young Lieutenant Goldmuir, saved his hide. He had never forgotten the young soldier and kept in touch. When he received news of Samuel's transfer to Benning he waited until the now Major Goldmuir was about to be bored silly training new recruits and then he offered him a position in the CIA. The army was Samuel Goldmuir's life. However, he didn't fancy spending his final years training 'bare-assed recruits'.

He joined the CIA. Propelled upward by Big Ron, he went to Iraq during both conflicts and learnt passable Arabic. When Ron Rawlins retired in 1998 he had groomed his protégé and friend, Samuel, to take his place. But the president was having none of it and appointed his own successor. Randolph Newlyn became the head of the CIA. It was two years before finally the White House relented, retired the incompetent Randolph and promoted Samuel. Goldmuir had been director of the CIA since and he knew Jack Clarke, his deputy, coveted his job.

"Right, Jacko, what have you got on this ExCy business?" He always got straight to the point.

Jack went through the visit to the UK, the photo ID of Belardi and the report by the Brits on the substance obtained in Somalia.

"Speaking of Somalia, Jack," – Samuel hated the loss of any of his operatives – "little lightweight sending in a rookie woman as their back-up, don't you think?" Samuel gazed over the top of his glasses.

"It was meant to be an easy op. In, get a sample, then out."

"You know nothing's that simple, Jack. You told the relatives?"

"Yes, yesterday," replied the deputy director.

"Don't envy that. Okay, let's do an in-depth on these folks; they've killed two of ours," said Samuel.

"I've prepared a plan to raid all the ExCy factories and warehouses we can, simultaneously," replied Jack.

The two men looked over the plan.

"Okay, go for it. But, Jack," Samuel looked up, "no rookies, and team strength on these raids."

"Right, boss." Jack picked up his papers.

"By the way, how's the woman," he paused, "Meredith?"

"Bit shaken up," replied Jack. "Raped – no, gang-raped, according to the doctor's report. The company psychiatrist also says some mental damage – may not be able to return to active duty," said Jack.

"Shame," Samuel replied. "I know her father. Keep me posted."

Jack got up and left to set up the operation to raid ExCy's known warehouses, factories and storage facilities.

11

Harry and Johno pressed the bell on the outside of The Kitty Club in London's Soho district. A flap opened in the centre of the door. Harry passed a fifty pound note to the large black man behind it. The door opened and they walked in. They headed past the hatcheck girl towards the club and the bar. Two Asian girls extracted themselves from a group at the end of the bar and linked their arms.

"Hello, boys, you buy us a drink?"

"Not just yet, darling," said Johno.

"Come back later, baby," replied Harry, attempting to extract himself from one of the girls.

"Champagne, sir?" asked a rather effeminate barman.

"No, mate, two beers," replied Johno.

The barman looked disappointed but produced two bottles of Stella Artois.

"Sixteen pounds, please," he said.

"How much?" echoed Johno and Harry.

"Sixteen pounds, please," repeated the barman, looking at his nails.

"Christ, I didn't know we were buying the whole bar a

drink," said Johno looking around but plonking a twenty pound note on the bar top.

Harry saw a booth that was in a good position to watch the bar and walked towards it. There was a stage at the end of the bar with a number of tables scattered around. A chromium pole was at the front of the stage.

"No prizes for guessing what goes on here, mate," said Johno.

"Bit slow at the moment," replied Harry, looking around.

Two other men sat near the stage with four olive-skinned girls. They were laughing and consuming the champagne being poured lavishly by one of the girls. Two more girls approached Harry and Johno. These were European. They slipped into the booth with them.

"Push off, darling," responded Johno. "We'll tell you when."

The girls didn't move.

"Look, darling, we don't want any company at the moment; we're talking business," said Harry.

"Bloody hell, Harry, these girls are blokes dressed up," said Johno.

"I thought they were," replied Harry.

"What sort of place is this then?" asked Johno.

"I think we're about to find out," replied Harry as music started playing from a sound system. A tall drag artist walked onto the stage swaying provocatively to the Shirley Bassey song *Big Spender* and mimed to the two men sitting at the nearest table. Three or four more men came into the club. Harry looked to see if the Arab they were seeking came in – but nothing.

The singer finished miming the first song and the music changed to Cilla Black singing *Anyone Who Had a Heart.*

"Christ, I can't stand too much of this," said Johno.

Harry laughed. More people came in: some men, some obvious transvestites.

"This is a right place, mate," said Johno.

The music changed again – *Girls Just Want to Have Fun* – the speakers blared out as the artist cavorted around the stage and slid around the metal pole. The club was slowly filling up. They were approached again.

"No offence, luv," Johno looked at the two 'girls', "but my mate and I would like our privacy, you know." He slipped them both a twenty pound note.

"What are you suggesting Johno?" laughed Harry.

The music blared out to the *YMCA* mimed by a group on the stage.

"Bloody hell!" said Johno. "Let's just ask some questions, mate, and get out of here."

They began to show the photograph of the Arab to the escorts in the club.

"Blimey, look at that one," said Harry, as a gorgeous transvestite dressed in a blond wig and a silver lycra dress, tight-fitting, with spaghetti straps showing her cleavage off to its full advantage, came into the club.

"You could almost fancy it," said Johno. "Blimey, mate, have you seen the size of her hands?" They laughed.

Johno looked at his watch.

"It's after 1pm, Harry. I don't think he'll be coming now. Shall we go?"

As they got up to leave there was a commotion near the bar. Two of the heavies that had been standing chatting up the hatcheck attendant moved towards the argument. Suddenly one of the escorts cried out as one of the men struck her. He then struck the tearful escort again and she cried. Harry was closest and as the bouncer, a stocky man with close-cropped hair, was about to strike her again he moved between the two of them.

"I think she's had enough, mate, don't you?" Harry said.

The bouncer, used to bullying escorts and transvestites, looked contemptuously at Harry.

“What’s it to you? Keep out of it,” he barked.

“No, I can’t do that. You’ve made your point, now leave it,” Harry said more menacingly.

The man looked at Harry then went to hit him with a right cross. Harry easily ducked under the punch and hit his kneecap with the sole of his shoe. The man cried out in agony and collapsed falling to the floor holding his kneecap. The other bouncer went to hit Harry but received a punch from Johno on the side of his face, then another in the gut. The bouncer doubled over and fell as Johno whipped his legs away. Harry looked at the sobbing escort.

"You all right, luv?” he asked.

She nodded, looking at Harry adoringly. Johno felt someone touch his hand then realised a piece of paper had been put into it. A door opened near the stage and two other burly-looking men and a shorter but nonetheless tough-looking man came out. They all had baseball bats.

“Time to say goodnight, ladies.” Johno blew them a kiss as they both scarpered up the stairs and out past the black doorman who had remained on the door. They laughed as they reached the corner of Wardour Street and slowed down.

“You shouldn’t be fighting with that wound healing, Harry,” said Johno.

“Couldn’t resist a damsel in distress.” They both laughed again.

Johno looked at the piece of paper thrust into his hand.

‘Meet me at the Starbucks bottom Tottenham Court Road tomorrow 3.30pm about photograph’ was scribbled in what looked like eyebrow pencil. Johno showed Harry.

“Well, we might have a lead after all. Time for a kip, though. Let’s share a cab on the firm,” said Harry, hailing a passing black cab.

★

Colonel Harriman had refused to move to one of Caroline's safe houses and remained in his mews cottage in Chelsea.

"If they try a hit I'll be ready this time," he said.

Caroline knew it was pointless arguing but had arranged for armed special response police to watch his house. The chief constable hadn't been very co-operative until the home secretary contacted him. Then Colonel Harriman, much to his annoyance, had twenty-four hour police protection.

They dined together most nights and tonight had called for a pizza to be delivered. The doorbell rang. Caroline looked out of the first floor window. A pizza man was standing holding their supper; his motor scooter was on its stand close by, the engine chugging away. The two policemen opposite in the unmarked Audi ignored the man. They had already been alerted by Caroline to expect a delivery.

The colonel went to the front door. As he opened it, two shots hit him in the chest and he fell backwards. Both policemen in the Audi opened the car doors. Phut, phut – the gunman fired at the policemen. A car window shattered. The pizza man jumped onto the scooter, the motor was still running, and he started to accelerate away from the house. More shots were fired. The assassin reached the top of the mews, turned left and was away.

Caroline found Colonel Harriman just inside the front door.

"John!" she cried out.

Gingerly, he sat up.

"Christ, it bloody well hurts getting shot at close range, even if you are wearing a Kevlar." The bulletproof vest under his shirt had saved his life.

"Thank God I made you wear that," said Caroline just as one of the police officers reached the front door.

"You okay, sir?"

"Yes, fine. Have you a description?"

"Only what you saw, sir, and I'm afraid he got away."

"Don't assume it was a man, sergeant," responded Caroline, now on her mobile.

Five minutes later, much to the annoyance of some of his neighbours, Colonel Harriman's mews house was being lit up by numerous blue police lights. Officers from the armed response unit and forensics searched for the bullet casings.

"Looks like a shell from a Walther to me," said one man in a white bodysuit holding up a shell case on the end of a pencil.

"You were lucky, sir," said a police superintendent. "If the man had chosen a head shot… well, need I say more?"

"Thank you, superintendent," replied the colonel. "Is it possible your men could turn off their blue lights? My neighbours will be complaining, and as several are members of parliament we don't want any repercussions, do we?"

The superintendent didn't look as though he cared but barked an order. Two of the vehicles left the mews and the others turned off the flashing lights.

"They've found the pizza delivery boy. Shot dead, I'm afraid," said a uniformed sergeant to the superintendent. Caroline had overheard the conversation.

"Bloody hell," was all she could say before talking to John Harriman.

"All right," he said. "I agree to come to your place for tonight. But I am not being driven into hiding – once your people and the police have finished here I'm going to get one of my team to sweep my house for bugs. They must have planted something to know we'd ordered pizza and the name of the firm."

"Yes, I was wondering that myself," said Caroline.

Later, a police car dropped them off at Caroline's flat in Putney.

Two armed uniformed policemen remained outside the street door; not exactly happy on a wet night.

12

Johno approached the coffee bar at 3pm, half an hour early. He knew Starbucks would be heaving at this time of day and waited to get a seat away from the window, facing the door. Harry followed him in five minutes later, queued up for a coffee, then sat on the opposite side and watched the door. At five minutes past the designated time, a man sashayed into the coffee bar. His effeminate look attracted stares from the other punters. Some smiled at him; others just stared. Part of his hair was dyed red and he wore too much make-up and heavy mascara. He bought a coffee and a chocolate muffin, looked around and moved towards Johno. He winked at Johno as he sat down next to him.

"Hello, sweetie," he said.

Johno grunted, well aware lots of people were staring.

"Come in disguise, why don't you?" said Johno.

The man picked up his muffin and carefully selected pieces, delicately putting them in his mouth between sips of coffee.

"Muffin, dear?" he asked, amusing himself with Johno's glances around.

"I think I'll stick to coffee, thanks," said Johno.

The man leaned forward.

"Thanks for helping Marilyn last night. That man Angus is a bully. As it is he's bruised the darling's face and she's had to put on a heavier make-up." He deliberated on whether to eat another piece of muffin. "Not good for your figure, these bad boys," he said, looking at what was left of the muffin.

Johno was getting tired of this, even though most people had stopped staring.

"Did you know the man in the photograph?" Johno asked.

"Well, not exactly, dear," he replied, licking his fingers.

"Let's have it then. What do you know?"

"Oh, you are manly." He crossed his legs extravagantly, attracting lots of attention.

"Look, chum, I helped your pal; now tell me what you know!"

"Don't get your knickers in a twist, sweetie." He passed Johno a piece of paper. "I'm Shirley, by the way. The man in the photograph is called Ali. He visits the club about once a month. He chats to several of the girls, then selects two to go with him." He took a sip of coffee.

"Go with him… Go where?"

"Ah, that's worth a couple of quid, duckie," the man's voice dropped deeper.

Johno had been expecting this and put two fifty pound notes on the coffee table.

"Bit cheap, aren't you, dear?" said Shirley.

Johno added two more notes.

"Now tell me," he said threateningly.

"Don't get upset, dear. It's just business," replied Shirley.

"Well, where do they go?" asked Johno.

"He has a penthouse flat in Marylebone. One of the old

Victorian mansions converted to flats. Lovely place. Gold and Arabic décor. Lots of rugs and statues. Mostly of naked men," he giggled.

"The address?" asked Johno.

"16 Bayswater Mansions, Marylebone Road."

"Anything else you can tell me?" asked Johno.

"Funny thing. No photographs. Nothing personal in the flat. Only a few clothes in the wardrobe. Uses Chanel aftershave. Likes kinky sex," he chuckled.

"What about a name?"

"He calls himself Ali, but I doubt that's his proper name. He has a suitcase in the wardrobe with gold initials on the outside – M H. He always pays in new fifties and wait for it," he paused, looking very pleased with himself.

"What?" said Johno.

"This is one of the fifty pound notes he paid me with last time."

"Careful," said Johno, taking the note by the edge.

"Ah, I wondered if you were a copper," said Shirley.

"Why did you keep this note?" asked Johno.

"I keep them all, my dear. Don't believe in banks. Do you know, some of our kinkier clients are bankers?" He laughed a short effeminate laugh.

Johno extracted four more fifties from his pocket.

"Here's my card," said Johno. "Phone me if the man comes to the club again."

"All right, sweetie."

"Where can I find you if need be?" Johno asked.

"I thought you'd never ask!" He winked at Johno and opened his shoulder bag.

"My address," Shirley said.

Johno read the card – Shirley Eaton, 6 Evelyn Terrace, Fulham SW6. A mobile phone number was shown.

"She's my favourite," Shirley said.

"Who's that then?" asked Johno.

"You know – Shirley Eaton in Goldfinger. Such glamour. They don't look like that these days." He swivelled in his seat, slung the strap of the bag over his shoulder, winked at Johno again and got up. As he left the coffee bar most of the customers turned and watched. *Such an actress*, thought Harry as he saw Johno get up. Harry followed ten seconds later when no one else did.

13

The French had not internally or publicly accepted that the Macedonian Airlines jet, which had crashed three hours out of Bogota, Colombia, bound for Paris, was anything but a terrible accident. Georges LeForge, the head of investigations for French customs, strongly suspected otherwise. But despite his meetings with Monsieur Philippe, the minister responsible for external security, no action had been taken.

He asked a friend in Interpol who the British MI6 person was at the Paris embassy and had telephoned for a meeting. Wishing to keep the meeting discreet, he had suggested a small, usually quiet, café in Montmartre, the popular area of Paris.

"Monsieur LeForge, you are welcome. May I offer coffee?" said the secret service agent.

"*Merci*, Monsieur Standing," replied LeForge.

Charles Standing was MI6's man in Paris and had arrived at the Café Rouge early. Working out of the Paris embassy as a trade envoy, he liaised with the French Secret Service and Interpol. Since 9/11, all of western Europe had increased its resources to intercept potential threats. Every day, thousands of Eastern Europeans, most without EU passports, travelled to Calais to attempt to stow aboard a lorry to get to the UK. On the face of it, the French did very little to stop this traffic. But in reality a team of Sécurité officers was surreptitiously taking photographs of many of the illegals queuing to enter the UK. French Algerian members of the Sécurité infiltrated the camps posing as desperate to get to the UK. The British paid handsomely, of course. A special fund had been created to pay for the French security officers and for the surveillance. Charles Standing administered the fund and tried to identify threats before forwarding all the photographs. Very occasionally a bad penny turned up, but usually they were wanted criminals posted by Interpol. This meeting, called by Monsieur LeForge, had been unexpected.

"Thank you for coming, Monsieur LeForge. How can I help you?"

"Monsieur Standing, please call me Georges. I am here on a delicate matter…" They sat sipping their coffee outside the quiet Montmartre café as the Frenchman explained the reason for the call. He elaborated on his department's worry about the ExCy plant outside Marseille and the sending of an investigator to Bogota to check the export of what…? The head of the French customs admitted his own government regarded the loss of the airliner as a *force majeure* – a loss by an unknown cause. He then showed the last text message from Serge on board the doomed aircraft.

Charles Standing was an experienced MI6 field officer and realised that politics with the French Sécurité could have a potential and disastrous impact on all the other work they were doing. But he had received a briefing from Caroline, the deputy head of MI6, regarding ExCy, and immediately realised that the downing of the jet was sabotage and that the substance referred to in the message might be crucial.

"Monsieur Standing, I cannot ask this on behalf of the French government but if the British were to use their submersible craft to investigate and try and retrieve Serge Votre's black briefcase, this might contain evidence of what activities ExCy are, as you British say, up to."

Both men knew the downed aircraft was sitting three miles below the surface and only two countries had the submersible craft that could go down that deep. The French did not want to ask the United States for their help, which left the British.

Charles was pondering this request from a junior French official to have a British destroyer take a submersible into the Atlantic Ocean and hunt for the downed Macedonian Airlines aeroplane when a motorcycle with two men roared up to the café. A man dressed head to toe in black jumped off the pillion and ran across to their table. Before Charles could react to the silenced pistol he saw in the man's hand, he was shot and then the gunman turned towards Georges LeForge and shot him at point blank range. The man ran back to the motorcycle which roared off.

The café owner was shocked. A passer-by called the police and an ambulance. Charles Standing was declared dead at the scene. Georges LeForge was still alive and rushed to the nearest hospital. For two hours surgeons struggled to save him, but his heart gave out shortly after 2pm.

⋆

Caroline Bland was reading some reports on the information Harry Sutherland had brought back from his visit as a VAT officer to ExCy's London headquarters. Shoreham Harbour Authority had been particularly helpful. A medium-sized tanker had docked at Shoreham in June 2007. A stevedore who had been working at the dock clearing a pile of timber was surprised to see the medium-sized tanker, as anything too big couldn't get in. He had watched a Filipino crew decline assistance and transfer the contents of their tanks to a fleet of four road tankers. One registration number had caught his eye – DOU55 633. He had laughed as his Christian name was Doug and his home phone number was 55633. That coincidence had helped Caroline trace one of the unmarked lorries and she was reading the report as her red telephone rang. The red scrambled telephone was used by embassies and calls from her operatives.

"Caroline Bland," she answered.

"Caroline, it's Ambassador Redman."

"Hello, Leonard. Problem?" Caroline knew the ambassador in Paris would not be telephoning her unless it was important.

"Sorry to tell you this, Caroline. Your man Charles Standing was shot dead an hour ago."

There was silence.

"Caroline, you there?"

"Sorry, Leonard, I was thinking. Any other information?"

"French police dealing. The officer in charge is Inspector Moreau. Charles was shot outside a café in Montmartre and so was the man he was meeting – no details on him yet," said the ambassador.

"Thank you for letting me know, Leonard. Any other info, please ring urgently."

Caroline used the house phone to call the internal security service. MI5 were closer to the French and she wanted to discuss the killing with them.

"Willy, I need to see you." She had buzzed the head of MI5, Sir William Villiers, responsible for UK internal security. Sir William had replaced another Oxford University graduate last year. Caroline had not got on with his predecessor but as she had been posted abroad by MI6 it didn't really matter. Sir William, on the other hand, was first-class. In their first meeting he had broken the ice – 'call me Willy,' he'd said.

Caroline went to the sixth floor and nodded to Sir William's PA, a crusty career woman, Meryl Dawes, who always reminded her of Agatha Christie.

"He's expecting me," said Caroline and was nodded towards Sir William's office.

Tapping on the door she went in.

"Ah, Caroline, sit," he said. "What have you got?"

As the acting liaison officer between the two branches of the British security services, Caroline went through the murder of Charles Standing in Paris.

"Must be connected with this ExCy business," said Caroline.

"Why do you think that?" asked Sir William, who had been investigating the pharmaceutical company at the behest of the home secretary.

"Just a hunch. We haven't lost a field officer for two years. Bit of a coincidence, don't you think? And then there's the man he was meeting. When we know who he was we may have more answers."

"Have you organised a replacement for Paris?" asked Sir William.

"Thinking about it, and I'll have to discuss it with Sir Anthony," she replied, thinking he would be her next call.

"Any other progress with this ExCy business?" asked Sir William.

"A few things are coming out, but nothing concrete."

"All right, keep me posted."

Caroline knew the meeting was over. Sir William wasted no time on pleasantries.

14

Louis Roussel, the head of the French security service, the DCRI, listened intently, smoke drifting across the table from the Gauloises cigarettes he chain-smoked.

"Have you enquired with British MI6 what this man Standing, if that's his real name, was meeting LeForge about?" he asked Inspector Moreau.

"No, I thought I would talk to you first. I think their meeting was connected to the Macedonian Airlines jet that crashed."

"*Pourquoi*?"

"His secretary, Madame Laurent, said he had been studying the report on the downed aircraft. He had a man on board."

"He did?" Roussel inhaled deeply as he pondered this information

"Yes, a customs inspector, Serge Votre, had become suspicious about tankers that had originated in Colombia arriving at Marseille from Bogota via the African ports of Mogadishu and Lagos."

"What did they think it was – drugs?"

"At first yes, but according to Madame Laurent, Serge Votre's last message was that he had obtained a sample of a liquid. I am obtaining a copy of all the reports and the phone transcript."

"Good, let me know quickly. I need to speak to the British," said Roussel, lighting up another cigarette.

15

Jack Clarke had flown to Mexico City to supervise the raid on two warehouses. He had given instructions authorised by the director to 'take out' the ExCy establishments in Somalia and Mexico. Preferably without the loss of further CIA operatives. This time, the raid was by Delta Forces and CIA agents – three groups of six members of the Delta Force and two CIA operatives at each location. The Delta Force was the name of the 1st Special Forces Operational Detachment set up to take direct action on counterterrorism. The raid in Mexico was a tricky one and Jack had welcomed that all the Delta operatives were dressed in civvies. They flew in two's to Mexico City International Airport, known locally as Benito Juarez International Airport, and met a CIA agent who had a people carrier. The Mexican government would not take it kindly if US army personnel were caught operating in its country and they all arrived as tourists from Miami and Atlanta on two separate flights.

The first Delta Force of six men was to break into the warehouse area in the north east of Mexico City, two operatives to hold the perimeter, whilst the four other

Delta members and the two CIA agents took a look inside the ExCy warehouse. When the agents had checked inside, the Delta specialists would plant explosive charges. Jack's plan for Somalia was similar – blow the place up, but see if there were any samples of liquid.

Things didn't entirely go to plan. When they arrived at the first warehouse in an industrial estate on the northern outskirts of Mexico City, it had been vacated and no guard on the gate. Only two large, empty vats were left in the warehouse. In frustration, Jack ordered that the vats be punctured with a small delayed explosive charge. Then he, and two CIA agents, went to the airport and travelled by an internal flight to Veracruz from Mexico City to meet the second Delta squad. The first Delta unit flew back from Mexico City to Miami and Atlanta using fictitious identities supplied by the CIA.

The second group of Delta operatives had flown as tourists in two groups from Houston to Veracruz airport, hired a people carrier using false papers, changed the plates, and met the three CIA agents at the airport. A recce had already been carried out by the CIA local agent in Mexico City. The group drove to the port of Veracruz where the second warehouse operated by ExCy Pharmaceuticals was situated at San Juanico Industrial Warehousing. When they arrived, the local CIA agent told them the warehouse was heavily guarded. An added complication was that Mexican police patrols regularly cruised the port area. Jack decided to continue the mission, sure that the extra security indicated something to hide.

At 2.15pm local time, two of the six-man Delta team put the guard at the entrance of the dock gates out of action using a stun gun and handcuffed and gagged him making sure he could breathe. The remainder of the group approached the ExCy warehouse. There were two armed guards patrolling the outside of the warehouse. One of the

Delta members had taken up a snipers position on the top of a large container five hundred yards from the warehouse. The guards were not expecting a problem that morning. Both men were smoking cheroots and gossiping about a bar they went to the previous night and didn't notice the two hooded men approaching until they were fifty yards away. They shouted a warning in Spanish not to come any closer and raised their weapons.

The Delta sniper spent hours every day practising and took out both of the guards with two shots from his favourite weapon a Remington M2010 ESC (an enhanced sniper weapons rifle). They had been briefed that an outer door might be locked, but the two guards were careless. They went inside and walked into another guard carrying two coffee cups. He was swiftly neutralised. He was shot but not before his cry had alerted another guard who came out of an office firing a Uzi sub-machine gun. One of the Delta men was wounded before the man was shot.

Then they heard sirens in the distance as the police arrived at the front gate of the port. The two Delta operatives left to guard the front entrance subdued the police officers who were no match for the soldiers, or rather had no stomach to fight a well-armed superior force. Jack entered the warehouse knowing time was running out; the Mexican police had almost certainly radioed in that shots had been heard from the dockside. A Delta specialist fixed explosives whilst Jack looked to obtain a sample of what was contained inside the huge vat, and another agent opened one of a huge stack of boxes.

Great, thought Jack, *no tap.* Then he spotted a ladder and climbed up the fifty-foot-high vat. A shot rang out and he felt a bullet whistle past his head. Then he heard the phut phut of a silenced sub-machine gun, he presumed from one of the Delta squad. He reached the top of the vat and looked down. Empty. *All this for nothing. Same as the Brits found in Somalia*, he thought. He climbed back down and told the Delta commander to set the timers for five minutes – at least they would blow up the storage facility. The other CIA agent showed him a bottle of Stardust shampoo he had taken from one of the pile of boxes. Jack grunted and put it in his pocket.

"Blow up the boxes as well," he told a Delta operative. The men retraced their steps back to the port entrance. The two members left there had now captured a second police car and two officers. All four policemen were unharmed but handcuffed to the steering wheel in their vehicles. They left in a hurry; driving quickly to the pick-up point.

Five bodies lay as they fell, two outside the ExCy warehouse, three more inside. Jack thought they looked Asian in appearance. They went straight to the pick-up point, along the coast to the Cabo Corrientes promontory down Highway 200 to a stretch of Mexico's Chamela beach. The local agent had chosen a stretch of beach hardly ever used by locals because of the rocky shoreline. Jack used his encrypted sat phone from the vehicle and, as they arrived down the end of a dirt road, a rubber inflatable grounded on the beach. Jack and the CIA agents were also exiting with the Delta Force.

The second Delta Force had come in two groups the previous day by a United Airlines flight to Veracruz from Miami and three members of the squad from Houston but had decided it might be too hot to return that way. The inflatable had to go a mile offshore before they were picked up by a US destroyer, the *Ulysses Grant*. The ship was meant to be participating in joint manoeuvres with the French and British to deter or capture drug runners using speedboats from Columbia into the Gulf of Mexico. The local CIA agent left to drive back to Mexico City and return the hired vehicle to a depot of the car hire firm at Mexico City International Airport.

Later, Jack was to report that ExCy would not be keeping any dangerous liquids in either the Mexican or the Somalian warehouses as the vats in all three, raided simultaneously, had been punctured or completely destroyed. Two guards had been killed in Somalia with no loss of personnel. One Delta operative had been wounded in the Mexican raids. The Mexican government had sought someone to blame for the atrocities. The CIA had leaked that they had intercepted a Colombian drug carrier who admitted the warehouses were being used to traffic drugs into the USA and it had been a fire fight between two drug cartels. The Mexicans were not convinced.

The company, ExCy, sought a detailed explanation. The Mexicans spluttered and promised better security, keen to placate such a large pharmaceutical company operating in Mexico.

The only really positive fact the CIA had taken away from Mexico and Somalia was that the men killed in the port warehouse raids all looked Middle Eastern or Asian. Photographs and fingerprints had been taken to check their database to ascertain if any of the dead men were known. The bottle of shampoo taken at the Veracruz warehouse was what it said on the label and didn't contain any other substance.

16

Twenty-four hours later, having got a flight from Ibiza to Nice, Daniel Ribert, another prominent member of the paparazzi, was scared. He knew he had some good photographs of the powerful launch and the men that had approached his rival Jason Long's speedboat just outside Ibiza harbour. But what to do with them? If he went to the authorities the photographs wouldn't be worth a euro. He sat on the bed, thinking. But anyone who was prepared to kill, even members of the paparazzi, was clearly ruthless. He didn't fancy approaching the killers and offering the memory card. Daniel was a member of the dreaded pack of the paparazzi.

When Daniel had learnt Jason Long, another member of the paparazzi, had hired a speedboat; he did likewise. Jason must be on to something big; hiring speedboats was expensive. When Daniel saw that Jason was following the magnificent yacht, the *Good Queen Bess*, at a distance, so did he. He had watched Jason take several 'run-by' shots of the people walking the deck of the luxurious yacht. Using his own telephoto lens, he didn't see any real 'faces' on board.

He'd been taking night shots of the yacht and several men walking around the deck, when Jason Long's speedboat was approached by another craft. Daniel was eight hundred yards away anchored nearer Ibiza Town harbour when suddenly two men on the launch that approached Jason's speedboat started shooting. Daniel nearly missed the photographs but recovered in time to take a stream of good shots of the killers. Now he was scared and for two days he was undecided as to what to do.

Finally he rang the editor of *Le Mistral,* a Paris newspaper, and offered him the shots of the murder of a Brit and a French citizen outside Ibiza Town harbour and the mysterious people on board the *Good Queen Bess*. The editor arranged a meeting in Nice; there might be a story. After all, you had to be rich to charter that particular yacht.

★

Paul Foncard had been editor of *Le Mistral* for five years. He began to sense a story when his reporter, Bridgette Corfour, told him the yacht, the *Good Queen Bess* was rumoured to be owned by the Saudi royal family. She had a useful contact at the Saudi embassy who wouldn't comment – why? Bridgette had begun to dig, but so far the yacht, its wealthy owners, and the people who were on board when Jason Long had been machine-gunned, remained elusive. Why did the yacht's captain not report the shooting? They were anchored 500 metres from the incident! He smelt a story and booked a flight to meet the photographer, Daniel, with Bridgette. It would be a good few days in Nice with Bridgette. She was very attractive and this time maybe she would…

★

Daniel had not left his apartment in the Rue de la Mere, Nice since his call to Paul Foncard. He thought the men on the speedboat who had machine-gunned Jason were Arabs and he had had a run-in with Arabs once before. At that time, he handed over prints showing a Saudi crown prince and a British princess embracing on the deck of the Saudi's magnificent cruiser. Worth one hundred thousand pounds, the prints were a life's work, but that's the point. If he hadn't handed them over, the Arab thugs would have cut his throat. As it was, they beat him senseless.

Daniel deadlocked and put the chain on the door of his first floor apartment. He always rented an apartment in Nice to cover the Cannes Film Festival and the summer. He spent part of his time in Paris, London and New York. Anywhere the paparazzi grouped together reduced the price of 'exclusives' as there were at any one time usually a dozen photographs from different photographers up for sale. Exclusives, where he had the only shot, were what he sought. This group of photographs he had now could be worth a tidy sum, he thought to himself. He opened another bottle of claret and sank back in the chair. There was a knock on the front door. Just a faint tap. He thought he heard the door opening – must be his imagination. He opened his eyes, trying to clear his head, when a man wearing something over his face burst into the room. Daniel tried to move but his legs seemed to be rooted to the spot. His mind took in a second man then the first man pointed a gun at him and fired.

⋆

Bridgette was getting a little annoyed. She had persuaded her editor to let her accompany him to Nice to view the photographs Daniel had told him about. He said they showed Arabs shooting and killing Jason Long and they had come from the *Good Queen Bess*. In addition, he had shots of several mysterious men on board. Scoops, Daniel had told Paul. Now he wouldn't answer his mobile. *I'll murder him if he's drunk again*, she thought.

They knew where Daniel lived and decided to visit in the morning.

★

Bridgette and Paul had been unable to reach Daniel Ribert on his mobile. Deciding to pay him a visit, they had breakfasted at the Hotel Orange and arranged for a taxi. Daniel rented an apartment in the Rue de la Mere; they paid the driver and walked towards number nineteen. Ringing the buzzer a number of times they were about to give up when the outside door was opened by another tenant. They slipped inside and went to apartment three. The outer door was ajar.

Paul called out, "Daniel, are you there?"

They walked slowly down the hallway. Music was playing – American rap. Pushing the first door they came to, they discovered an untidy bedroom with no sign of Daniel.

"Daniel," shouted Bridgette.

Moving down the hall they passed another bedroom, this time articles were strewn all around the bed. They reached another door they found to be the lounge. Bridgette screamed. Lying in a pool of blood was Daniel's body.

Paul took out his phone and began to photograph the scene.

"What are you doing?" asked Bridgette.

"Still a story here," he replied. "Let's make the most of it before the police arrive." Bridgette felt sick. She could see that half of Daniel's head was missing.

"Come on, let's phone the police and get out of here. What if the killer comes back?" she said

"I doubt that. He's been dead for at least a few hours; look, the blood is nearly dry."

"Don't touch him."

They could see the room had been ransacked.

"The killer must have found his photographs," said Bridgette.

"Not necessarily. Let's have a look around," replied Paul, keen to find the photographs.

"Come on, Paul, we must phone the police and wait in the street."

Outside the apartment block, having phoned the police, they heard a siren in the distance.

"I wonder if Daniel still went everywhere on that old British Triumph motorcycle?" Bridgette began to search down the road. She beckoned Paul.

"Look, that's his motorbike."

Quickly, as the sirens were getting louder, Paul undid the strap for the pannier on one side. Emptying the contents he found only an old *Figaro* newspaper and a dirty pair of jeans. He went around the other side as a police car roared down the road, siren blaring. Opening the pannier he found a notebook and a memory card; he pocketed both.

"Are you sure that's wise?" Bridgette glanced nervously at the police as they reached the apartment.

"Who's going to know?" replied Paul. "Come on, let's introduce ourselves and see if we can involve ourselves in the investigation."

Another police car arrived and two men dressed in dark suits both wearing blue open neck shirts walked towards the apartment.

"*Bonjour,*" said Paul. "We are from *Le Mistral* and telephoned when we discovered the body."

"Come with me, please," said one of the men, not bothering to introduce himself.

They went back upstairs where the police had already entered the apartment, and one of them was talking to the first suited man. The other man turned to Paul.

"I am Inspector Gaston. This is Sergeant Choud. Tell me, when did you find this man?"

After twenty minutes explaining partly what they were doing at the deceased person's apartment, the inspector asked them to come to Nice Central Police Station.

"Immediately," he said.

Four hours later they left having admitted that Daniel had told them that he had photographs of the killers of Jason Long and his colleague in Ibiza. They told the police the entire story, omitting they had the memory card.

"He thought the killers were Arabs," said Bridgette.

Paul glared at her.

"What else did he say?" asked the police inspector.

"Nothing; he was frightened," replied Bridgette.

"Why?"

"He thought they might come after him," replied Bridgette.

Paul sat impassively, not mentioning Daniel's motorcycle or the items he had taken.

Finally they left, having given their fingerprints, 'for elimination', said the inspector. They were asked not to leave Nice for twenty-four hours in case they were required again, and went back to their hotel. They didn't notice the dark-haired man following them, went through the lobby, collected their keys – Bridgette had insisted on a separate room – and went upstairs. The dark-haired man joined them in the lift. As they walked towards Paul's room they realised the man was following them.

"Don't be alarmed," he said in passable French. "My name is Adam. I'm a private investigator." He showed them a card.

"What do you want?" asked Paul.

"You were at the apartment of the murdered man, Daniel?" he asked.

"What is your interest?" Paul was sensing another aspect of this story.

"I was asked to investigate the destruction of a speedboat outside Ibiza Town by the AXA insurance company. Here's my card."

"And?" said Paul.

"A friend of one of the murdered men in Ibiza told me that this man Daniel knew something. I traced him to that apartment in Nice and was about to call when you both came out."

Paul thought quickly. Did he see him go to the motorcycle?

"So how can we help?" asked Paul.

"Well, you can let me have a look at what you took from his motorcycle pannier for a start."

Paul thought for a second. No point denying it and he invited the insurance investigator into his hotel room.

17

Adam Runfold, who had used his insurance claims inspector identity to get what information he could from the editor of *Le Mistral* and the reporter, Bridgette Corfour, sent an encrypted email to Caroline Bland in London.

> Daniel Ribert had photographed the men who attacked Jason Long's speedboat, killing him. Also I have other photographs of the 'guests' on the Good Queen Bess outside Ibiza Town. I am on six minutes past four easyJet flight to Gatwick. Daniel is now dead – killed before I got there.'

Adam was one of the senior MI6 officers investigating ExCy's activities; nevertheless, he had to travel second-class and as cheap as possible. He was returning to Gatwick from Nice on the easyJet flight, with the photographs he had acquired. He had noticed the Arab earlier as he sat in the departure lounge. The man had looked at him several times. Adam made sure he sat at the rear of the plane in order to observe everybody on board and was the last to leave the cabin at Gatwick.

He intended to board the Gatwick Express to London's Victoria Station, and walked down the airport escalator. He couldn't see the Arab and was beginning to think he might be imagining things when he instinctively turned and saw the same man three steps behind. Suddenly he felt a hand push him in the back he lost his footing and tumbled crashing to the bottom of the escalator. As he tried to regain his balance, he had let go of his overnight bag and as passengers crowded around he grimaced as he tried to get up and find the bag. One of the policemen on airport duty, who had been at the top of the escalator coming down to patrol the station, felt sure he had seen a dark-skinned man carrying a dark blue overnight bag going up as he came down. CCTV in the station and airport tracked the man to the bus station where he disappeared. Adam was badly bruised and annoyed with himself but as his superior officer Caroline Bland said, "Well, at least you'd backed-up the photographs and already sent us copies. The opposition may think they've got all the photographs of the people on the boat now and that might give us a chance to trace them."

⋆

Belardi read the encrypted email concerning the British interference and MI6. He was concerned about Caroline Bland who was a career spy and had advanced up MI6 to the position of deputy director. Belardi noted the comment that Caroline was the more public figure, with Sir Anthony preferring a background and virtually reclusive role. It had been the tendency for senior officers in MI5 and MI6 to maintain a low profile but after the publication of books by some of their predecessors, both Caroline and Sir Anthony were particularly known to his source. It was because of the interference from

MI6 that Belardi was contemplating a hit. He knew from Saudi intelligence sources that Caroline Bland was leading the investigation of ExCy and her lover, Colonel Harriman, who ran a security firm, was also interfering in their affairs. He knew that the British and Americans had discovered nothing. All the vats in Somalia, Mexico and France had been emptied and cleaned. The French customs man had obtained a sample in Columbia – but that was at the bottom of the Atlantic. They also had to eliminate a girl, who had been asking uncomfortable questions. They had already arranged for two of the people who worked with her to be killed. Now he sent a hit order.

He instructed the Libyan and the Iranian to kill the MI6 woman Bland first, then the interfering Colonel Harriman, then the girl at the university.

18

When John Harriman had first told her about the meeting with his goddaughter, the death of two of her work colleagues and what she was investigating, Caroline hadn't taken the situation seriously. More as a favour to John, she arranged for one of her best field agents, Adam Runfold, to try to obtain a sample of what the pharmaceutical company ExCy was holding in vats in Somalia. But Adam's sorté into Somalia and the subsequent interest of the CIA had changed her mind. Now on full alert, she sensed something was seriously wrong. Samples of ExCy cosmetics, widely on sale in the UK, were being analysed by government scientists. Several bottles of their products, all obtained by John's goddaughter six months ago, were being examined. She was reading the early report prepared by the boffins at Porton Down.

REPORT ON EXCY PHARMACEUTICALS' STARDUST RANGE

ExCy Pharmaceuticals manufacture a range of cosmetics using the trade name Stardust. These cosmetics are imported already made up in dispensers or as bulk liquid and sent to a bottling plant in Birmingham for distribution. The bulk container ships come in to Harwich and Shoreham. The cosmetics are available from major supermarkets throughout the UK. A substantial marketing campaign (estimated cost of TV advertising £10 million) promotes the Stardust range using well-known celebrities to front the advertisements. Billboard advertising is extensive as is 'off the page' ads in most newspapers and women's magazines.

ANALYSING SAMPLES OF SHAMPOO

The Stardust shampoo sent to us contained the following ingredients: aqua, sodium laureth sulfate, cocamidopropyl betaine, sodium cocoamphoacetate, panthenol…

Caroline's concentration began to waiver. She skipped the next fifteen ingredients, finishing on *propylparaben and methylparaben.*

ANALYSING SAMPLES OF DEODORANT FOR WOMEN – A ROLL-ON AND A SPRAY ALSO MARKETED UNDER THE STARDUST RANGE

Cyclopentasiloxane, aluminium zirconium, PPG-14 butyl ether, seed oil, parfum, dimethicone.

Caroline skipped the next twenty ingredients, finishing on *carboxaldehyde and limone.*

Must make a note to check my cosmetics when I get home, she thought. *No idea all these chemicals were included in shampoo and deodorant.* She read on.

ANALYSING SAMPLES OF HAIRSPRAY

Another long list of ingredients.

ANALYSING SAMPLES OF LIQUID SOAP, TOOTHPASTE, SUNSCREEN, SHAVING CREAM AND NAIL POLISH

Five long lists followed, some with similar ingredients. All prompted Caroline to make a mental note to check her bathroom cabinet.

NOTE

The ingredients for the men and women's shampoo, toothpaste, shaving cream, deodorant and hairspray are similar *except*:

In the samples marked H1, H2, H3 and H4 (women's shampoo, hairspray, toothpaste and deodorant) we discovered some ingredients not included in the list of chemicals stated on the packaging. These we suspect are nanoparticles, possibly fullerenes.

Fullerenes are minute, hollow-shaped particles made of carbon atoms that are bio-available. This nanotechnology is being used by other cosmetic manufacturers – see appendix.

Government scientists are endeavouring to isolate the particles and/or fullerenes we believe are included in samples H1, H2, H3 and H4 with the assistance of Essex University.

Most of the samples obtained from supermarkets DID NOT contain the additional ingredients that we suspect are nanoparticles. So our conclusion is that the samples (H1, H2, H3 and H4) obtained some months ago for laboratory testing at Imperial College ARE DIFFERENT to the cosmetics available today. The NANOPARTICLES ARE NOT PRESENT IN THE LATEST SAMPLES. Under laboratory conditions, when you remove the stated ingredients in the earlier samples H1, H2, H3 and H4, an ingredient(s) is left behind in each. We believe nanoparticles are included but not stated on the list of ingredients on the packaging.

Caroline had not excelled in the sciences at school and had asked a government chemist working at Porton Down, the government military science park situated near Salisbury, to come and see her. There was a knock on her door.

"Come."

Joseph Dyer, one of the new MI6 intakes from Cambridge, came in, followed by a middle-aged man.

"This is Mr Partridge from Porton Down," he said.

After the formalities Caroline asked, "Have you seen the report?"

"Yes, and I must say I'm very surprised."

"Why?"

"The nanotechnology referred to in the report is at a very early stage of development. I wouldn't have thought anyone was manufacturing day-to-day cosmetics using nanoparticles or fullerenes."

"Well, it seems some are," replied Caroline.

"This has a deeply disturbing conclusion. If manufacturers are already using nanoparticles then we must isolate who they are and challenge them as to why they're not including reference to them in the list of ingredients. The public has a right to know."

"Quite so. They are potentially dangerous, then?"

"There have been a number of papers." He opened his briefcase and extracted two A4 sheets. "Here is a list of articles you'll find on the internet. Notably work done by the Japanese exposing the risk of titanium dioxide nanoparticles which the researcher declares had a detrimental effect on pregnant mice and caused males to have reduced sperm production."

"Could nanoparticles or fullerenes used in cosmetics be a health hazard to human beings?" asked Caroline, as she studied the report.

The chemist thought for a moment. "Without evidence to the contrary, I wouldn't like to take the risk of using cosmetics with potential toxic chemicals in the ingredients."

"Thank you, Mr Partridge."

Disturbed by what Partridge had said, Caroline went onto the internet to study the articles he had listed. Then she arranged a meeting with Sir Anthony, she needed his backing to achieve what she had in mind.

19

THE HOME OFFICE – LONDON

Colonel Harriman was not a stupid man but these scientific people got on his nerves. They spoke a language he couldn't understand and even though his goddaughter had briefed him on these nanoparticles he was having great difficulty keeping up.

Caroline had invited him to a meeting at the Home Office attended by a junior minister, David Gilby, the heads of MI5 and MI6, three government scientists, two academics from Essex University and a senior minister from the Department of Health. Caroline spent the first twenty minutes using the screen on the wall and her laptop explaining why she had asked for the meeting. This introduction was causing John Harriman to concentrate fully and glance surreptitiously at the notes Caroline had given out. It seemed these nanoparticles (or fullerenes), he was still not certain what was what, were present in some cosmetic samples his goddaughter had obtained six months ago but were not present in recently purchased samples.

Sir Anthony Greenwood and Caroline had concluded that after Harriman's goddaughter and the other academics at Imperial College had queried the ingredients and began asking questions, two things happened. One, was two deaths, the other, the complete range of products now available from ExCy using the trade name Stardust and Stardust Pure had been changed. They could only conclude this was deliberate and the deaths were murder.

Caroline pointed out that until it was established exactly what nanoparticles or fullerenes had been used and their composition, the chemists and scientists were unable to determine the possible risk to the public. She said that as far as they could estimate, over one million cosmetics from the Stardust brand had been sold during the past six months. Caroline set out in chronological order the events that led to her requesting this meeting and updated the group on the CIA's action to destroy warehouses, vats and manufacturing plants. She pointed out that despite the CIA and British Intelligence efforts, the evidence against ExCy was flimsy but the series of coincidences, murders and attempted murders suggested the company was up to no good.

There was some debate on nanoparticles and fullerenes by the academics; they agreed that some of the cosmetic industry was, according to several recent reports, including nanos in its cosmetics – some very big names were on the list.

The meeting broke up with the health minister requiring the 'fullest investigation'. The heads of MI5 and MI6, Caroline and Colonel Harriman were asked to stay behind after the meeting and it was this request that John Harriman was now considering.

The minister had implied that a course of action was to bring into custody the UK Managing Director of ExCy, Abdul Suleman. It was left to the assembled group to decide if this was a practical course of action and John Harriman sat contemplating that. He knew that Suleman was a distant cousin of the Saudi royal family. This was likely to preclude official action. Should Harriman Security make the snatch and take him to the farm they leased in Essex for interrogation?

He decided to call a board meeting for tomorrow, but not discuss the possible action to snatch Suleman with anyone, except Sir Anthony and Caroline.

20

Abdul Suleman, who controlled the European operations for ExCy, had driven to Heathrow and picked up two men. One, an Iranian, Ali Omar, the other a Libyan, Amadou Masrat. These two men had been sent to the UK to kill Bland, Harriman who had been interfering, and a girl at Imperial College in London. He didn't propose to have any link with these men other than the initial briefing. He took them to a house ExCy owned in Knightsbridge. There both men received an Uzi sub-machine gun, a pistol and a quantity of Semtex. They were familiar with the use of weapons and making bombs – they had been seconded from al-Qaeda. Details of the three targets were on a laptop given to the men. A black Mini Cooper S was put at their disposal and six disposable mobile phones – everything was untraceable; the car had been bought for cash by a bogus Pakistani in Bradford and the phones 'off the shelf' in Tesco.

*

Abdul Suleman had a penchant for transvestites and regularly visited The Kitty Club in Soho. Normally he picked up one or more of the 'girls' and paid for a night participating in his sexual fantasies. Harry Sutherland got a call from Johno that Shirley had rung him to say Suleman was in the club tonight.

Seven members of Harriman Security sped to the club in three vehicles. Harry and Captain Norlington were to snatch Suleman as he came out of the club, and went to his car. Suleman's security guards were to be tazered by Captain Johnston. Four other members of the team were to block both directions of the road outside the club, one with an apparently broken-down lorry, the other faking a car crash.

Suleman left the club with two 'girls' and used his mobile. His black Mercedes E350 came up the road and stopped outside the club. As Suleman went to open the door two men got out, both wearing balaclavas and brandishing pistols.

"You," one of the men pointed to the 'girls', "disappear."

They were only too happy to oblige and ran back to the club frantically knocking on the door.

"Get in."

Suleman was shoved into the back of the car. One of the men followed him, keeping the gun pointed at his chest. Another man appeared and got in the front seat. The offside rear passenger door opened and a further armed man got in. Suleman was flanked either side and didn't resist. His security was trussed up in the back of a furniture van. The convoy headed out of Soho up Shaftesbury Avenue, down Charing Cross Road onto the Strand and then the Embankment. The convoy moved slowly, observing speed limits, and headed north of the river to pick up the A13. Destination – the farm Harriman Security rented near Colchester, Essex.

Suleman had gathered his wits and began to talk.

"This will go very badly for you. Don't think my friends won't find you – they will, and then you are horsemeat."

Harry hit him with the barrel of the gun.

"Shut your mouth until we ask you to talk." He remembered Susan's brother Edward, who had saved his life when an assassin tried to kill him on Wandsworth Common, and was seriously tempted to shoot the bastard that the colonel thought had hired the hit man.

"Listen, pal," said Captain Norlington who flanked Suleman on the other side, "I would shut your mouth if I was you," and stuck his gun barrel in Suleman's mouth. Captain Johnston who was driving Suleman's Mercedes said, "Steady, boys, we don't need to damage him yet."

When they reached the A13 they put a hood over Suleman's head and handcuffed him.

21

The two men had been studying Caroline Bland's flat in Eaton Square. The building was a large house divided into four flats. The woman, their target, resided in the first floor flat and after much debate they decided to plant the Semtex in the hall inside her flat and remotely detonate it as she walked in. Gaining access had been easy. As one of the other tenants had come out, the Iranian had breezed in. He picked the lock of her flat and went in. Deciding to leave the device under a telephone table in the hall, he set it up, and left the way he came. He had unknowingly triggered a silent alarm to MI6 headquarters at Vauxhall Cross.

Caroline Bland and John Harriman had a longstanding arrangement. They did not stay at each other's home, but tonight, after an early and excellent dinner at Rules Restaurant near the Strand, and as it was only 9pm, Caroline had invited John for a nightcap. She opened the street door to the house. John always joked about the old-fashioned lift with metal gates and the snail's pace it went to the first floor, but they had decided to take the lift as he had a slight calf muscle tear.

Her telephone rang.

The two al-Qaeda assassins had watched Caroline Bland go into the main door with the man. *With Allah's blessing the man would be the infidel Harriman*, thought the Libyan. The Iranian had counted how long it took to reach the first floor flat then added five seconds. That should mean they were in the hall of her flat – he pressed the remote. A huge explosion interrupted the silence in the street and a fire started on the first floor which could be seen through the window. The two men decided to leave before the fire brigade and police arrived. Lights were coming on all along the road as they drove sedately out of the square – a job well done.

Later, Caroline was to reflect how lucky they were. Just for once they had decided not to use the stairs and the old-fashioned lift had jammed with them locked inside.

They had been joking about the irony of the lift jamming, serving them right for being so lazy, when the bomb went off – neither was hurt and the phone call to her mobile would have been too late. Bomb disposal later reported a sophisticated remote had been used to trigger a Semtex bomb.

★

John Harriman had not yet told Caroline that his organisation had grabbed Suleman. He figured that the security services, MI5 and MI6, would prefer a third party to do the work and find out what this man Suleman knew. If the Saudi ambassador caused a rumpus then the British government could, in all honesty, deny any knowledge of Suleman's whereabouts.

This latest attempt on Caroline's life demonstrated that the enemy was prepared to kill high-ranking members of the British Secret Service. They had been lucky – the lift jammed on the ground floor leaving them unable to open the gates. They had laughed, kissed, and then the bomb went off. The fire brigade eventually freed them after Special Branch arrived. An attempt on the life of the deputy head of MI6 promoted special measures. Caroline was taken to a safe house; John was left to his own devices. He knew, though, from the earlier attempts, that they (whoever 'they' were) were after him as well. Time to also leave his much-loved Chelsea mews house. Smithy, his second-in-command Major Smith, had offered a bed at his house in Epsom, Surrey, which he decided to accept.

Meanwhile, he also decided to move his goddaughter. He spoke to Amanda, one of his operatives, who was babysitting Dee, and she agreed she could move in with her at her flat in Putney. His mobile rang.

"Hello."

"Colonel, it's Captain Norlington. We've started to question Suleman."

"Good. Keep me up-to-date."

Colonel Harriman was used to violent conflicts, having served, and then commanded, the SAS before retiring in 2002. His resources were getting thin on the ground as now he was being shadowed by Sergeant Quick; his goddaughter Dee, by Amanda, as well as double-ups on Harry Sutherland who they had also tried to kill.

Hopefully, he thought, *Suleman would crack and tell them what this was all about.*

22

From the earlier samples that Dee had obtained, she had isolated missing ingredients not mentioned on the packaging. At first she had assumed that the missing ingredients were chemical. Then her tutor, Professor Dolen, had discussed the increasing use by the pharmaceutical industry of nanos and fullerenes. He had pointed out that parabens were very widely used which had provoked an ongoing investigation by the US Food and Drug Administration (FDA). Professor Dolen had given her a list of commonly used ingredients that were openly included in a broad number of cosmetics. Dee was astounded that many of the popular cosmetics included ingredients that were really questionable substances. Then she had started to concentrate on the Stardust range, produced and manufactured by ExCy, and had found many of these questionable ingredients, but also had concluded that there were other ingredients not marked on the packaging. Her tutor had agreed. One of the senior laboratory technicians had also been unable to break down the complete content of various Stardust cosmetics.

Their combined efforts to persuade ExCy to divulge

the list of ingredients had met with a stony silence. Dee had even visited the London office of ExCy, but had been abruptly informed that nobody could answer her queries. When Professor Dolen had died in what was reported to be a freak accident she hadn't connected the accident to her investigations. But when Toby Marshall, the laboratory technician who had been helping her, was murdered in broad daylight in Kensington, she joined the dots. Her godfather, John Harriman, agreed that the deaths were much too coincidental and had assigned Amanda to guard her. This was a little invasive. Her boyfriend, Jake, was fed up with Amanda following them everywhere and she hadn't seen him for days. Dee liked Amanda and welcomed her company, but tonight she was meeting her boyfriend Jake and had devised a plan to lose Amanda for the night.

The new head of chemistry at Imperial College had made it clear he did not want Amanda in the laboratory so she had to sit outside the door of the lab. It was 7pm before Amanda realised Dee was not in the lab. One of the other students, who knew Amanda was Dee's bodyguard, smiled as he told her she went out the fire exit. Amanda phoned Colonel Harriman.

"I'm sorry, Colonel. Dee has deliberately given me the slip."

"Where are you now?"

"At Imperial College."

"Go to your flat; she may have gone there to change. Check where that boyfriend, Jake isn't it, is at the moment. Latch onto him and I bet you find Dee. I'm coming over myself with Sergeant Quick to help."

Amanda phoned Jake. She had insisted Dee gave her his number.

"Hello."

"Jake?"

"Yes, who's that?"

"It's Amanda. Is Dee with you?"

"Yes, I'll put her on."

Dee knew Amanda would eventually put two and two together but they had had two and a half hours alone – better than nothing.

"Hi Amanda."

"Dee, where are you?"

"The Grapes, Kensington High Street."

"Wait there, I'm coming." Amanda phoned Colonel Harriman.

*

The two men had been watching Dee for an hour since their attempt to kill the MI6 woman Caroline Bland. They hadn't had the opportunity to fake an accident as she hadn't left the man's side. Now they decided when they left the bar to shoot them both. The Iranian went outside to bring the car nearer. The girl from Suleman's office had tailed the woman and man to the bar but the Iranian told her to leave and return to her flat by underground.

*

Amanda scanned the area around the pub. There was a black Mini Cooper parked on double yellow lines, but the glass was darkened and she couldn't see if there were any occupants. Best not take chances. She approached the pub, went into the Bristol Bar and spotted Dee and Jake in a booth in the corner.

"Sorry to interrupt, guys, but we're concerned for your safety, Dee. There's just been another attempt on the deputy head of MI6 and Colonel Harriman."

"John – my God, is he all right?" asked Dee.

"Yes," Amanda smiled, "they were lucky," knowing they had been stuck in the broken-down lift which had saved their lives. "The colonel and Sergeant Quick are going to join us shortly, then we will go to my flat. Jake, you can come if you wish."

Jake looked a little churlish. He fancied Dee but didn't like the idea of men trying to kill people around her.

"Nah, it's okay. I'll go." He gave Dee a peck on the cheek, got up and left.

"I see," said Amanda as she saw a look on Dee's face she had experienced herself – let down by a man. Her mobile rang. "Okay, we're in the Bristol Bar." She glanced around the bar again. "That was the colonel. They'll be ten minutes," said Amanda opening her shoulder bag for quick access to her Walther PPK. The bar was getting crowded. *They're unlikely to try anything inside*, she thought.

Colonel Harriman and Sergeant Quick walked in and, working their way through the late evening crowd, they sat in the booth.

"Hello Dee," said the colonel.

"John, are you okay?" Dee asked.

"Oh, you've heard about the explosion?" he replied.

"I didn't know it was an explosion," Dee replied, glancing at Amanda.

"Anyway, I'm fine. Sergeant Quick did a recce before we came in. He doesn't like the look of a Mini parked almost opposite."

"I saw it – darkened windows," said Amanda. "I couldn't see any occupants."

"Well, there are," Sergeant Quick said. "Someone is inside, they're smoking and the window is slightly open."

"Is there a back way out, Amanda?" the colonel asked,

"Yes," she replied. "It leads into an alley, but the problem is the alley comes back out front alongside the pub."

"Okay, this is what we'll do."

Sergeant Quick got up after synchronising watches. Five minutes later, at 10pm, they left by the front door. Colonel

Harriman went first with his Browning pistol drawn. Followed by Dee, Amanda had gone out the back and down the alley alongside the pub exactly at ten. Sergeant Quick, driving a BMW pulled up outside, Dee came out the front and was bundled in. Just then one man got out of the Mini. Amanda saw he had a machine pistol and opened fire. Colonel Harriman shouted to Sergeant Quick to drive and took up a firing position. The man who had got out of the Mini got off a burst at Amanda. Colonel Harriman shot him. The Mini roared off down the High Street, turning left at Warwick Gardens, with Amanda and the colonel firing after it.

Amanda walked towards the man on the road, kicked the machine pistol away and felt his pulse. Dead. Not surprised. She knew Colonel Harriman was a dead shot who beat her at the range every time. She turned around as Sergeant Quick pulled up in the BMW. Amanda got in the back, Colonel Harriman the passenger front seat.

"I think the driver's gone but let's not take chances," said the colonel.

He used his mobile to phone Superintendent Day of Special Branch who was in charge of the current investigation, and reported the attempt on Dee, the second attack that evening. Probably the same team, they agreed.

The colonel phoned the farm.

"Any news, Captain?" He spoke to Captain Johnston about the interrogation of the man Suleman at the Essex farm.

"Not yet. He's proving a tough nut."

"Okay, let me know when you've got something."

"Right. I'll go to Caroline's new safe house and check her security. Dee, you stay with Amanda at her flat. Later, Sergeant Quick will take me to Epsom to the safe house where I'll be staying." Colonel Harriman made a call to Caroline. He knew she would arrange for Special Branch to watch her safe house in Longstone Avenue, Willesden but wanted to see it for himself.

23

Suleman was proving to be obstinate. Doheny and Mack had slung him up, hanging upside down from a beam in the barn with his head two feet off the ground. A man they did not know had met them at the farm and taken over the interrogation. They suspected he was one of Caroline Bland's people or perhaps MI5 (he was not). This man, he told them to call him Suggs (they suspected this was not his real name), was short, strong and stocky, with a tattoo on his arm. He beat the legs, back and testicles of a now nude Suleman with a long cane. Harriman's two operatives admired the Arab's courage but knew it was only a matter of time. Both Doheny and Mack had been in the SAS. They had seen torture before and on occasion, if necessary, inflicted it themselves.

"Okay, Suleman, let's do it the hard way. Take him down and get the plank and tin," said the man calling himself Suggs.

Suleman suspected worse was to come – and he was right. He was bound by leather straps to a wooden plank with his head over the end of the wood. A chair was placed in the middle of the barn and the plank placed on it. One of his captors then brought a large metal container and began to roll out a hosepipe. Suleman had heard of this torture. The CIA used it and had taught the Taliban in Afghanistan – he had seen the technique before. He was blindfolded then felt the plank being tilted – he knew what was next. The hosepipe was turned on and directed at his nose and mouth. He tried to close his mouth but the water went up his nose and he began to choke. Suleman imagined he was going to drown and began to silently pray. They stopped.

"Tell us your name," one of his captors asked.

Suleman didn't reply and the plank was tilted again. The water began to pour down his face again. He spluttered, and felt he was drowning. Choking, he raised his hand. The water stopped.

"Tell us your name," the same voice asked.

"Abdul Suleman," he whispered.

"Louder."

"Abdul Suleman."

"Good. Now let's talk without unpleasantness," said the voice.

One of his captors released the straps binding him to the plank. The man must have been very strong as he lifted Suleman and plonked him on a chair. A spotlight was turned on, it shone in his eyes, and his arms were secured to the chair.

"Who do you work for?" asked the voice.

Abdul Suleman knew as soon as he started giving them information he would be unable to stop. Again he said a silent prayer and then bit down hard into the tooth.

It was several seconds before Doheny realised what he had done.

"Quick, make him sick! Put your fingers down his throat. He's just taken poison."

Suleman spasmed and bubbles appeared at the corner of his mouth; he slumped to the floor.

Mack felt for his pulse, looked up and shook his head – he was dead.

The boss would not be pleased, but how were they supposed to know the man had a capsule in a false tooth.

The man calling himself Suggs phoned Colonel Harriman.

"Suleman has killed himself. He had a hidden poison capsule in a tooth. By the smell I think it was a cyanide capsule."

"Did you get anything?" asked the colonel.

"No, sorry, he was silent. I suspect he was Taliban or al-Qaeda. I've dealt with them before." Suggs didn't need to remind Colonel Harriman, he had worked with him in Iraq during the first desert war and subsequently he had been an MI6 operative in Afghanistan. He was now retired and was going home unable to help any further.

*

Colonel Harriman reported the death of Suleman to Caroline Bland at MI6 and verified his goddaughter had arrived at Amanda's flat. They decided to lift Suleman's secretary. The woman had been identified from employment records as Safiyah Jamil and was thought to be a Lebanese national. The unit watching ExCy's London office had noted her leaving at midday but had not seen her since. Special Branch officers were briefed and raided the offices at 2pm, taking away two laptop computers and a filing cabinet. No sign of the woman.

Later a woman wearing a full burka, the one-piece veil that covers the face and body leaving only a mesh screen to see through, passed through passport control at Heathrow on a flight to Beirut. Her passport stated she was Karim Basilah.

24

Ibrahim had received a coded message from the woman, Safiyah Jamil, who was Suleman's number two in London. Suleman was missing – she thought probably taken by British security services. She updated him on the bomb left for Bland, but didn't know if she was dead. Two hits had been arranged for last night – one on the girl who had started the investigation of their Stardust range in London and forced a costly withdrawal, and one on Harriman; both attempts had failed. One of the assassins had been shot, the Iranian, and was presumed dead. The Libyan would continue with his orders to kill Bland, Harriman and the girl. Ibrahim had instructed Safiyah to leave the UK and fly to Beirut where she would be met at the airport. He proposed to hide her for the moment until she could be of use again.

*

A meeting had been called in Karachi. The principals were meeting to discuss strategy.

Five years ago Osama bin Laden had met one of his key lieutenants, Belardi (also known as Mansur Ahmedi), on the border between Pakistan and Afghanistan. He had in mind a daring scheme that would seriously punish the infidel Americans, their British lapdogs and other western countries. It would also generate huge wealth for the participants. But the plan needed at least four immensely wealthy principals. When he instigated the plan, Osama bin Laden included a high-ranking official in Pakistan's ISI (The Inter Services Intelligence Service), an important Saudi, a Russian, an Indian and a Chinese man. The Saudi, Russian, Indian and Chinese principals were all billionaires and their contribution had been an initial one billion dollars each. The group met in secret, usually in Pakistan, where the ISI Director, a lieutenant general, monitored security with the group's head of security, Belardi.

Ibrahim, one of bin Laden's longstanding supporters, had been appointed by the group as the managing director. He was tasked to set up initial operations in the USA, Mexico, Colombia, France, Somalia, Oman, Lebanon, the UK and Nigeria. This involved leasing warehouses, buying containers and organising worldwide local managers to oversee the operation. A new company with assets of two billion dollars, called ExCy, was also set up to build or lease refineries and storage areas in ports in all these countries. A further one billion dollars was used to acquire a chemical company, legitimately trading in Switzerland, called Lausanne Chemicals. On acquiring all the shares the name of this company was changed to the Ulema Corporation, which traded as ExCy Pharmaceuticals.

The Ulema Corporation was a shell company operating through a series of holding companies which led to the Cayman Islands, then to Belize City, where the Cayman company, a holding company called Yesara Consolidated, was in its turn owned by Ferza Consolidated. The trail didn't quite end there. Ferza was owned by four other companies. One in the Caymans, another in China, the third in India and the final owner was a Saudi company. All the owners were untraceable.

The front company, Ulema Corporation, manufactured cosmetics and produced all the Stardust range promoted by ExCy. Manufacturing the cosmetics in Switzerland, India, the Middle East, Somalia and Nigeria, the Ulema Corporation transported the part-finished or complete liquids, soaps or creams as bulk liquid. Another ingredient was added at bottling and fulfilment plants in Somalia, Mexico, Nigeria, France, the UK or Colombia if the ingredients were incomplete. Some of the cosmetics were already packaged and the extra ingredient added earlier. Toothpaste was already packaged as Stardust Extra Whitening, shaving foam and gel already packaged in pressurised containers as Stardust with aloe vera, deodorant as a roll-on called Stardust Sensitive. Perfume and nail polish were also packaged and shipped complete; shampoo and liquid soap were shipped as bulk liquid, including the extra ingredient, and bottled at the various plants they controlled worldwide; all under the brand name Stardust.

*

The board members assembled in Karachi on the coast of Pakistan.

The Russian, Alexail Pankov, had been a low-ranking member of the KGB. Then came detente and with it opportunity as Gorbachov and Yeltsin changed Russia. Pankov, mostly through bribes and murder, acquired a state petro-chemical company and Siberian oil wells. He also shared the ownership of a gas pipeline into Poland. His new oligarch status made him a target for both the liberals and the Mafia in Russia, so he moved to London. He sold his holdings of gas, chemicals and oil, and was reputed to be worth fifteen billion dollars.

The Chinese man, Cheng Kuang, was a front for state money. Through skilful manipulation he acquired much of the wholesale trade manufacturing clothing in China and Hong Kong, and a large chemical plant in Shanghai. His connections enabled him to have licences to import certain western goods. He also owned a huge IT company which fronted many western software houses. He was a wealthy man but most of his profits were returned to the state.

The third member – a Saudi, Farid Al-Kazaz – had many connections but no obvious business interests. Ibrahim knew this man from previous dealings and, as he had the connections and wealth, he enrolled him in the group.

The Indian, Madura Chatterjee, was one of the richest men in India. He owned a diverse group of businesses ranging from the Delhi Bank and India Autos to India Phosphates, Delhi Chemicals and Chatterjee Pharmaceuticals. Most of the materials for the cosmetics were sourced through his businesses and sent to Switzerland, Somalia, Nigeria, Mexico or Marseille, or packaged and sent complete to distribution centres.

*

Ibrahim had called the meeting in Karachi following the capture of Abdul Suleman in London, and the disruption to their plan caused by the CIA attacking their warehouses in Mexico City and Somalia. Fortunately, these holding warehouses had been cleared when the three British university people began sending emails asking for the ingredients of their products to the London office of ExCy. As a precaution, the Stardust range had reverted to conventional cosmetics three months ago. The interfering British and Americans were too late.

Six men sat around a large table in the house on the outskirts of Karachi. Each man had his own bodyguards but security was provided by the ISI, Lt General Akif Gandapur and members of al-Qaeda. The house had been swept for bugs five times as each of the board members insisted that their own people double-check.

The board members were taking risks in different ways. The Chinese man knew his government would disown him, the Indian that he would be eliminated, as would the Russian. Only the Saudi man felt confident that if it leaked he was involved, he would be protected.

The idea was first mooted to each of the board members in 2005 and codenamed Tears of the West. Three of the board members were only interested in the fantastic wealth that the scheme would bring them all. The Saudi had a dual interest in the disruption the plan would cause – the money was secondary to his hatred of the West. Hiding behind the mask of friendship, the Saudi had many business dealings with western countries but secretly he loathed their decadence, their Christian beliefs and their arrogance.

The meetings were held in English to avoid having translators.

"A welcome to everybody," said Ibrahim. "I have called this meeting at the request of our leader," (he referred to Osama bin Laden). All the four men around the table said very little. Each feared being recorded. Only the Saudi really trusted Osama bin Laden, the instigator, and the Russian, Indian and Chinese board members were always reluctant to meet.

"I appreciate your prompt agreement to meet. Here is our business report." He handed out laptops with a slip of paper confirming the start-up procedure. Each board member had a report of the business affairs in their own language. They didn't receive operational details – all had agreed early on that Ibrahim as MD, and the head of security

Belardi, would handle the operation. They only required information if it directly affected them. The four men read the report.

Alexail Pankov spoke first. "The initial capital injected by us," he looked around the table, "has been used?"

"That is the principal reason I called the meeting," said Ibrahim.

"The operation fronted worldwide by ExCy has been a great success, but we had to change production from the special ingredients to conventional cosmetics as we had a minor interference from a university in the UK."

"This minor interference," asked Cheng Kuang. "Have the British identified the ingredients?"

"They have not been able to," replied Ibrahim.

"But if they do," said Pankov, "the plan changes, yes?"

"We are taking steps to prevent the British being a threat," said Belardi. He did not propose to tell them that two of the British academics were dead and the last one, a woman, was being targeted as they spoke.

"I leave the operational details to you," said the Saudi, Farid Al-Kazaz.

Ibrahim nodded. "What I wanted to tell you was that we are opening up the second company owned by the Ulema Corporation under the promotional name of Celebrity Cosmetics. The turnover for the Stardust range means we are breaking even in the USA, but losing money in the UK and Europe. You will see from screen 6," they all scrolled down, "a breakdown of overheads which initially were set-up costs, but now are mainly transport, packaging and marketing."

"Are we intending to continue marketing the Stardust range?" asked Pankov.

"Yes, because we will use it, as – how do the British describe it – as a smokescreen."

"Pardon?" said Cheng Kuang.

"The Americans and British will be chasing shadows as the cosmetics purchased as the Stardust range will all be clean," replied Ibrahim.

"When are you intending to start production of the new range – you called it Celebrity?" asked the Saudi.

"We have purchased a small cosmetics business in Germany and will be using this company, Oriel Cosmetics, to front the production of the Celebrity range," replied Ibrahim.

"Good," said Madura Chatterjee, who had been very quiet. Chatterjee had initially been reluctant to be in business with Arabs and Pakistanis, but the potential returns coupled with the intention to use his chemical company to supply materials and ingredients had changed his mind.

"Will my company in New Delhi still supply?" Chatterjee asked.

"Yes, of course," replied Ibrahim.

Chatterjee nodded, pleased to hear his business would continue to profit whatever happened down the line.

"Are we intending to use the same distribution outlets and depots for the new range?" asked Farid Al-Kazaz.

"Yes, but we have taken new warehouses in Nigeria, Oman, Belize City, Marseille, Cartagena, Colombia, Puerto de Manzanillo, Mexico, Yemen, Holland and the Port of Houston in the USA."

"Where will the cosmetics be produced?" asked Cheng Kuang.

"From our friend," he looked at Chatterjee, "some of the cosmetics will be sent by oceangoing bulk tanker to Oman and Yemen where extra ingredients" he referred to the nanoparticles "will be added. Then by bulk tanker to each distribution port. The initial range will be shampoo, hairspray, deodorant, toothpaste and perfume. Later we will prepare a range for men. Packaging will be sent from Germany via Marseille to all the distribution ports to bottle and package the shampoo and perfume. The German factory will also fill the deodorants, hairspray and toothpaste, having been supplied the complete ingredients by the factories in Oman and Yemen, using sea and road tankers. Transporters will then take the packaged toothpaste, hairspray and deodorants to Marseille for shipment in container ships to the USA and Europe. Later, shampoo and perfume will be sent in liquid form to the distribution centres to package and bottle the products," replied Ibrahim.

"We will need to commence a marketing campaign and sales people from the German company, Oriel, will have to sell the new range to the supermarkets and shops in the USA and Europe," he added. "In fact, our sales team has already started to approach the buyers for the leading supermarket chains and shops."

"Clearly," said Chatterjee, "these measures will require more investment?"

"Yes, as I told you at the start of this venture, you would all be required to contribute three billion dollars in the first year of operation. We are looking for you to send the balance of two billion to the Belsize bank account in the next few days."

The four business men looked at each other; it was Chatterjee who spoke first.

"It will take longer than two days. I for one have to make certain arrangements."

"I believe I can send the money in one week," said the Saudi.

"I also can do so in one week," said Cheng Kuang. He knew he could send the money tomorrow, but why hurry?

"Okay," said the Russian Pankov reluctantly. He was probably the poorest of the multi-billionaires and knew that one-third of his capital was being put at risk.

"Thank you," said Ibrahim. "Unless you have any questions the meeting is concluded." He looked around the table.

"I have one," said Chatterjee. They all turned to look at him. "When do you require the shipments to the depots in Oman and Yemen to begin?"

"Immediately," replied Ibrahim. "I intend that the Celebrity range of cosmetics is on the shelves in the USA and throughout Europe by December this year to meet their pagan festivities."

He refers to the purchase of cosmetics as Christmas gifts, thought the Russian.

The men left the house separately; three of the board members had arrived by private jet landing at Karachi's Jinnah International Airport. Chatterjee had come by train and car.

Ibrahim had asked the Saudi to stay behind.

"My friend, I hear that the prince is becoming concerned as British MI6 have asked about ExCy and the cosmetics," said Ibrahim.

Farid Al-Kazaz thought for a few seconds before answering.

"My blessed prince is a wise man who understands the British. You will be aware that he studied at Oxford University and went to Sandhurst Military College. He knows that the British are tenacious and is concerned that they will not give up trying to find out what is going on. Can I assure him that Belardi and you have taken measures?"

"I did not wish to discuss operations with the board, as it is all in hand, but reassure the prince that the academics at the London university who enquired about the ingredients in the Stardust cosmetics have been eliminated. The French customs man who acquired a sample of the cosmetics in Bogota is at the bottom of the ocean. The CIA has nothing and neither do the British."

"Thank you. I am sure the prince will be reassured." He bowed and left.

*

Belardi was the group's head of security and had been charged with eliminating the three British university people, the interfering Colonel Harriman and the MI6 woman, Caroline Bland. He was journeying to the north of Pakistan by train to meet Osama bin Laden – he wondered if he would make the reverse journey, as matters were far from satisfactory even if the Saudi prince had been reassured.

25

Jack Clarke was contemplating the meeting in thirty minutes with Samuel Goldmuir, and Bud Ruskin, the director of the FBI. The CIA, ably assisted by Delta Forces, had destroyed the Mexican and Somalian operations of the chemical company ExCy. But he felt uncomfortable. Despite an extensive investigation of the Stardust cosmetics in fifty states, with government analysts examining the ingredients, only the usual substances, some on the FDA's 'might be dangerous' list, had been identified. The Federal Drug Agency had told him that in common with virtually all other cosmetics, the Stardust range had parabens, sodium hexametaphosphate, Methylisothiazolinone and butylphenyl methylpropional.

The chemists at FDA reassured him that no actual proof existed that these chemicals were a health risk but they were being investigated. He was also reassured that these ingredients were included in a number of cosmetics his wife and, he suspected, the First Lady used. So, they had turned up nothing. They had disabled a number of vats inside large warehouses, but had lost two agents and had a badly damaged rookie female agent – so something was amiss. Trouble was, he didn't know what it was. The Brits continued to keep their cards close to their chest but he knew that they were continuing to investigate. He had also had a report on the explosion in the apartment block of the MI6 woman, Caroline Bland. Someone was still trying to knock off some of the Brits. He knocked at the director's door.

"Enter."

"Ah, Jack, you know Bud?" Samuel Goldmuir already knew the answer.

"Yes." They shook hands.

"Well, what progress?" asked Samuel.

Jack presented both the senior security officers with his report.

"So, nothing new. We have busted some ass but not established what's going on?" said Samuel.

Jack had to nod in agreement.

"What about the Brits – can we tap into their intel?" asked Bud Ruskin.

"Sure, but I don't think they've got anything we haven't," Jack replied.

"Well, liaise, Jack. Let's remember we're on the same side."

"Sure, but they won't take direct action. They're far too concerned about upsetting many of the Middle Eastern countries."

"Fine," said Samuel, "but they are good at what they do."

Jack nodded as he began gathering up his papers.

"Keep testing the cosmetics from this Stardust range and make sure you put the word out that we are interested in any rumours of activity by al-Qaeda," said Samuel.

Jack took that as his cue to leave.

26

Colonel Harriman had scheduled a meeting with Caroline Bland at MI6 headquarters. Harriman Security was on red alert which meant all operatives doubled-up and extra precautions were taken. Captain Harrington travelled with him in the reinforced Mercedes 320 but as Malcolm Ridge, the driver, scanned the road behind for a tail, nobody spoke. Colonel Harriman was no stranger to danger, but when someone threatened his goddaughter Dee, he got mad – very mad. They pulled up outside the building known, due to it's odd shape, as Babylon-on-Thames, the offices of MI6 on the Albert Embankment the south bank of the River Thames. Passing through security they gave up their weapons and were met by Caroline at the lift.

"Hi, come on up. I've asked Simon Tomlinson of MI5 to join us."

Caroline, Colonel Harriman, Simon and Captain Harrington listened as Marcus Welch, one of Caroline's assistants, summarised.

"The bomb in your flat," he glanced at Caroline, "was crude but effective using Semtex which was wired to a remote. It was probably triggered by a mobile phone within five hundred yards of your property. The person who planted the bomb was later shot outside the pub in Kensington High Street. We know that as his fingerprints matched a set left on the door of your flat. His identity is not known to us, CIA or Interpol. We've traced his entry to the UK through Heathrow on the 15th January. We're assuming the unidentified driver – we have a grainy photograph through the darkened Mini windows – also came in the same way and we're checking CCTV to try and match. The Mini was found abandoned in a station car park in Feltham. From CCTV ,a man is seen exiting the car but he is careful to cover his face; he walked away from the station so we're checking all cameras around the area to try and pick him up again. The list of items on the VAT inspection of ExCy which we were given to follow up produced a couple of interesting things." He switched on a large wall television screen.

"Shewards Bank – there was a deposit of one hundred million dollars. We have it on good authority that this money was later transferred to a bank in Zurich. We're working on where it went after that. Ergon Oil – Special Branch interviewed the managing director who eventually produced paid invoices showing the hire of road tankers to transport, we presume, the Stardust product to their bottling plant in Birmingham. A bulk liquid carrying ship would arrive in Shoreham, Sussex. We believe the ship originated in Oman but it stopped in Marseille before coming to the UK. It would be a small tanker as there's a restriction on size. Other container ships arrived at Harwich, much larger, and papers reveal they came from Marseille. There's an ExCy depot there. The oil company has hired out empty road tankers and obtained lorries from a haulage company for ExCy to arrange pick-ups at Tilbury Docks, Shoreham and Harwich. They then transport the cosmetics to large supermarket holding depots all over the country or the bottling plant in Birmingham. We're checking if the oil company has any link to al-Qaeda."

"John, have you anything to add?" Caroline asked.

"We checked out the solicitors, Wright, Smith and King. They're based in Fenchurch Street. Our computer boffin broke into their computer. They dealt with the lease obtained by ExCy on their Mayfair office. The signature is Suleman's – nothing else of interest," he replied.

"The road tankers which left Shoreham, Harwich and Tilbury harbours have also been tracked by Special Branch, using motorway CCTV, to Birmingham where ExCy has a pharmaceutical plant bottling shampoo. Special Branch raided their plant, took samples, files and computers but this has yielded nothing," said Simon.

"They presumably use goods vehicles to transport the finished articles," said Caroline.

"Yes, major logistics companies deliver their boxes of product to supermarket distribution centres from the ExCy distribution centre in Birmingham. We have CCTV from near their plant in Birmingham," replied Simon, who continued. "BMW in Park Lane co-operated and gave us copies of the car hire agreements for three BMWs, all 520s with darkened windows, and a motorbike. Each vehicle was hired for a week at least twenty times. They're still going back over their records."

"The name D Ali, hasn't turned up anything either here, with Interpol or the CIA but our contact in the Pakistan Security Service has told us that a man with the same initial and, bearing in mind Ali is a common name in Pakistan, is reported to be a minor al-Qaeda member," said Caroline. She added, "We have photographs of Suleman arriving at Battersea helipad. He had come from Heathrow on a flight from Cyprus. We think this links with the murder of a photographer in the South of France."

"What about the photographs your agent got from the French newspaper reporter?" asked Simon Tomlinson.

"They've proved quite useful." Caroline handed out a folder containing stills with a note attached.

"You can see we have identified three men. Suleman, who we already knew about, Belardi (also known as Mansur Ahmedi) who we believe is a senior member of bin Laden's inner circle, and Ibrahim who has been linked with terrorist activities in Afghanistan. We think he is also al-Qaeda." Caroline paused to let the men read the reports. "A cheque was also paid to Mr A Ibrahim for fifty thousand pounds in the ExCy account records. We don't know what this was for."

"Do we know the whereabouts of this man Ibrahim?" asked Colonel Harriman.

"No, but we believe he visits Pakistan and Afghanistan regularly and we have asked the intelligence services of both countries to notify us if he surfaces," said Caroline.

"I wouldn't hold your breath with that lot," said Simon Tomlinson.

"Maybe not, but several ISI officers in Pakistan are leaning towards the USA and trying to help – you never can tell," Caroline replied.

"That ship, the *Good Queen Bess*, where is it now?" asked Simon.

"Tied up in Cannes," replied Caroline.

"Might be worth keeping a close eye on its movements – they've used it once and might again," said Simon.

"Good point. We'll put a request to the French," said Caroline.

"Speaking of which," said Simon, "what about that officer of yours killed in Paris?"

"He was meeting a man called Georges LeForge who was head of investigations for French customs," replied Caroline.

"Any idea what about?" asked Colonel Harriman.

"Yes, it seems that the French wanted to ask if the British Navy would help retrieve the black box from that Macedonian jet that disappeared a few hours out of Bogota, Colombia." Caroline replied.

"And?" asked an astute Simon.

"They wanted a submersible to try and retrieve a leather case chained to the wrist of one of their customs investigators. It seems they believe he had obtained some liquid from the ExCy warehouse in Bogota."

"Are they saying the jet was sabotaged?" asked Colonel Harriman.

"The French are cagey but that's the impression I get," Caroline replied.

"Are we going to do it?" asked Simon.

"Waiting on a response from the Ministry of Defence, but it seems likely. The plane sank in very deep water and may not be accessible," said Caroline.

"Other than blowing up the ExCy warehouses, has the CIA added anything new?" asked Simon.

"No, and I have a meeting scheduled with Jack Clarke in New York in two days to review where we are," she replied. "Last but not least," Caroline pressed a button to light up the wall screen, "this woman, known as Safiyah Jamil, working at the London office of ExCy, travelled from Heathrow to Beirut as Karim Basilah. We have a contact in Beirut who accessed the CCTV at the airport. She was met by this man." They all looked at the screen. "His name is Hassam El Iraqi, a prominent Hezbollah member living in Beirut. Our contact is trying to track where they went and if we find her we'll consider asking the CIA to lift her." Caroline paused. "Is there anything else?"

"Yes," replied Colonel Harriman. "The second assassin – any news?"

He referred to the other man who had driven away in

a black Mini after the attempt on their lives in Kensington. One of Caroline's assistants brought a note for Simon.

"Ah, the second man – the CCTV picked him up at Feltham, where he dumped the car. We're checking CCTV at all rail stations on the south west train line to Waterloo," said Simon.

There was a knock on the door and a fair-haired young woman walked in.

"Yes, Jo?" said Caroline.

"This report has just come from the government chemists at Porton Down and a professor specialising in microbiology at Essex University."

Caroline briefly studied the document. "At last something concrete." She read from the A4 sheet. "The samples of products from the Stardust range, picked at random from supermarkets in the UK, only reveal the expected chemical content shown on the packaging. However, the samples which were sent marked 'several months old' were different to the latest batch. We've been able to determine that there are ingredients in each sample not listed. We believe it is one or more nanoparticles and are endeavouring to isolate the particles and identify the ingredient."

"So Dee was right; there is something not listed as an ingredient?" said Colonel Harriman.

"It does appear so," said Simon.

"It's becoming increasingly important to establish what has been added," said Caroline. "I'll speak with the Home Office minister to get additional resources."

The meeting closed with John Harriman warning Caroline to take particular care, as the second assassin had not been caught.

⋆

Caroline left the south bank office with the two armed Special Branch officers. She thought she was well able to take care of herself but bowed to pressure from her boss, Sir Anthony. A black BMW X5 with darkened windows pulled up and all three got in. Discreetly following in a black cab he had hijacked earlier was the Libyan; he fell behind the target's car, staying two vehicles away. He knew it would be difficult to follow the BMW in the heavy London traffic and, as he suspected, he lost them at the top of a slip road off the Embankment. He decided to park the cab somewhere and maybe use it tomorrow – the driver lay dead on the floor under a blanket in front of the back seat; he had shot him with a silenced pistol. He headed south over Lambeth Bridge towards Brixton to find somewhere to leave the black cab overnight, preferably near a tube station to enable him to return to the safe house in Knightsbridge.

27

Uhmed Abaid had to be really careful. He had received a message from the CIA HQ at Langley to help the Brits find this woman Safiyah Jamil now travelling as Karim Basilah. Syrian by birth, Uhmed's parents had immigrated to the USA in 1975 when a war broke out in Lebanon between Maronite Christians and Muslims. His father, a lecturer in physics at Beirut University, decided that their Syrian background would not help them with either group and applied for, and obtained, American citizenship. Uhmed was born in San Diego in 1980. He studied Chinese at UC San Diego before going to Harvard to study political science. He was fluent in modern standard Arabic, Urdu and Levantine Arabic, all taught by his mother and father.

It wasn't long before the CIA recruited him and after a year of intensive training he was sent back to the Lebanon. There were many Syrians in Beirut so he integrated easily, but it was very dangerous. The Christians still resented power-sharing with the Muslims, and the Lebanese Muslims resented the role Syria had played before the UN established an uneasy truce.

He tracked the man who met Karim Basilah, through a lucky break. The man who picked her up was known to him as a Hezbollah leader living in downtown Beirut. He had been discreetly watching the building where the man lived, for two days – nothing. She could be inside; that's when he dreamed up the raid. Many Lebanese were still trafficking illegal drugs and a police raid on the house would not be unusual. He bribed a policeman and appropriated four uniforms.

The CIA snatch team from the Special Activities Division was led by an Iraqi who had been recruited after the first Iraq war. Saddam Hussein had murdered his father and mother. After applying, as a Christian, for political asylum in the USA, he was befriended by a church group in Charleston. When he finished his studies at the University of Charleston, he applied to join the CIA. He became an expert shot and after initial postings at Langley he had been undercover in Afghanistan, Iraq and Syria. His reputation as a cool-headed leader led to his transfer into the Special Activities Division. Uhmed and he were to lead the 'police raid' on the house – the other two operatives were to cover their exit and drive the Citroen van they were using for the snatch.

Police raids were not unusual in Lebanon and when there was a loud banging on the door Safiyah opened it. Uhmed pushed her inside, but she tried to scream when the other policemen produced a hypodermic syringe. They put her in a rolled up carpet and carried her to the van parked outside and headed towards the arranged pick-up point on the coast near the Sidon District.

A CH-53E Super Stallion helicopter arrived on time and all the snatch squad and the unconscious Safiyah took off for the light aircraft carrier USS *Simon*, cruising fifty miles offshore. Uhmed dumped the van at Beirut airport.

The carrier headed north and transferred their prisoner to a fishing boat off the Turkish coast at Izmir.

★

Safiyah Jamil had been passed to a speedboat in the Black Sea and taken to a secluded bay. She was then transferred to a waiting vehicle which drove to a CIA black-op holding centre in Medgidia, Romania. They had examined her mouth when she was out cold and removed a false tooth containing a cyanide pill. She had tried to use the deadly pill as soon as she woke up.

Now stripped naked, soaking wet and deprived of sleep by loud music in her cell, she shivered uncontrollably. Her interrogator was a burly man she did not recognise with a tattoo on his forearm. He had black penetrating eyes but was not the worst of her captors. Another man beat her and burned her breasts with cigarettes. It didn't take long before she broke.

An encrypted email was sent to Langley.

28

Ibrahim was very angry. He had expected the group head of security, Belardi, one of their commanders, to take care of Suleman's deputy – Safiyah Jamil. Hide her or kill her had been the leader's instructions. Now he was hearing she had been lifted, probably by the CIA, in Beirut. He considered what she might know. Suleman, he knew, preferred boys and transvestites, so he doubted there had been any pillow talk. But she needed to have certain information to manage the logistics of moving the chemicals from various ports to the bottling plants, and also some of the packaged Stardust range to warehouses to be picked up by supermarkets in Britain and Europe. *Hopefully,* he thought, *that's all she knew,* because he felt sure the British already had that information.

*

Jack Clarke read the coded message from the CIA internment unit in Romania.

Safiyah Jamil, known as Karim Basilah, was really a Palestinian woman Eshraq Urduni. Age twenty-eight, she had joined the PLO when her mother, father and two brothers had been killed by an Israeli bombing attack on the Southbank near the small village Nabi Saleh. She had been groomed from eight years of age. Growing up an extremist, prepared to do anything, she had lured several Israeli soldiers to their death in Palestine. It was then that she was transferred, that's how the interrogator put it, to Hezbollah and then to al-Qaeda for further training in Libya. She had been involved in bombings in Spain and Iraq. She was then sent to London to assist Suleman who ran the UK and European operation for a group she knew owned and ran the ExCy cosmetics company. She dealt with logistics; providing tankers to deliver chemicals to Birmingham in the UK and Marseille in France.

The chemicals and cosmetics arrived by sea in containers docking at ports in the UK named as Shoreham, Tilbury and Harwich, usually from Marseille in France. She did not know what the chemicals were, except she had been instructed to make sure the bottling plants in Birmingham and Marseille were under strict instructions not to touch the chemicals; gloves to be worn at all times. She had recruited Pakistanis, Somalians, Moroccans, Tunisian and other male and female African labour in both locations to bottle the cosmetics. A Somalian in Birmingham was shot when he stole two bottles of shampoo from the Birmingham UK plant.

She had arranged transport for Suleman, her immediate superior, and once for another man who was more senior than Suleman. He landed at Heathrow Airport, England and had travelled by helicopter to London. She had quickly realised he was one of the leaders and Suleman had told her not to talk to him, unless he asked her something. He was given a hire car – a BMW (details in appendix). She arranged for banking transfers. One hundred million pounds sterling from Shewards Bank to a bank in Zurich, Switzerland. Smaller sums to Suleman. That's how she discovered the name of the other supposed senior person – a bank draft was made out in his name for fifty thousand pounds sterling – it was to an A Ibrahim. He left after three days. She booked him on Pakistan Airways out of Heathrow to Karachi, Pakistan (see appendix for date and his description). She has given us the names of a number of active al-Qaeda trainers and camps in Pakistan and earlier Libya. Also a Hezbollah cell in Israel (unknown to PLO).

She also gave up an al-Qaeda agent in London, Umed Zamal, a Professor of Arab studies at the London School of Economics. She had been required to report to him all actions carried out by Suleman – it seems his bosses didn't entirely trust him. We pressed her on what was going on with the ExCy cosmetics but other than they used the trading name Stardust and had spent ten million dollars in the UK and five million dollars in France and Germany advertising and marketing, she knew nothing as to the ingredients or the purpose. She told us that there are nine items in the Stardust range – these are: toothpaste, nail polish, deodorant (roll-on and spray), shampoo, hairspray, soap (liquid), shaving cream, sunscreen and perfume. She was told by Suleman never to be tempted to sample them. One day, when she had picked him up from a club in London (see appendix for The Kitty Club), he was drunk and said the cosmetics were deadly. Suleman went on a number of trips overseas. She booked him British Airways and Emirates flights to Cyprus, Marseille, Zurich and Geneva. He also flew to Karachi and Mombasa by Emirates. She had destroyed the hard drives of three laptop computers before leaving London. Finally, she told us that two assassins had been sent by al-Qaeda to kill the deputy head of MI6, Colonel Harriman and a woman who was at Imperial College, London.

We await instructions.

Jack responded, 'Hold for now,' and sent a report to his boss, Samuel Goldmuir, and Bud Ruskin. He intended to brief the British when Caroline came in two days' time.

29

The Libyan had watched the Southbank headquarters of MI6 for two days. He had seen the woman come out flanked by two men on both occasions but there was no opportunity to kill her if he was to survive. He knew that in the end he would have to take a risk, as he could not return to Libya if he did not complete the mission. The problem was she kept erratic hours. She did not arrive at the same time every day and left the building at night between 7pm and 11pm. He used the black cab as his cover, keeping the light off so nobody tried to hire him (even then, several people did). He had dumped the body of the taxi driver on a common in Streatham and knew the police would have found it by now. The taxi was becoming a danger to him so he decided to use it only one more time.

*

Caroline was meeting John Harriman for a drink tonight and then dinner at Quaglino's, one of their favourite restaurants. The two Special Branch men met her at the front door. Her driver pulled up in the BMW X6 with the darkened windows and she strode towards the rear door. There was a blinding flash and a loud explosion. She felt something hit her head then blacked out.

John Harriman received a call on his mobile from his old friend Sir Anthony Greenwood informing him that Caroline had been taken to Chelsea Hospital. An explosion on the Embankment – she had been hit by shrapnel. His driver must have broken all records as he raced from Park Lane to Chelsea.

He rushed into the hospital, found out where she had been taken and ran up the stairs. Sir Anthony was already sitting in a small reception area with three other suited men the colonel did not know.

"They're operating on her at the moment, John," said a sombre Sir Anthony. "She has a head wound; it looks as though nails have penetrated her brain, and she has injuries to her arms and legs. She was wearing Kevlar body armour which stopped any further damage." Sir Anthony did not expect Caroline to survive but he wouldn't tell his old friend that now. For just under two hours the men waited; tense, sometimes pacing up and down, almost as though they were waiting for a baby to be born. Then the surgeon came through a set of double doors.

"Sir Anthony, would you come with me?" he asked.

Colonel Harriman had seen death many times in Iraq, Ireland and Afghanistan but nothing prepared him for this. His friend came back from the meeting with the surgeon.

"I'm so sorry, John. Caroline died at 9.45pm. She received multiple injuries to her brain, head and neck. The surgeon said she wouldn't have felt any pain."

John Harriman had never cried, even in Iraq when members of his unit were caught in a dogfight with Republican Guards and he had lost friends. Even when Mack had been tortured by that sadist Russian. But now he sobbed.

Linda, Caroline's sister, arrived, realised immediately she was too late and also broke down. They clung to each other in pain and support. Sir Anthony stopped him going to see her – "Remember her as she was, John," he said – her face was blown away by the destructive force of the nail bomb.

★

The funeral of Caroline Bland was, at her request, family and close friends only. The Reverend Jonathan Ridge introduced firstly Sir Anthony and then John Harriman, who both eulogised on the life and times of an outstanding woman. John told Linda, but not the assembled mourners, that he had intended to propose marriage that night. He had bought the ring which he had asked the undertaker to put on her finger. As the coffin moved slowly towards the curtain John Harriman vowed to avenge her – and when he caught up with the people responsible, God help them.

★

Two days later, Colonel Harriman sat in his office contemplating his next move. A meeting had taken place in Washington between Sir Anthony and Jack Clarke. Sir Anthony had passed on as much intel as he could and John knew that al-Qaeda was firmly involved, if not behind, whatever was going on. That was the problem – neither the Americans nor the British Secret Service knew what this was all about. ExCy was still trading in the States and Europe but its Stardust range was continually monitored and given a clean bill of health. The girl the CIA had captured had some useful intelligence but she did not know what was really going on. The man, Ibrahim, had been spotted in Pakistan but so far had not left that country. The CIA and MI6 were reluctant to try to kidnap him in

Pakistan – but Colonel Harriman was not so restricted. If he could get a fix on that man and had enough advance information as to his whereabouts, he was determined to have a go at lifting him. An MI6 agent, who had been particularly close to Caroline Bland, had unofficially told him that a CIA undercover operative was expecting shortly to pinpoint the whereabouts of Belardi. This man seemed very cosy with an ISI lieutenant general, one of Pakistan's main security services, and was photographed on the *Good Queen Bess* by the photographer who had been killed in the Med. Colonel Harriman knew if either target stepped outside Pakistan he would make an attempt to capture them – with or without the CIA or MI6.

★

As Colonel Harriman mourned Caroline in London, Belardi was meeting Osama bin Laden in Abbottabad, north west Pakistan. Bin Laden lived there unbeknown to local people but watched over by Akif Gandapur, a lieutenant general in the Pakistan Secret Service. Most of Pakistan's politicians would deny that al-Qaeda or bin Laden operated from Pakistan, but Akif Gandapur knew different. Belardi had been one of bin Laden's main followers for a decade but still feared meeting him. He knew bin Laden hated failure and he had little positive news.

"*As-salaam 'alaykum,*" bin Laden greeted his trusted lieutenant. "What news have you?"

Belardi replied to his leader's greeting, "*Wa 'alaykum salaam.*" He paused. "The Americans and British have interrupted our plan using the ExCy Chemicals' Stardust range of cosmetics. Ibrahim has activated the alternative brand Celebrity through a German company, Oriel Cosmetics."

"This is going to require a great deal more money. Have our friends given their support?" asked bin Laden.

"Yes, although it is going to take seven days for them all to forward the money. Ibrahim has requested they invest a further three billion dollars each."

"A significant sum," replied bin Laden, stroking his beard. "The killing of the British MI6 woman – was that really necessary?" he asked.

Belardi knew that the leader's view was that a low profile should be maintained. He hesitated before answering.

"Ibrahim did not consult me but gave the order to eliminate the woman and the troublesome Colonel Harriman. They were both interfering in the operation."

Bin Laden nodded. Belardi continued.

"Both our operatives sent to manage the operation in England have been killed. Ibrahim does not propose to send anyone else at the moment."

"The girl the CIA has, Karim Basilah – can we extract her or kill her?" asked bin Laden.

"We haven't found out where they have taken her. In any case," Belardi continued, "we don't believe she knows anything to compromise our operation."

"Sometimes people know more than you think. Eliminate her if you can," replied bin Laden. "Tell me about the arrangements to manufacture and supply the new cosmetics to the West," he asked.

They spent twenty minutes examining the new plan to supply the new brand, Celebrity Cosmetics, to the USA, Canada and Europe. Bin Laden nodded as he listened to the plan.

"Good," said bin Laden. "Tell Ibrahim to send me a message when our friends have all contributed the sum required."

Belardi left, relieved he had not been held responsible for the collapse of the earlier operation involving Stardust cosmetics.

30

The death of Caroline Bland had left a huge void in John Harriman's life. He didn't know what to do now that he had nobody with whom to share a visit to the theatre or a meal at Quaglino's or Rules Restaurant. He threw himself into work and became a hard taskmaster. Business as usual was all-consuming. The services he provided to the rich and famous of bodyguards and security were always in demand. He employed seventy-five people and most had served in the SAS, SBS, Special Branch or the military. Despite the demand for his services, he continued to guard his goddaughter Dee.

She was stubborn like his friend, her father, Martin, and insisted on going to Imperial College despite the security risk. Amanda, one of his best female operatives, accompanied her everywhere but was finding the time she wasted waiting for Dee outside a laboratory boring. Amanda wasn't the only one. Harry Sutherland was Amanda's back-up and mainly stayed in the shadows watching out for danger. Harry didn't like 'babysitting' as he called it. Not that he complained to the colonel. That wouldn't do;

a soldier obeyed orders even if he didn't like them much. But this job gave him too much time to think about Susan Croucher – the sister of the man who saved his life on Wandsworth Common. Those brown eyes, a smile that lit up the room, petite, yet beautifully proportioned – Harry was in love and all this hanging around made him think, should he contact her? It had been a month; but she had been quite emphatic he thought about what she had said, *Every time I saw you I would be reminded of the circumstances of the death of my brother.*

Harry's mobile rang; he recognised the number. "Colonel."

"Harry, I'm changing your shift."

"Sir?"

"Maloney is taking over for a short while. I need you on something else. Wait for him to replace you then come to HQ."

Harry was delighted and went to find Amanda. He knew she was bored as well and would probably not be pleased he was being moved and she had to stay put.

*

Colonel Harriman was not a man to wait for things to happen. These people who had killed Caroline, two university bods, a photographer in France and probably downed a jet carrying several hundred passengers were actively doing something. He thought Dee was on to what it was connected to – the ingredients of the cosmetics manufactured under the Stardust banner. But the boffins said the cosmetics were clean. *At least now they are,* he thought. The colonel always believed action produced better results than waiting for a break. Captain Harry Sutherland knocked on his door.

"Come," he answered.

"Afternoon, Colonel," said Harry.

"I've got a job for you, Harry, in France. I want you to replace the captain of this yacht." He passed Harry a photograph of the *Good Queen Bess*.

"Sir?" Harry looked at Colonel Harriman.

"This man," he showed Harry another photograph, "is going to go missing. He's the captain of the boat I showed you. I've arranged with the owners that you will replace him as skipper. You can sail this boat? She's the old Royal Yacht *Britannia*."

Harry whistled.

"Sure, I've skippered during my holidays a number of the world's biggest yachts based in Cannes two years ago for the charter company, Sail Luxury. A friend of mine," he didn't add also ex-SBS, "runs the company and was short of a skipper."

The colonel already knew Harry had a Master Mariner certificate he obtained after he left the Royal Navy.

"Good. I'm hoping the group of people that hired the yacht were so taken with her they'll do so again. Their advantage of meeting on the yacht is multi-point pick-ups and drop-offs; also, eavesdropping is very difficult. They might have been scared off by the photographer incident, but I doubt it. After all, they dealt with him."

"When do you want me to go?" asked Harry.

"Immediately. I've arranged for you to take over in three days' time. You will be an Australian, Thomas Mitchell, originally from England but you've been living in Australia for ten years. Here are your documents: passport, driving licence, certificates from the Australian navy, a bank account and a London flat with some supporting information left around if they check up on you. They might prohibit mobiles so we'd like to implant one of MI6's gizmos in your back." Harry looked startled.

"It's okay; they can take it out again. It's a minute tracker that enables a satellite to pinpoint precisely where you are.

Once we have a suitable fix, we'll raid the yacht and get all the occupants. The Royal Navy frigate, *Newcastle*, will be shadowing the yacht. Helicopters will enable the SAS to drop in and take off the occupants."

"Just a small point, sir," asked Harry, "is any of this legal?"

The colonel cleared his throat. "Let's not worry about that; Sir Anthony is helping us. Incidentally, Commander Cunningham, who Harriman Security recruited when he retired from the Special Boat Services, will be your second-in-command."

★

Using the new Chinese encrypted code, Belardi sent an email message to the men who ran the operations worldwide. These men – codenamed Blue, Red, Black and Green – were summoned to two different pick-up points around the Mediterranean. At the request of Ibrahim, Belardi had once again chartered the big yacht from Cannes, the *Good Queen Bess*. He knew Ibrahim loved the luxury and the food was superb. Belardi knew it was a risk but his contact in the DCRI, the French Central Directorate of Interior Intelligence, assured him that the investigation by the French police *judiciaire* of the murder of the photographer had got nowhere. He also wanted to bring in a new man to cover Europe, as he presumed Suleman, who had been based in London, had committed suicide (he was known as Blue). As usual, Belardi asked the charter company for a crew list and was surprised to see the skipper was Australian. *What happened to the Lebanese man who captained the yacht on the last cruise?* He emailed his contact in France and his associate in the Pakistan Security Service and asked them to check out the captain and all the crew members.

★

Harry Sutherland was not familiar with taking on the identification of someone else. As ex-Special Boat Services he was used to undertaking dangerous missions, but as acting captain of the *Good Queen Bess* he would have preferred to have kept his own name. Luckily he had worked in Australia with their special services for over a year and was able to impersonate a Brit who had been based in Sydney for ten years. It was not in his nature to be gregarious but he thought an Aussie yacht skipper would be less inclined to be as extroverted as many Australians he had met. After all, the man was in command and had been in the Aussie navy, so he played his part.

It was a week before the charter company informed him that the ship had been hired for a ten-day cruise around the Mediterranean. It was mysterious as, despite his enquiries, they didn't seem to know who had hired the yacht. He used a payphone in a café near the marina in Cannes to brief the colonel. The charter company received instructions to go to Palma, Majorca to pick up six passengers. Harry was able to send a coded text on his mobile before dumping it over the side. He had hidden another in his cabin.

He was excited about skippering this fabulous yacht and enjoyed the cruise to Palma. They berthed in the morning and waited for their passengers. Four Middle Eastern-looking men arrived the following morning showing charter documents and, at Harry's insistence, their passports. Two were Iranian and two Pakistani. One of the Pakistanis, seemingly their leader, called all the forty-two members of the crew and six officers to a meeting in the lounge. He introduced himself as Ursaan and insisted that his principals, who they would be picking up in Cyprus and Beirut, would require the utmost security. Ursaan insisted on the crew giving up their mobile phones. Each crew member was sent to his cabin with two of the Iranians and his belongings were searched and mobiles confiscated. Harry tried to object but in the scheme of things he knew that a captain would accede to the customer's request – the charter was for two million dollars and contracts like that didn't grow on trees.

Harry's cabin was also searched – he made it clear he was far from happy and very reluctantly gave up his mobile. They left Palma for Cyprus that afternoon. The remainder of that day and for the next two days they averaged twenty-one knots and approached Larnaca at 4.30pm. Instructed to drop anchor and not to berth, Harry watched as a rubber dingy came alongside and four men came aboard. Harry went to meet them. One of the men Harry thought was a Pakistani, the other three he wasn't sure. None of the faces were familiar. Harry topped up the fuel tanks and left at 6pm, heading for Beirut and aiming to arrive at 9pm. They berthed in the harbour and a further four men came on board. This time Harry recognised the man who had been photographed on this boat before by the French paparazzi and also in London coming out of the ExCy office. He was later confirmed as al-Qaeda by the CIA – his name was Belardi, a known al-Qaeda terrorist.

*

Belardi examined the list of crew members. He had been careful to check out the new captain, an Australian. The Saudi secret service man who had broken into this man's flat in London confirmed he appeared genuine. Belardi recognised the names of seventeen of the other crew members and three officers who had been on the yacht on their previous charter. Three others were Filipinos; two in the galley, one a cabin steward. The other men on board were all French except the second-in-command, an Englishman called Barry Sheppard, who had also been checked out by the Saudi secret service in London. His flat had also been broken into and his possessions scrutinised. Again, nothing suspicious – he appeared to be a jobbing sailor who had worked in the South of France, West Indies and Miami. Still, best be safe than sorry. Belardi smiled and spoke in Pakistani to Ursaan, saying Sheppard had studied at the LSE, a London university, where he majored in politics, and they should keep a particular eye on him. He ordered another sweep of the yacht for bugs and listening devices. All cabins to be searched again. The crew wouldn't like it – but tough, he was not trying to win a popularity contest. He instructed Ursaan, who the crew thought was in charge, to tell the captain and the crew to remain on board at each stopover.

★

The captain of the British frigate, HMS *Newcastle*, had stood off but had been tracking the yacht as she left Palma Harbour. Instructions from the Ministry of Defence were simple: keep out of sight and off the radar, so they were over two hundred nautical miles away. A long-range plane, a Boeing E-3 Sentry, commonly known as an AWAC, was shadowing the yacht. He knew the yacht well; he had had the privilege of escorting it on a tour of Australia five years ago. He was, therefore, a little concerned as he knew the yacht's top speed was twenty-two knots and he would have a job closing the gap if the SAS were to be sent in. However, the two helicopters on board the frigate could close the distance quickly if the man on board needed support, but their approach would not be silent. Now they cruised slowly towards Lebanon and no instructions had been received.

31

Belardi read the encrypted email from his source in the Chinese Secret Service. A Chinese satellite reported a British warship identified as a Type 23 frigate was standing off about two hundred nautical miles north. It might be nothing, but Belardi had not remained alive in Afghanistan and Pakistan by ignoring his instincts. He sent a message to Ibrahim not to join the yacht in Beirut. He knew he would be furious as he enjoyed the luxury of the yacht. *But the British,* he thought, *had a saying he had heard in London – better be safe than sorry.*

Belardi decided to leave the yacht and hold the meeting here in Beirut. He had to brief the four men who ran the worldwide operation, particularly Abail, the Saudi he had appointed as the new European operations manager: code name Blue. Belardi issued instructions to Ursaan who escorted the important men they were guarding to four vehicles brought to the gangplank. Each vehicle had blacked-out windows. All of these men were accompanied by two bodyguards in each vehicle. Ursaan neither knew nor cared who they were; he feared Belardi, who he had once seen blow a subordinate's brains out for questioning an order. Belardi had already slipped ashore with two others heading for a house on the outskirts of Beirut. He had contacted a leading Hezbollah commander and was being escorted to downtown Beirut. The man, Fadi Maboob, was on the payroll of Osama bin Laden. Lebanon had become one of the world's largest narcotics producers after the civil war, with much of the hashish production centred around the Bekaa Valley. Hezbollah and al-Qaeda co-operated in the establishment of distribution to Europe through Syria and Turkey. Whilst the Taif Agreement stabilised the country in 1989, and the committee appointed by the Arab league formulated solutions which they proposed to Christians and Muslims, al-Qaeda and Hezbollah continued to ship hashish. Belardi had been a key person bribing the Lebanese militia and Hezbollah. It was one of the Hezbollah commanders who joined him in the black Ford Galaxy and escorted him to the meeting place.

★

Harry Sutherland, as Captain Mitchell, enquired when the guests would be returning to the yacht, but the man Ursaan was non-committal. Harry left the yacht on the pretext of arranging for fuel and supplies. As he walked alongside containers stacked by the harbour side a man caught up with him. He was dressed in traditional Arab dress.

"You want hashish?"

Harry ignored him.

"You want cigarettes?" The man carried a plastic bag.

Harry knew Beirut was a major smuggling port used to ship cheap cigarettes to Cyprus and onwards.

"No, I don't," Harry replied, stepping up his pace. He expected to be met by a CIA agent, Uhmed Abaid.

"You like a young woman?" *The man was persistent,*

thought Harry. "Keep walking and talk about obtaining some cigarettes," the man said. "Uhmed, CIA."

Harry walked towards the buildings on his left and began to barter with the man for four thousand cigarettes.

"Good. Listen. Belardi and several bodyguards have joined a Hezbollah commander and driven off. Langley has a satellite overhead and will track the vehicle."

"It's likely the other cars are going to the same place," said Uhmed.

"Is there any possibility we can get to that meeting and try to listen in?" asked Harry.

"No chance. You see the three men ahead?" Harry nodded.

"Hezbollah. Stopping anyone leaving the harbour, and probably working with Fadi Maboob who controls downtown Lebanon.

"Okay, give me some of your cigarettes. I'll return to the yacht and we'll try to capture them on the return leg to Cyprus. Please notify London to tell the SAS to stand by. I'll signal them to launch the mission by zigzagging."

Uhmed made a show of passing Harry several packs of cigarettes and they parted company, Harry heading for the port office to arrange refuelling.

*

Belardi called the meeting to order. He had arranged for a large flat screen to be secured to the wall and linked to his laptop. Moments later the face of Osama bin Laden appeared on the screen.

"Welcome to Beirut, brothers," he said.

All the men in the room were silent, clearly in awe of the great man. The bodyguards remained outside the house but had scanned the rooms for bugs before the transmission.

"Belardi will instruct you on the next phase of our

operation, Allah be praised. You are all about to help us punish the infidels, so listen carefully to Belardi and don't fail me."

At that the screen went blank. All four men in the room looked towards Belardi.

For the next hour he relayed to the four controllers their instructions. Each had distribution responsibilities for the new cosmetics that they learnt were called Celebrity, a brand distributed by Oriel Cosmetics, a German company. The men were given briefing notes written in their native language. Each set of notes contained details of the new warehouses and bottling plants acquired in their territory and the equipment being installed. They were told to burn the note when they had familiarised themselves with the contents. Belardi did not elaborate where the cosmetics would be made, only that ships would bring containers either with the cosmetics already packaged or, if the warehouse was to act as a bottling plant, there would be liquid containers and machinery for bottling and labelling. Each man had instructions where to send the packaged cosmetics. If cosmetics were to be bottled, mainly shampoo, they also had to package the bottles and send them to a distribution centre, usually a port in the USA or Europe. Belardi waited until the four men had read the notes.

"You must handpick the workers at your warehouses or bottling plants. Use the ten men I will send each of you as security. One of these men will act as your deputy but do not inform them of our plans, only what they need to know. Substantial sums have been spent on equipping each warehouse, so these sites must be kept secret from the Americans and British."

Belardi told the four men they would not be travelling back to their region by sea. He handed each of them a ticket for a flight from different airports. Red, who was the manager of Mexico, the USA and Canada, would fly by

Etihad to Hartsfield–Jackson Atlanta Airport from Beirut and onward to Mexico City. Black, a Pakistani who acted for the group in the Middle East, would take a fast boat to Cyprus and board a Cyprus Air flight out of Larnaca to Bahrain. Green, an Iranian who ran the African continent, would fly by Qatar Air from Beirut to Dubai and then onward to Cape Town. Blue, who managed Europe, having taken over from the previous manager captured in London, was going by Qatar Air from Beirut to Zurich where he was to be based. Belardi was driving across the border to Amman and flying by Etihad Airways to Karachi. All the commanders destroyed their notes and were escorted to cars and then driven to their embarkation point.

Belardi had bribed a border guard and entered Jordan later that evening without showing his passport. He was due to meet Osama bin Laden in north Pakistan in four days time to discuss phase two of the operation the leader called: Tears of the West.

32

John Harriman lined up the four-foot putt on the eighteenth green at the prestigious golf club in Sunningdale, Berkshire.

"Good putt, John," said Anthony as the ball dropped into the hole. "Drinks on me. That puts you two up."

Colonel Harriman laughed; a rare thing since the death of Caroline, his longstanding partner. Sir Anthony didn't find much time to play golf these days but he knew his friend was hurting, even if he didn't show it. The security team shadowing both men breathed a collective sigh of relief as Sir Anthony and the colonel entered the clubhouse. Caroline Bland's killer had not been apprehended and a game of golf entailed a great risk for Anthony's bodyguards and the colonel's men. The two men showered changed and went into the bar. Four security men followed and positioned themselves covering the door, two more men guarded the entrance and four patrolled around the building.

Colonel Harriman hadn't relaxed much but had found himself enjoying the game and the company of his old friend. Now down to business.

"Any news on the missing assassin, Tony?"

"Nothing I'm afraid. Gone to ground it seems," replied Sir Anthony.

"My goddaughter is causing me a bit of a headache with security but insists she's getting results," said the colonel.

"She's still working on the nanoparticles angle?"

"Better than that. Cheers." He raised his glass. "She's travelling to Essex University every day. Apparently they have specialist equipment for detecting these particles. She's now closing in on the size of the particles and their composition."

"Clever girl. The senior government scientific bods are also working on the content of the products Dee provided," said Sir Anthony.

"The new Stardust cosmetics on the shelves still clear of the mystery ingredients she found?"

"Yes – continuous testing is going on but no nanoparticles found."

"It's pretty clear that after the CIA raids on the ExCy warehouses, they have reverted to normal ingredients – if you can call some of the strange things in cosmetics normal," said the colonel.

"The home secretary is reluctant to instruct ExCy to withdraw its products. Let's face it – he has no evidence to force the company to stop trading in the UK, and the attorney general has been muttering about international law and common trading platforms."

"Bloody politicians and bureaucrats; why can't they act when there's clearly something seriously wrong?"

"Well let's concentrate on what we're doing," said Anthony.

"We had a call from Harry Sutherland on the *Good Queen Bess* via the CIA. He reports the men who boarded in Palma and Cyprus all left the yacht in Beirut Harbour. He saw Belardi, who came on board briefly, but he also left," replied the colonel.

"Yes, I also heard from CIA who are watching the harbour," replied Sir Anthony. The colonel's mobile rang, he answered and rang off.

"Harry has received instructions to return to Cannes. Only the original four men picked up in France are remaining on board."

"Okay, let's pick them up when they refuel in Palma, or if they can, take them at sea," said Sir Anthony. "I'll send a message to my man Adam to back up Harry and Roland Cunningham."

"Adam's on board?"

"Yes. Thought it best he remained incognito from your two boys until he was needed," replied Sir Anthony.

Colonel Harriman was a little taken aback, but then reflected on what Caroline had always said to him – a spook likes to work alone and invisibly.

"At sea or Palma it is then," said the colonel.

"I'll have the team of SAS men on the frigate briefed to meet the yacht when the terrorists are captured. They can then transfer the four men to HMS *Newcastle* and bring them to England."

"Another swift half?" asked the colonel.

"No, I must get on. Good to have a round with you. Let's do it again soon."

Colonel Harriman doubted that Sir Anthony's or his own men would appreciate both of them out in the open again whilst the assassin who killed Caroline was still on the loose.

33

Professor Endleson had been a little miffed to be summoned to Whitehall and then asked to go to the USA, but after the government chief scientific officer, Sir Henry Park, told him the problem, his interest picked up. If a manufacturer was adding nanoparticles to its range of cosmetics he wasn't unduly surprised, as several of the world's leading brands were already doing so. What was interesting was the connection with terrorists. He had written a paper two years ago pointing out that all western countries were susceptible to a biological terrorist attack. He had thought they would contaminate water supplies. But this was something very interesting.

He was on his way to Heathrow to fly by British Airways to Boston. He was pleased as he was travelling first class and he could study the student Deidre's initial findings in relative comfort. The Home Office was footing the bill, and he was delighted to be going to meet Eugene Rendle, a Professor of Chemistry, Chemical Biology and Physics at Harvard University, the US centre for nanoscale applications. It was a real pleasure to meet Rendle whom he had heard lecture on toxicokinetics in London. In June 2002 the UK government had commissioned the Royal Society, the UK Academy of Science and the Royal Academy of Engineering to carry out an independent study of likely developments and whether nanotechnology raised, or was likely to raise, new ethical, health or safety, or social issues which were not covered by current regulations. Professor Endleson had been a member of the Royal Academy Committee. The report in 2004 from the committee highlighted the immediate need for research to address uncertainties about health and environmental issues. It also made recommendations about legislation to control exposure to nanoparticles. The professor knew that strict regulations had not been put into place.

Landing at Boston Logan International at 13.45 local time, Professor Endleson walked out of arrivals and saw a man holding a board with his name. He wearily walked towards the young man holding up the sign, 'Harvard University Welcomes Professor G Endleson'. He hadn't slept on the flight as he was studying the latest email from Dee Cox, who was working with him at Essex University on secondment from Imperial College. Dee and the team of researchers had, using the Condensation Particle Counter (CPC), determined the concentration of nanoparticles in a sample of Stardust shampoo. They had enlarged a number of the hundred thousand particles detected by the optical detector and were now trying to analyse their content.

Not an easy task when you consider that, as he had explained to Humphrey Dawes, the Home Office minister, the aspect ratio between a nanoparticle and a football is similar to that between a football and the planet earth.

"Hello, I'm Professor Endleson," he said to the young man holding up the board.

"Oh, hi there. Todd Newby. I'm one of the team at the centre."

They shook hands and Todd relieved the rather weary-looking professor of his trolley and luggage.

"I have a vehicle in the car park. Follow me, sir."

The journey to Harvard University was uneventful and forty minutes later they drove onto the campus. The professor was glad that this young man had been sent to bring him to the centre as he looked around the impressive, sprawling campus and thought how easy it would be to get lost.

"Here we are, sir. They're expecting you." Todd stopped outside a modern two-storey building, got out, opened the boot and gave the professor his hand luggage and overnight bag.

Professor Endleson had not been to Harvard University before, although he had visited Michigan State University and Boston College of Engineering for conferences. He walked in and was greeted by a security guard and shown to reception. He knew he wasn't at his best – the flight and a lack of sleep, plus he hadn't slept well the previous night contemplating Dee's early findings. He sat waiting, a slight headache beginning to irritate. A middle-aged man approached.

"Hi, Professor Endleson. I am Eugene Rendle."

The two academics shook hands as Eugene enquired about his journey. Professor Endleson covered up his fatigue, curious to hear what their findings were.

"Come and meet the guys," said Eugene.

Professor Endleson knew Professor Eugene Rendle was one of the most eminent men working on nanoparticle projects at the Harvard centre and in the world. He was a Professor of Biology and Physics who he had previously heard in the UK at a lecture at the Royal Academy of Engineering on measuring the type and quantity of nanoparticles. Professor Endleson was introduced to two other academics that he also knew by name and reputation were leading experts on nanotechnology, Professor Brian Flavier and Norton Tresargo, a senior engineer in nanofabrication.

"Come and meet the other members of the team," said Eugene.

Professor Endleson shook hands with the twenty men and women without registering their names.

"I expect you'd like to rest up before we get down to business?" asked Eugene.

Professor Endleson drew on all his strength. "No, I wouldn't mind seeing what you chaps have got now."

The three men he had met originally led him through to a laboratory, one of many from what he could see.

"Take a seat," said Eugene. "I know you Brits have an expression I believe is 'teaching grandmother to suck eggs', but forgive me if I go over ground that's obvious."

He proceeded to detail the process the research team had undergone since receiving twenty-three thousand samples of Stardust products.

"Most of the samples, in fact 80%, didn't surprise us – the usual cocktail of ingredients. Then we discovered a bottle of shampoo that definitely contained something in addition. The team narrowed the ingredients down using image metrology and a particle pore analysis. There were particles, pores and grains in the shampoo. We measured the radius of the particles and distribution using a Photon Correlation Spectroscopy – I guess you call it a PCS? Isolating the nanoparticles, we used small-angle x-ray scattering and small-angle neutron scattering. As you know, the advantage of these techniques is that they're able to simultaneously sample and average very large numbers of nanoparticles. This led us to identify several different particles with compounds formulating or coating the nanoparticles. Silver, silicon, mercury, diethyl phthalate, dibutyl phthalate, titanium dioxide and lead were all present. This was a rather shocking discovery in a bottle of hair shampoo. But when we went on to discover parabens were also present, we were frankly astonished. What manufacturer would include some of these most deadly substances in a hair shampoo, hidden as nanoparticles, and why? In fact, out of 2,417 bottles of shampoo chosen at random from all over the States, 227 contained nanoparticles and with the recipe I have detailed."

"Did you test any of the other Stardust range of cosmetics?" asked Professor Endleson.

"Yes, but as you can imagine screening thousands of samples has been time-consuming." Eugene looked at his notes. "The hairspray, because it's a fluid, enabled us to test using the Photon Correlation Spectroscopy and once again we measured the radius and distribution of particles present in 8.9% of the samples, 392 hairspray cans."

"Were the ingredients you identified in the shampoo present in the rogue hairspray?" asked Professor Endleson.

"Slightly different. We used a Nanoparticle Surface Area Monitor (NSAM) as it measures the charge of an aerosol sample that has gone through a diffusion chamber. We then made a calculation to work out the deposited surface area the sample particles would reach in respect of the regions of the human lung; mainly trachea, bronchial and alveolar. The hairspray ingredients could also penetrate the scalp, as well as be inhaled," said Eugene.

Brian Flavier added, "We wouldn't have been surprised if the particles were exactly the same as the shampoo samples – but they weren't." He looked at his notebook. "In fact, the particles in the hairspray consisted of, or were coated with, the bio-accumulate phthalates, DEHP, DBP, DEP and DBCP, as well as benzene, silver and silicon; not a very healthy mixture of particles."

"Someone has gone to a great deal of trouble," muttered Professor Endleson.

"Yes, we agree, but who and why?" replied Brian Flavier.

"George, – may I call you George?" Professor Endleson nodded. "Shall we continue discussing our findings over dinner? I'm sure you're fatigued from your journey."

Professor Endleson was staying at the Marriott hotel and it was Todd who drove him there. He chatted about nanoparticles and some of the work they had been doing on biological engineering. George Endleson was happy to reach the hotel and check in – the group was meeting at Mano's, a popular restaurant, for a 7pm dinner.

Professor Endleson didn't have a nap but sent an email to his team at Essex University. The Americans had broken down the particles and identified the ingredients in at least two of the cosmetics. He had scribbled notes, as Eugene and Brian told him their processes and listed the ingredients. He sent the email to his deputy and copied in Dee Cox, who had started this worldwide investigation in London.

34

Dee Cox read the email, nodded to herself and printed off the file attached. The time difference meant she would have to wait until tomorrow to discuss the findings from Harvard with the other members of the team at Essex University. There were only three members of her team and whereas they were analysing samples of the products, they hadn't broken down the nanoparticles sufficiently to identify ingredients. They had discovered over one billion nanoparticles in a shampoo sample but interestingly only three hundred thousand in the nail polish. They had therefore decided to concentrate on the nail polish and now had a result which tomorrow they would email to Professor Endleson.

*

Jack Clarke and Bud Ruskin studied the document they had received from Professor Eugene Rendle of Harvard University.

"Do you get any of this, Bud?" asked Jack.

"I gave up chemistry in the second trimester." Bud laughed.

"The important point is, we must be of one on this," said Jack. "The Stardust cosmetics from these ExCy people were contaminated and toxic."

"What are you thinking – total ban?" asked Bud.

"Yep – and all of the range to be taken off the shelves."

"I agree. After all, it's possible some old stock remains, especially in out of the way places," said Jack, as Bud nodded his agreement.

"It's up to the State Department to decide how to implement a ban," said Bud. "So, how is the action in capturing the people behind this thing?"

"We're tracking one of the prime movers – a guy named Belardi." He pressed a button and on the wall-mounted screen a photograph appeared. "And the Brits are trying to capture some of the members of a group on board a yacht as we speak."

"Have they analysed exactly what effect on the body there would be by using these Stardust cosmetics?" asked Bud, looking at the documents on the desk.

"We have scientific and biological analysts looking at that at Langley and Harvard," said Jack.

"Okay, let's go and see the president and the secretary of state. The chief of staff should also be briefed."

⋆

Colonel Harriman had been unable to take his customary early morning run since the explosion killed Caroline Bland. One of the assassins continued to elude Special Branch, the police and MI5. He had been advised not to take risks and he had curtailed his usual routine. Now he had made a decision and called Major Smith, his deputy at Harriman Security. Since 2007, when the government decided to privatise the security for the royal family and certain embassies, some security companies were licensed to carry firearms. Harriman Security was one such firm. Of course there was annoying red tape if a weapon was discharged but the colonel put up with the bureaucratic process because carrying weapons in his line of business was vital.

Arriving at his Park Lane headquarters accompanied by Sergeant Quick, his bodyguard for today, he summoned all his officers on duty.

Fifteen men and two women squashed around the boardroom table.

"I have made a decision." They all listened attentively. "We must catch the assassin who murdered Caroline and it seems the authorities are no nearer collaring him or her. I propose to act as bait to lure the assassin out."

There was a gasp from several of the personnel around the table.

"I realise the risk, especially if the assassin is a sniper as well as a bomber. But my goddaughter remains in danger, as does Harry Sutherland, and I feel some action is needed. This is what I'm going to do." The colonel explained his plan, made the arrangements and returned to his office.

*

Adam Runfold had been acting as a steward on board the *Good Queen Bess*. Even Harry Sutherland and Roland Cunningham hadn't been informed an MI6 agent was on board. He unscrewed the metal skirting board in his cabin and took out the three Sig Sauer P230 pistols the silencers, handcuffs and the two stun guns. When the yacht was underway from Beirut to Palma for the three-day return cruise he left his cabin. It was a dark, starry night with a clear sky and a gentle swell. The man patrolling the main deck didn't see Adam as he fired 50,000 volts into his back. He handcuffed the man and hauled him to a storage cupboard where had had earlier left a gag and some rope to tie his legs. He picked up the small silver tray, covered it with the white linen tea towel and went towards the steps leading to the bridge. He knew another of the guards would be on the bridge with one of the Harriman Security employees, Cunningham or Sutherland. Entering the bridge by the door from the main deck stairs, the guard reacted by pointing his mini Uzi sub-machine gun. Adam, looking suitably demure and shocked said, "You ordered a steak sandwich at 2am, Captain?"

Harry looked at this man and nodded, and the guard lowered his weapon. Adam suddenly fired the stun gun and the man dropped shaking to the deck.

"Hi, I am Adam, MI6," he said.

"Didn't know we had company. I was just figuring out how to disable him." He looked at the man on the floor as Adam secured his hands with the plastic handcuffs.

"I have a nice storage cupboard for our friend," he said as he dragged the hapless man to the door.

"Do you need a hand? The yacht's on autopilot."

"Yes, he weighs a ton," replied Adam.

They carried the man to the storage cupboard, gagged him and secured his legs.

"See you've been busy," Harry laughed. "What about the man Ursaan? He's sleeping in the purser's cabin."

"I'm going to deal with him now," replied Adam.

"Need a hand?"

"No harm, as long as the yacht's secure."

"I'll wake up Roland Cunningham to man the bridge," replied Harry.

He tapped quietly on Roland's door. The cabin door inched open.

"It's me, Roland. Can you go up to the bridge?"

Harry quickly explained that Adam had captured two of the men left on board and now they were going after the others.

Adam, continuing to pose as a steward, knocked twice on the cabin door where Ursaan was sleeping. He opened the door gingerly, with a Browning pistol in his hand. Adam looked down at the gun.

"Sorry to disturb you. The captain requests you come to the bridge. A large ship is closing on us and has been following our course for the past hour."

This wasn't a lie as HMS *Newcastle* was indeed closing rapidly as Harry had deliberately begun to reduce speed, and zigzagging gave the signal to the frigate shadowing them to close in. Ursaan went back into his cabin to find his jumper; he had already put on his trousers. He left the cabin, following Adam, toward the stairs to the bridge, his sub-machine gun slung over his shoulder. He didn't have time to react as Harry fired the stun gun. Immobilised by 50,000 volts, his body convulsed. Adam handcuffed him and they carried him downstairs to a now crowded storage cupboard.

"One to go," said Adam.

They did the same trick again, knocking on the door, this time instructing the guard that Ursaan wanted him on the bridge.

Having secured all four of the men left to accompany the yacht to Palma, Adam asked Harry to contact the captain of HMS *Newcastle*. They arranged for the frigate to come alongside and set up a breeches buoy to transfer the four men to the warship. Adam was to accompany the prisoners. There was already a team of six SAS men on board the frigate to maintain guard duty. The frigate would then sail to Portsmouth and the four men would be taken to the SIS house off the M23 motorway, north of Gatwick Airport, for interrogation. Firstly, Ursaan, who was apparently the leader, had been tranquilised in case he had a false tooth and intended to bite into the hidden capsule of cyanide. The four men and Adam were transferred successfully to the frigate in a slight swirl, with half the crew of the yacht reassured by Harry that the four Arab-looking men were terrorists wanted by British Intelligence. It was easy to convince the crew who had seen the men patrolling the yacht with sub-machine guns.

Harry phoned the colonel with the news of the capture.

"MI6 will take over their interrogation," said the colonel. "Fly back as soon as possible from France as I might need you both if the missing assassin takes another crack at me."

35

Colonel Harriman drove into the Chelsea mews where he had a small house. He had now returned from the safe house MI6 had provided after Caroline Bland was killed. He was alone and almost dreaded going in. The rain beat down. It was a filthy night. *Just the sort of night to die,* he thought. Carefully, he opened the front door. The bomb squad had briefed him that the intruder had been inside for long enough to set up a trip wire – but it was likely he would use the same technique as earlier and set a bomb off remotely. They were right, that was his intention.

"The bandit is on a motorbike at the end of the mews," reported Captain Johnston.

"Take him out using the stun guns," said Colonel Harriman as he inched gingerly up the hall in his house.

Harry Sutherland opened the front door to number 15. The rider on the motorbike looked across the road. Captain Norlington, who had been hidden in an Audi parked in the mews, slipped out of the passenger front seat – he left the door ajar – and approached the black-clad motorcyclist. At the same time Sergeant Quick and Corporal Williams blocked the top of the mews with a transit van. The assassin instantly realised he was in trouble, started the motorbike and was about to roar off when 50,000 volts hit him. He flinched but continued to accelerate, pulling the stun gun out of Captain Norlington's hand. Captain Johnston took the shot. The rider dropped the bike as the bullet passed through his leg. The bike clattered along the road; the rider lay prone on the tarmac.

"Rider down, repeat, rider down," said Captain Johnston. The four men approached the man on the ground cautiously. He moaned but remained motionless. Captain Norlington turned him over. Suddenly he reacted, pulling out a pistol, but before he could fire Captain Johnston shot him in the head at point blank range.

Colonel Harriman reversed the way he had entered his house. He had decided to let the bomb squad find the device he thought was inside.

"Ah, pity," said the colonel as he looked at the dead assassin.

"No choice, I'm afraid. He was about to shoot Norlington," said Captain Johnston.

The colonel phoned Sir Anthony at MI6 to organise a clean-up and get the bomb squad, then went to placate two of his neighbours who were nervously approaching.

★

Osama bin Laden had been living in the large house in Abbottabad, northwest Pakistan for some time. Security was good as there was a large Pakistani army base five miles away, and one of his followers, Akif Gandapur, a lieutenant general in the Pakistan Secret Service, monitored activity in the area. He was planning a major attack on a US embassy in Kenya but the Tears of the West was his most significant achievement. The fools had no idea even though they had raided most of the ExCy warehouses and bottling plants. He knew the Americans and British were examining the Stardust cosmetics. But he also knew from his last remaining agent in London that MI5 and MI6 did not know what was happening, as he had an MI6 employee in his pocket. Belardi had been his most trusted lieutenant for over ten years. He was due at the compound in two hours. Osama never invited both his key commanders, Belardi and Ibrahim, to come to the compound at the same time. He felt secure because he took precautions. But the Americans had their satellites and drones and probably knew Belardi was involved in the ExCy operation.

Ibrahim dealt with the money – buying businesses, leasing warehouses, arranging tankers and all the logistics of moving millions of bottles of cosmetics to North America and Europe. Belardi ran the security for the operation using his contact in the ISI, some helpful Saudi contacts and, most importantly, the Chinese. Neither of his lieutenants knew his key contact in Beijing who had given him a new Chinese secure email program, to date not penetrated by the Americans. Nor did they realise he had received help from the Chinese in other ways. Bin Laden pondered the problem. If he didn't confide in one or both of his commanders, the Tears of the West operation would grind to a halt if he, the leader, were captured or killed. Both of his commanders knew the plan but neither knew who provided the nanoparticles. When the Chinese businessman had first approached him he hadn't really understood. But now – he knew the scheme could decimate the West and he wanted it to continue even if he was discovered, captured or killed. Belardi or Ibrahim – who should he empower? He couldn't decide; perhaps both?

36

Jack Clarke read the report which had been delivered by the boffins at Harvard simultaneously to the head of the FBI and the secretary of state. His internal phone rang.

"Jack, I'm coming down," said Samuel Goldmuir.

An hour later, Samuel, Jack, Sheila Franklyn a senior analyst, and Morgan Harrison the CIA's leading scientist, sat around the boardroom table.

"Sheila has prepared a number of scenarios concerning these nanoparticles in the Stardust range of cosmetics," said Samuel.

Sheila Franklyn had graduated from Harvard with a degree in biology and taken a Masters at Yale in applied physics. Recruited by the CIA five years ago she specialised in indentifying biological warfare threats to America. All eyes turned to her.

"Okay, these nanoparticles added to the usual ingredients of shampoo and hairspray – this is not a biological attack in the usual sense of the phrase. But that's what it is. I've examined all the nanoparticles reported by Eugene Rendle at Harvard as being present and one thing stands out." She paused for effect. "They are nasty, particularly to pregnant women or women trying to conceive, or to a guy's fertility."

"Elaborate," asked Samuel.

"Look at the list of nanoparticles in the hairspray." She displayed a list on the screen on the wall. "First of all you have to understand that this plan, probably by al-Qaeda terrorists, is long-term and different from anything we've encountered before. These nanoparticles are being absorbed either through the skin, swallowed or inhaled into the lungs. Either way, they reach the bloodstream and are a deadly toxic cocktail targeted we suspect towards the reproductive system." She read out the list of nanoparticles. "Silver is usually used in nanoparticles to control the crystallinity of silicon. Silver nanos cause damage to testicular cells, according to a recent study by the Norwegian Institute of Public Health, with possible consequences for fertility." She continued. "Bio-accumulate phthalates known as DEHP, DBP, DEP and DBCP are absorbed through the skin causing a reduced sperm count, they interfere with hormone function and are likely to cause harm to an unborn child."

Sheila paused to allow the men to take in what she was saying.

"DEP is suspected of interfering with hormone function, disrupting the endocrine system, causing reproductive and development problems as well as other health effects. Phthalates are linked to lower testosterone levels, decreased sperm counts and poor sperm quality. Benzene can shrink ovaries and cause menstrual irregularity. In other words, gentlemen, this nanoparticle cocktail included in a bottle of Stardust shampoo or sprayed on the hair and absorbed through the scalp is very, very nasty." Sheila continued. "If that wasn't bad enough there are parabens which also affect sperm production."

"So," said Director Goldmuir, "absorbing these

nanoparticles is likely to have a serious and damaging effect on a woman's reproductive system and a man's sperm?"

"In a nutshell, you've got it," said Sheila.

"But why is anyone going to all this trouble?" asked Jack Clarke.

"We're working on that one," said Sheila as she switched to the next visual.

"Now take a look at what reproductive toxins delivered by coated nanoparticles are included in the ingredients of the shampoo." She read out loud the list and added her comments.

"Again, silver and silicon particles; DEP, which remember is suspected of interfering with hormone functions causing reproductive and development problems; DBP, also in the hairspray; titanium dioxide, thought to affect the reproductive system; and most notably lead nanoparticles which if you are pregnant the exposure can cause miscarriage, premature birth or smaller babies. They also found mercury nanoparticles which may cause miscarriage, and again parabens."

"Let me get this straight – these nanoparticles are so small the human eye cannot identify them and there are large numbers of different toxic ingredients in the composition of these nanoparticles and as a catalyst shampoo and hairspray carry these particles into the bloodstream by absorption through the skin, swallowed or inhaled into the lungs," said Director Goldmuir. "And the effect of these things is interference with normal birth by affecting the woman's reproductive system or the male's sperm?"

"That is the conclusion of Morgan, who is the CIA's leading scientist, and myself," replied Sheila.

"Then, there you have the reason. The fertility of our nation is under attack. This isn't their normal method of attack but it's just as dangerous to our citizens," said Director Goldmuir.

"This may sound a stupid question," said Jack Clarke, "but how many of these nanoparticles are getting into the bloodstream and can they be removed?"

"That's the worst thing of all," replied Sheila. "We don't know any way to remove the nanoparticles from the human body. As to how many, the centre at Harvard estimated a billion nanoparticles were in each bottle of shampoo and tin of hairspray."

"Jesus Christ," said Jack.

"It's clear we have to close down this Stardust range and get them off the shelves of supermarkets. We know ExCy has reverted to cosmetics not containing these nanoparticles, but old stock which contain the toxins may remain in distributors' warehouses," said Goldmuir. "I'll ask for a meet with the president and the secretary of state today. You had all better accompany me."

37

Dee Cox had concentrated on the Stardust nail polish since receiving Professor Endleson's report on what the Americans had discovered. Using image metrology and a particle and pore analysis at Essex University, she determined glycol ethers, DBP, DEP and butyl parabens were all contained in or coated nanoparticles included in the range of nail polishes. Examining what scientists, various online information websites and universities had to say about these particles, she concluded that terrorism had reached a whole new meaning and telephoned her godfather, Colonel Harriman.

★

Dee's telephone call requesting a meeting was timely. Colonel Harriman had just left Sir Anthony Greenwood. 'Keeping the wraps on this thing' had been the instruction from the Home Office. 'Mustn't let people find out about the problem with this Stardust range of cosmetics – ignorance is bliss and all that,' the minister had said. But Anthony

Greenwood and Simon Tomlinson did not agree. Analysts in Simon Tomlinson's department had calculated, using data collected from the major supermarkets, that three-quarters of a million bottles of the Stardust shampoo had been sold and a similar number of cans of ladies hairspray. They knew from recent samples that the cosmetics were no longer toxic. But during the time that they had been they were widely marketed and only recently had their toxic content changed. The commercial TV companies confirmed that ExCy had spent ten million pounds advertising the cosmetics on national TV. The supermarkets confirmed that the Stardust range was keenly priced, which they felt had increased sales. Colonel Harriman also knew that when all the ingredients of these products were known, the collective sales would likely mean millions of people in Britain would have absorbed, inhaled or swallowed toxic nanoparticles.

Professor Endleson had submitted a preliminary report following his visit to Harvard. Colonel Harriman thought the government was not acting properly and were indicating that a cover-up was the best option. What he wanted more than anything else, since the death of Caroline Bland, was the perpetrators of this appalling biological attack to be brought to justice, including Bin Laden.

★

Umed Zamal, a Professor in Arab studies at the London School of Economics, left his flat in Bethnal Green at his usual time of 7.30am. Travelling by London underground from Bethnal Green station on the Central Line, he travelled one stop to Liverpool Street, walked to the Circle Line and got on a train to Embankment where he changed onto a Northern Line train getting off at Leicester Square. He changed again onto the Piccadilly Line, alighting at

Holborn. All this was to check if he was being followed as he could simply travel straight to Holborn from Bethnal Green. He walked, stopping to look in shop windows as they had shown him in Tripoli during al-Qaeda training. From Holborn tube station he walked down Kingsway to the LSE in Houghton Street, he checked if he was being followed. Satisfied, he doubled-back up to Southampton Row and went to the British Museum in Great Russell Street. He was due to meet Joseph Dyer at 9am in the Court Café on the north east corner of the Great Court. He usually arranged to meet there as very few people were in the café so early in the morning and afterwards he enjoyed visiting the Egyptian Room.

Sitting in the corner, he studied the people in the café. Two women seemingly engaged in an interesting conversation about a man were sitting two tables away. A group of Americans chatted noisily around a table. An elderly couple sat across the café and a single man studied what Umed thought was a map of the museum. Joseph Dyer came in at 9.05am and walked through the self-service ordering a coffee. He sat at Umed's table. This would be their last meeting. Since Suleman had been taken and Safiyah Jamil had been recalled to Beirut, Umed had known his time at LSE and in the UK was limited. The trouble was he had got used to the lifestyle – his students looked up to him. He even had a brief affair with one of them, a very attractive French girl. He had studied at Oxford University twenty years ago; he liked England and its traditions. Now the encrypted email yesterday from Belardi – 'leave immediately'. But he had arranged the meeting with Dyer two days ago, and thought it prudent to meet him once more. He would find out where the British security services were in relation to discovering the real purpose of the Stardust range of cosmetics.

"Hello again, Joseph."

Dyer looked at him with undisguised hatred. "What do you want?"

"First things first. Sabrine sends her love. She said to tell you she is safe and being looked after." He passed a newspaper to Dyer who picked it up and put it in his briefcase – he knew it contained a dozen packets of cocaine.

"Now tell me where you are with the investigation of ExCy and the cosmetics range Stardust," said Umed.

Joseph Dyer had been recruited into MI6 after he graduated from Oxford in 2003. He had been proud to pass the selection process and when he was appointed as an analyst in Caroline Bland's department he was delighted. Now he was a wreck. Hooked on cocaine and in love with a woman who seemed to be in the control of terrorists, he dreaded going to work. He looked down at his coffee cup pondering what to tell this man. He tried not to give much away, but he needed the cocaine and the now infrequent meetings with Sabrine.

"Come, Joseph, what have you got for me?" asked Umed, slightly changing the tone of his voice.

"MI6 has captured four men from a yacht sailing in the Mediterranean. We believe they're connected to whatever's going on," he replied.

"What have they said about the cosmetics?" asked Umed.

"Very little, but there are a number of people working on what is believed to be ingredients not stated on each cosmetic packaging."

"Who are these people?"

Joseph thought for a moment. Caroline had been murdered because he told this man she was leading the investigation and the door she used as she exited the building. A young woman, the girl Dee Cox, was being targeted by terrorists and he thought he was responsible.

"I don't know. That's above my authorisation," Joseph replied.

"Come now, remember Sabrine needs you to help us," said Umed.

Joseph was sweating, partly as a result of needing a fix, but also because he was scared – scared of these people and of betraying his country.

"All I know is several universities and laboratories at Porton Down are analysing the cosmetics. I don't know any more."

"All right, Joseph, calm down," said a more conciliatory Umed. "Where have they taken the four men captured on the yacht?"

"I don't know. Probably West End Central police station for Special Branch to interrogate them," Joseph lied smoothly.

"Okay, is there anything else?"

"No," replied Joseph.

"I have given you extra supplies of cocaine as I may not meet you for a while. A new friend may contact you. If so, he will introduce himself as a friend of Sabrine. You leave first."

Joseph got up without finishing his coffee and headed for the exit.

Umed sat for a few minutes watching. The table of Americans were still animated. The man studying a map picked up his cup but didn't look around. Other people were coming into the café now. He waited until Joseph had left the room then followed him out. He went down Southampton Row to his rooms at the LSE. He thought to himself how much he would miss London and particularly teaching his students. But the message yesterday was simple: leave immediately. He kept a small suitcase in his office already packed with his basic essentials. He checked his desk and drawers removing a notepad and his favourite Mont Blanc pen. He always carried his passport and credit cards but checked his inside pocket. He used a mobile he had bought on a pay-as-you-go basis yesterday and phoned Sabrine, she answered after three rings.

"I am going on a visit and will be away a short while. I gave you three weeks' supply of the drug yesterday. Someone will contact you soon. Remember you are being watched. Don't meet Joseph." He didn't wait for a response and dialled the Emirates Airline desk in London.

"Do you have a flight to Dubai this afternoon?" Satisfied, he booked business class on the 3pm flight – time to head to Heathrow and have a light lunch in the Emirates Executive Lounge where they served halal food.

The team shadowing Umed Zamal had followed him into the British Museum. He was using anti-surveillance techniques but they had an eight-person team who easily shadowed him. Unfortunately the MI5 officer who followed him into the café could not sit close enough to hear the conversation with Joseph Dyer. But the directional microphone placed earlier under his usual corner table would record everything. They had nearly been caught out when Dyer came into the museum. Two of the agents following Zamal knew Dyer and he would recognise them. Luckily they spotted him first and ducked out of sight. When Dyer left, two agents followed him whilst the remaining six continued to follow Zamal to where he worked. Dressed in casual clothes as students, two of the team followed until they were satisfied he was in his room. Several bugs had been placed in his room at the LSE as soon as the Americans told MI5 he was al-Qaeda. Zamal didn't stay long in his room leaving with an overnight bag.

"Looks like he's running," said Simon Tomlinson having picked up Zamal's conversation with Emirates from the hidden bug in his office. "Hugo, Linda, Nick and Bruce – continue tailing him. Dan and Mary – go now to Heathrow. I'll brief Special Branch and the airport police and arrange transport to take him to Saxon Court when we pick him up." The security services' mansion was just off the M23 motorway and was where prisoners were taken who would not end up in a court of law.

Umed Zamal was not a professional spy or terrorist. His training in Tripoli and later in Pakistan gave him basic field skills but he didn't spot any of the four remaining MI5 agents following him.

Umed travelled uneventfully on the Heathrow Express, feigning sleep but keeping a watchful eye on the people in the carriage. Getting off he went to terminal three and picked up his ticket at the Emirates desk. He decided to check in immediately and go to the Emirates Executive Lounge. As he was about to go through to the departure lounge and through security, four armed police appeared in front of him pointing their machineguns. "Arms in the air. Drop the suitcase." Umed was not a brave man – he did what he was told. He was handcuffed and taken through an unmarked door, along a passageway, down three flights of steps, all the time flanked by the four policemen and several other men. They left the terminal – he could see they were on the airport side – and he was shoved into a black unmarked van. Inside he had a hood put over his head. Nobody said anything. He felt a sharp prick in his arm and then blacked out.

"Hugo, here. We have him and are travelling to Saxon Court," was the message to the head of MI5.

*

Sir Anthony Greenwood wasn't often surprised by anything, but the meeting he had just attended with Sir William Villiers, his opposite number at MI5, was one of these occasions. MI5 had irrefutable evidence one of his MI6 staff, Joseph Dyer, had been photographed talking to a known al-Qaeda agent this morning. Dyer had been picked up by MI5 and the SIS and was on his way to Saxon Court in Surrey, the house used when Special Branch weren't involved, This could embarrass the service terribly if Dyer turned out to be a traitor. After the debacle a year ago, when MI6 exposed a long-term mole in MI5, this was just what Sir William Villiers had been waiting for.

One of Caroline Bland's people to boot, he thought. Sir Anthony knew that he could not be involved in the questioning of Joseph Dyer or the al-Qaeda suspect Umed Zamal. Luckily, HMS *Newcastle*, the frigate bringing the four suspected al-Qaeda prisoners back to the UK, had not docked yet, so Sir Anthony diverted the prisoners to Colonel Harriman's farm in Essex. He wanted to keep some control over this investigation as MI5 would be cock-a-hoop now and try to take over completely.

38

Belardi had taken an internal flight from Karachi to Islamabad. He met Lt Colonel Akif Gandapur of the Pakistan ISI and travelled by car, with his two-man bodyguard, towards the Afghanistan border. Osama bin Laden had been living and running al-Qaeda from Abbottabad for a year now and Belardi knew he felt secure, the first time since the 9/11 attack on America. The large compound in Abbottabad was non-descript. If the locals were curious they had the sense to keep away. Even the large antenna on the flat roof of the two-storey building didn't prompt discussion in the local mosque or cafés. As far as they knew it was a military occupied building. The Sheikh, Osama bin Laden, greeted his friend and trusted commander. He had made up his mind to introduce Belardi to his Chinese connections and thoroughly brief him on stage three of the Tears of the West programme. Strong coffee was brought and the two men sat on the floor.

"Belardi, my most trusted friend, I feel the time is right to introduce you to my Chinese friends. You will fly to Beijing where you will be met by Lihua Nha Ping. He is a high-ranking officer in the Chinese Secret Service. He is able to divert Chinese satellites if we wish to monitor our enemies and has agents all over the world. You will also meet one of our important benefactors, Cheng, whom you already know. This man devised the nanotechnology that enables us to mix toxic chemicals with cosmetics used by western women and men. He supplies us through his company, Shanghai Chemicals, with the toxic impregnated particles. I have decided you should know these trusted friends. If something happens to me I would want our work to continue. We must defeat the infidels at all cost." He paused and sipped his strong black coffee. Belardi waited until he was invited to speak. Osama gestured to him. "Consider what is at stake." He turned around the screen of the laptop in front of him.

Belardi knew the Stardust range of cosmetics being sold in the West had been doctored by including toxic nanoparticles in the ingredients. He did not entirely appreciate the implications. He read the screen,

> Between eight and eight and a half million Americans have purchased an item of contaminated Stardust shampoo. A similar number has used the hairspray. One million decadent women have painted their fingernails with the nail polish. Six million have purchased the perfume spray. Four million have purchased toothpaste and deodorant. A further three million have purchased shaving cream and three million, liquid soap and sunscreen. Even if some of these items were purchased by the same person or family, the nanoparticles we have impregnated in the cosmetics will be in the bloodstream of millions of the infidels. And in Europe we have struck a blow for Allah. In the UK, two million units of shampoo, hairspray and deodorant have been purchased. One million shaving cream, two million toothpaste and five hundred thousand nail polish. In addition, large quantities of liquid soap, sunscreen and

> perfume. France, Holland, Germany, Italy and Scandinavian countries have purchased similar quantities. In Canada, there is also considerable success. Our plan is working.

"Forgive me, but is it possible the American scientists will discover the toxic ingredients soon?" asked Belardi.

"Yes, but what can they do? Remember, once the nanoparticles are in the bloodstream they have no way of removing them." He laughed a long mocking laugh. "Forever the infidels have the particles in their bodies and our Indian and Chinese friends have a commercial proposition that will fall into place."

"I am sorry, I don't understand," said Belardi.

Osama laughed again – not something he readily did since the Americans had been hunting him.

"Our benefactors in China and India are going to sell babies to the western infidels."

"Sell them babies?" Belardi was completely surprised by this revelation.

"Yes. Soon the infidels' women will discover they cannot conceive because the nano cocktail has destroyed their eggs or blocked ovulation, the men because their sperm has been diluted or destroyed. They will be desperate for a child." He laughed again. "Just think of it, Chinese and Indian children will, in twenty years, outnumber the infidel."

"Ah, I wondered why our four benefactors readily supplied so much money," said Belardi.

"It is capitalism, but if we find more ways of introducing toxic nanoparticles to the West, eventually we will destroy their bloodlines."

"We have other ways of delivering the nanoparticles?" asked Belardi

"Yes. The new Celebrity Cosmetics range will continue the good work. We will plan other attacks. For example, we are buying dairies in Europe, America and Canada. We will introduce a new nano ingredient into their milk, cream and cheese. That is phase three of our operation. In the next twelve months our Chinese friends have calculated that five million women and two million men in the UK will be infertile. The figures are much the same in the European countries. But the Americans will be hit hardest. The Chinese estimate that forty million women will be infertile and a similar number of men with a low or non-existent sperm count."

"That is a lasting legacy." Belardi looked in awe at the leader.

"Yes, and we can continue to attack them. If we think laterally we can buy food manufacturers, water companies, bottled water companies, soft drink manufacturers, alcohol manufacturers; the list is never ending. As soon as the infidel realise one product is toxic we will launch another." Osama looked suitably dignified. "My master plan will achieve what centuries of Muslims have been unable to contemplate – the end of the American and European bloodlines."

"Do you think they will find a way of countering the threat?" asked Belardi.

"I never underestimate the Americans, or the British for that matter, but our Chinese friends tell me the world is many years away from understanding these nanoparticles and how to control or rid oneself of them. After all, western companies have been including nanoparticles in cosmetics for some time and now some manufacturers are including particles in creamers."

"What can I do to further this great quest?" asked Belardi.

"I have told you all of this in case the Americans find me. You are tasked with continuing the work even if I am gone." He looked at Belardi solemnly.

"And I shall complete the great work," said Belardi, as he fell to his knees and kissed Osama bin Laden's hand.

39

Colonel John Harriman had started Harriman Security in 2001. He left the SAS and decided that personal security was going to become a lucrative new business and invested some of his capital. He recruited retired ex-SAS and SBS personnel, people he had worked with, and others whom he had earlier had dealings with in the army and Special Branch. Recognising the need for employees to have a wide-ranging skill set, and in some instances unique skills, he heard about Jafar Bhutani and his cousin Raza leaving the SAS and the Pakistan army respectively at about the same time.

Jafar was born in 1972 to Pakistani immigrants who had settled with their family in the UK. He was very intelligent and went to Leeds University before applying to join the regular army as a graduate trainee when he was twenty-one. He went to Sandhurst and after passing out as a second lieutenant joined the Grenadier Guards. His fluency in his native language, Pashtu and Urdu brought him to the attention of the SAS, particularly when he won the fifteen hundred metres rifle shooting tournament at Bisley on behalf of the army. He was invited to join the SAS in 1999 and his commanding officer was Colonel Harriman, then an acting brigadier and commander of the SAS. Jafar had served with distinction in Northern Ireland, frequently undercover, and was part of the SAS battalion's activities in the invasion of Iraq in 2003. He also worked across the border into Pakistan during Afghanistan's struggle with the Taliban. John Harriman recruited him when he was forced to leave the SAS under a slight cloud in 2006. Two Taliban prisoners had been shot near the border by an SAS unit Jafar commanded. He was cleared at the court martial of acting outside his authority but resented the inquiry and, principally, the lack of support by the army. The two Taliban fighters his unit had captured had escaped when the SAS unit was ambushed. Jafar and two troopers followed them and under fire shot them both. His superiors and the CIA were not happy as both members of the Taliban were senior commanders and supposed to be CIA informants. When he resigned his commission, John Harriman approached him with an offer which he accepted immediately.

Raza Bhutani, his cousin, was born in Bradford in 1981. He was a wayward young man and at fifteen ran with a gang of men who used local girls as prostitutes. Eventually the police arrested the gang and the leaders were all sent to prison. Raza was a lookout for the gang and helped target unsuspecting young girls. His father and mother were horrified and gave him an ultimatum – change his ways or be sent to Pakistan under the care of one of his father's brothers who was in the Pakistan army. He chose to go to Pakistan. During the early days of the conflict in Afghanistan some of the officers in the Pakistan army and members of the Military Intelligence, the ISI, tried desperately to control the increasing influence of the Taliban in Northern Pakistan. Raza had joined the army in 2001 influenced by his uncle, a colonel in the Inter Services Intelligence. As a lieutenant he was stationed on the border with Afghanistan. That was when he met his future wife Anoosheh, an Afghan woman. She was the daughter of an Afghan chieftain who smuggled goods from Pakistan to Afghanistan and hashish in the opposite direction. Patrolling the border meant Raza had to turn a blind eye, or challenge the Afghan smugglers. He turned a blind eye considering the items being smuggled not worth a firefight.

The Afghan chieftain and Raza became business partners and it was during this period that he fell in love with the Afghan's daughter. A marriage was brokered by Raza's uncle. Tragedy struck shortly after they were married. A group of Taliban fighters ambushed Raza's father-in-law and killed all the smugglers, including Anoosheh, Raza's wife. The Taliban senior commander controlling the area had decided his authority was being undermined – his solution: kill everybody. Raza was broken-hearted and swore revenge. That was when he deserted and crossed the border to pursue the murderer of his wife. He found the Taliban in caves near the border and killed six men, including the commander. Knowing he would also now be hunted, he returned to Pakistan and was arrested. During his court martial, his uncle and other officers vigorously mounted a defence, but he was found guilty and cashiered out of the army. Returning to the UK, a far different man, he met his cousin, Jafar, who worked for Colonel Harriman. An introduction was made and the colonel offered him a job which he accepted.

Now both men sat in Colonel Harriman's office in Park Lane, London.

"Gentlemen, I have a mission for you both which you may choose to turn down." Both the men looked at Colonel Harriman quizzically. They had never heard him give anyone an opportunity to turn down an order. "As you know, the four men who were captured by Captain

Sutherland and Commander Cunningham are being interrogated at the farm. All of them were recruited by this man." A television screen flickered and Belardi's picture appeared. "His name is Belardi. We believe he's a Pakistan national and is also al-Qaeda – we suspect a senior member of that organisation. MI6 believes he operates out of Pakistan and together with this man," – a picture appeared of Ibrahim – "helps Osama bin Laden run the terrorist network al-Qaeda. We need to find and extract one or both of these men." He paused and changed the screen to a map of Pakistan. "MI6 has a man at the embassy in Islamabad and they have informants in most of the major cities. Unfortunately, their man has been taken ill and was flown back to the UK two days ago. They're sending a replacement but he will have no local knowledge, and, putting it bluntly, be obviously English. He won't be able to travel without creating some suspicion. The informants might be reluctant to meet him. So this is the idea. You will both fly to Karachi and then on to Peshawar. Your job will be to meet the local informant in Peshawar, then go and meet the other MI6 agents in Quetta, Zhob, Rawalpindi, Chaman and Islamabad, seeking information on either of these men we want."

The two men looked at each other, each one waiting for the other to speak. Finally Raza said, "Will we have a cover? We can't just go to all these places without some plausible reason."

"Yes. Sir Anthony Greenwood has arranged that you will be buyers for the Midlands firm, Dunstan's. As you know, they have thirty department stores in the Midlands and the north east. You will be in Pakistan to seek out garments, bed linen, leather goods, carpets, rugs and cutlery aimed at the growing Pakistani population in the UK. You will travel to certain firms that already have connections with other outlets in the UK and Dunstan's – appointments will be made in advance to provide a cover story." The cousins pondered on what Colonel Harriman had said.

"Okay," said Raza, "I will go. When do you want me to leave?"

"Hold on, cousin, you're not going to have fun in Pakistan without me," said Jafar.

Colonel Harriman grunted expecting no less than their commitment, "Thank you. Now, gentlemen, Major Smith will brief you further and arrange the documentation."

"Will we know the identity of the MI6 person in Islamabad if we need them?" asked Raza.

"Not initially. If you get intel on the whereabouts of either of these men you will email the company you are fronting for with the message, 'We have found one main supplier'. That will prompt the MI6 person to contact you on your satellite phone."

The two men left for a meeting with Major Smith, and Colonel Harriman phoned Sir Anthony with the good news – his two men were willing to go.

40

Belardi had left the upbeat Osama bin Laden and travelled to Islamabad. He was due to depart on a Pakistan International Airlines flight to Beijing, via Lahore, and had flown on an internal flight from Peshawar. He was accompanied by Lt General Akif Gandapur, a high-ranking officer in the ISI. Belardi didn't pass through passport control or security at either Peshawar Airport or Islamabad. Boarding the flight to Beijing he was very pleased. Osama had trusted him with this most important information and he was shortly to meet their connection in the Chinese Secret Service who had protected them on several occasions.

Landing in Beijing after the eight-hour flight, Belardi was met at arrivals by a Chinese man holding up a sign with a picture of a large eye with a tear running down the page. The pre-arranged signal had amused Osama. He was driven to an impressive, detached, two-storey villa on the outskirts of Beijing and was greeted by a beautiful Chinese woman who spoke to him in English.

"Cheng Kuang welcomes you to his house. He has been delayed but will join you shortly. Please come in." The woman led him into a large room with western furniture – a large leather-bound desk was in the centre of the room facing three leather chairs.

"Please to sit." She clapped her hands and a door opened. Three more women came in. One brought cold flannels, another tea on a silver tray with delicate china cups. The other woman spoke.

"My name is Mei. I am a translator and also your companion for the duration of your stay."

Belardi was not a ladies' man but found the prospect of this charming and beautiful Chinese girl looking after him a pleasant thought. The door at the far end of the room opened and a Chinese man he had not seen before entered followed by Cheng Kuang. Belardi had met Cheng previously at a meeting hosted by Ibrahim in Karachi. He was one of their principal partners and immensely wealthy. Cheng bowed and introduced the other man as Lihua Nha Ping. Belardi knew by reputation that this man was one of the most powerful and dreaded men in China, heading up the Chinese Secret Service. Belardi bowed and spoke some words he had learnt in Chinese. Osama had insisted he treat these men very reverently and do whatever was necessary to retain their goodwill. After the initial introduction he was invited to relax in the sauna and swimming pool in the basement before dinner. Two of the women remained in attendance, washing him in a sunken bath. He had never been a flirtatious man but these women, each dressed seductively in a black bikini, were engaging his mind and it wasn't about the forthcoming meeting with Cheng. They brought hot towels and dried him. Thoroughly relaxed, he was shown by the delightful Mei into a large lounge. Mei explained that Cheng was a collector of rare antiques and pointed out the three Tibetan bowls, bone-laid cabinet pieces and silver-edged furniture purchased in India. At one end of the room was a large oak dining table and on the wall a huge flat screen television which was out of place in this lavish room full of antiques. Cheng and Lihua entered and the three men sat at the dining table.

"You are honoured guest," said Cheng. "Please ask Mei for anything you want. We must regrettably talk some business." He nodded to Lihua who used a remote which activated the television screen.

"You will see from our satellite image that a British frigate went alongside the yacht you hired and five men were transferred to the warship. We assume the four were the men you left on board. Are those men any threat to our security?" asked Lihua.

"No," replied Belardi. "They are bodyguards and do not know our business."

Lihua nodded as though this was the answer he expected.

"We have sent two tankers from Shanghai, one to Nigeria, the other to Yemen and Oman to the new factories," said Cheng.

He referred to the factories leased to manufacture, bottle and label the new Celebrity range of cosmetics. Belardi knew that the Chinese factory in Shanghai manufactured and engineered the nanoparticles which contained the toxic chemicals which were then mixed with the cosmetics in India, Mexico, Yemen, Somalia and the other bottling plants. The new factories in Nigeria and Oman were to bottle the new range of Celebrity shampoo. The factory in Yemen would mix the ingredients for the content of the roll-on deodorant bottles and liquid soap containers, and later fill the pressurised shaving cream and hairspray in metal containers. The German factory would receive the liquid from Yemen to fill the roll-on deodorants, the liquid soap and, later, toothpaste, and send it to Marseille for transporting on container ships.

"We will also ship the special liquid to Belize City and Marseille," said Cheng, knowing that the perfume was bottled in Marseille, the sunscreen lotion, hairspray and nail varnish in Belize and Germany. Belardi made a mental note to check with Ibrahim, who was in charge of logistics, that all the factories were ready to mix the ingredients, had the bottling equipment and were ready to manufacture the cosmetics to send to the USA and Europe.

"All is going very well," said Belardi.

"Yes, but you should be aware that the CIA and the British have discovered the original content of the Stardust shampoo and hairspray," said Lihua.

"You know this for sure?" asked Belardi.

"We have people in key positions," said a rather indignant Lihua. "Also, the British MI5 has your man Umed Zamal. They picked him up at Heathrow Airport – he has a capsule?" Lihua referred to the false tooth that most of the important al-Qaeda operatives had in their mouth which contained cyanide.

"No, regrettably not. But he knows very little," replied Belardi.

"I am getting concerned that the CIA and British are penetrating your organisation," said Lihua.

"We all must expect minor persons to be captured from time to time. Suleman was taken in London and killed himself with the cyanide. Whilst the CIA and British have some success it is only an inconvenience and not serious," replied Belardi.

"The Americans can be headstrong. What do you anticipate will be their next move against us?" asked Cheng

"What can they do? They have raided the Stardust factories. But I expect they will ban the range shortly and endeavour to track the originator," Belardi replied.

"Does your principal still believe he is secure where he is living?" asked Cheng, referring to Osama bin Laden's hideaway in Pakistan.

"Yes, but he has briefed me on the entire operation

to make certain that if he is discovered our plans would continue," said Belardi.

"Excellent. I think that concludes our business. Let us enjoy a pleasant dinner," said Cheng.

The two Chinese men left the house at 11pm and Belardi retired to his room. Two of the Chinese women, whose names he found out were Li-Hua and Bao, meaning pear blossom and precious, joined him. He was not sexually active in Pakistan but the close attention of the two girls aroused him and he spent several hours in delights he had not previously imagined.

In the morning, he reluctantly left the villa and went to the airport. Belardi was flying Air China to Shanghai to view Cheng's factory, then later that day he would fly overnight to Karachi via Chengdu.

*

Liu Hong had reported directly to the premier of the State Council that Lihua Nha Ping had met Cheng and an unknown Pakistani at his house in Beijing. Lihua Nha Ping, a Politburo member, was a senior Ministry of State security officer, which was the main civilian foreign intelligence service. The premier arranged to meet several of his trusted allies in the Politburo and the general secretary of the Communist Party – he knew the risk to China was increasing as Cheng and Lihua conspired with Osama bin Laden. They may have to act soon and stop whatever was going on before the Americans found out the Chinese involvement.

41

Sir Anthony Greenwood expected nothing else – the rivalry between MI5 and MI6 had increased since a senior MI5 officer was discovered by MI6 spying for the Russians. The man had been in situ for over twenty years; it was a terribly damaging admission by MI5 that they had failed to uncover the spy and had damaged relationships with our cousins in the US for a short while. Now they had some revenge for the humiliation. Simon Tomlinson had discovered that a junior MI6 officer was passing on information to an al-Qaeda agent in London. Tomlinson had collared both. Sir Anthony had been presented with the transcript of young Joseph Dyer's confession – it was grim reading. What a fool he had been – a drug addict caught in a honey trap. Sir Anthony started to read the report gleefully handed to him by his opposite number at MI5.

Interview with Joseph Dyer – Present: Simon Tomlinson and Sebastian Masters-Buchanan

"So, Joseph, have you considered what I said?" Simon had

spelled out to Joseph Dyer that he was caught cold. Joseph was frightened and thought for a moment. They said that they had the photographs and a recording of his conversation with the spy Umed Zamal, made when he met him twice at the British Museum. Simon offered Joseph an opportunity to tell his story – as he put it, a chance to put things right.

"All right, I'll tell you," replied Joseph. He paused to compose himself. "It was coming towards that time of year when everybody is either so bloody happy or pissed. December – a month that I usually hated – but that day in 2005 everything changed. That's when I first met her. She came into the Black Prince in Chelsea with a group of girls. At first I just fancied the pants off her, then I loved Sabrine with every fibre of my being; she seemed to mesmerise me." He seemed to visualise her once again and a tear ran down his face and said, "the long black hair, the dark brown eyes, the cute nose and her smile. What a smile she had – it always melted him. Perhaps she had been too young? He was twenty-eight and she was coming up to twenty. He had graduated from Cambridge with a first-class honours degree in business studies and Arab affairs. She had gone to theatre school." He continued. "Despite her radiant looks she hadn't fulfilled her ambition to star in the West End. She was an actress, you see," he said proudly. "She aimed to be the leading lady in a film. I felt her rejections, as directors simply wanted to bed her; not give her the part in the film or play. But it was that day that fate led me to her – the 20th of December. Yes, the date is burnt into my heart, into my soul. The day we first went out I knew I wanted her, and not just a quick shag. I couldn't stop thinking about her. I began to be the shoulder she cried on. I tried to woo her, as my dad had put it, in the old-fashioned way."

Simon let him talk; he was in full flow.

"My dad had given me a tip early on – don't rush her into bed; she needs to be wooed. I didn't really understand the meaning of the word but he explained. Take her to nice places, surprise her with small gifts, always treat her well, make her laugh, hold the door for her, kiss her tenderly – save the lust. I thought the technique might be working when in March 2006 we shared a bed together at my friend Alastair's flat. She had taken off her dress but not her underwear. Nevertheless, I felt her physical presence and yearned to make love. But she said, 'No, not tonight, Joseph. I am having a period.' I was devastated, but what can you do? During the next month I dated her regularly. We went to concerts, to art galleries, skating, to the cinema, restaurants but I never got beyond the settee in her flat. She kissed wonderfully and I always thought I was courting her towards marriage and a lifetime of lovemaking. But then she broke my heart. I knew she had been seeing an actor, an Asian, who was appearing in one of the West End plays. They had met at stage school but I thought he was gay – at least that was the impression she gave. I was stunned when she told me she was going to India with him. He had got a minor part in a Bollywood film and she was going with him to New Delhi. Perhaps it was the glitz, the glamour – I don't know the why and wherefore. All I know is I was devastated. She promised to write regularly but that didn't happen. Whilst the man, according to his Facebook entry – and I now accepted he was her boyfriend – began to get bigger and better parts, she didn't make it.

"I lost touch and resumed my life and didn't even realise she'd come back to the UK. I saw her in the winter of 2006 from a distance on the High Street in Putney, and my very soul cried out. But I knew I was wasting my time so I didn't cross the road. I couldn't stand the pain again.

"Then a friend told me he'd seen her with a child. There was no sign of the father, whom I presumed to be the actor who had now graduated to supporting leads in blockbuster Bollywood films."

He stopped and sipped some water. Simon let him continue.

"It had now been many months since I'd seen her. I'd dated a string of women and I knew my parents despaired I would ever marry. I'd set the bar too high and that proved to be the case. I saw her once more, later that year, and it ironically was when I was dating a woman from work. We were dining in Rules Restaurant just off the Strand when she came in with an Arab man I didn't recognise. She glanced in my direction but there wasn't even a flicker of recognition. That made up my mind and I recited to myself, 'Better to have loved and lost than never have loved at all'. My companion looked at me and smiled, 'Ah, I know that look. Let's toast unrequited love'."

He continued. "Later that week, I was at my gym in Chelsea. It was a Thursday night. I remember it well; Chelsea was playing a champions league match I was watching on a large screen, when she walked in. She began to exercise on a running machine. I had to go and say hello. Yes, she was free for a coffee. We chatted for an hour and I arranged to meet her for lunch in two days time. Our romance began to blossom and I fell in love all over again. Then she began asking me questions about my work. Had I remained at MI6? Gentle questions. It never occurred to me she was extracting secrets; she was so lovely and I adored her. Then she suggested we go to a Turkish restaurant for dinner. She wanted to introduce me to a friend."

"What about the drugs?" asked Simon.

"I thought it was harmless."

"What – sniffing cocaine?" said Simon.

"You already know I became addicted." He began crying.

"Come on, Joseph, get a grip and continue your story."

"I first met the Middle Eastern man Zamal in a Turkish restaurant in Acton. In the beginning he was charming like Sabrine. They talked about her acting career and how he could help her get parts in the West End. They seemed like old friends. Then Sabrine introduced me to cocaine. She said that the high I would get would enhance our lovemaking – yes, at last we were lovers. Zamal, Sabrine and I met at least twice a week – I didn't know he was supplying the drugs. I should have been suspicious but I loved her. Later I discovered the child I thought was hers was in fact a friend's – she had no children. She lived in Shoreditch, yet came to a gym where I met her again, in Chelsea. I should have been suspicious," he kept repeating. "I should have been suspicious. But she was so convincing. I loved her." A pause whilst he drank some water.

"Tell me about the man Zamal."

"We had met as usual for dinner. He began asking me questions in a private room at our usual Turkish restaurant about my job at MI6. At first I didn't answer, then two other men came in and began beating me. Sabrine begged me to answer, to help them – they were her dear friends – and then one of them twisted her arm. Zamal told me that if I wanted to keep being supplied with cocaine and keep seeing Sabrine without her pretty face being scarred I had no choice but to help him. One of the men had a knife at her throat." A pause again.

(Dyer began weeping – interview suspended).

Interview recommenced:

"So what did you do when these men attacked and threatened you?"

Joseph sobbed. "I told him about our investigation of ExCy; that Colonel Harriman had a goddaughter who had discovered ingredients in Stardust cosmetics that were not listed. When she tried to find out what they were, her tutor and a laboratory assistant were apparently murdered. He asked what the connection was between Colonel Harriman and Sir Anthony Greenwood, which I explained. He asked about Caroline – Caroline Bland. God help me, I didn't know they would kill Caroline." He broke down again.

"All right, Joseph. You're being very co-operative. So what else did this man Zamal ask you?"

"Did MI6 have any idea what was going on."

"What did he mean – 'what was going on'?"

"He asked me did I know what was meant by the words Tears of the West. I said I'd never heard those words."

"What else did he ask?"

"What had Colonel Harriman discovered when his man had visited the ExCy office in London?"

"What did you tell him?"

"I gave him a list of items we were investigating."

"What items?"

"Colonel Harriman's man had gone to the office of ExCy as a VAT inspector and looked at the payments ExCy had made. I listed as many as I could remember from a meeting with Caroline Bland."

"Please continue."

"He asked me where Colonel Harriman and Caroline Bland lived and if they were lovers."

"You told him?"

"Yes." Joseph began to cry again. "I didn't know they would kill Caroline." He continued sobbing.

"So, the man Zamal gave you cocaine which you shared with the woman, Sabrine?"

"Yes."

"Did you share an address?"

"Yes."

"Write down her full name and address."

Joseph wrote down Sabrine La Tour, which was her stage name, and an address in Shoreditch, London.

"Is there anything else you can tell us about the man Zamal?"

Joseph thought for a moment then answered, "No."

Interview terminated 21.35.

Sir Anthony put down the report and sighed. That young man had sealed his own fate. He would not intervene.

42

The British prime minister was a worried man. This business the security forces and Harriman had uncovered was political dynamite and yet he still didn't entirely understand the implications. Liaising with the president of the United States they had decided to discuss the problem again after meeting with their respective key personnel, and to schedule a meeting with the premiers of France, Germany, Canada, Holland and Belgium, all of whom were likely to be as seriously affected as they were. Initially they had thought of calling a G7 meeting. But the security services could not confirm the Russians were not involved in the conspiracy as both the Soviets and the Japanese had not been on the receiving end of a marketing campaign for the Stardust cosmetics.

★

The seriousness of the situation was growing and the prime minister convened a Cobra meeting at 10 Downing Street. He was in the chair and in attendance were the deputy prime minister, foreign secretary, home secretary, defence secretary, minister of health and the attorney general. He had also summoned the head of the Civil Service, the director general of MI5, the chief of the Secret Intelligence Service MI6, the chief scientific officer, boffins from Porton Down and Professor Endleson from Essex University. In effect, he had activated the National Security Council, whose task was to deal with threats, hazards, resilience and contingences.

Professor Endleson started the meeting by describing nano-encapsulation. "The coating or enclosing of a substance, as if within a capsule, with another material at the nanoscale level." He had produced a screenshot which he showed on the giant screen on the wall. "What we think they have done, using the metallic nanotubes or fullerenes probably made of a silver compound, is fill or coat these with toxic chemicals and close the ends. You would probably call these fullerenes." He showed a picture of a fullerene on the screen. "What causes the closed end to open we don't know, but the nanoshells or nanotubes, transport what we believe to be toxic chemical material. They also seem to be using liposomes which are spherical closed colloidal structures. Am I getting too technical?"

The prime minister said, "Well, as I understand it, extremely small receptacles are being used to transport toxic chemicals."

"That's it, Prime Minister, except they are also making nanoparticles out of toxic material; for example, lead nanos have been found."

He explained that persons unknown had developed this technique he called 'self-assembled nano structures of different materials' and they had included toxic chemical materials in the nanoparticles which were present in very large numbers in the cosmetic range Stardust. He continued, "The threat to human reproduction is very serious. Many women would have been contaminated, using the Stardust range, by absorbing the lethal toxins in nanoparticles through the skin or breathing them into the lungs or swallowing them as toothpaste. These nano toxins attack a woman's reproductive system and act particularly as an endocrine disrupter. In addition, any male who used the contaminated shampoo, deodorant, shaving cream or toothpaste, or who breathed droplets from a hairspray, would suffer a serious deficiency in his sperm count." He added, "Perhaps the nano toxins would also go on to develop other dangerous illnesses or cancers. The mobility of nano-materials also gives them potential access to all areas of the body. A list of the ingredients we have identified is annexed at the back of my report and their possible effect on the human body."

There was silence around the table.

"It's important we all understand the size of these nanoparticles," said the prime minister, looking at Professor Endleson.

"Micro-measurement quotes that a unit measurement of a nanometre is one-billionth of a metre. For example, a sheet of A4 paper is about 100,000 nanometres thick. Another popular description is that one billion nanoparticles can fit on the head of a pin."

Several of the ministers shifted uncomfortably and the home secretary turned to the prime minister. "The House of Lords Select Committee on Science and Technology, and the Food Standard Agency, have both taken the view that no food product or packaging using nanotechnology should be allowed into the market without proof it's safe."

"But what about cosmetics?" asked the deputy prime minister.

"You have to understand that biotechnology is regarded as one of the most important future methods for disease control and already has many other potential applications," replied the chief scientific officer.

"That's all very well, but who's controlling the use of nanoparticles?" asked the prime minister.

"Well, technically, I suppose, as some of the proposed applications are concerned with health, it's the MHRA," replied the health minister.

"Sorry, what is the MHRA?" asked the deputy prime minister.

"The Medicines and Healthcare Product Regulatory Agency," replied the health minister. "Also The European Medicine Agency is mandated to investigate healthcare products."

"Hmm... what you are telling us isn't much comfort as it seems to me that there isn't a specific body examining every product which might contain nanoparticles," the prime minister said, holding up his hand "And let's face it, these Stardust cosmetics could be the tip of a very ugly iceberg."

"Oh, come, Prime Minister," said the chief scientific officer. "I'm sure this is an isolated situation."

Several people tried to speak at once.

"Professor," said the prime minister.

"Well, actually, this cosmetic range may be using the most toxic chemical nanoparticles as ingredients for a particularly terrifying reason, but several very famous cosmetic companies are also including nanoparticles in their ladies' face creams and sunscreens, and a certain brand of toothpaste uses nanoparticles to add an ingredient to help whiten teeth."

An excited babble broke out around the table and the PM had a job bringing order.

"Gentlemen, we have some decisions to make and it seems to me they are as follows." As much as he disliked putting anything on paper he had his secretary prepare a list of issues, which he handed out in a file headed 'Most Secret'.

"Let me go through these one by one for comment. Firstly, do we know how many women and men have been affected by using the Stardust range of cosmetics?" He looked towards the home secretary who he knew had been working on likely figures with the chemists at Porton Down and the government's chief scientific officer.

Somewhat sheepishly, the home secretary looking at his file said, "Circa two million bottles of shampoo have been sold, and a similar number of women's hairspray applicators and deodorants. In addition, circa two million tubes of toothpaste and a half a million nail polish bottles. Our figures also show over one million dispensers of shaving cream. We're awaiting figures for perfume, sunscreen and liquid soap."

The foreign secretary raised his hand attracting the PM's attention.

"Yes, Jonathan?"

"There is a possibility that some of the products may have been used by the same person."

"True," replied the home secretary, annoyed because he was going to make this point later.

"That's no consolation," said Sir Geoffrey, the attorney general. "Millions of our citizens have been exposed to what I understand to be a cocktail of deadly nanoparticles during our watch." Pandemonium broke out around the table.

"Gentlemen, please." The prime minister banged his hand on the table.

"Sir Geoffrey may be correct, but we cannot assume all these cosmetics were sold whilst we were in power."

"Yes we can, Prime Minister," replied the home secretary. "The range first appeared on the shelves of supermarkets and in the shops eleven months ago."

The prime minister ignored the answer and moved on. "My next point is: can these toxic nanoparticles be removed from the body and if so would the person's health be affected?"

Professor Endleson replied, "We don't know of any way the nanoparticles that are in the bloodstream or in the body's organs can be removed."

The answer was greeted with a stony silence.

"Then we had better start working on finding a solution," said the prime minister, addressing his comment to the health minister, Keith Landers.

"Keith, the Ministry of Health liaising with Porton Down, the chief scientific officer and all the universities with expertise in this field must immediately begin to investigate how these nanoparticles can be removed, negated or treated in the human body." The health minister scribbled a note on the file in front of him.

"Thirdly," began the PM, "we have to consider how we deal with the announcement of this situation to the public. I've already asked Constance, Matthew and Susan," who were the PM's personal spin doctors, "to come up with a way of announcing the situation." He didn't add the thought that was in all the politicians' minds around the table – without blaming us.

"Clearly," he added, "this is a global problem. I'm in discussions with the American president about calling a meeting of the leaders of all the countries affected. Foreign secretary, you were preparing a list."

"Yes," replied Jonathan Gould. "The countries affected are the USA, Canada, France, Germany, Holland and Belgium. Some of the population of the Scandinavian countries, Spain and Italy may also have been infected."

"Fourthly," the prime minister said, "our secret service has to find the people behind this attack on our citizens, Sir Anthony."

Sir Anthony Greenwood had been sitting quietly

listening to the information he had earlier provided to the Home Office and the prime minister.

"We have reason to suspect this is a terrorist attack by Osama bin Laden and al-Qaeda. They don't have the financial resources to mount such a global attack alone. Somebody with elaborate technology must be helping them and they must have substantial financial backing. Consider the advertising cost of marketing this Stardust range in the UK – it was twenty million pounds. Add to this the cost of a US and European marketing campaign and one starts to see an extremely large budget. Then there is logistics: the transport, packaging, bottling and distribution of all these cosmetics. We believe the budget so far is over two billion pounds," said Sir Anthony.

"So what are you saying, Sir Anthony?" asked the deputy prime minister.

"It would only be speculation," he replied.

"Yes, but who do you think could help al-Qaeda mount this attack?" asked the PM.

"Well," he paused, "the technology suggests possibly China, Russia, Japan, Iran or the USA. As the Americans are unlikely to attack themselves we are investigating the others."

"Are you making any progress finding the perpetrators?" asked the deputy prime minister.

"Yes. I cannot discuss specifics, as I'm sure you appreciate, but we have a number of leads we are following," replied Sir Anthony.

"Come now, you must do better than that," said the deputy prime minister, who had repeatedly criticised the need for Britain to spend such a large amount of the Home Office budget on the security services. The ministers around the table, each looking for a scapegoat to eventually blame for this mess, looked at Sir Anthony.

"The terrorists who are perpetrating this attack have

a code name for their atrocity called Tears of the West. This code was first picked up a year ago in an email by a high-ranking officer in the ISI. He relayed the email to us – but we had no idea what it referred to. Then nine months ago the goddaughter of Colonel Harriman, the managing director of Harriman Security, was preparing her PhD thesis on the chemical ingredients in cosmetics when she discovered that nanoparticles were present in some cosmetics she had purchased. These cosmetics were manufactured by ExCy using the marketing name Stardust. Despite her best efforts to get the manufacturers ExCy to discuss or even confirm that nanoparticles were included in their cosmetics she hit a brick wall. Her tutor Professor Dolen, and a senior laboratory assistant, also tried by email to arrange an interview with the management of ExCy in London. Within a week, both these men were dead. The professor 'fell' under a tube train and the senior laboratory assistant was murdered in an apparently failed mugging.

"Colonel Harriman contacted me – he and I were at Cambridge together. He also began to investigate ExCy and sent one of his operatives undercover to the headquarters of this firm in London. He found nothing of immediate use. When there was an attempt on his operative's life – he was shot on Wandsworth Common – it was obvious that the terrorists had discovered Harriman's man was investigating them. Liaising with the CIA, we set about investigating ExCy's worldwide manufacture of the Stardust cosmetics. CIA agents attempted a raid on a plant in Somalia – two of their men were killed and a third seriously attacked. One of our agents successfully brought back from Somalia a sample of a liquid from vats in the Somalian warehouse. This turned out to be ordinary shampoo with no added nanoparticles. Likewise when the CIA raided a Mexican warehouse used by ExCy all they found was liquid soap. Meanwhile, samples Harriman's goddaughter had obtained had been passed to Essex University which was also convinced nanoparticles were included in the cosmetics. Simultaneously, the Americans passed samples they had collected to Harvard biotechnology unit. They were the first to confirm the number and nature of the nanoparticles. Page twenty-one of the prime minister's report shows their findings.

Meanwhile, Harriman picked up the managing director of ExCy in London, a Mr Suleman. Unfortunately, he had a false tooth containing cyanide and committed suicide rather than give up any secrets. Suleman's assistant, a young woman, escaped to the Lebanon but a combined CIA and MI6 operation captured her. The Americans obtained some interesting information from her, including the name of another al-Qaeda agent in London who has subsequently been picked up by MI5. Several months ago a French customs officer went to Colombia to investigate the suspected liquid being exported to France. It seems he obtained a sample but the plane he was returning to Paris on exploded in mid-air and his evidence lies deep in the Atlantic Ocean. Another incident in France, when one of their paparazzi photographed men on a large yacht in the Mediterranean, attracted our attention – as the photographer was murdered. Another paparazzi photographer had been tailing the dead man and also had photographs of some men on the yacht. He was also killed but one of our agents discovered the hiding place where he had hidden his photographs and brought them back to the UK. Our agent was attacked and the photographs stolen, but he had already emailed copies to Caroline Bland. We identified two senior al-Qaeda commanders and sent details to the CIA, which has a sophisticated facial tracking system that can be linked to airport security. There had been several attempts to kill Colonel Harriman and Caroline Bland before a bomb, planted in a stolen black cab left outside MI6 headquarters, blew up and Caroline was killed."

The table went quiet as Sir Anthony continued.

"We have, together with our American friends, examined the evidence at our disposal and both the CIA and our security services are concentrating on finding Osama bin Laden and his two senior commanders. We also suspect that al-Qaeda has other senior agents worldwide, as this operation would not be able to be managed by one or two people. The CIA, which has more people in the field than MI6, is hunting these agents."

Sir Anthony chose not to mention the four terrorists being interrogated by Colonel Harriman's men in Essex, or the Harriman officers currently undercover in Pakistan. He was right not to. Since the last government had decided that the special protection unit, deployed to protect the royal family and embassies, should be disbanded to save money, private security firms had taken over. Harriman Security had recruited most of the redundant police protection officers and had obtained a special licence to carry firearms. They now provided protection for most of the royal family, countless embassies and rich people. The deputy prime minister, who was a vocal opponent of private firms having guns, even though the discharge of a weapon was as controlled as the regulations which applied to the police, didn't like Colonel Harriman having had a public spat with him at an embassy a year ago.

"Anything else, Sir Anthony?" asked the prime minister.

"No," replied Sir Anthony.

"Can I just ask," said the deputy prime minister, "the involvement of Harriman and his merry men – is that really necessary?"

Sir Anthony had been expecting this question. "Yes. It was his goddaughter who first discovered the inclusion of nanoparticles in the Stardust cosmetics. She was a target for the terrorists and two of her senior colleagues killed. Harriman was also on to this attack on our citizens ahead of the homeland security services, the police or Special Branch; and his manpower, with experienced personnel, is massively larger than ours since the cutbacks."

The home secretary raised his hand. "The deputy prime minister will recollect how vocal he was when debating the need to streamline an 'overstaffed MI5 and MI6', as he put it."

Laughter broke out from the ministers around the table. The prime minister restored order.

"Gentlemen, it is clear Harriman is doing a job in the national interest. Let's leave it at that. Sir William," he looked at the Head of MI5, "anything to add to the MI6 report?"

"Only that we have taken into custody an al-Qaeda sympathiser in London and are using all available resources to shadow several other suspects." Sir William would have clearly loved to have mentioned the capture and interrogation of an MI6 employee who had leaked secrets to al-Qaeda, but had been warned against doing so by the home secretary.

"Right, let's get on then," said the prime minister. "My next heading, point five – what use, if any, have we made of this nanotechnology. That's why I have asked the senior operations director from Porton Down to attend today's meeting. There will be no names."

One of the men at the end of the table began speaking.

"We've been working with nanoparticles for some years. Not, I hasten to add, in connection with cosmetics, but it's clear that microbiology has an important part to play in defence. For example, we're working on body armour that will contain nanoparticles, which our early day experiments suggest will stop an AK-47 bullet up to 300 metres." He didn't add that they were also examining using nanoparticles as a biological warfare weapon.

"Thank you," said the prime minister. "The seriousness of this situation cannot be understated but we must not throw the baby out with the bathwater."

Several of the ministers laughed. *Very misplaced,* thought Sir Anthony.

"Point six. This concerns the impact on the health service. I have asked Keith to prepare a report – Keith."

Keith Landers had been appointed as health minister principally as his wife was the PM's cousin. His background in health matters was even less than normal for a minister, so he read from his notes.

"I have obtained figures on the actual number of these cosmetics sold, which we've already discussed. This leads us to assume that at least two million people, many are women of childbearing age, have used one or more of the cosmetics in the Stardust range. The figure could be as high as four and a half million. In addition, we calculated that at least one million men have used a Stardust product, which includes shaving cream, deodorant and shampoo. Once again, this is a best estimate – it could easily be more. Then we have the children."

A silence descended around the table. Even the deputy prime minister sat forward.

"Yes, I'm afraid that we calculate up to two million children may have been impregnated as parents use the shampoo to wash children's hair or use liquid soap in the bathroom or sunscreen, and many of the older children use a deodorant." He paused, feeling pleased with himself that this hitherto terrible scenario had not occurred to anybody. "If our figures are accurate, then we estimate up to five million childbearing females will be seeking reassurance from healthcare professionals that they remain fertile and a similar number of children will be brought for reassurance by parents to doctors. We believe men will not react in as great a number as they won't initially believe they may have become infertile. But there are likely to be one million men seeking sperm tests.

"Our analysts do not believe the National Health Service will be able to cope with this sudden dramatic influx of new patients requesting screening for fertility confirmation. We, therefore, propose that a budget of one billion pounds be allocated to set up temporary screening facilities in ten strategic centres – details are in my report. We feel that this screening facility must be a priority and recommend that we seek to recruit several hundred further fertility specialists and an equal number of paediatricians from around the world. We'll need to purchase additional equipment for each centre and do so quickly, as we do envisage a large demand when our European partners and other countries realise the significance of these terrorist attacks. Furthermore, up to ten thousand more beds will need to be provided in NHS hospitals when already pregnant women get complications as a result of the toxic chemicals introduced to their body and require urgent attention. This figure may be conservative as we don't really know the effect on pregnant women. Our estimated budget of one billion pounds may have to be topped up if a simple method of determining the existence of the deadly toxins in the body isn't discovered. If women are required to stay at our new centres it will take nearly a year to examine every potentially affected person."

Pandemonium broke out around the table. The health minister looked taken aback.

"You cannot seriously be suggesting that a woman would wait up to a year to find out if she is infertile as a result of using a Stardust cosmetic – there will be riots, marches, media hostility," said the deputy prime minister.

The prime minister, who had already seen the figures, banged on the table.

"Those figures are early day estimates. Our colleague has had little time to consider the ramifications of this attack on our population. Let us say that this is an initial report and that by tomorrow we will have it fine-tuned."

"Fine-tune he had better, or we'll face incredible hostility," said the deputy prime minister.

"I agree," said the home secretary. "Can I suggest, Prime Minister, that the health minister ratchet-up the response and doesn't worry about the budget? After all, we must move quickly to acquire the equipment, find new premises to temporarily equip and also attract new staff. I suggest a special pay scale is devised to attract personnel."

"Agreed," said the PM. "I'm also proposing, in point seven, a new minister be appointed to deal with all aspects of this crisis. If you agree, I'll make the appointment today."

The PM had already sounded out Lord Jeffries, a health minister in the 1980s, to join the cabinet. He was seventy-two now but had been held in high esteem by the public.

"Gentlemen, point eight." The prime minister went on to discuss the timing of an announcement to the media as he intended to do a broadcast to the nation. He felt they had ten days and said that until purpose-built new units could be set up (which he had been told would take at least a year) he had asked the health minister to approach the heads of all private hospitals and clinics to seek secondments of their premises. He said a bill would pass through the House of Commons, called The Emergency and Disaster Bill, which would give the government powers to carry out any action thought in the public good on this matter. He didn't add that he had recalled ten thousand members of the armed forces in case of serious rioting, and set up a meeting with chief constables for the home secretary to host in two days' time.

"Finally, I cannot stress on you all how important it is that nothing we have discussed leaks to the media before my announcement. You'll note that I have drawn to your attention in the penultimate paragraph that all the information which has been given is subject to the Official Secrets Act. In two days' time, I will be meeting the heads of foreign governments affected by these terrorist attacks. I hope we'll all agree a timetable to announce this atrocity to our nations. But, if not, we must move quickly to acquire equipment and staff. Are there any other matters arising?" He had learnt early in politics that if six people knew a secret that was five too many and was apprehensive this disaster would remain a secret until his broadcast.

But there was a silence as his colleagues reflected.

"Incidentally, the home secretary is about to instruct all the supermarkets to place a recall notice on all Stardust cosmetics by advertising in the national press. The reason being given is that a rogue employee of the manufacturer may have placed something in the cosmetics at a processing plant overseas. The warning will say that it is a precautionary measure. We'll also hope that other retailers will take the cosmetics off the shelf – we've written to their trade associations. All the unused and unopened bottles will be transported by the supermarkets to a warehouse facility in Wolverhampton that the Home Office has leased. That's it, gentlemen. Thank you for your attention."

The meeting broke up, with a small group discussing how it was going to deal with this disaster, and the chief scientific officer curious as to why the PM had not mentioned the potential effect on all consumers of kidney failure, cancers of the liver, stomach, colon, and heart problems which he had highlighted in a report. *Politicians*, he thought, *always have an agenda*.

43

On the same day the UK prime minister held his Cobra meeting, the president of the United States had called a meeting of the National Security Council, which was the president's forum for considering national security matters. Seated around the large table were the vice president, the secretary of state, secretary of the treasury, secretary of defence, chairman of the joint chiefs of staff, the assistant to the president for national security, director of National Intelligence, the health secretary, the attorney general and the secretary of the Environment Protection Agency (EPA). He had also invited Professor Eugene Rendle and Professor Brian Flavier from Harvard University and the Directors of the CIA and FBI.

"Eugene, I would like you to brief us on what has happened here," said the president.

Eugene Rendle handed out a green folder. "Thank you, Mr President. You will read in the notes I have provided, 'What is a Nanoparticle?' I suggest you all familiarise yourself with the explanation." He clicked on his laptop and the massive screen at the end of the room displayed the first paragraph of his report.

"The size is the key, gentlemen. The Environmental Policy Agency, the regulatory body that protects the environment and public health, describes the size of a nanoparticle as 100,000 times thinner than a strand of hair. The British have a useful explanation: one billion nanoparticles can fit on the head of a pin. I can also tell you that a nanometre, we call them by the initials NM, is a billionth of a metre. Now – you can imagine that it takes a very sophisticated analytical technique, called Field-Flow Fractionation, which we combine with Dynamic Light Scattering, to measure mass and size of nanoparticles. This image metrology and a particle pore analysis showed us that there were particles in a bottle of shampoo from a range called Stardust. We then identified the compounds either carried by hollowed-out nanoparticles, which are called fullerenes, or nanoparticles coated or made of the chemical/material which we discovered.

"The list of ingredients was sent to the FBI, CIA, the State Department, EPA and the health secretary. At the request of the State Department we also copied in several other universities who were analysing the samples of the cosmetics from the Stardust range. The British have made similar discoveries in nail polish, shampoo and deodorant, and we have now broken down the ingredients of the hairspray, shampoo, perfume, liquid soap, shaving cream and sunscreen. I won't bore you with the process as there are different procedures to analyse liquids. My colleague, Brian Flavier, has, on page six of the notes, prepared a detailed list of the chemical content of the nanoparticles in each of the Stardust cosmetics. And he has, as a biological chemist, explained what effect each of the ingredients might have on reproduction in the human body; the area we consider being attacked."

He clicked the hand-held control and a list of ingredients appeared on the screen, product by product. As he scrolled down the screen he referred to the names of the chemicals and repeated the known effects on females and males.

"I might add that we don't know for certain how radically some of these chemicals will affect the foetus, or act as endocrine disrupters, or whether the female ovulation if interrupted might be prevented. However, most of the chemicals present in these nanoparticles are known to us as massive toxic inhibitors of normal fertility and pregnancy, and they can be targeted to specific parts of the body. Some of my colleagues, specialists in human biology, state that every woman who has absorbed these chemicals through the bloodstream, swallowed, or inhaled these particles into the lungs is 90% likely to be infertile or unable to conceive a healthy baby. And the chemicals contained in these cosmetics are endocrine-disrupting chemicals and can cause poor sperm quality and testicular cancer."

The members of the National Security Council began to react.

"Mr President, I don't wish to interrupt the professor, but a little elaboration would be helpful," said the vice president.

"What's your point, Hal?" asked the president.

"Well, maybe it's me, but what I think the professor is saying is that all the women that have used these Stardust products are now probably infertile – is that right?" The president turned towards Eugene Rendle and Brian Flavier. Brian responded.

"That's about the size of it, Mr President."

Pandemonium broke out around the table. The president had to raise his voice to bring order.

"Gentlemen, please let Eugene and Brian finish their part of this report."

Eugene continued.

"The effect of these chemicals on the male reproduction system is also as deadly. Some of the chemicals contained in the particles have been tested by different countries on rats and mice that showed a marked reduction in sperm, and we know that certain chemicals will destroy male fertility."

"So, it's women *and* men?" asked the president.

"Yes, sir."

"Well, what can we do to eradicate these chemicals from a person's body and will their normal reproductive system return?" asked the president.

"We have no method of cleansing the body of these nanoparticles. They'll remain in the body's organs and bloodstream," replied Brian Flavier.

Again there was an outcry and this time the health secretary spoke.

"It is important to state, Mr President, that we have not been working on toxic nanoparticles having to be removed from the body. Now we know the problem, we can instruct all our scientific agencies, the universities and private companies to concentrate on finding a method to remove them."

"Thank you, Maxwell, but that's for the future. I'm very concerned about the now."

"Eugene, you say that considerable numbers of toxic nanoparticles have been detected in each of these cosmetics – how many are we talking about?"

"Millions, sometimes billions, in each one, Mr President." The president sighed and sat back in his chair. Then just as his composure appeared to be lost he leaned forward.

"Okay. Two things – have we prevented any more of these cosmetics being used and, secondly, how many people are likely to be affected?"

The director of National Intelligence, Walter Fairchild, raised his hand.

"Mr President, both the FBI and CIA have been working on Operation Stardust since it became apparent something was up. Samuel will elaborate." He referred to Samuel Goldmuir, the director of the CIA.

"Mr President, I have added a report to the file excluding certain ongoing operations. A brief outline is that the British gave us a heads-up nine months ago that there may be a problem with this range of cosmetics. We asked the FBI and the Border Agency to monitor shipments into the US and we passed samples of the cosmetics to the FDA to analyse. At first the samples seemed clean. But then the nanobiologists at Harvard discovered nanoparticles in a bottle of shampoo. There were no specifics as to what they were or did. We decided to take a look at the manufacturer and went to Mexico City and later Somalia." He didn't elaborate that they had lost two men in Mogadishu. "We didn't find anything except normal soap but we had such a hostile reception – armed guards aren't usually necessary to guard soap – that we dug deeper. The ExCy Corporation, which manufactures these Stardust cosmetics on behalf of a Swiss company, was a dummy corporation. We traced it back to an outfit called the Ulema Corporation, a holding company based in the Caymans. Again, a dead end, but we tracked this Ulema Corporation to Belize – they were owned by Yesara Consolidated. At the moment that's as far as we've got but these Yesara people are also a dummy. We've been liaising with the British and French, and have turned up several al-Qaeda people. There was a meeting in Europe on board a yacht in the Mediterranean. Several of the guys on board were photographed and we identified these two men."

He clicked on the device in front of him.

"We know this guy as Mansur Ahmedi, also as Belardi – definitely a key al-Qaeda player. This other guy is known to us as Kadar, an al-Qaeda banker. The Brits identified him as Al-Rashid-Bin Ibrahim. The Brits picked up a guy in London, Abdul Suleman, who was photographed on the boat and was a director of the ExCy Corporation in the UK – he took cyanide rather than face questions. We then tracked Suleman's second-in-command, a woman, as she fled the UK to Lebanon." He showed her photograph on the screen.

"Her name is Safiyah Jamil but she travelled as Karim Basilah. The Brits tracked her to a house in the Lebanon and we arranged to snatch her. We have her now in a secure location, and she is being helpful. The operation is most certainly being orchestrated by Osama bin Laden, under the code name Tears of the West, we think from Pakistan. We've intensified our search in Pakistan for Osama bin Laden, Belardi and Ibrahim. This is a worldwide op. Our analysts believe this ExCy outfit couldn't, alone, have manufactured the toxic cocktail, injected nanoparticles into cosmetics and delivered a huge marketing exercise to sell the cosmetics in the US, Canada and Europe. We estimate the cost to the terrorists, and make no mistake this is a terrorist attack, is at least two billion dollars and that's not including the manufacture of the nanoparticles."

"Sorry to interrupt, Samuel," said the president, "but who's helping these guys – any idea?"

"We don't know, but our analysts think the biotechnology is beyond al-Qaeda. Best guess is a rogue state, like Iran or North Vietnam, but we know the Russians, Chinese and Japanese have the capability," he replied.

"Does the FBI have anything to add, Bud?" asked the president.

The director of the FBI, nodded.

"When we were first alerted to this rogue cosmetic, we picked up samples from all the states and passed then to Eugene at Harvard and the FDA. It became clear that they'd stopped sending the contaminated cosmetics to the States, as all the new samples were clean. Then, samples taken from smaller outlets in malls and small towns were examined.

These samples proved to be positive for nanoparticles, including the ingredients shown. We then realised they had tried to divert us by switching their shipments to clean cosmetics. We've continued to monitor both the border with Mexico and through the Port of Houston where many of the deliveries enter the States. The lorries from Mexico head up the West Coast and western states; the shipments into Houston are sent by rail or truck to the eastern and mid-states. We have all known al-Qaeda sympathisers under surveillance."

"Thanks, Bud. Franklyn, can State give us some intel on how much damage has been caused by these cosmetics?" Franklyn Andrew Browne was the secretary of state and a close personal friend of the president. When elected in 2008 the president had surrounded himself with his supporters and friends.

"Sure, Mr President. We've taken an inventory of sales of the Stardust cosmetics from eight months ago by the supermarket top ten chains with over 13,000 stores and the regional supermarkets with 140 chains, as well as retailer co-operatives, deep discount stores, Ethnic, Hispanic and Latino stores. The list of sales is as follows: shampoo – circa 32 million bottles, ladies hairspray – circa 26 million cans, deodorant roll-on and spray – circa 22 million, nail polish (a kit of 4) – circa 10 million, ladies perfume – circa 17 million bottles, shaving cream or gel – circa 15 million, sunscreen – circa 16 million bottles and circa 10 million bottles of liquid soap."

The president was busily writing down the figures.

"I make that over one hundred and thirty million bottles, cans or tubes," he said.

"Yes, Mr President, and we cannot be certain more haven't been sold on the internet or by out-of-town small stores," replied Franklyn Browne.

"Are we to assume, Mr President, that one hundred and

thirty million of our citizens have been infected – I think that's the right word – by these Stardust cosmetics?" asked the chairman of the joint chiefs of staff, in his southern drawl. This was the first time General Bradley Paterson had appreciated the seriousness of the situation.

"Yes, Bradley," replied the president, looking sombre.

"Well, not quite, if you don't mind my saying, Mr President," said Bud Ruskin. They all turned to look at him. "Well, our figures suggest substantially less. Look at it like this – a woman buys a shampoo, hairspray, soap, nail polish, perfume and deodorant for herself. I believe she can only be contaminated by the toxins once. Likewise the sunscreen may be bought by the same woman. We think that a better figure is close to forty million women and twenty million men have been contaminated by this stuff."

The health secretary, who had sat impassively throughout the meeting, leaned forward and raised his hand. Maxwell Liddle was the eldest son of Jeremiah Liddle, one of the richest men in America, and had been a major benefactor for the campaign to elect the president. The president knew the Liddle clan was grooming Maxwell to stand as a future president.

"Mr President, I believe, as does the FDA, that the FBI's figures are closer to the number of women and men likely to be infected by using these cosmetics. But we also have calculated that 27% of the women and 22% of the men are likely to be over forty years of age and may be past childbearing age." There was a murmur from around the table.

He continued, "But, and this is pure conjecture," his law degree obtained at Princeton, and subsequent five years in practice at the prominent Wall Street practice of Marshall Downs, made him qualify every statement he made, "we think at least thirty million children have been contaminated."

Pandemonium broke out around the table again as the president tried to wrestle back control of the meeting.

"Gentlemen, gentlemen, please." He had forgotten Maggie Leighton, a senior White House administrator working for the State Department, sitting in the shadows taking notes. "Professor Rendle, is this possible?" he asked the Harvard academic.

"I see where the health secretary is coming from," he said. "If mothers have used their own shampoo, liquid soap, sunscreen or any of the Stardust cosmetics on their children – then they are likely to be impregnated with the nanoparticles."

"Good God," said General Paterson out loud. The vice president interceded.

"Mr President, we need to establish a set of concrete facts – of primary importance being how many and what age-range are infected."

"I agree," he replied and turned towards the health secretary. "Maxwell, you and the FDA must, in the next twenty-four hours, give us all a definitive list of the sales of these cosmetics, the likely number of people affected by toxic contamination, their age-range, and the approximate distribution state by state. The latter is important as we work out how we're going to deal with this situation."

The health secretary nodded.

"We also have a massive logistics problem, Mr President," said the secretary of state.

"Go on."

"Let's assume that forty million, and that may be conservative, are infected by these nanoparticles. We have a major problem." They all waited. "State governments maintain their own health departments and the local governments in counties and municipalities usually have their own, using branches of state health departments. This catastrophe is a state-wide time bomb. If forty million of our citizens spread around the US find out that they have been impregnated by these toxic particles, they're going to want medical advice straight away. Each state will have a different medical capability. But you bet your life none of them will be able to cope with their share of forty million concerned new patients, and that's without the panic that will set in about the children being infected."

Once again the meeting descended into a babble of voices as the implications of this catastrophe sank in.

"All right, guys, let's look at the logistics," said the president. "Lance, I want your department to consider how each state will cope with this tragedy. Examine medical capacity; look at private hospitals and clinics. You can also consider military hospitals in each state. Prepare a definitive and have it on my desk in two days." Lance Manley, the secretary to the Environment Protection Agency, nodded.

Maxwell Liddle raised his hand. "Mr President, we simply do not have enough medical equipment or qualified staff to handle forty million anxious folk angry and frightened about fertility and pregnancy."

"What's your point, Max?" asked the president.

"Resources, Mr President – we need to buy more equipment and seek additional obstetricians urgently."

"Agreed. Unlimited federal budget for that, Max – start the ball rolling," replied the president.

"In addition, you need to recruit hundreds of additional paediatricians," said the vice president.

"Sure, go ahead with that, Max. State-wide numbers are likely to be hundreds if not thousands required. Widen the recruitment net to South America, Australia, New Zealand, Italy and Spain," replied the president.

"Why those countries, Mr President?" asked Max.

"None of them were targeted by the terrorists according to the Brits," said the president. "Now, Ryan," he turned to the attorney general, "we need to prevent any further dangerous substances entering the States and get all these Stardust cosmetics off every shelf. We also need to exclude any further cosmetics from this outfit ExCy or any linked corporation."

"I've already issued a federal warrant to seize all Stardust cosmetics through the FBI and the EPA's national enforcement team. The Toxic Substances Control Act is already a federal law, we have environmental laws and Presidential Executive Orders connected to nanotechnology. E013045 is an Executive Order for the Protection of Children from Environmental Health Risks and Safety. We also have the Federal Food, Drug and Cosmetic Act. All these federal laws enable us to act," Ryan replied.

"Thank you," replied the president. "I've called a meeting of the state governors tomorrow; many are travelling as we speak. I intend to ask each governor to oversee the administration and deal with what's likely to be general panic once this terrorist attack becomes common knowledge. The FBI will provide support to the police in each state and if necessary the state governor will call out the National Guard."

"You think things are going to get ugly, then?" asked General Paterson.

The president thought for a second. "I do. Anyone who attacks the USA will provoke a severe reaction. Attack our families, our women, our children – this will provoke a massive angry retaliation. People will look for revenge; find someone to blame."

"Yeah, and it could be this administration," said the vice president.

"I've also asked the Speaker of the House of Representatives and the Senate party leaders to a meeting and convened a closed session of the Senate in eight days," said the president. "I'll address the nation in ten days unless anything breaks in the media – and I trust it won't. The State Department will be preparing briefing notes which we'll give to all senators and representatives. We'll also issue a press pack and a video of the complex nature of this attack on our citizens and we'll design a website."

"Mr President," General Paterson interrupted.

"Bradley," said the president, looking slightly annoyed.

"Since the CIA hasn't yet pinpointed who is helping these al-Qaeda terrorists, should we ratchet-up to DEFCON 3? It will sure as hell send a message to any of the people involved that we know what they have done and will react severely."

The president thought for one second.

"No, Bradley, let's keep our powder dry until we know who has helped al-Qaeda. Then we'll review what action to take."

General Paterson was disappointed but knew better than to argue.

"The Brits are hosting a meeting of the other nations who have been attacked, in two days. We're intending to coordinate announcements to all our citizens in ten days time," said the president.

"Mr President, I meant to ask Professor Flavier earlier. These toxic nanoparticles – can they have any other effect on the organs of the human body? I know they seem to be directed towards fertility but what about other effects on health?" asked the vice president.

"Good point," replied the president. "Professor?"

"We're not entirely sure if the toxic nanoparticles, which remember remain in the body, will cause long-term liver failure, cancer or other organs to fail. We've started a full toxicokinetics analysis and our specialist biotechnology department will be examining the bio-distribution."

"Which means?" asked the vice president.

"To examine the possible locations of the nanoparticles

in the body and the mathematical account of their absorption, distribution and metabolism, and to determine the fate of these chemical substances in relation to human organs," Professor Flavier replied.

"So, this whole mess could get worse," said the vice president.

"Well, yes, I guess so," replied Professor Flavier.

General Paterson banged his fist on the table.

"By God, we're gonna have to deal with who has done this to us."

The president, sensing no further advantage in debate, decided to close the meeting. "Gentlemen, we will reconvene in three days."

⋆

After the meeting, the president remained with the secretary of state and Samuel Goldmuir.

"Samuel, you need to find bin Laden and these other two guys urgently," said Franklyn Browne.

"We are trying, Mr Secretary, and so are the Brits. Hopefully we'll have something soon."

"Use all resources at your disposal, Samuel," said the president. "We need a win or the publicity will bring down the administration."

44

Colonel Harriman had extracted all the intel he could from the four men captured on the *Good Queen Bess*. The men had now been passed to the CIA at RAF Northolt in west London. He suspected they would be transported to Guantanamo Bay or Romania. He read the report by his interrogation team headed up by Smithy, a man who specialised in interrogating prisoners. He had initially crossed paths with Smithy in the first Iraq war when his SAS unit captured an Iraqi general. Smithy was in charge of the General's debrief and, whilst John Harriman was not involved, he met the sergeant known as Smithy several times. When he heard he had left the service he made him an offer to work from time to time for Harriman Security.

Smithy reported that only one of the men, Ursaan Alvi, was of any interest. The other three were merely foot soldiers, bodyguards employed on occasion in the Lebanon or Pakistan. Ursaan, on the other hand, had a great deal to reveal as he had been one of Belardi and Ibrahim's principal bodyguards, travelling with either of them in Pakistan and worldwide. Ursaan had accompanied Belardi twice to Zurich – they had gone to a meeting at the ExCy Corporation office. Ursaan said that Belardi had met a man he thought was based in London. He hadn't been present at the meeting. The second time Ursaan accompanied Belardi to Zurich he went to a bank. He thought the name of the bank was the de Courcy Merchant Bank. Ursaan also accompanied Belardi on trips to the Lebanon when they met leading Hezbollah commanders.

Smithy let Ursaan talk – after he had spent three days in solitary, with no sleep, and was periodically drenched with cold water from a high-pressure hose he had had enough. There had been no need for more extreme measures, reported Smithy. A note was highlighted on Smithy's report – *accompanied Belardi and Ibrahim to northern Pakistan.* This interested Colonel Harriman as he had just sent two of his men undercover at the request of MI6 into Pakistan. Both Belardi and Ibrahim had flown from Karachi to Islamabad before meeting a high-ranking army officer in the Pakistan Intelligence Service. Ursaan had to wait at a hotel in Islamabad for three days on each occasion. But he didn't know where the two commanders in al-Qaeda had gone. Ursaan also accompanied Ibrahim to London. They flew to Heathrow, with Ibrahim using a false passport. He knew that because the tickets were in the name of Sameer Jagirani. Ibrahim also went to Somalia, Belize, Oman and Mexico accompanied by Ursaan. He did not attend any of the meetings with Ibrahim but they did visit a bank in Belize Town called the Central American Trust. Ursaan admitted his men had killed the two French photographers as they had been spotted taking photographs of the people on the *Good Queen Bess*. One of the photographers had got as far as Cannes before they found him, but initially not the photographs. Then one of Ursaan's men spotted a man take something from the photographer's motorcycle. The man seen in Cannes had been followed to Paris with a woman and another man they met to London and all three were mugged – the photographs were stolen and had been destroyed.

There was a note that Ursaan Alvi was a Pakistani who travelled under several aliases. He had worked for the ISI until recruited by Belardi two years ago. The report concluded Ursaan was a bit player but some of the places where he accompanied Belardi and Ibrahim might prove interesting.

I bet both Belardi and Ibrahim were meeting Osama bin Laden in northern Pakistan, thought Colonel Harriman, *but where?* He put the report in a confidential packet and sent it 'eyes only' to Sir Anthony Greenwood.

Sir Anthony sent a copy of the report to Samuel Goldmuir via the CIA officer at the American embassy in Grosvenor Square.

45

Ibrahim decided to sleep and lowered his seat to make the chair lay flat. As he lay he thought, *the advantage of first-class air travel is you can enjoy a good night's sleep*. Travelling Emirates from Karachi to Zurich, he was going to their bank to arrange for the transfer of some funds to Belize. He preferred to carry out these transactions face-to-face – no paper trail. As he lay still in semi-darkness, there was a man across the aisle reading with a light on. He considered his position. He knew Belardi had gone to see Osama but not what the meeting was about, and that concerned him. Until recently he had shared responsibility with Belardi but it seemed to him he was being edged out – and that was a massive concern. He knew Osama was a ruthless leader and if for some reason he was no longer in favour, he needed to know. He lay wondering what the reason for this change was. *Perhaps it was the stupid leasing of the yacht for the second time after those French photographers, who Belardi had eliminated, had taken shots of everyone who went on deck? Or was it the loss of Suleman, the London manager – code name Blue?* he thought.

London was turning into a disaster. He had switched the European operation to Marseille and appointed a Saudi to run the region. *Was Osama annoyed he had lost many operatives in London? But they were only minor players, foot soldiers, and they had successfully killed the deputy head of MI6, and several of the university academics who were nosing into their affairs.* He turned on his side hoping the light from across the cabin would not keep him awake. But it was not the light that night – he couldn't sleep contemplating his fate if he was no longer in favour.

★

Belardi had arranged for an Iranian, Navid Sassan, to act as Ibrahim's bodyguard on his trip to Zurich. He was concerned that Ibrahim's security was not good enough and he seemed oblivious to the risk he ran by flying to Europe and not electronically transferring money. True, it eliminated a paper trail to go personally to their bank, but the Americans would probably know by now the ingredients of the Stardust range of cosmetics and be searching for any al-Qaeda members. If Ibrahim was on their watch list then he could be spotted at Zurich Airport. If he was caught, Belardi doubted Ibrahim would bite into the false tooth and commit suicide. Belardi's instructions to Navid were simple. If Ibrahim looks as though he is going to be picked up – kill him.

★

The Saudi, Abail, who had taken over as code name Blue, manager of the European operation, had arranged for the replacement labels, and one million bottles of shampoo labelled Celebrity were now sitting in warehouses in Tilbury, England. He had arranged for five leading supermarkets to take the entire stock promising, through the London advertising agents he used, that a three million pound advertising campaign using a well-known female singer would launch the Celebrity range next month. He knew that a tanker was heading to Marseille from Oman where a further batch of shampoo had been prepared. The French bottling plant had been expecting the liquid but there had been a slight delay which forced him to postpone the launch of the nationwide advertising in the UK. *How typical,* he thought, *the British were so keen to take all he could supply at fifty pence a bottle to sell at seven times as much. Even then the shampoo would be very competitively priced and they greedily thought they would sell out quickly.*

★

Ibrahim was finally nodding off when a stewardess apologised and handed him a note. He turned on a sidelight.

Business rival knows you are coming. Get off at Dubai. Other arrangements have been made. Someone will contact you. B

He unfastened his seatbelt and went into the toilet. Tearing up the note he flushed it down the toilet and then he walked into economy and found his bodyguard. He spoke to him quietly in Pakistani to get off the plane with him and follow him when they reached Dubai.

46

Jack Clarke was furious. The systems analysts at Langley had reported Ibrahim on an Emirates flight from Karachi to Zurich. A picture of him going through passport control had not been forwarded by the Pakistan Intelligence Services but by the Chinese Secret Service. Why, he did not know, but didn't at this point in time care. They wanted Ibrahim and now had him on a plate so to speak. But no! Willis Coogan, his number two reported that Ibrahim had got off the flight at Dubai. Fine; it was a stop-off en route to Zurich. Trouble is, he didn't get back on. Despite the co-operation of the UAE Secret Service they could only track him as arriving in Dubai. Jack suspected they knew precisely where he had gone but were stalling. He made a call to his boss, who in turn phoned the director of National Intelligence and asked him to contact the UAE ambassador in Washington to exert some pressure – they must find out where Ibrahim went. He can't have disappeared.

⋆

Ibrahim had followed the instructions and left the Emirates flight at Dubai Airport. He was first off the plane and walked up the apron. An Arab was walking towards him and he spoke to him in English.

"You are Ibrahim?" Ibrahim nodded. "Follow me."

The man led him to the end of the apron then abruptly turned left, the opposite direction to the departure or transit lounge. He opened a door and Ibrahim followed him down to the airport tarmac. Walking swiftly they reached a four-seater cart. The man got in and Ibrahim and his bodyguard followed. They drove in the electric vehicle in silence, hugging the contours of the buildings then, abruptly, the man changed direction towards a number of stationary executive jets. One of the planes had the steps down and the buggy driver pulled up alongside.

"Up you go. Luggage will follow."

Ibrahim walked up the steps. A steward greeted him.

"You are welcome. Please take any seat and fasten your seatbelt; we will be leaving immediately."

Ibrahim was pensive but followed instructions. He wondered whose plane he was on and where he was going.

★

Jack's pressure had paid off. An email, with an attachment, had been sent from Dubai by the UAE secret police showing Ibrahim leaving the airport building, getting in an electric cart and driving alongside the terminal. The airport cameras picked him up boarding an executive jet. Urgent enquiries were taking place as to the owners of the jet and to find out the flight plan the pilot had logged.

★

Ibrahim decided, after thirty minutes in the air, to start asking questions and pressed his call bell. An Arab approached him – not the flight attendant that had welcomed him on board.

"My master sends his compliments. He appreciates you will have many questions; some I can answer, some I cannot."

"Whose plane am I travelling in?" asked Ibrahim.

"A friend's," replied the man.

"Where am I going?"

"Yemen."

"Why Yemen?" asked Ibrahim.

"My master believes the Americans are tracking you and by now will know you are on this plane. My master cannot be implicated in a dispute with the Americans so we have arranged that the plane was chartered by you at short notice. The flight plan given to Dubai Air Traffic Control is to Karachi. We will shortly drop under radar and fly at a low altitude around the Arabian Sea and eventually land at Aden. I believe you have an office in the city? My master suggests you wait several weeks before leaving Yemen, and use a private charter. Now I suggest you enjoy the flight. A steward will attend you shortly. Please ask for anything you want, your bodyguard is at the rear."

Ibrahim settled back in the luxurious leather recliner. He was thankful to whoever had saved him – perhaps this meant Osama still held him in high regard.

*

After Jack Clarke reported that the known al-Qaeda terrorist Ibrahim had escaped capture in Dubai, the president of the United States had personally called the Saudis. The CIA had traced the ownership of the executive jet to a member of the Saudi royal family. Normal diplomatic enquiries had not produced an answer. Where did the jet take Ibrahim?

Now Jack had the answer – Yemen. It was good news that they knew where Ibrahim had gone – bad news that someone high up in the Saudi government had helped him. Now he was pulling out all the stops to find Ibrahim – his agents had been alerted and Willis Coogan was on his way to Aden in the Yemen, by the CIA Lear jet 35, to take charge. If Ibrahim was still there they would find him. An aircraft carrier, a cruiser and two destroyers had been deployed to the Arabian Sea in case anyone doubted the American intention.

★

Belardi opened the email. An encrypted message from their Chinese friend – *American sixth fleet off Yemen. CIA travelling there now. Suggest our friend moves.*

He used a disposable mobile and contacted Ibrahim.

★

Ibrahim moved quickly to leave Yemen. He had landed at Aden International Airport and had been escorted out of the airport by an army officer – not passing through immigration. Now he was being driven up one of the major roads in Yemen, the N2, towards Al-Hudaydah, a seaport to the east. On arrival he would charter a boat to Djibouti and then find another ship going to Karachi. He was travelling, using a different set of false papers, as Syed Jagir, a Pakistani businessman.

47

10TH APRIL, 2011

The British prime minister had called the summit meeting in London and only the Americans and Canadians of the countries affected, did not attend in person. The president of France already knew most of what the British and Americans were going to tell him. The German, Dutch, Belgian, Norwegian, Swedish, Italian and Spanish leaders were attending this hastily called meeting with their foreign and Home Office ministers.

The prime minister chose his country house, Chequers, to hold the meeting – easier for security to keep out the prying eyes of the world's press. That didn't stop several hundred camping outside the gates. They all knew something extremely important was happening. Intrigued and curious many were suggesting the British were about to give notice on pulling out of the EU. Others scoffed at this suggestion, saying that the British had not held a referendum and would be unable to leave the EU without this mandate. Other speculation included the break-up of NATO – after all the British had reduced its army to such a small number of full-time soldiers it was felt that they could not support the treaty any longer. Speculation and intrigue was the food and drink of the media, and excitement gripped the news feeds to their countries as they considered all possibilities.

When the British prime minister commenced the meeting he was in a sombre mood. He started by explaining that, as he had indicated to each of the leaders, the meeting was about a terrorist attack on all their countries. Then with the help of a huge plasma screen on the wall he elaborated. Each country had been given a thick bound document, with a translation into their native language, as he recounted the awful discovery that the Stardust range of cosmetics on sale in all their countries contained deadly toxic nanoparticles. He handed the discussion over to Professor Endleson.

The professor elaborated on the findings of the Americans and the British team at Essex University. At this point the prime minister invited the American president to comment – he had been participating in the meeting by satellite link on another screen at the end of the room. The president of the United States introduced the Canadian prime minister, who was with him in the White House, and his secretary of state, Franklyn Browne. The secretary of state confirmed the findings by their universities and Federal Agency that the nanoparticles in the cosmetics were toxic and would very likely prevent normal birth or harm a pregnant woman and reduce a male's sperm count.

The group had remained relatively passive as the British had explained the reason for the meeting, but when the Americans said that they calculated up to sixty million of their citizens were infected, pandemonium broke out. It was as though a lecture on biotechnology had suddenly been interrupted with a shocking truth. A recess was called by the British to restore order. Thirty minutes later the president of the United States continued to talk to the assembled leaders.

"You'll need to examine the market penetration of these cosmetics in your own country and determine the steps you must take. The British, Canadians, French and ourselves are speaking to our own nations, on national TV Friday of next week. We suggest we all coordinate our announcements of this atrocity on the same day and time. This way we'll at least control the media frenzy that will result once this barbaric act becomes public knowledge. We also suggest you consider your medical resources to field the numerous enquiries your citizens are going to make into fertility and their general wellbeing. We've drafted our speech and are sending you all a copy. This appalling crime has, in our view, been carried out by Osama bin Laden and al-Qaeda. But they must have had significant scientific and financial support. When we find out who and how, we will act – make no mistake. We consider this attack on our citizens to be the most serious threat to world peace since the Second World War. In the document the British have given you are full details of the cosmetics, what we know of the company trading this brand and photographs of our most wanted – the men we believe are organising this attack. I'm aware that on occasion we don't all share information on the activities of our secret services, but this crime against humanity requires we all co-operate to capture the terrorists and bring them to justice."

The German chancellor, a former research scientist, was the first to react.

"Mr President, do your security services know how these terrorists have been distributing these cosmetics in our countries?"

"We've discovered facilities run by the ExCy Corporation in Mexico and Somalia. Our agents suspect they have manufacturing and distribution outlets in many countries. I suggest your police and security services investigate how the manufacturer, ExCy, has been distributing the cosmetics in your country. This may lead to warehouses, or offices to raid and to detain suspected criminals and terrorists. If you need our help please contact Langley – details are in the folder. You'll probably discover an extensive marketing campaign to promote the sale of the Stardust range of cosmetics. The payment for the advertising is made to a respected advertising agency and comes from a Swiss bank, the Cayman Islands or Belize," replied the president.

"Have you arranged for the Swiss to investigate this bank?" asked the French president.

"Yes. It's proving difficult to penetrate their usual security, but we're working on it," he replied.

A general agreement was reached for the leaders to broadcast to their nation on the same day and, except for the different time zones, at the same time. Each leader left, fearing what they might find on further investigation and how their citizens would react to the atrocity.

Afterwards, the German foreign minister approached the British prime minister.

"Can I have a quiet word?"

He was shown into an office on the first floor.

"Prime Minister, the German government appreciates the work the British have done to bring this terrible matter to our attention. But we wonder if a public admission of our collective failings to prevent the catastrophe is the right way to proceed. You British have a saying I like, 'Let sleeping dogs lie'. Perhaps we all might consider a delay before we admit that worldwide one hundred million women and fifty million men, not to mention the children, are infected with these nanoparticles?"

The prime minister had considered this option himself, but the cabinet had narrowly voted to come clean – reveal all to the British public.

"I appreciate your candour, but the British government feels that the attack on our citizens would eventually leak – and that would be a public relations disaster. Can you imagine each of our countries under attack by the media for our failure to be honest with our citizens? No – we dismissed the option to do nothing and I think the approach we're taking is the right course of action."

"Understandably so, Prime Minister. We believe likewise," replied the German.

He left with the British PM, curious as to what would have been proposed if he had agreed to a delay.

48

12TH APRIL, 2011

Raza and his cousin Jafar had been in Pakistan for two weeks. Dressed in a grey shalwar kameez, a type of long fitting shirt, with a waistcoat, both had non-descript brown quetta style chappal sandals and looked every inch the Pakistani businessman. Travelling as buyers for the British department store, Dunstan's, they had met agents of MI6 in Karachi, Peshawar, Quetta and Zhob, and were now travelling to Rawalpindi. The men they had met all worked in public services. One worked at Karachi Airport as a passport control officer, another at Peshawar Airport in immigration control. In Quetta and Zhob, their contacts were a garage proprietor and a police officer. But nobody had any information about Belardi, Ibrahim or Osama bin Laden. Their journey around Pakistan was not without danger – al-Qaeda and Taliban sympathisers were everywhere and the closer they went to the border the more dangerous their operation was. Reaching Rawalpindi late in the afternoon, having travelled by hire car from Peshawar, they checked into the Karim Hotel. The following morning they met their contact – an elderly man who worked in a garage.

He studied the photographs then much to Raza's surprise said, "This one. I have seen him," he pointed to the picture of Belardi. The cousins looked at each other.

"When and where?" asked Jafar, speaking in Hindko, a dialect used locally.

The man was from Peshawar where many of the population spoke in this Punjabi dialect. He thought for a minute. "Maybe two weeks ago. A military vehicle pulled into the garage for petrol – he got out and went to the toilet." He studied the photograph. "Yes, I am certain it was him." He looked pleased with himself. This was the first time he had been of any assistance to the British, despite receiving fifty pounds from his non-existent brother in England each month for the past two years.

"You say it was a military vehicle?" asked Raza.

"Yes. I am not sure what division – but it was army. The driver got out to pay and another man sat in the back – I did not see his face but he wore a uniform."

"Which direction did they go?" asked Jafar, trying not to appear too excited.

"North, towards Islamabad."

"And what was the time of day?" asked Raza.

The man scratched his head. "I am not certain, but I think it was late dusk."

"Is there anything else you can tell us?" asked Raza.

"I can find out if my cousin in the traffic police keeps the film of the crossroads camera on the main road to Islamabad. Sometimes they have film in the camera, sometimes not," he laughed. "If the police have been putting film in the camera I will have to buy it."

"How much?" asked Jafar.

"Ten thousand Pakistani rupees."

"Okay, go ahead," replied Jafar.

An hour later the man returned. Unfortunately the camera on the crossroads had no film. The cousins studied the map of the area.

"He could have headed north from Islamabad," said Raza.

"Or east," said Jafar.

"I'm inclined towards Haripur, which is getting close to the border," replied Raza.

"I see what you mean. Let's travel up the N35. We have another contact to see at a garage in Haripur," said Jafar.

"Let's hope the aroma in Rawalpindi hasn't reached Islamabad." Raza referred to the smell of the sacrificed animal markets that seemed to permeate up your nose and throat in Rawalpindi. The cousins laughed and set off for Islamabad; east on the N5.

Reaching Islamabad in the early evening they stopped at the Islamabad Serena Hotel, near Constitution Avenue, and planned their journey for the next day. Raza sent a message to Sir Anthony Greenwood via Colonel Harriman.

*

Sir Anthony studied the map of Pakistan. If Belardi had been heading north towards Islamabad, either bin Laden was holed-up in that modern city or he had a hideaway nearer the border. He put in a call to a colonel in the Pakistan Intelligence Service, a friend of John Harriman, who usually co-operated with the west.

Who was the uniformed man who accompanied Belardi in a military vehicle? Likely to be a senior officer, he thought. Sir Anthony sent a message to Langley requesting the CIA divert a satellite or a drone to Islamabad and north towards the border.

49

13TH APRIL, 2011

Ibrahim had a most uncomfortable journey from Djibouti to Karachi in an aging, rusty steamer carrying sheep and coffee. The stench of the animals overwhelmed the pleasant smell of coffee, and with the rough sea and the stink he had been sick numerous times on the journey – he almost wished the Americans had caught him.

Hiring a car using his alias, Syed Jagir, he travelled from Karachi on the M-9 planning to join the N5 to Rawalpindi then on towards Islamabad. He had decided to stay overnight in Rawalpindi or Islamabad before journeying on to Abbottabad to meet the leader. Still nervous as to whether he would receive a warm welcome, he mulled over the security of his position. *Only he knew all the banking arrangements – surely this was sufficient to save him?* he thought. *Yes, that would be the test. If they intended to extract details of the bank accounts in Zurich, Belize and the Caymans he would know they had decided to eliminate him. Had they already summoned his clerks from Karachi, his main office? Three men in Karachi knew a little – what if they had been summoned to Abbottabad?*

He knew he would not die bravely by biting the tooth and releasing the poison. He stopped for petrol just outside Rawalpindi.

★

The man nearly fell off the threadbare leather stool as Ibrahim came to the window to pay for petrol. As the car, a black Toyota Land Cruiser with darkened windows, left the forecourt, he copied down the registration number and phoned his contact in Islamabad.

Adam Runfold, the MI6 agent who was on duty at the embassy, asked the man to repeat the message. One of the men in the photographs he had been given, called Ibrahim, had just filled up his tank with petrol and was now heading north towards Islamabad. Adam acted immediately, sending a text to Raza and contacting the CIA.

★

Willis Coogan had been sent to Pakistan several weeks ago to find Belardi, Ibrahim or bin Laden. Despite the extensive number of paid informants nothing had turned up. The Pakistan Secret Service had been no help – lots of platitudes but no sightings of any of the targets. Now Adam Runfold of the British Secret Service had called him with a sighting of Ibrahim on the N5 outside Rawalpindi heading north towards Islamabad where Willis was based. He summoned the other CIA members to the embassy boardroom.

★

From the moment Ibrahim's black Toyota was picked up fifty kilometres from Islamabad, a CIA team consisting of three cars and a motorbike tailed him. The silver Toyota Prado was now sitting back three hundred metres behind a convoy of colourful lorries. These highly customised decorated lorries, commonly known as jingle trucks, have paintings, calligraphy and ornamental decor all over the surface and front of the vehicle. The Prado driver had just overtaken the second of the CIA agents who was driving an old red Maruti Suzuki. A third car, an aging silver BMW 3 series, was four lorries further back on the crowded highway and the motorcyclist remained at the rear. Langley was also tracking the Toyota, having positioned a satellite, the KH-11 Kennan, the most advanced surveillance satellite ever launched. Jack Clarke had personally taken over this operation and had been in communication with the trackers through the satellite. His orders to Willis Coogan, his senior agent, were simple – let him lead you to bin Laden.

Raza and Jafar, two of Colonel Harriman's operatives loaned to MI6, had not been briefed by the CIA. Following Adam's message they were waiting in a lorry stop for the Black Toyota to appear on the N5 south of Islamabad. They picked him up, joined a convoy of lorries and began their tail.

Ibrahim, oblivious to the CIA or MI6 tail, kept his speed at under 80 km/h, driving sedately so as not to attract attention. It was difficult to drive much faster anyway with the convoy of colourful lorries in front of him. There was a silver car in between lorries at least four hundred metres away, and two lorries behind him was a newer silver coloured car driven by a Pakistani man that had been there for thirty minutes. He had no field craft but decided to test if he was being followed and stopped at a roadside café. Typically, several men sat in the open on charpoys with a small table in front of them. The small charpoys, rope beds that double as couches or chairs, faced a concrete hut with the proprietor sitting outside cutting meat into chunks for a stew. Ibrahim spoke to the two other men. It would be hours before the meal would be ready, so he decided to buy oranges. He put a pinch of salt on each slice, as was the tradition, and studied the road. The black and silver cars had passed without stopping followed by several others. He did not notice the BMW or motorcycle pull up before reaching the café five hundred metres down the road. Satisfied, Ibrahim resumed his journey on the N5 driving slowly, typically behind several lorries. Raza had stopped in a lay-by, spotted him and tucked in three lorries behind. The cousins had no idea they were in a CIA operation.

Langley detected the silver Suzuki three vehicles behind Ibrahim, but were unaware that two MI6 operatives were also tailing their quarry. Ibrahim decided to check into a hotel in Islamabad before going to Abbottabad. The leader did not like visitors turning up early and his appointment was tomorrow at 2pm. Deciding on his favourite hotel in Islamabad, Ibrahim checked in to the Marriott. He had dinner in his room and dealt with the numerous emails he had received from the four managers who controlled the world distribution of cosmetics. He gave the go ahead to start the advertising campaign in the USA and UK of the Celebrity brand, initially shampoo.

Raza and Jafar had shadowed Ibrahim's Toyota and when he pulled into the Marriott car park they decided to sleep in their car, taking turns to watch just in case he tried to leave during the night.

*

Jack Clarke was considering what action to take. Two men, who appeared to be of Pakistani origin, had followed Ibrahim since the outskirts of Islamabad in a silver Suzuki and were now parked in the car park of the hotel where he had checked in. Both the men remained in the car. He considered his options. Take out the two men or disable their vehicle to prevent their pursuit. He argued that if they were Ibrahim's bodyguards they would be staying in the hotel. So – they were most likely ISI, or military intelligence working undercover. Jack knew there was a leak in the ISI and did not trust them. He had phoned the commander of military intelligence and been assured none of his men were on an operation in Islamabad. Jack had not elaborated on the CIA operation or what their interest was as he was uncertain as to who were al-Qaeda or Taliban sympathisers in the army. His internal phone buzzed.

"What? The car is a Hertz hire car… out to a Brit, Raza Bhutani? What the hell?" he said angrily.

He put in a call to Sir Anthony Greenwood and solved his problem.

★

Raza's mobile beeped: a message from Dunstan's. The cousins' cover touring Pakistan was as buyers for Dunstan's who operated a chain of department stores in the UK. The message read: *The buyer you have identified is being pursued by a rival. Break off and move on tonight.* Raza showed his cousin. They started up their car and moved off, deciding to drive to the British embassy in Islamabad to speak to their MI6 contact.

Jack Clarke nodded to himself as he watched the Suzuki leave the car park – *What would they do without satellites?* he thought.

★

Ibrahim had spent a restless night – he couldn't shake off his fear that he was going to his death. Leaving the hotel shortly after 10am, he drove onto the road to Haripur where he intended to stop for lunch and to check if he was being followed. He had two hours to reach Haripur then onto Abbottabad and drove within the speed limit on the N125. He passed the now familiar military base on his left – clever of Osama to have a house so near the Pakistan army. He was stopped two miles outside Abbottabad by an old, battered Mitsubishi four-wheel drive that had seen better days, overtaking him and flagging him down. Two men got out with AK-47s slung over their shoulders. He opened the driver's window.

"*As-salamu Alaykum*, brothers. Al-Rashid-Bin Ibrahim. I have a 2pm appointment."

The man on the driver's side studied him; the other checked the rear seats and boot then nodded. Both of the men returned to their beat-up vehicle – Ibrahim drove on.

*

Jack Clarke had watched the other car overtake and block Ibrahim's Toyota. The satellite image showed two figures getting out of the other vehicle then a few minutes later get back in. He spoke to Willis Coogan on the ground in Pakistan.

"Hang back, there's a roadblock ahead. He must be getting close to bin Laden's hideout."

Willis was in the silver BMW and pulled over two kilometres behind Ibrahim's car. The other CIA agents also stopped; one in a garage forecourt, another parked on the other side of the road, with the motorcycle stopping two hundred metres behind, all before the army base was reached.

50

Ibrahim, oblivious to the satellite tracking his every move, reached the leader's house in Abbottabad. As he pulled up, the tall, metal security gates were manually pulled back by two men, each with an AK-47 slung over his shoulder. Another man signalled Ibrahim to park alongside the wall opposite the house. Then another younger man searched the car again. Ibrahim was told to get out and lean against the car. He was used to this, being patted down; Osama didn't allow anyone to bring weapons into the house, except his bodyguards. He was greeted by a burly bodyguard with a full beard who he knew had been with bin Laden since his days of hiding out in caves in Afghanistan.

"The master will see you now."

Ibrahim was sweating; the house was not air conditioned in every room. The first time he had visited bin Laden in Abbottabad he had not expected the minimalistic rooms lacking furnishings – but then he did like luxury. Today, as he was shown into a plain room with no furniture, just large cushions on the floor, he marvelled at the man who he knew was very wealthy. His crusade against the infidels was pure; he had no trappings of the West he hated. This man was a true soldier of Islam.

Osama bin Laden came into the room flanked by the bodyguard Ibrahim had seen earlier.

"*As-salamu Alaykum*. Welcome to my home."

After the formality of tea, Ibrahim began to feel more relaxed. He answered bin Laden's questions on distribution of the new Celebrity range of cosmetics and confirmed that advertising campaigns would commence shortly in the USA and UK. One million bottles of shampoo were waiting at their collection point in the UK and a tanker containing the toxic shampoo was at sea on its way to Colombia for bottling and sending to the US. Ibrahim produced a written account of the financial position of the project Osama had called Tears of the West. All the partners had transferred the additional funds that had been called for and the banks in the Caymans, Belize and Zurich all had substantial deposits.

"Belardi informs me that you were nearly taken by the Americans on your trip to Zurich," said bin Laden.

"Yes, I was fortunate Belardi has an excellent security team," Ibrahim replied.

"And you were very close to being apprehended in Yemen."

"The infidels were trying to catch me, but I eluded them."

"Thanks be to Allah, but you are a marked man and you must cease flying until Belardi informs you it is safe, and then only use an alias and false documents."

"I listen and obey," replied Ibrahim, thinking this was a crunch moment.

"Very well. You will go to a safe house in Karachi and work from the office there. Remain in the house at all other times. One of my guards will drive you and remain with you. The money transfers can be made electronically?"

"Yes, but I have always preferred to instruct the banks

personally rather than create an electronic, traceable signature," replied Ibrahim.

"I understand, but you are now at great risk. The infidels are seeking you as we speak and we cannot afford any other close calls. You will deal with the money transactions electronically. Our software and email encryption is excellent – use it."

"I will obey," replied Ibrahim.

Bin Laden got up from the cushion and Ibrahim breathed a sigh of relief.

*

Jack Clarke watched the screen as the green metal gates opened and the black Toyota drove out.

"Send a message to Willis – tail him but don't intercept," he instructed his associate.

The CIA agents used the same tactics as before but this time the motorcycle was closer to the Toyota but remained four hundred metres behind. The CIA agents switched positions periodically and when they reached Rawalpindi two different vehicles went on station. Ibrahim and his driver were completely unaware of the tail and had decided to drive to Karachi without an overnight stop.

*

Jack asked for a meeting with Samuel Goldmuir, Walter Fairchild, Franklyn Browne, General Paterson and the president.

51

"Gentlemen," the five men sat around the long table and looked towards Jack Clarke, "I've asked for this meeting as I believe we have pinpointed the hideout of Osama bin Laden."

The president who had already been briefed by Samuel Goldmuir said, "Okay, Jack, show us what you've got."

Jack indicated to an associate to lower the lights, and the screen at the end of the room came to life.

"This is a satellite picture of a compound in north Pakistan at a place called Abbottabad. We received a tip-off that Ibrahim," a photograph appeared on the screen, "was travelling from Rawalpindi heading north towards Islamabad. We had time to divert a satellite and get together a team to carry out surveillance. We picked up a black Toyota outside Islamabad which we had been informed had a single male occupant – we believed to be Ibrahim. The team, keeping a good distance as we were tracking the vehicle by satellite, followed the vehicle to the Marriott hotel in Islamabad. Ibrahim was photographed leaving the vehicle in the hotel car park." He showed the still photograph of Ibrahim getting out of the vehicle and several other photographs as he walked towards the hotel.

"We positively identified Ibrahim who has been on our most wanted list for six months. Deciding to follow the target and see where he led us, we continued satellite surveillance and the ground team carried on following him. As he passed by a Pakistan army military base and near Abbottabad, another vehicle forced our target to stop. Two men, you can see on the screen, approached the vehicle. We thought this was a stop and search and suspected we were getting close to where Ibrahim was going. He then turned off the main road and pulled up at a large, triangular-shaped compound." Jack let the picture sink in before continuing. "We think this is where bin Laden has been hiding."

The president interrupted, "Have you any aerial photographs or other intel confirming that he's there?"

"No, but we've diverted a drone to circle over the building taking photographs and beaming back live visual, and hope to confirm a sighting shortly."

The president knew that the CIA used a sophisticated stealth drone called a RQ170 Sentinel that could fly high above the area without detection by the Pakistan army.

"Okay, so what's your next step, Jack?"

"I'd like permission to put together a team to go in," Jack replied.

"With respect, Mr President, I don't see how we can mount a mission a hundred miles inside Pakistan's border unless we have concrete proof bin Laden is in that building," said Franklyn Browne.

"Mr President, if there is the slightest chance bin Laden is there we must act," said General Paterson.

The president of the United States was, by nature, a cautious man and reacted how Samuel Goldmuir had predicted he would when talking to Jack earlier.

"I take Franklyn's point. Jack, get your people on the

ground, back to Abbottabad and bring us proof he's there – then we'll talk again," said the president.

The president discussed his address to the nation in three days' time and reminded Samuel and Jack that the capture or death of bin Laden would have a major impact to redress the negative publicity the administration was going to get when the significance of the toxic nanoparticle attack on US citizens was realised.

After leaving the meeting, Jack went to Langley to meet Sir Anthony Greenwood who had flown in that morning. He had realised more evidence of bin Laden's presence in the compound was necessary and hoped the Brits would co-operate.

★

Sir Anthony telephoned Colonel Harriman on the secure phone at the British embassy.

"Hello, John, I'm on the embassy telephone. Is your scrambler on?"

Colonel Harriman was one of the few, outside the security service or the PM's office, who had a secure landline.

"Yes, Tony, how can I help?"

"Your two men – are they still touring?"

"Yes," the colonel replied.

"Good. I'd like to extend their stay. Jack Clarke has requested that they concentrate on a particular area. I'm sending you details and a new cover story. Can you loan them for a little longer?"

"Sure. Send me details," replied the colonel.

"Be in touch," said Sir Anthony as he rang off.

Thirty minutes later, a courier from MI6 arrived at Colonel Harriman's HQ on Park Lane. Raza and Jafar were about to go house-hunting, looking for a property to buy for their grandmother who wanted to return to the northeast of Pakistan where she was born.

52

16TH APRIL, 2011

Belardi was furious. Ibrahim had travelled from Karachi to Abbottabad with only one bodyguard and no real security to check he wasn't followed. The risk to the leader was unacceptable. If he had a free hand he would eliminate Ibrahim – he was proving careless. The problem was, as the leader had explained, they needed an accountant and administrator to oversee the team of people at their office in Karachi and the four men managing the operation in Europe, the USA, South America and Africa. The logistics were complicated and Belardi knew he could not manage that side of the operation. So Ibrahim lived – but he sent an email reiterating that he must not leave the office in Karachi. He was to sleep in the building until further notice.

*

Ibrahim was not surprised to receive Belardi's instructions; the two men did not get on. He also knew that he had survived purely because he alone knew the logistics and, importantly, all the bank details. To placate an angry bin Laden he had activated the third part of the plan to further flood the infidels with infected cosmetics and dairy products. The new Celebrity range of cosmetics was being manufactured and Stardust shampoo bottles had been relabelled in the UK. The marketing campaign was underway to promote the sale of the shampoo; two million bottles in the USA and one million in the UK. He had recently, through nominee corporations, purchased two dairies in the UK, one in Poland and three in the USA. They planned to impregnate firstly small capsules of cream, and then milk with toxic nanoparticles. The inclusion of the particles in creamer and milk would be another anonymous attack. Their Indian backer had already started deliveries of Celebrity deodorant and hairspray to Nigeria to be bottled and put in pressurised cans and then sent to the UK and USA. The Chinese backer was preparing the impregnated nanoparticles to send to the dairies to be included in creamer and milk.

Belardi was in Islamabad; he was meeting his contact in the ISI.

53

The prime minister had spent the last three hours with his press secretary, Justin Hayward, William Morgan, his chief spin doctor, and the deputy prime minister, writing his speech for the televised broadcast in two days' time. They were all surprised that the world's media had not, to date, latched on to the fact that eight western leaders were all broadcasting unexpectedly. The president of the United States would broadcast ahead of the European leaders due to the time difference. All the men sitting around the cabinet office table knew that the world news and the internet would be awash with comments before the prime minister's broadcast.

*

THURSDAY 18TH APRIL 1820HRS
(1320HRS WASHINGTON TIME)

The prime minister was nervously pacing the cabinet office. He had deliberately arranged for the broadcast to be made from this room where he felt comfortable – but viewing the earlier reaction to the president's speech he was nervous. The early American press reports were critical. 'Where were their security services?' demanded a late edition of the *New York Times*. 'Why did the Environment Protection Agency not have tougher product controls?' asked a reporter from *The Washington Post*. CBS reporters interviewed numerous experts on biotechnology and toxicokinetics. State governors declared that it was a federal matter covered by toxic substance legislation and the mayor of New York quoted the Federal Food, Drug and Cosmetic Act (his researchers must have been doing overtime). One clever reporter even listed the cost of the Stardust range: shampoo – $4.80, Hairspray – $2.70, deodorant – $2.55, shaving cream – $2.15. His point being that these prices were so competitive federal agencies should have been more vigilant and suspicious. Naturally the president had not revealed all he knew during his midday broadcast but television channels had reacted quickly and 'experts' had been discussing the catastrophic effect of this bio-attack, which was how it was being described, since the president's broadcast. Nanotechnology was being debated and discussed across the States – and blame was being apportioned. Several hospitals reported a surge in pregnant women visiting A&E. Angry women blocked an afternoon chat show's telephone lines and, as yet, the public at large didn't really understand the terrible consequences.

⋆

Number 10 Downing Street was a hive of activity. After news of the American president's broadcast had reached the media in the UK, the prime minister's press secretary wisely arranged a press conference after the PM's broadcast to the nation at 2030hrs GMT. The TV crews for both main channels had to position cameras and lighting in the cabinet office and a normal Thursday had become frantic. The prime minister wisely remained in his private quarters practising his TV broadcast and fine-tuning the press conference speech he was to make afterwards. At 1930hrs GMT his make-up was carefully applied, so as not to notice or mark his shirt. His hair was brushed and sprayed to remain in position; he picked up the aerosol making sure it was not, ironically, a Stardust product. The time had come to take up his position at the boardroom table in the cabinet office. The deputy prime minister and the leader of the main opposition in the house had been briefed earlier that morning and both offered to join him at the table to show solidarity – but he had declined. He knew that the news he was about to impart to the country would probably mean he would be unable to stand for a second term of office, but at least he would face the onslaught and he wouldn't hide. The lights facing him were bright but after a practice he was able to read the autocue without hesitation and felt he was ready. The transmission would be live on prime time television and last for three minutes.

"We're going live in five everybody," shouted a floor manager; the BBC and ITV seemed to be collaborating with lighting and some personnel. That five minutes seemed like an hour to the PM – but then the same man said "one minute" and a woman dabbed his brow and moved out of shot.

"Five, four, three, two, one." A man signalled to the prime minister who began to speak...

"I am talking to you this evening about something that has happened recently. You will remember the terrible bombing in London at the tube station in July 2005. I am afraid that the perpetrators, al-Qaeda, led by Osama bin Laden, have done something as appalling. In order to explain what has happened, I must tell you about the new biotechnology. It is called nanotechnology. This enables minute particles, which are undetectable by the human eye, to be injected into our bodies to help to cure illness. Work is being carried out to use this new biotechnology to help fight cancer. But this new technology has been corrupted by terrorists, who have used the principle but added toxic materials. This is the first bio-attack, using nanoparticles, that the West has had to endure and it is most of Europe, the USA and Canada that are bearing the brunt of this evil. What the terrorists have done is to add toxic chemical nanoparticles to everyday items such as shampoo, deodorant, toothpaste, shaving cream and other cosmetics using the brand name of Stardust. This brand of cosmetics, seemingly manufactured in Europe, is not what it appears. All their cosmetics contain nanoparticles which our scientists and universities have now identified as likely to be dangerous to human beings. This despicable attack on our very fabric will not go unpunished but in the meantime please take all unused Stardust cosmetics back to the supermarket or shop you bought them. Do not use them again. The government has prepared extensive briefing notes explaining this new bio-attack on our nation and you can go online – the web address will be shown after this broadcast – where you can view a film and notes explaining this terrorist atrocity. Lessons have been learnt and I can assure you that steps have been taken to control this new technology. Our friends in America and Europe will also be reporting today this attack on all their citizens. Rest assured we will find those responsible and bring them to justice."

The transmission ended with complete silence in the room. The television crews had not been briefed and there was a stunned silence.

The prime minister got up and left. Now he had to speak to the world's media.

54

The first broadcast by the president of the United States had been shown to the premier of the State Council in China, members of the Politburo and the general secretary of the Communist Party. The premier was the first to speak.

"If the Americans find out, and I believe they will, that the chemicals added to these nanoparticles were designed, added and manufactured by one of our chemical companies in Shanghai, we can expect retaliation. An analysis has been carried out as to what their reaction will be, as follows..."

The six men present at the meeting read the conclusions:

The Americans will order an attack on the factory manufacturing the toxic nanoparticles; probably an airstrike by Tomahawk missiles launched from their sixth fleet entering the China Sea.

The Americans will order a nuclear attack on Shanghai and the surrounding area – the missiles will be launched from submarines.

The Americans will ask the other members of the UN Security Council to expel China and for the UN to impose economic sanctions which would be damaging commercially and restrict trade.

The Americans will expel all Chinese diplomats and restrict travel by all Chinese nationals. Other UN states would be similarly encouraged to expel diplomats and Chinese business assets could be impounded.

The Americans may ask that all UN members seize and confiscate Chinese assets and impound our currency held in their banks.

A combination of the previously mentioned.

"We know that the president is a reserved, prudent man but his advisors, particularly the head of the armed forces, are not," said the state premier. "I have ordered our military to be on the highest alert. Our warships are all being moved, as we speak, to strategic defensive positions. What we have to decide is if they launch a nuclear attack, do we retaliate?"

The normally reserved general secretary of the Communist Party replied.

"The Americans have a far superior fire power and nuclear arsenal. If we retaliate they will surely obliterate us."

"But are we then to stand by and take no action?" asked a senior Politburo member.

"No. I suggest we move to a defensive strategy but act to hand over the bodies of the two men who have caused this situation. In addition, we will offer financial restitution to all the countries that have been attacked," said the premier. "We will have to take this matter to a full meeting of the Politburo, and if my suggestion is approved, we will approach the Americans first."

They all nodded and left, most with an apprehension about how their place in the world order was likely to have dramatically changed.

*

Cheng Kuang, the Chinese entrepreneur and owner of the industrial chemical manufacturing plant in Shanghai, was arrested and taken to Qincheng Prison, a maximum security prison located in the Changping district of Beijing. The Ministry of Public Security was chosen by the premier to carry out the arrests and Lihua Nha Ping, the head of the Ministry of State Security, followed Cheng Kuang into custody. Liu Hong, the head of the Ministry of Public Security, supervised the interrogation of both men. It did not take long to reveal that Cheng Kuang had been manufacturing and supplying al-Qaeda with the toxic nanoparticles and shipping them by tanker to Marseille, Colombia, Somalia, Nigeria, Yemen and Mexico. Lihua Nha Ping had been providing al-Qaeda with information on US and British naval activities and monitoring emails and telephone calls from the secret services of both countries concerning bin Laden or al-Qaeda. Cheng Kuang could not admit that some members of the Politburo knew of his activities, as he was informed that all his family would be eliminated if he spread those foul rumours.

The Chinese admired the achievements of Cheng Kuang in manufacturing lethal nanoparticles, and transferred the scientists and biologists that had developed the process to another facility far from Shanghai to continue working on biochemicals, toxicokinetics and biotechnology. Cheng Kuang and Lihua Nha Ping were both executed and their bodies kept in cold storage in the event the West required positive sight of their punishment.

55

Belardi had no warning that the Chinese supplier of the lethal concoction of nanoparticles had been arrested. Ibrahim had tried to contact him to verify that two tankers were en route to deliver the liquid containing the nanoparticles to Nigeria and Colombia – he had not received a reply. The regular encrypted emails from Lihua Nha Ping of the Chinese Secret Service had also stopped.

★

Raza and Jafar were systematically sweeping north east Pakistan between Islamabad as far as Abbottabad. Using their cover as seeking to buy a house for their grandmother who was born in the region, they were accompanied by a genuine associate of Plantinum, an Islamabad estate agent. The cousins did not immediately concentrate on the Abbottabad area but started their supposed search for property in Haripur, Murree and Birote. The estate agent was completely taken in by their cover story but when they proposed to travel up the N35 towards Abbottabad he was very reluctant. The lure of a commission persuaded him, and the three men travelled towards the target area. They had passed a military base some two kilometres back when a battered four-wheel drive cut them up and forced them to stop. Raza and Jafar were both armed but had already agreed with Adam, the MI6 agent in Islamabad, to only use the weapons in self-defence. Two Pakistani men approached their hire car. Speaking in Hindko, their driver explained what they were doing, whilst nervously eyeing the AK-47 rifle casually slung over the man's shoulder. The men told them to turn around – this area was a security region and had no houses for sale. They complied.

★

Colonel Harriman studied the email from Raza. *Had to stop searching for grandmother's house three kilometres from the army base on the Kakul road in Abbottabad. Feel Abbottabad could be a key area to search for a property – do you require we continue?* The colonel called Sir Anthony and arranged a meeting.

★

Jack Clarke was aware that the two Brits had been stopped as Ibrahim had been. The drone circled the area and sent real-time pictures to Langley. He had already pinpointed a large compound with a house in the centre as a possible and now concentrated the aerial spy on this property. His senior operative in the area, Willis, was attempting to penetrate the area and eyeball the house by approaching the compound across country from the south. He could only travel at night, so it was taking him some time to get into position. Jack took the call from Sir Anthony.

"Okay, will Harriman let his guys try and get closer?" Jack asked.

"They are planning to do just that," replied Sir Anthony.

"Good. Keep me in the loop," replied Jack, not bothering to tell Sir Anthony about Willis.

★

Raza and Jafar studied the map. If the house was, as suspected, near Abbottabad, al-Qaeda had chosen well. Only one main road with a large army barracks on the Kakul road nearby. The men who stopped their car earlier had made it clear that nobody was going down the Kakul road. That meant the only way to study the house and the compound was to approach from Kakul, the nearest village, going across ploughed fields with no cover. They knew that the triangle-shaped compound hid a substantial house. Adam had told them it was at the end of a dirt road, 1.3km southwest of the army base and north east of the city centre of Abbottabad. They used the cover of night to reach a row of trees east of the property and dug-in using camouflage nets to conceal their position.

Willis Coogan had approached the compound from the south, also at night, but finding no cover found a derelict house about a thousand metres away and waited for other CIA agents to arrive.

56

20TH APRIL, 2011

The US president had taken a battering from the news channels which had obtained more information about the penetration of the Stardust cosmetics than he had admitted in his television broadcast. Most TV channels and newspapers had found biochemists to elaborate on the formation of nanoparticles and the possible toxic chemicals that had been introduced to Americans by using the Stardust range. The media deliberated on the number of people exposed. Some estimates were wildly out but others, by collecting data from supermarket chains, began to piece together the awful truth. The president knew that his advisors would not be able to deny the substantial exposure of American citizens for much longer. He needed a quick win and the obvious target was al-Qaeda and bin Laden.

The president summoned his National Security Council to a meeting at the White House.

"Gentlemen, the CIA has a laudable case for a raid on

a compound in north west Pakistan where they believe bin Laden is hiding. Samuel, please elaborate."

Samuel Goldmuir activated the large screen at the end of the room. "This is the compound at a place called Abbottabad where we believe bin Laden is holed-up. One of his commanders, Ibrahim, was tracked by CIA operatives and our satellite to this compound a week ago. He left after a short whilst, returning to Karachi where he has an office. This is now under surveillance. We also have agents on the ground watching the compound in Abbottabad and they report armed men intercepting all approaching vehicles and gunmen at the gate of the compound. You can see the layout of this compound. The metal entrance gates lead to an outer area and a small building. This leads through a gate to the larger three-storey building with a flat roof. You will see two satellite dishes but strangely there is no telephone line or internet connection. The residents of this building are elusive but we have a photograph of a man on the balcony of the main building who we believe to be Osama bin Laden." He brought up a picture on the screen.

"We also followed this man, a known al-Qaeda courier we know as Abu Khan, a Kuwait-born Pakistani, to this property."

Another picture of a bearded man was shown.

"Our conclusion is that this is the hideout of Osama bin Laden and we recommend a task force raid the compound as soon as possible."

⋆

Sir Anthony Greenwood had spent a rather unpleasant meeting with the home secretary who had criticised the fact that a spy for al-Qaeda had been discovered working at MI6. There was no defence and sadly Sir Anthony had lost the argument. The young man, Joseph Dyer, would not stand trial. MI5 would deal with the matter – the government simply could not afford a public scandal hot on the heels of the prime minister's broadcast, which had already created a media frenzy. Sir Anthony knew the unfortunate wretch would be found having committed suicide. There would be some speculation, but nobody would know what he actually did at MI6, and the police investigation would reveal a troubled man who decided to end it all.

Sir Anthony left Whitehall to meet John Harriman; he needed another favour.

Colonel Harriman had not been surprised when Sir Anthony requested a meeting. Two of his operatives had been watching, from a hide, the compound in Abbottabad in north west Pakistan for several days. On the first night they checked the trash cans for clues as to the occupants but no rubbish was put out and none the next day. There was minimal movement to report except a woman, accompanied by a bearded man, who went to the nearby village on the second day and bought groceries. Raza, one of Colonel Harriman's observers, said that they bought a great deal of groceries for the one family rumoured in the locality to occupy the compound. The only other movement was the arrival of a man who was photographed and details sent through Adam, an MI6 agent, then onward to London and forwarded to the CIA at Langley.

Colonel Harriman and Sir Anthony studied the map on the table.

"A destroyer will be docked here." Sir Anthony pointed to Karachi Port. "Raza, Jafar and Adam Runfold," he referred to John Harriman's two operatives and the MI6 agent in Pakistan, "with members of the Pakistan Secret Intelligence Special Forces, commanded by your friend Colonel Akrim, will grab Ibrahim at his office in Karachi. They will take him to the dockside to be put on board HMS *Coventry*. The ship will sail immediately for Muscat where Ibrahim will be transferred at the international airport to an RAF VC10 and flown to Brize Norton. Your men, Adam and four of Akrim's special forces, will gain access to Ibrahim's office, drug him and hopefully prevent him taking the cyanide, assuming he also has a hollowed-out tooth."

"Do we tell the Americans?" asked Colonel Harriman.

Sir Anthony thought for a moment. "No, I don't think so. Let's keep it a British affair."

The two men parted, Sir Anthony to arrange for HMS *Coventry* to steam to Karachi from the Indian Ocean where she was on a goodwill tour of India. Colonel Harriman returned to his HQ on Park Lane and put in a call to his friend Colonel Akrim. Later he called a meeting in the boardroom with his number two, Major Smith, and the two other men he was sending to help capture Ibrahim, Captains Harrington and Johnston. He arranged for his two men and himself a reservation on a British Airways flight from Heathrow to Karachi.

57

Raza and Jafar were delighted that their uncomfortable stakeout of bin Laden's probable hideout in Abbottabad had been called off. Adam Runfold had contacted them on a satellite phone and told them to drive to Karachi. A day later and having driven all night, Adam met both men at the Ramada Plaza at the airport. Having briefed them on the forthcoming raid on Ibrahim's office, Adam left them to sleep and went to seek a rental property close to Ibrahim's office block in Saddar Town, a district of Karachi. Adam had not been told that the CIA was already tracking Ibrahim and when he had the chance at the hotel in Islamabad, where Ibrahim stayed a week ago, he got Raza to place a tracking device on his SUV. This had led MI6 back to Karachi and Ibrahim's office.

★

Colonel Harriman, having flown to Karachi from London, was looking forward to meeting his old friend. He had already discussed the operation over a secure line and knew Colonel Akrim could be relied upon to help him.

The man he was meeting in Karachi, Colonel Akrim, had brought a special forces unit to the SAS training base in Hereford in 1983. Captain Harriman had been the liaison and he made a lifelong friend. He entered the bar of the Pearl Continental Hotel in Karachi city centre dressed in civvies and smiled as he held out his hand.

"John, how good to see you – and looking fit and well," said Colonel Akrim, as the two men warmly shook hands.

"And you, Usman, the world is being kind?" asked Colonel Harriman.

"Oh, I can't complain, although I am becoming increasingly anxious that I retire in one piece," Colonel Akrim replied.

John Harriman knew that his friend operated on the high-risk border between Pakistan and Afghanistan; Indian country as many of his colleagues in the SAS had called the lawless areas.

"You heard about Caroline?"

"Yes, I am so sorry. She was a fine woman." Colonel Akrim had been introduced to Caroline Bland by John Harriman early in 2001, when the British were occupying and policing parts of Afghanistan. Then, acting Brigadier Harriman had gone to Afghanistan to see for himself the conditions his SAS units would face.

The two men ordered coffee and a serious look came over Akrim's face. "I have made arrangements for six of my most trusted special forces to assist with the raid. But bear in mind that some members of the ISI are Taliban sympathisers and it is rumoured several senior officers actively assist them. We must therefore carry out this operation the day after tomorrow."

"I agree; the sooner the better, and the destroyer, HMS *Coventry*, will be docked at Karachi Port by then."

They discussed the operational details and parted. Colonel Harriman would not be involved in the raid on Ibrahim's office, but Colonel Akrim would lead the operation himself.

★

Posing as revenue officers from the Pakistan Federal Board of Revenue, two of Colonel Akrim's men in civvies pressed the intercom on the wall of Ibrahim's office. It was common knowledge that the Federal Board was proactively seeking the 2.3 million wealthy tax defaulters and that the Pakistan government had granted them unparalleled authority to investigate suspected individuals and firms. Ibrahim's front was import and export of carpets and would be a revenue officer's target. The receptionist checked with the second floor – should she let them in? Two men went to the front door to question the reason for the unannounced call. Both men were shot with silenced pistols and two soldiers followed by Captain Harrington, Raza, Jafar and Adam swiftly neutralised the receptionist with a stun gun and raced up the stairs to the first floor. Three other members of the Pakistan Intelligence Service Special Forces went up the fire escape with Captain Johnston.

Ibrahim realised something was wrong and sent two of his men down to the first floor whilst he hastily tried to disable his computer. He thought for a brief second about biting into the false tooth then his instinct for survival took over.

"Come," he ordered his last two men, and they opened the fire door and began to descend. A burst of the Uzi submachine gun by the first of the special forces killed both Ibrahim's bodyguards, and he was zapped by 50,000 volts from Captain Johnston's stun gun. When he reached the prone figure, Captain Johnston injected him with sodium pentothal which would subdue him until he was aboard the destroyer. He smelt his breath – garlic, not the acrylic smell if he had taken cyanide.

"Okay, we have him," reported Captain Johnston to Colonel Akrim as he carried the prone Ibrahim with another soldier down the metal stairs.

Captain Harrington, Raza, Jafar and Adam had not encountered any resistance but one of Colonel Akrim's men had taken a bullet, a shoulder wound, as they reached the first floor. They began to pack up all the computer equipment. Raza and Jafar read paper files – some they kept, others they dropped on the floor. The operation was over in eight minutes. Ibrahim was dumped on the back seat of a black SUV, and Captain Johnston got in with him. The ISI soldiers got in another vehicle and the British left in the third. Colonel Akrim watched from an alleyway opposite from a parked BMW. He phoned John Harriman. "Merchandise on its way."

The convoy of vehicles reached the port and pulled up alongside the gangplank from HMS *Coventry*. Two marines helped carry Ibrahim up the gangplank followed by the four Brits. Captain Harrington shook hands with the five Pakistani men and followed Colonel Harriman, who had joined him on board the destroyer.

⋆

Wilson McCourt watched the raid on Ibrahim's office with some incredulity. The CIA had occupied the third floor of offices opposite, not intending to grab Ibrahim but to keep him under surveillance. Now some guys had raided the office and bundled Ibrahim into a black SUV. McCourt had sent Mitchell on his motorbike to tail them, and then contacted Langley.

Jack Clarke muttered out loud as the message reached him.

"Who the fuck has taken him? ISI? Taliban? Find out quickly." he instructed McCourt in Karachi.

58

28TH APRIL, 2011

Belardi was not an indecisive man but he was faced with a problem. There had been no communications from the Chinese for over a week. Osama bin Laden had replied to the message he sent through the courier, Abu Khan, that he hadn't detected any activity in the Abbottabad area and the ISI, through Lt General Akif Gandapur, had no reports of American activity. But nevertheless he was nervous. Ibrahim's office was not answering its satellite phone – he decided to send one of his men, Alvi, to Karachi to investigate.

Alvi contacted him the following day. "The office is closed. No sign of anyone," he reported.

"Any sign of forced entry?" asked Belardi.

"No. And none of the occupants of the offices in the vicinity reported anything."

Belardi didn't like Ibrahim, or his naivety concerning personal security, but where was he?

His instinct was to move from the Islamabad office. He retrieved a false passport, driving licence and credit cards in the name of Asad Meshgi, made a call to Lt General Gandapur and drove to Jhelum. He had a safe house there, and it was close to the Indian border – nobody would expect him to go to India. Encrypted messages had been sent to the four managers of the worldwide operations asking them when they had last had an email or phone call from Ibrahim. The replies concerned him – it had been three days since Ibrahim had been in touch with any of the operational managers. That was very significant. Should he suggest Osama leave his compound?

★

Ibrahim had been flown from Muscat to Brize Norton on an RAF VC10 and then transferred to Saxon Court, a mansion in Surrey, minutes from the M23 motorway but completely hidden from the road. The doctor on HMS *Coventry*, the destroyer that had taken Ibrahim to Muscat, had removed the false tooth that contained a lethal dose of cyanide. Now Ibrahim was being interrogated.

★

McCourt, the CIA senior operative in Karachi, had phoned Jack Clarke at Langley with the news. Jack banged his fist on the table and went upstairs to talk to Director Goldmuir. A planning meeting was underway concerning the raid on bin Laden's supposed hideout in Abbottabad, which he interrupted. He explained what had happened.

"What? Surely not!" exclaimed the director of the CIA.

"No doubt about it – taken on board one of their destroyers, which we satellite-tracked to Muscat. We suspect he was flown to the UK, landing at any one of three possible places. I have alerted London to find out where they're holding him."

Director Goldmuir didn't explain to the group meeting, convened to discuss killing or lifting bin Laden, why his mood had changed. But he knew he had to suggest to the president that the date for the raid was brought forward. *Christ, what a mess-up,* he thought.

*

The president, the secretary of state and the chairman of the Joint Chiefs of Staff listened as Samuel Goldmuir outlined the proposal planned by the CIA and the special operations commander, Vice Admiral Dearing. He talked over the screenshot on the giant television. "Called Operation Neptune Spear, our Special Activities Division and a detachment of the Naval Special Warfare Development Group will be supported by the Special Operations Aviation Regiment."

The director of the CIA outlined the plan and answered questions from the three men. Finally, the president asked, "Why have you brought the date forward a week? Surely that's unnecessary. Bin Laden seems to have been there for some time. Why are we rushing the plan to take him?"

The director of the CIA had anticipated the question. "Unfortunately, Mr President, the Brits have lifted Ibrahim, one of bin Laden's senior commanders, and we think this might spook him to run."

The president looked quizzical. "The Brits have Ibrahim? Surely we had him under surveillance to pick him up after Operation Neptune Spear?"

"Yes, but regrettably nobody told the Brits, is that it?" asked the secretary of state.

"In a nutshell," replied Samuel Goldmuir.

"Christ, what a foul-up," said General Paterson.

"It was a mistake not including the Brits in the loop, but we were concerned about the security of the whole operation. One of their MI6 guys was an al-Qaeda spy," replied Goldmuir.

"All right, I'll phone the British prime minister and ask him to keep Ibrahim on ice without mentioning the forthcoming raid," said the president.

"Is it possible Ibrahim could be passed to us? We have more resources to interrogate him," asked General Paterson.

"I'll mention it," said the president.

The meeting closed agreeing the revised timetable of Operation Neptune Spear, with Samuel Goldmuir figuring he had got off lightly. Luckily he knew about the MI6 mole from an indiscreet MI5 man in London.

59

2ND MAY, 2011

The president watched the massive screen as the black images of four helicopters closed in on what he had been told was bin Laden's compound. The briefing earlier had informed him that the helicopters would fly from Afghanistan with two teams of US Navy SEALs arriving at around 0030hrs on Monday. The two Black Hawk helicopters would set down in the compound and the twenty-four SEALs would capture the occupants. The president knew the risks – they were operating 100 miles inside Pakistan and there was a military barracks close to the area in Abbottabad. He had joined the national security officials in the situation room watching the night vision images sent by the Sentinel drone flying high above the target area. The video links with the CIA headquarters were fed to the president and his team as the raid unfolded. Suddenly he was alerted to a potential disaster. One of the Black Hawks had a malfunction as its tail grazed the wall of the compound – but skilfully the pilot managed a soft crash landing and all the navy SEALs successfully left the stricken helicopter. He was receiving a commentary from the CIA.

"A team has just breached the walls and doors. They are in the block building where we believe bin Laden is hiding. Gun fire from the compound."

Minutes, which seemed like hours to the anxious president, passed then he heard one of the Chinook helicopters had arrived to take off the SEALs and any computer kit they had found. Then the code word he had been waiting for: Geronimo EKIA. He was relieved yet found himself saddened that he was responsible for the death of another man, as the code meant bin Laden was dead and they had his body. He hated being responsible for the death of another human being but it went with the pay grade. He knew the body would be taken to USS *Carl Vinson*, an aircraft carrier, in the Arabian Sea. He had instructed that if bin Laden was killed he would be buried at sea, but in accordance with Islamic precepts and practice. The stricken Black Hawk was blown-up and the command room of the CIA cheered as the last of the raiding party left.

60

Belardi heard his mobile bleep – incoming email from Lt General Gandapur, his contact in the Pakistan Security Service.

> Osama bin Laden captured or dead. American raid shortly after midnight. Suggest you move on.

Belardi thumped the table with his fist, said a silent prayer then began to clear his desk – no time for sentiment. At 1.15am, Belardi was on the move. With only a driver he crossed the border into India and drove to Srinagar. His contact in Srinagar provided a different car and he drove on towards New Delhi. It was a long journey of over 850 kilometres and he chose to stop at Jalandhar and booked into the Maya Hotel. Reaching New Delhi late the following day he found a flight to Mumbai. Using his new identity, as a Saudi businessman Mohamed Sarraf, he boarded the two-hour flight. There was no first class so he sat at the rear of the plane in economy. For once he had to go through normal arrivals showing his false passport. He knew that all passengers were photographed but he had cut his hair and shaved his beard. He now had a small goatee beard, typical of a Saudi national. Belardi had contacted the Indian billionaire, Madura Chatterjee, who met him at the dock at Mumbai.

"Welcome, my friend," said Madura. "It is a sad day." He referred to the death of bin Laden killed by the Americans nearly two days ago.

"Yes, but he will have taken his rightful place in the kingdom of heaven," replied Belardi.

"I have arranged for you to travel as a passenger on one of my tankers sailing to Beirut. The captain has given up his cabin, but the conditions will reflect that this is not a passenger ship," said Madura.

Belardi nodded.

"I advise you to go into hiding as the Americans will have taken computer data and I believe they have Ibrahim. I have briefed my three sons who will take over our enterprise," said Madura. "And I intend to disappear. Have you warned our other friends?" He referred to the billionaire backers of the enterprise, the Saudi, Farid Al-Kazaz, and the Russian, Alexail Pankov. He knew the fourth backer of the Tears of the West, a Chinese man, had gone off the radar.

"Yes, they have been warned. Alexail will have a problem because he lives in London and the Russians would like to kill him for other indiscretions. Farid is well-protected." Belardi knew that Farid had a close connection with the Saudi royal family.

"It is goodbye then. If you wish to communicate with me do so through my sons. You have their details?"

"Yes. May Allah be with you," said Belardi and followed by his bodyguard boarded the Indian-registered tanker.

The ship steamed at a leisurely ten knots through the Arabian Sea to the Gulf of Aden hugging the coast then into the Red Sea. They passed through the Suez Canal and after nearly fifteen days at sea Belardi was happy to see the port of Beirut.

He was met by two men from Hezbollah who took him to a safe house in Rashid Nakhle Street in a suburb of Beirut. The non-descript white house had a fast internet connection as the district also had a police station and a courthouse. Belardi sent encrypted messages to the worldwide commanders who organised the distribution of cosmetics. Black, a Pakistani who was the al-Qaeda commander in the Middle East, Green, an Iranian based in Cape Town, Blue based in Marseille and Zurich and Red based in Mexico City would all be expecting instructions following bin Laden's death. Belardi instructed the European commander Blue and Red the American commander to send the new Celebrity shampoo to the supermarkets in Britain and America, then go to a safe house. Each commander had an elaborate network of safe houses and false passports. He instructed Green and Black to go into hiding immediately fearing Ibrahim was in American hands and would reveal many secrets.

61

Ibrahim had not endured the torture for very long. He had never considered he would die for the cause; in any event they had removed his false tooth making it impossible for him to commit suicide. He was surprised to find his captors were British but this initially gave him renewed hope. He did not think the British would act as aggressively as the Americans – but he was surprised.

The torture had started after he had been taken from the aircraft. A very uncomfortable flight handcuffed to a seat and then driven for about an hour, hooded, to some sort of house with cells. Kept in a cell for twenty-four hours with loud noise keeping him from sleeping and men continually waking him and beating him with rubber pipes was bad enough. But then they stripped him and began to soak him with a high powered hose and freezing cold water. After each session they took him back to the cell that only had a dirty mattress on the floor. He endured but then he was taken to another room. Powerful lights were shone in his face and leads strapped to his naked body. They began to question him. At first he gave them nothing – but then they started the torture using electricity. He could not withstand the intense pain. He gave them what they probably already knew: his name, rank in al-Qaeda, and his connection with bin Laden. He spoke about meeting other al-Qaeda operatives in Mexico, Somalia, Zurich and Lebanon.

He told them about the two meetings on the *Good Queen Bess* in the Mediterranean. He gave them Suleman's name in London but said that other men he met had code names: Blue, Black, Red and Green; and he didn't know their real names. He confirmed that they had been impregnating Stardust cosmetics with toxic nanoparticles. He tried to maintain he did not know the ingredients in the nanoparticles, but when they started the electric torture again he admitted he knew the chemical company in Shanghai, who manufactured the particles and added the toxic chemicals. He gave up the name of the company and the Chinese businessman who ran the firm. They did not seem to know much about the distribution so he kept quiet. He found once he started to talk that his cell was changed and a bed provided with a mattress.

He was given hot food and clothes. Then the bombshell – they told him bin Laden was dead. At first he didn't believe them, but they showed him film on a TV screen and told him where he had been captured. He knew the information was correct. He prayed, but was not delivered. They began to press him on the system of communications. He knew they must have his laptop computer but probably couldn't break the encrypted code. He tried to resist but the threat of more torture…

He tried to bargain, but his tormentors simply beat him or reattached him to the electrical wires that he feared most. He gave them the code. They began to ask questions about Belardi. They showed him his photograph. They knew a great deal about him. There seemed little point denying Belardi's existence or involvement as they had a photograph of them together on the boat. He sobbed when they attached him to the chair and the electrical wires.

"What more can I tell you? I have given you everything."

But they continued and he gave more: the ports where the deliveries entered each country and then finally the names of the four billionaire backers and the reason why they provided the money for the attack on the West. He thought, *It is the first time I have surprised them.*

62

The prime minister presided over the Cobra meeting. Present were the home secretary, the secretary of state for defence, the deputy prime minister, the secretary of state for health, the attorney general and the chief of the defence staff. The emergency council met to discuss issues which crossed over department borders and the subject today certainly did that. The prime minister brought the meeting to order.

"Gentlemen, this is a meeting to bring you up to speed on developments concerning the attack on our citizens by al-Qaeda terrorists using toxic chemical nanoparticles mixed with off-the-shelf cosmetics. MI6 has given me information, which suggests that the attack is far from over. We know that al-Qaeda must have a backer or backers with considerable biotechnology skills and resources. We have information," – he didn't disclose that MI6 was interrogating Ibrahim at a security services' property in Surrey – "that points to a Chinese billionaire businessman who owns a factory in Shanghai which is producing all the toxic nanoparticles. These nanoparticles are transported by tanker to pharmaceutical factories at various locations for mixing with the cosmetics. They are then included in various cosmetic products and marketed under the Stardust range through supermarkets and other outlets."

The prime minster took a sip of water, glanced at his notes and continued.

"Since the death of bin Laden, MI6 believes that one of his commanders, Belardi, also known as Mansur Ahmedi, has taken over the attack on us, continuing to use the code name Tears of the West. The other countries we know have been subject to these terrorist atrocities are America, Canada, Germany, France, Holland, Belgium, Norway and now, we believe, Israel. Others inadvertently have exposed their citizens by importing this brand of cosmetics, including Spain, Italy, Greece, Cyprus, Austria and Portugal. We were deliberately targeted and the secretary of state for health will shortly tell us how many of our citizens are likely to have been contaminated. Since my broadcast there has been a march of ten thousand female students culminating in an open air meeting in Trafalgar Square. There were a number of arrests for public disorder offences but there have been very few hostile demonstrations. A number of mosques have been attacked which I abhor. The media has, as expected, conducted a thorough analysis of the atrocity and is continuing to examine the crime and whose fault it all is. I have noted several journalists beginning to point the finger at this government. The general election in three months time is the only reason I have not resigned."

They all began to gush and object to the prime minister's suggestion.

"No. I would have gone but for one simple fact: the party's chances of winning the general election are minimal on the back of this outrage. The government will be blamed, and it is preferable for the party that I take the responsibility and fall on my sword after the election."

The attorney general, a rather sombre and serious man, spoke first. "Prime Minister, the media is not, in the main, blaming you. Surely you will survive this setback and lead us with confidence into the election?"

"Thank you, Sir Geoffrey, for your confidence, but we are destined to lose by a significant margin. Consider this: up until now, the opposition has kept its powder dry, preferring to let the media reach its own conclusion, and that will be that our security services and others under this administration have failed. It's only a matter of time before they discover the true extent of the damage, the prospect of two million women being unable to conceive, the effect on the foetus for those that are pregnant and a million impotent men who are likely to develop testicular cancer. And then the children impregnated with toxic chemicals we cannot remove. There will be an outcry. But enough speculation, home secretary – you have some news for us?"

"Thank you, prime minister. Yes, we and the Americans have tracked bin Laden's second-in-command to Lebanon. The CIA is hot on his tail and hope to capture him soon. Concerning public outrage, there have been meetings, mainly of women's groups in various parts of the country, but police reports confirm that so far the speakers have delivered information, not rhetoric. What I am about to tell you is one of the worst aspects of this terrorist attack."

He paused for effect as the ministers looked at him expectantly. "Not only is the terrorist attack designed to destabilise our nation's natural birth rate, but we now understand that the backers of al-Qaeda expect, in the years to come, to recuperate their expenditure by selling babies to our citizens."

The normally unflappable prime minister spoke gravely, "Elaborate please."

"Information has come to hand that next year the backers intend to advertise babies for sale; Chinese and

Indian babies to be precise, sold for up to twenty thousand pounds each."

"That's utterly outrageous. Is the intel reliable?" asked the deputy prime minister.

"Yes, and they have a business plan anticipating the sale each month of one hundred thousand babies in the UK, two million in America and at least one hundred thousand in all the European countries affected by the bio-attack on the childbearing women and men," he replied. "The backers of this outrage have set up dozens of medical centres where women will conceive in India and China and then they will advertise the babies on the internet."

"I suppose people will be desperate," said the attorney general.

"That, gentlemen, is my point, and why this administration will be blamed," said the prime minister.

"Al-Qaeda was expecting to potentially increase the numbers of women unable to conceive and sterile men each year, thus making the West virtually sterile. To maintain our population, we would have to open our borders to unlimited immigration and not only within the EU. We would be competing with other countries seeking unaffected people who were able to reproduce. Our own citizens would have to adopt a child or accept that their death was the end of their family line. Remember, even their children are likely to be impregnated."

"What a doomsday scenario," said the chief of defence staff.

"They only succeed if we are unable to find an antidote," said the health minister. "And all our pharmaceutical companies, universities and our friends worldwide are working on a solution."

"That's the positive viewpoint we must endeavour to explain to the media which will do us most good," said the deputy prime minister.

"I agree," said the prime minister. "But Newsnight and Panorama last night were enjoying explaining toxicokinetics and biotechnology – it increased their ratings. Look at last night's programme discussing how some particles containing toxic substances could block both female egg growth and ovulation, and they showed that our Department of Health had many failings in preventing chemicals, such as phthalates, being included in cosmetics prior to this attack."

"Surely we can show that the Department of Health examined these issues?" asked the deputy prime minister. The health minister glanced at his notes. He knew that this question would be posed by someone.

"There is a committee on mutagenicity of chemicals in food, consumer products and the environment." But he knew this was a weak response as it was an advisory non-departmental public body.

"What about the House of Lords' Select Committee on Science and Technology?" asked the home secretary.

"The committee and the Food Standards Authority have both taken the view that no food product or packaging using nanotechnology should be allowed into the market without proof of safety," replied the health minister.

"Yes, that's all very well, but who is monitoring the situation? What body specifically can we say examines products and food for any breach of what appears to be some sort of voluntary code?" asked the deputy prime minister.

"In short, we have no such body with the teeth to ban products or food that is actively analysing the market," replied the attorney general.

"We're setting up, through the Department of Health and the Environment Agency, a department which will prepare a database of hazard in food or any goods sold to the public," said the health minister.

"Gentlemen, all this will be sadly seen as locking the stable door after the horse has bolted," said the home secretary.

"What I believe is essential, is that we continue to encourage all our universities and pharmaceutical companies to design and engineer nano-materials to eliminate adverse health effects and to develop nanotechnology in a reasonable and sustainable manner," said the prime minister.

"Why?" asked the deputy prime minister. "Haven't we seen the devastating effect of this biotechnology?"

"That's the point. If we don't do it somebody else will and they could hold a gun to our head if we don't understand the technology, not to mention keeping our place in the development of these new biotechnologies," replied the prime minister.

"Have we decided how to deal with the involvement of the Chinese chemical company in manufacturing and producing these toxic nanoparticles?" asked the chief of defence staff, who had sat listening to the politicians as they tried to find a way out of the mess.

"I'm more concerned as to how the Americans will react," replied the prime minister. "When you consider that they have upwards of forty million of their citizens impregnated with these toxic nanoparticles, they could easily overreact."

"Do they know about the Chinese chemical company?" asked the deputy prime minister.

"Not yet, but we have the intel and have little choice than to share," replied the prime minister. "I intend to make a personal call to the president before MI6 sends the CIA the dossier we have prepared."

"We also have other information leading us to the other backers of the al-Qaeda bio-attack," said the home secretary. "There are three other backers: one an Indian billionaire who owns a number of global companies, including subsidiaries in the UK, another backer, a Saudi, a close confidant of their royal family, and finally a Russian oligarch living in London."

"Has the Russian been arrested?" asked the attorney general.

"No. For the moment he has escaped the net," replied the home secretary.

Damn good job, thought the attorney general, *because I haven't a clue what he would be charged with.*

The telephone rang in the meeting room. They all looked at each other as the prime minister's secretary knocked and entered.

"Sorry about that – the foreign secretary is on the secure line for you, prime minister."

The prime minister excused himself and left the room. A few minutes later he returned, looking ashen.

"I regret to advise, gentlemen, that CBS, the American worldwide news network, is running a story in four hours time on the actual toxic chemicals used in the bio-attack. It is intending to describe in great detail the biological implications of each chemical to the female and male reproductive systems and the risks associated with heart problems, liver, kidney, lung, testicular and brain cancer," said the prime minister.

"Oh dear." The deputy prime minister looked glum.

"I think we can expect our television channels to pick up on this tonight and our press tomorrow," said the prime minister.

"Well, we can't deny it, if it's accurate," said the home secretary.

"No, I think we need to be prepared for a battering tomorrow," said the deputy prime minister.

"I'm wondering if all the bad news shouldn't be delivered at once," said the prime minister.

They all looked at him.

"Perhaps now the timing is right for me to broadcast again and reveal the numbers of people we believe are infected."

A debate followed and they all finally agreed that the prime minster was right. They concluded that as there would be a huge public backlash led by television commentators and the popular press, why not reveal all the bad news?

The prime minister closed the meeting, went to his private flat and contemplated his resignation. When he told two million women they were unable to conceive and a million men they were impotent and what about the children! He knew his days leading the party were over.

The deputy prime minister and home secretary walked to their cars together.

"Do you think he'll go?" asked the deputy prime minister.

"I would think so. He's getting several thousand hate mail letters every day and attacked on social media. His children have been kept back from school. Who do you think will stand against you?" prompted the home secretary.

"You?" He laughed and got in his car.

Out of every political setback is an opportunity, thought the home secretary.

63

Belardi took the call from a Hezbollah commander in Beirut and reacted immediately. Calling his bodyguard, they collected some belongings, went to the car, which pulled up outside, and left. A light aircraft would fly them from the nearby airport outside Beirut to Arak in Iraq. He had already arranged a safe house.

★

"Ten minutes; how close can you get?" said Jack Clarke. A team of CIA analysts and agents in Lebanon was endeavouring to track where Belardi had gone – but so far a dead end.

"Tell Willis in Beirut to pick up Hezbollah commanders. I'll call the State Department and get them to pressurise the Lebanese army to help. Somebody got him out. He cannot have gone to Israel, so I would lay a bet on Iran or Iraq."

★

The Chinese ambassador, Chang Liu, sat with Franklyn Browne, declined the offer of tea, and quickly got to the point. Speaking in good English, he said, "Mr Secretary, I have come to offer an apology on behalf of the Chinese people for not realising that one of our citizens was helping the terrorist organisation al-Qaeda."

"Chang Liu, please be explicit – what are you saying?" asked Franklyn Browne, the secretary of state.

"We have recently discovered that Cheng Kuang, one of our citizens who runs a chemical company in Shanghai, was producing the toxic nanoparticles which we believe were included in the cosmetics called Stardust."

"What you are saying is grave, Mr Ambassador."

Chang Liu bowed his head.

"My government has instructed me to inform you that the criminal has been tried and found guilty of treason against the state – he was executed."

The secretary of state sat impassively for a few seconds.

"This is extremely serious, Mr Ambassador. You realise, of course, how many of our citizens were impregnated with the lethal nanoparticles manufactured in your country?"

"My government has instructed me to inform you that it is putting all state institutions on immediate instructions to help find an antidote or some method of removing the offensive material."

"We appreciate your help, Mr Ambassador, but I feel that forty million Americans are not going to find that enough."

"I have also been instructed to offer, as a gesture of our goodwill, financial restitution to your citizens or your government. The figure of one hundred billion dollars has been suggested."

At first, Franklyn Browne's blood began to boil; he had a job calming himself down. Then he considered the situation. The money would be useful to cover the cost of the medical facilities having to be set up to deal with this crisis. Also, he wanted to avoid the hawks in the administration provoking a world war. He believed the Chinese did not know exactly what had been going on, but he doubted they had done all that could have been done to prevent a rogue industrialist dealing with al-Qaeda.

"Very well, I will convey your apologies and the offer to the president." The diplomat got up, bowed and left.

★

Later that day, all of the European countries attacked by the al-Qaeda biotechnology were approached by a Chinese ambassador. The story was the same: the Chinese were completely unaware of the traitor Cheng Kuang's terrible arrangements with al-Qaeda. Each country was also offered twenty billion dollars as financial restitution – several took this amount. The British asked for fifty billion dollars, which was eventually paid.

64

Colonel Harriman sat at his desk. He picked up the silver-framed photograph of Caroline as the telephone rang.

"The code is green," said a voice on the other end of the line.

John Harriman had not been content with the prime minister's resignation or the rumour of billions of dollars paid by the Chinese as compensation. As the Russian, Alexail Pankov, paid for his involvement with a bullet in his head in Cyprus, and Chatterjee, the Indian billionaire, was shot by a firing squad in India, he doubted the Saudi billionaire would ever be found. He had therefore acted in the only way he knew.

Eight of his men volunteered. They planned and executed a raid on the MI6 safe house in Surrey. Using stun guns they overpowered the guards and found Ibrahim in a cell downstairs. He was shot twice. Sir Anthony Greenwood did not participate in his friend's killing of Ibrahim, but secretly he was relieved. The Americans had been pressing the acting prime minister to extradite Ibrahim. But Sir Anthony did not want a public trial in America. It might placate their citizens' hunger for blood and a public execution but the media frenzy would start all over again. His greatest fear was the Americans overreacting against the Chinese. He did not want that, especially as one of the world's largest pharmaceutical companies was reporting good progress in extracting nanoparticles from the human body – at a price, of course.

Special Branch investigated the killing of Ibrahim, but there were no clues as to who had carried out the attack. Sir Anthony let it be known he thought it was the Israelis, as 50,000 of its citizens had been impregnated by the deadly toxins.

*

Belardi had closed down all operations – for now. He had transferred four billion dollars (luckily he had insisted Ibrahim give him the banking details) before the Americans tracked down the bank accounts. Through a nominee company he was buying dairies in Europe and the USA, intending to follow through bin Laden's second phase of Tears of the West by impregnating creamers and milk. He kept hidden the tons of toxic nanoparticles that were still held in Somalia. He decided to hold back the attack using the Celebrity brand.

*

The deputy prime minister led the party to a massive defeat at the general election. He also lost the leadership election, and the incoming opposition leader was not surprised that the defeated party replaced all previous cabinet members, saying they were tainted by the biotech crisis.

The American president survived a number of calls for his impeachment on the grounds of negligence. He finally accepted two hundred billion dollars from the Chinese but sent a team of SEALs into Shanghai, which blew up the warehouse where the deadly nanoparticles were produced. The Chinese happily turned the other cheek. The president's ratings were so low he knew he would not contest the next election but hung on 'to maintain continuity in these difficult times'.

The director of the CIA, Samuel Goldmuir, was forced to resign and the president also replaced Bud Ruskin at the FBI – it was his opportunity to deflect some of the heat. The new CIA spymaster tracked down the four directors of operations, codenamed Blue, Green, Red and Black. Two were taken to Guantanamo Bay, one committed suicide, and the other was shot dead after a gun battle in Cape Town.

Colonel Harriman's goddaughter obtained a first-class honours degree in biotechnology.

None of the countries introduced a robust investigation division to analyse all products used by their citizens for dangerous substances. The USA and EU talked a great deal about a Kite mark demonstrating a product that had been analysed thoroughly and was safe – but haven't got around to implementing the process yet…

65

John Harriman hadn't accepted a dinner date for several months. He simply couldn't face going to dinner without Caroline – the hurt was too much to bear. Caroline's sister had to work really hard to get him to agree to meet her at Rules, the restaurant he enjoyed most in London.

She's late, he thought, as he sat mindlessly pondering the menu and not welcoming the return to the restaurant where Caroline and he had enjoyed many wonderful evenings. He vaguely noticed a woman come in wearing a headscarf but didn't take any notice until she sat down at his table. He looked at her for the first time then began to shake uncontrollably.

"John... John, it's okay – it is me."

Caroline Bland held his hand as tears began to roll down his face.

"But, you're dead. I attended your funeral," he said.

"I'm so sorry. Sir Anthony knew that you, of all people, had to be convinced I was dead, otherwise it would leak and I would be in the firing line again."

"But, the bomb? Fragments penetrated your skull. I was at the hospital – I saw the damage."

"Yes, I was very badly hurt, but plastic surgery has helped and I've grown my hair but still use a headscarf as I am conscious of the scars on my scalp."

John Harriman studied her face and hair.

"Oh, Caroline, I've been to hell and back without you but I'm not sure I can forgive the deception – you broke my heart."

"I know." There was silence for a moment then Caroline said, "I'll understand if you don't wish to resume our relationship, but I wanted to at least try. I love you and missed you like hell as well."

John looked at her.

"Let's see what happens. I would like to try to rekindle the love; my life has been empty without you."

Later that year they married – a quiet ceremony at Chelsea Registry Office. Only Sir Anthony, Caroline's sister and Major Smith attended. Caroline had returned to work at MI6 but John insisted she remained deskbound – no more risks.

66

Belardi had not been idle since his self-imposed exile in Iraq and his flight to the UAE as the CIA closed in. From his safe house in Al Fujairah one of the seven Emirates not well known by the tourists or oil industry he set up four new operation managers worldwide, sending new al-Qaeda commanders to Marseille, Mogadishu, Houston and Belize City. Then he arranged for the supply of the remaining liquid containing the nanoparticles to be divided and sent to Belize then on to Houston Port, and the other half to Marseille. He had arranged for tankers to take the liquid to the dairies he had purchased in the USA, Poland and England.

He had replaced the management at all the dairies and placed his own men in key positions. Two of the new commanders were Lebanese, the others from Saudi Arabia and Pakistan. Each was a highly qualified biochemist. When the tankers arrived at the dairies the liquid was mixed with coffee creamer, then packaged in small capsules – the type of small pots used in the USA and Europe – and larger containers principally for the US market. The pots were packaged with the name of the dairy as Café Blanc, a luxury long-life coffee creamer. He laughed at the title of the product he had chosen – *long-life, that is really amusing*. The creamers were sold to supermarkets, chains of coffee bars, offices, hotels and hospitals – anywhere that could inflict most harm to the target population, from children to age forty-five. The fools were not checking foodstuffs and it was a simple matter to continue the leader's good work.

He changed the email heading from Tears of the West as he suspected Ibrahim would have given up the code name. He had arranged with Chatterjee's three sons to work on creating more of the toxic nanoparticles and they were having some success following the formula supplied by Cheng before he died. Belardi knew the Russian, Pankov, Cheng and Chatterjee were all dead but no problem, it meant he could continue to use the billions of dollars they had provided and was not required to account to anyone. The sons of Chatterjee hated their government for executing their father and were only too happy to help.

His only problem was an interfering postgraduate student at Wolverhampton University who had written a paper on nanoparticles included in coffee creamers. But his attack on the West continued.

He prayed he would have the time to continue his work – the Chatterjee brothers had started advertising 'adopting an Indian baby' and money was pouring in.

They were now supplying non-dairy creamers in addition to the standard variety and no agency or government questioned the ingredients – it was all too easy.

Epilogue

The president of the United States, the most powerful man in the world, sat despondently in the oval office. Should he resign or continue and see out his term of office? He had battled months of negativity from the media concerning the responsibility of his administration not to have detected the threat biochemistry presented to the American people. Since his live broadcasts, he had made three further broadcasts endeavouring to distance his administration from the unforeseen acts of terrorists, but the first admission that al-Qaeda had included toxic chemicals in cosmetics available throughout the States had started a witch-hunt. It didn't matter that these nanoparticles were virtually undetectable. He had clung to power but had sent for Franklyn Browne, the secretary of state, to discuss the latest threat to his office. He sat contemplating the actions he had taken. He had replaced Samuel Goldmuir and Bud Ruskin the directors of the CIA and FBI and dismissed Maxwell Liddle the health secretary whose family had donated large sums to his earlier presidential election. Other heads had rolled – but it wasn't enough. He had given the go ahead to destroy the

Chinese factory in Shanghai that had produced the toxic nanoparticles, the Chinese had not reacted. Now this latest report.

"Good afternoon Mr President," said Franklyn Browne trying to be cheerful.

"Please sit Franklyn, I want to read you this report," he glanced down at the paper on his desktop.

"This is from the Division of Statistics at the Department of Public Health," he continued reading out loud, "there has been a significant rise in babies born with birth defects reported by the state-wide data collection system. Although it is recognised that statistics can vary from one source to the next, national estimates state that pregnancies ending in miscarriage have quadrupled in the past three months." He had no idea that in the States roughly fifteen to twenty per cent of all pregnancies end in miscarriage defined as loss of the foetus before the twentieth week. "Now," he continued, "forty-five per cent of all pregnancies are ending in miscarriage, many in the first seven weeks". He continued reading out loud to Franklyn who said nothing. "There are usually four point four million confirmed pregnancies in the US every year 1995–2005. This year the number of births will dramatically reduce." He paused and took a drink of water. "Furthermore, the number of stillbirths (considered stillbirth after twenty weeks) has increased from twenty-six thousand (state-wide) in a year to that number over a three month period. Infant death during the first month up from nineteen thousand (state-wide) in a year to over fourteen thousand in a three month period. Another alarming figure is the number of women having abortions, presumably after discovering a birth defect during the early weeks of pregnancy. The number of abortions (state-wide) last year was two hundred and fifty thousand."

The president stopped reading shocked by that figure and sipped his water, he continued, "there have been two hundred and twenty-seven thousand terminations in the previous three months" The report writer added a note, *there have been one billion abortions worldwide since 1980*, which was cold comfort to the president. He continued reading out loud, "It is clear that the nanoparticles targeting the reproductive system of women are having a marked effect. Evidence of babies born with birth defects have increased to over four hundred and fifty thousand (state-wide) in the last three months." He finished reading now in a very sombre mood.

"But who's going to see this report?" Asked the astute secretary of state.

"That's the problem Franklyn, *The Washington Post* have a copy. They phoned my press secretary for an interview this morning. I shall have to tender my resignation, there's no other way." They debated the situation for an hour but the president knew he had to go.

He knew he would go down in history as the man who failed the American people.

Some of the toxic chemicals that can be found in various products

BIO-ACCUMULATE PHTHALATES

DEP – A man-made colourless liquid with a slight odour and a bitter, unpleasant taste. Trade names can be looked up online. It is used in cosmetics and fragrances. Some studies suggest it can cause damage to reproductive organs and fertility in males. Technical name: Diethyl Phthalates.

DEHP – A common class of phthalates used in plastics, including some medical devices. It is an androgen antagonist found in many cosmetics and fragrances as well as numerous other cosmetic products. It is thought that it can cause lower sperm counts in men. Technical name: Bis (2 – ethylhexyl).

DBP – A colourless substance previously used in cosmetics (may still be somewhere), including nail polish. It is banned in the EU. Technical name: Dibutyl phthalate

DBCP – A pesticide found to cause infertility in male workers who handle it regularly over long periods.

No longer used in the US. Technical name: Dibromochloropropane.

Phthalates – regarded as suspected endocrine disrupters and can cause lower levels of sperm counts.

Benzene – A colourless chemical or pale yellow liquid and at room temperature has a sweet odour. It is inflammable. It is connected with causing cells not to work correctly and can damage the immune system. It is reported that some women who breathed high levels of benzene for many months had irregular menstrual periods and a decrease in the size of their ovaries. Reported to be found in some shower gels and shampoos.

Lead – Thought to affect unborn babies and can cause miscarriage, premature birth and low birth rate. It is in some lipsticks, sunscreens and whitening toothpaste.

Mercury – It is reported that some skin products contain the toxic chemical mercury chloride as an active ingredient. When applied, the chemical apparently absorbs through the skin into the bloodstream. Use of mercury in cosmetics is illegal in some parts of the world.

Parabens – Four are reported to be frequently used in cosmetics: ethylparaben, butylparaben, methylparaben and propylparaben. Health concerns are that they can be endocrine disrupters which are thought to be linked to a risk of breast cancer and infertility.

Silicon – Found in some suntan, hand lotion and soaps, and used for breast implants. The jury is out as to its harmful qualities.

Silver – Silver nanoparticles can be created by synthesis and are sometimes used as a carrier for other nanoparticles.

Titanium Dioxide – Recently classified by the International Agency for Research on Cancer (IARC) as Group 2B carcinogen: "possibly carcinogenic to humans". Widely used as a whiteness provider in toothpaste, in cosmetic skincare products and sun block as a UV blocker. This sunscreen blocker is usually nanoparticle titanium dioxide. The jury is out on health effects.

At Wolverhampton University studies have been carried out regarding nanoparticles in coffee creamer – see articles online.

Look up chemicals online on websites that report chemicals which may affect fertility. Even if there are no warning statements on labels this does not necessarily mean that there is no risk.

Other chemicals to watch out for not in the story are:

DEA. Diethanolamine – A chemical used as a wetting or thickening agent in shampoos, soaps, hairsprays and sunscreens. It blocks absorption of the nutrient choline which is essential to brain development in a foetus.

D & C Yellow II – Found in a wide variety of cosmetics. The jury is out if digested.

Elastin – Found in facial creams and body lotions. Reported to suffocate skin by not allowing moisture in or out.

Formaldehyde – Thought to be carcinogenic and a neurotoxin. It may be fatal if swallowed, absorbed through the skin or inhaled. Sometimes found in baby shampoo, bubble bath, deodorant, perfume, hair dye, mouthwash, toothpaste, hairspray and nail polish.

Isobutylparaben – Reported to be a potential breast cancer risk. Found in body products.

PEG Stearates – Check PEG online for a list. Some found in body products, creams, lotions and cosmetics.

Toluene – Reported to be a poison to humans and an endocrine disrupter and potential carcinogen linked to brain cancer. Found in some nail polish.

These are just a few of the ingredients in some cosmetics and beauty products. Go online yourself – it might be an eye-opener.

See the David Suzuki Foundation website for useful information on nanoparticles.

Writer's Notes

First and foremost, other than known historical events, this is a work of fiction. Biochemists, bio-technicians and chemists – please forgive any latitude in explaining how nanoparticles could be included in cosmetics without indication on the packaging. None of the world's pharmaceutical companies would do such a thing – or would they?

Some people and organisations, notably Greenpeace and Friends of the Earth, have been trying for some time to force politicians to create a standard for the inclusion of nanoparticles in food, cosmetics and other products used by the public. The reader can research all the personal products they use and in my view should do so. Some very nasty chemicals are included in day-to-day cosmetics and I believe nanoparticles are included in some coffee creamers and cosmetics.

There is no doubt that biotechnology is going to play an important part in medicine, alleviating disease, and in other areas. But a system of control should be established to measure chemical content in food and cosmetics, and some chemicals should be banned.

The Baby Factory

Reported by the *Daily Mail,* 2nd October 2013 – The world's first baby factory is being built in India to house hundreds of women who will be paid to conceive children for western couples. The multi-million pound clinic will have self-catering apartments for visiting western couples intending to buy a baby for just under £20,000.

★

My thanks to Google and Wikipedia for, as usual, providing a superb tool to find information, some of which I have included in my story. I recommend the reader goes online and types 'nanoparticles – the use in cosmetics' and 'chemicals to avoid in day-to-day cosmetics' or 'nanotechnology in food'.

★

Nanoencapsulation is the coating or enclosing of a substance, like, say, a capsule, within another material at the nanoscale level. So what I have written about is fiction but it seems to me quite possible. I hope you enjoyed the story.

★

The Royal Yacht *Britannia* is presently berthed in Edinburgh and is open to the public.

What do you think of nanotechnology?

I would be interested to post your comments online.

Visit Ted York at www.tedyork.com

Also from Ted York

Born in 1878 to an east London docker's family, Rosie finds herself a mysterious benefactor who pays for both her and her sister to be privately educated. Whilst undoubtedly talented in the school room, Rosie longs to take to the stage at the Britannia Theatre in Shoreditch, London. As a beautiful, intelligent and talented actress she is popular with the Britannia Theatre crowd and, thanks again to her benefactor, is offered a part at the Theatre Royal, Drury Lane. In 1900, Rosie accompanies the cast of *Much Ado About Nothing* to Paris. The excitement of the world fair, the Exposition Universelle, and the summer Olympics is surpassed when Rosie meets Frederick, the son of a rich Swiss merchant banker. A whirlwind courtship leads to a grand wedding in Westminster Abbey.

As her life changes from actress to society lady, she mixes with lords and ladies, princes and kings. Flirting with the early feminist movement, Rosie's life unfolds with relentless excitement as she works for the early forerunner of the British Secret Service.

Rosie is a woman of the twentieth century. A charming and likeable heroine, she will appeal to readers looking for a heart-warming 'rags to riches' saga.

As he settled down to try to sleep, the colonel saw the light flashing on his bedside warning system. His instincts, honed over forty years, made him freeze...

Ludvig Korotski is the ex-station head of the KGB in Berlin. During the early '80s he trained a ruthless team of saboteurs, assassins and overseas agents. A cruel, ruthless man, he had left mother Russia when the 'soft liberals' began to root out the hardliners. He earned a living based in Sweden, offering his freelance 'services' to all-comers, including Iran, Libya and the militant al-Qaeda.

Out of the blue, he is approached by an old adversary, an ex-CIA operative, who offers him a contract to put together a new team to kill people in Britain. Ludvig doesn't care what they've done – his only concern is the £6,000,000 he is offered to fulfil the contract. All is going well until one of his agents tries to kill ex-SAS Colonel Harriman.

Harriman is now running his own security firm and, after the failed attempt on his life, begins to investigate why he has been targeted. Was it an old grudge? He sets about finding out why the murders are being committed and unravels a frightening story...